The SteelMaster of Indwallin

Book 2 of *The Gods Within*

Can one ever rule both the steel within, and the shadows with-out?

by

J. L. Doty

TELEMACHUS PRESS

Cover designed by Telemachus Press, LLC

Cover art:
Copyright © ThinkstockPhoto/96635409/iStockPhoto
Copyright © ThinkstockPhoto/89908712/iStockPhoto
Copyright © ThinkstockPhoto/77005529/Stockbyte
Copyright © iStockPhoto/2537945/jimikuk

Published by Telemachus Press, LLC
http://www.telemachuspress.com

Visit the author's website:
http://www.jldoty.com

ISBN: 978–1–938701–87–0 (eBook)
ISBN: 978–1–953757–02–9 (paperback)
ISBN: 978–1–953757–10–4 (hardcover)

Version 2023.11.23

KEpuz!po!EFTLUPQ.6CV292J:
Formatted using eTools for Writers 3.8.8, Nov 22 2023, 14:45:26
Copyright © 2013–2016 by J. L. Doty

Printed in the United States of America

10 9 8 7 6 5 4 3 2 1

The SteelMaster of Indwallin

Book 2 of *The Gods Within*

Prologue:
The Tenets of Steel

Beware the power of the self-forged blade,
for the heart of the steel is ice,
the soul of the steel is fire,
and the child of the steel is blood.

Only the master knows the steel as the steel was meant to be known.
Only the master shapes the steel as the steel was meant to be shaped.
Only the master rules the steel as the steel was meant to be ruled.
But the heart of the master is the steel, for the steel was ever meant to rule.

The strength of the steel is the master,
the power of the steel is the master,
the glory of the steel is the master,
but always the life of the master is the steel.

Beware the power of the self-forged blade.

1

An Inappropriate Rival

MORGIN LOOKED AT his reflection in the mirror and nodded with satisfaction. It had taken some doing, and of course careful planning, but he'd managed to alter the outfit Olivia had chosen for him into something more to his liking. He'd cut away the white lace at the cuffs, replaced the bright red vest with a soft brown leather one, then discarded the skin-tight red pants in favor of a pair of well-made, loose-fitting, tan breeches. He'd kept the knee high black boots, and as a concession to Olivia he'd decided not to discard the bright red coat. He completely ignored the pretty little blade she wanted him to wear, and instead buckled on his own sword. As another concession, he'd polished and cleaned both the sword and sheath; though try as he might the old steel refused to shine.

He looked in the mirror, and decided that while he was not up on the latest fashions, he was at least dressed well, and in good taste. Avis would be a little upset at his modifications, and Olivia would be downright furious, but she wouldn't know about it until they stood face-to-face in public, and then it would be too late for her to demand a change.

At a discreet knock on the door Morgin called out, "Enter."

The door swung open and Avis stepped into the room. He stopped beside Morgin, and looking at them both in the mirror Morgin noticed he stood more than a head taller than the servant. He'd grown a great deal in the last few years, and was now taller than most of the other young men. And while he didn't carry the bulk of a Malka, he was stronger than most, with a lean and wiry frame not unlike that of Tulellcoe.

Avis looked at the changes Morgin had made to his clothing and raised an eyebrow. "Your Lordship, I am to inform you the banquet will begin shortly, and the Lady Olivia would like you there early so you can greet the other clan lords as they arrive."

Morgin nodded. The title of warmaster carried with it certain responsibilities, and he had accepted them, if only Olivia would accept him. "Would you tell the Lady Rhianne I'll stop by her apartments shortly to escort her downstairs?"

Avis's eyebrows shot up happily. "Yes, my lord. Will that be all?"

"Yes," Morgin said, "And thank you."

"Certainly, my lord." Avis bowed and left the room.

Morgin hesitated for a few minutes to give Avis a good head start, then followed. He wasn't sure how he'd handle the situation with Rhianne. She still spurned him, was still angry that he'd believed she had betrayed him, and the foul way he'd treated her certainly hadn't helped matters. They were both trying to start over, but the best they could do was a strictly civil and polite peace. There remained a wall of formality between them they couldn't breach.

He tapped lightly on the door to her apartments. A wide-eyed young girl answered and quickly admitted him to a waiting room, then she nervously offered him some wine. He declined politely and added, "Tell my wife I'm here."

"Yes, my lord," the girl said, curtsied, then disappeared into another room.

Morgin's appearance threw Rhianne's staff into an uproar. He heard muffled voices in her boudoir, then Rhianne entered the room alone. Morgin was left with the impression her servants hovered out of sight just beyond the door. She paused, composed herself, and when she spoke her tone was cold and indifferent. "My lord, it is gracious of you to come."

Morgin almost melted. As he looked at her a small lock of hair broke loose from the elaborate tangle atop her head and floated down over one eye. He'd seen the same lock of hair floating over her eye a hundred times, and he wondered sometimes if it wasn't a subconscious manifestation of her magic. He said, "I thought it would be . . . proper." He winced at his poor choice of words, though it didn't seem to bother her.

She nodded. "Yes. A husband and wife should be seen together, especially at times such as this."

Morgin winced again. He turned toward the door, opened it, and held it. She took his arm and they walked out into the hall, then down the long procession of stone steps. They walked in silence, and Morgin sensed that, like he, she wanted to say something, but could think of nothing that wouldn't sound forced, or trite. Instead he took those few moments to prepare for Olivia.

The old woman had spent a busy winter trading messengers with all of the Lesser Clans, carefully negotiating the conditions of the yearly meeting of the Council. Using Morgin's newfound notoriety and his victory at Csairne Glen, she'd arranged to have the Council meet at Elhiyne this year. And with the arrival of spring, the walls of Elhiyne had quickly filled with the nobility of the four Lesser Clans.

On the surface nothing had happened during the first two weeks, mostly a lot of entertainment, and of course they all went hunting, most often in small groups, though sometimes in large expeditions. It was on these hunting trips, or in small rooms in the back of the village inn, or on a pleasant stroll through the forest, that clan leaders conducted most of the serious business, though hunting did seem to be the preferred method of getting someone alone for a quiet chat.

Three days ago that stage of the negotiations ended when the more formal and public meetings in the Hall of Wills had begun, though Morgin came away from the preliminary negotiations with the impression that Olivia was not pleased with the results. She wanted the other clans to back Elhiyne in a bid to crush the Greater Council, but Penda and Tosk and Inetka were skeptical of her chances at victory. Tomorrow they would meet for the last time in the Hall, and there was little doubt Olivia had failed to achieve her desires, though everyone could see she blamed Morgin for that failure.

The old woman had had the Hall arrayed in splendor for this night's banquet. The servants had spent days cleaning everything they could find to clean, and at Olivia's orders had positioned a grouping of long tables in the shape of a horseshoe at the center of the Hall. When Morgin and Rhianne entered the Hall, Olivia, in the midst of giving some poor servant a tongue-lashing, interrupted her tirade to bark at Morgin, "In another moment you would have been late."

Morgin looked at her for a moment. "But I'm not late, am I?"

"Well that's about the only thing you've done right."

Morgin tried to ignore the rebuke. "Where do you want me to sit tonight?"

"Why, at the head of the table, of course, oh ShadowLord."

Rhianne looked at him kindly, and for the first time in a long time showed him some sympathy. "I'm sorry, Morgin."

He shrugged. "We're all sorry I can't be what she wants, aren't we?"

Rhianne's face saddened. "I didn't mean it that way."

Morgin said, "I know."

In short order the other lords and ladies of the Lesser Clans arrived and were seated. As Olivia had instructed, Morgin sat at the head of the table. On his right sat Olivia, then BlakeDown and Tulellcoe and a long line of noble men and women. At the far end of the table sat Valso and Illalla, each with a heavily armed guard standing behind him. On Morgin's left sat Rhianne, and next to her BlakeDown's son ErrinCastle—the heir to Penda was about Morgin's age, and he paid far too much attention to Rhianne. JohnEngine had seen to it that he and France were seated far down the table where they could get drunk and enjoy themselves.

The servants moved to fill everyone's goblet or tankard with wine or ale. When the servants stopped moving about Olivia stood slowly and all eyes fell on her. She waited for some moments until the room was absolutely still. "My Lords and Ladies of Penda, and Tosk, and Inetka. We of House Elhiyne welcome you. We give you thanks for the wisdom you have lent to this council of equals, and we are humbled by the sage council of the Lords BlakeDown et Penda, PaulStaff et Tosk, and Wylow et Inetka . . ."

Olivia's words dropped to the back of Morgin's thoughts as he noticed ErrinCastle whispering something in Rhianne's ear. The Penda looked Morgin's way and their eyes met. ErrinCastle grinned and leered, though Rhianne, with her head turned to listen to the whisper, did not see his face. The Penda was a handsome young man, and could have had a dozen of the most desirable young women at the drop of a hat, but he focused his attentions on Rhianne. And more than that, his advances were so blatant he seemed to be trying to goad Morgin into jealous anger, as if challenging Morgin to confront him. It was absolutely idiotic, for nothing good could come of such a public display. So for the good of Elhiyne, Morgin was determined to swallow his pride and avoid making an issue of it. At least Rhianne had been careful not to encourage the fellow, though if he continued to be so obvious, Morgin might have to do something. If only Rhianne would do more to discourage him.

Morgin became conscious of Olivia's eyes upon him.

". . . And so, my lords," Olivia finished. "Tomorrow will be the last day of the Council. We have come to many agreements and disagreements, but we have not lost our unity, and I believe we all agree the unity of the Lesser Council is the only thing that keeps the jackals off our backs. So let those jackals be warned." She looked down the table at Valso and Illalla. "If our enemies seek contest with us, they will again face the shadows of Elhiyne."

Someone in the back of the Hall—Morgin suspected one of Olivia's lackeys—shouted, "ShadowLord!" Several Elhiyne clansmen took up the cry, and a few Inetkas as well, but Morgin didn't encourage it, and none of the Pendas or Tosks joined in, so it died quickly.

"Enjoy the hospitality of Elhiyne," Olivia said, and sat down.

The servants moved quickly, filling the tables with food while the Hall filled with the buzz of laughter and idle conversation. Morgin wanted to talk to Rhianne, but while ErrinCastle monopolized her time, Olivia was determined to monopolize Morgin's.

"Lord BlakeDown was speaking to you," Olivia chided him.

"I'm sorry," Morgin said. Olivia's eyes narrowed angrily; she'd told him time and again he must never apologize in public. The ShadowLord, the Warmaster of Elhiyne, should never appear to debase himself before another. Morgin tried to sound less apologetic as he asked, "What were you saying?"

BlakeDown smiled. "I was wondering what ransom you will demand for the Decouixs."

Morgin looked at Valso and wondered how the Decouix prince could maintain such an air of unconcern in captivity. "I don't know," Morgin said flatly. "I think if I really took what I wanted, it would be their heads. But I'm afraid I'll have to be content with something less."

ErrinCastle demanded, "And why is that? Why don't you just kill them?"

Morgin shrugged. "They're more valuable alive."

"Is it because of the story I heard about you?" ErrinCastle demanded loudly, glancing about the table at several of his friends with a sly grin. "Is it because of these gods I'm told you speak with? I've heard they told you not to kill the Decouixs. But then perhaps I heard the story wrong. Please. Tell me about it." One of ErrinCastle's friends smirked into his handkerchief.

Morgin reached for a piece of roast pheasant and said flatly, "Maybe I'm just tired of killing in general."

Rhianne tried to rescue him. "Well now, in my opinion, that's a very good thing to be tired of."

"I believe it's your power," Olivia said, knowing full well his power was dead. "I believe it's giving you wise council, though it's quite common for one to be unaware of such a subtle manifestation."

"You know it's the oddest thing!" ErrinCastle observed to no one in particular. "I've heard so much about your power, Lord AethonLaw, and yet I've never seen the slightest hint of it."

Morgin wanted to show him the power of his fist, but had to be satisfied with a simple comment. "I see no reason to flaunt my abilities."

Most of the evening went that way, with ErrinCastle baiting him, BlakeDown looking on like an observer at a cock fight, Rhianne trying to rescue him, and Olivia always trying to gain some advantage from even the slightest tension. Morgin was relieved when he finally got away. He wanted to find JohnEngine and France and have a little fun, but they'd disappeared somewhere so he drifted toward the stables where Mortiss, at least, would not talk back to him.

He didn't scratch her between the ears as he'd done with poor old SarahGirl. Mortiss had no need of such comforting. "What a rotten evening this has been!" he said to her.

She snorted, as if she didn't really feel like listening to his troubles.

"I know," he said, "I know. But I have to talk to someone."

She rolled her eyes and shook her head.

"I wish you could tell me what happened to my power," he said. "And I wish I knew what to do with Rhianne. Ellowyn was right. I do still love her, even if I don't want to admit it."

"And why don't you want to admit it?"

For an instant Morgin thought Mortiss had actually spoken, but then Rhianne stepped out of the shadows. "Why don't you want to admit it? Tell me. I do want to know. And who is this Ellowyn you speak of? And what did you mean when you said you wished the horse could tell you what happened to your power. What did happen to your power?"

Morgin shook his head. "I don't know. It's just gone. It died some place; I think at Csairne Glen."

Rhianne stepped closer and frowned. "What do you mean died?"

He wondered for a moment if he should be telling her this, but if he ever hoped to trust her at all, he must trust her now. "Just that! My power is dead. It's as if I've lost an arm, or a leg. No! It's as if I've lost my sight along with both arms and legs. I'm almost helpless."

She reached up and touched his cheek. "I'm so sorry."

"That makes two of us."

She looked into his eyes for a long moment, then she withdrew her hand from his cheek. "And why don't you want to admit you still love me?"

He didn't try to answer that question, but instead asked one of his own. "Aren't you getting a little tired of ErrinCastle?"

"Of course I'm getting tired of him. I don't like it when he baits you, and he's mooning over me like a puppy. His advances are getting downright embarrassing."

"Then why don't you get rid of him?"

"I would if I could," she said, frustration in every word. "If he were at least discreet I could turn him down discreetly, but he's become so blatant I'd have to openly insult him in public to discourage him. And your grandmother has specifically forbidden that. So I'm doing the best I can."

Morgin said, "I do know what it's like to be caught between my grandmother's desires and my own."

"It's maddening," she said.

This was the first time in years they'd actually spoken more than a few words in a private setting. More frightened than he'd ever been in any battle, more fearful of this moment than he'd ever feared death, he took a chance. She stood within arm's reach, so, looking into her eyes, he reached out carefully and put his hand behind her, pressed it into the small of her back and pulled her toward him. He did so carefully, gently and tentatively, ready to yield if she showed the slightest bit of resistance. But she came to him gladly, and as he drowned in her eyes he saw that twinkle appear, the twinkle he hadn't seen in so long a time. She pressed her body lightly against him and stopped with her lips almost brushing his, her arms still at her sides, the soft scent of her skin washing over him.

He hesitated, not sure where to go with this, and in that instant she smiled and said, "Well husband, are you going to kiss me or not?"

He said, "I wasn't sure if—"

She didn't let him finish, but wrapped her arms around his neck and pressed her lips to his. As their tongues danced together, he pulled her tightly against him, and he realized they had never kissed before, not like this, not hot and passionate, both of them sensing each other's desperate need. When the kiss ended and their lips parted she rested her chin on his shoulder, and they held each other tightly for a long moment. Then she leaned back, looked at him carefully and smiled.

He blurted out, "I'm sorry I was stupid enough to believe you went to Valso's bed. I was a fool."

Her eyes narrowed, though the twinkle remained. "Yes, you are." She stepped out of his arms, turned and walked out of the stables.

He was alone again, with only Mortiss to keep him company. She snorted and shook her head, as if telling him she agreed with Rhianne.

2

The Steel Within

"YOU PROMISED ME you'd discredit him," DaNoel said. Then, thinking of the en-spelled guard dozing in the corridor, he lowered his voice. "You promised."

Valso sat down on the cot in his cell and spoke as if lecturing a child. "And I fully intend to keep that promise. My methods are effective, but they cannot be rushed. Take, for instance, the Penda whelp ErrinCastle."

"What does he have to do with discrediting my bro—the whoreson? He's a fool who can't keep his head about women. That's all."

Valso shook his head carefully. "You don't actually believe he's that much of a fool, do you? He's making a complete ass of himself over Rhianne. His father has told him more than once to stop being such an idiot, and each night he resolves to maintain his dignity the next time he sees her. But the next morning, when he does see her, my spell takes over, and he loses all control."

"So you're responsible for that?" DaNoel laughed and looked at Valso with new re-spect. "That's driving the whoreson crazy."

Valso nodded happily. "Yes, it is. ErrinCastle's advances are putting him under a great deal of stress right now, and tomorrow that will be very important."

"Why?" DaNoel demanded. "What's going to happen tomorrow?"

Valso intertwined the fingers of his hands, cupped them behind his head and leaned back comfortably on his cot. "I really can't tell you that, though I will tell you the whoreson has two very carefully kept secrets, both of which will be revealed tomorrow and create quite a bit of excitement. Don't miss the final session of the Council in the Hall of Wills, or you'll miss all the fun."

"Listen to me, Decouix," DaNoel said. "I want to know what's going to happen, and you're not going to evade the answer."

Valso sat up and his eyes narrowed. "I'm not, am I?" he asked through an unpleas-ant smile, and DaNoel's eyes grew heavy. He felt very tired . . .

••••

In seconds DaNoel drifted off to sleep standing on his feet. Valso stood, approached him, and spoke softly. "You can't even conceive of the power I command, you ignorant fool. I've a mind to kill you where you stand, but traitors can be a valuable commodity so I'll let you live, for the time being.

"Now you'll remember nothing of this. You'll leave here, return to your room and go to sleep. And tomorrow you'll not remember coming to me, nor leaving, nor anything that happened between. But you'll instruct the stable boy to saddle and provision a horse for you, and to hold it ready. And when the excitement begins in the Hall of Wills you'll come to me immediately. Is that clear?"

DaNoel's eyes opened and his head straightened. There was no hint in his features that he was not fully in control of himself. "Is that clear?" Valso repeated.

"Yes, my lord. Will that be all?"

"Yes. You may go."

DaNoel bowed. "Thank you, my lord." He turned and left.

Valso laughed openly. He controlled that one so easily, and some day it would be just as easy to control them all. Someday, he and his god would rule the Mortal Plane as it was meant to be ruled.

••••

Morgin had trouble getting up the next morning. He had had a fitful night's sleep, filled with dreams he couldn't remember and a struggle he couldn't name. He awoke late, groggy and slowwitted, and found it impossible to move with any degree of haste. His sword filled him with unease, and he couldn't put it out of his thoughts. But he pulled himself together, headed for the kitchens, wolfed down some food, then made his way to the Hall of Wills.

The central floor of the Hall was recessed three steps below the periphery, with a high vaulted ceiling overhead. With everyone packed around the edges of the Hall the difference in elevation gave the central floor the air of a stage, while the three steps surrounding it formed a boundary beyond which mere observers dare not pass.

The last session of the Council was well under way when Morgin arrived. The twelve council members—three chosen from each of the Lesser Clans—were seated at a heavy, wooden table placed in the center of the main floor. Everyone else stood along the outer periphery, and anyone who wished to address the council would step forth and do so from that floor.

As was customary, though not required, none of the clan leaders placed themselves on the Council, perhaps feeling they could be more effective addressing the Council from the floor. To address the Council one needed to walk down the three steps to the central floor and wait patiently to be recognized. At any given moment there were usually two or three clansmen or clanswomen, already recognized, standing before the Council, discussing or arguing the topic of the moment, while a half dozen more waited quietly to be recognized along the edges of the floor. Morgin had observed that the speed with which one was recognized was quite dependent upon one's status within the Lesser Clans—status through rank, money, power, birth, it really didn't matter. And if one weren't highly placed, it would be foolish to speak without proper recognition.

He slipped quietly through the observers and headed toward the back of the Hall. There were more than a few eyebrows raised at his tardiness, though Olivia showed no reaction. But Morgin knew that steel-gray stare too well, and there was no doubt in his mind she would have words with him later.

It was customary to come armed to the Council, but to place one's weapons aside once there. At the back of the Hall Morgin unbuckled his sheathed sword and placed it on a rack among a great number of weapons. But just as he put it down his fingers refused to release it, and it took a decided effort to let go, though doing so increased his unease. He turned back toward the crowd feeling almost ill, spotted JohnEngine not too far away and moved quietly to his brother's side.

JohnEngine looked worse than Morgin felt. "What's the trouble?" Morgin whispered.

JohnEngine took a ragged breath and exhaled it slowly. "Too much wine last night. Or not enough. I'm not sure which."

"Be silent!" someone hissed at them.

At the moment a Penda lord named Tarare argued some subject with Alcoa, marchlord of the western Elhiyne lands that bordered Penda. Morgin knew Alcoa only vaguely, for the man kept to his own lands. Nor did he personally know Tarare, but it was common knowledge the Penda lord was simply a mouthpiece for BlakeDown.

"They are always a threat," Alcoa said loudly, "And until they are taught the proper lesson, they will always be a threat."

"And what lesson would you teach them?" Tarare demanded. "That you can take our hands from the fields and turn them into soldiers? That you can march them off to a war in a distant land while our crops wither without care? That you can—"

"Enough of this," Alcoa said angrily.

AnnaRail stepped onto the edge of the central floor, and a Penda councilman recognized her immediately. A Penda! "My lords," she said carefully. "We speak of war, and we speak of peace, as if our lives are carried on in either one or the other state. But that is rarely the case, for most often we live in a gray limbo between the two . . ."

While AnnaRail debated with Tarare, Olivia ambled her way through the crowd of observers. She paused here and there, had a whispered word with this lord or that, but she worked her way purposefully toward Morgin. When she reached him she took him by the arm and pulled him to an empty corner of the Hall. He was careful not to make a scene by resisting.

"That wife of yours," she hissed. "You need to control her better. She's allowing ErrinCastle to make a fool of himself."

For the first time Morgin realized he now towered over the old woman. He had spent so many years as a young boy looking up at her, but now she had to look up at him. He stepped in close to her to emphasize the difference in their heights. "My wife has done nothing untoward or inappropriate, but ErrinCastle has certainly come close to crossing the line. Tell BlakeDown ErrinCastle needs to control himself, because if he doesn't I'll kill him."

Morgin yanked his arm out of Olivia's hand and turned away from her. But she stepped quickly around him. "Oh Lord of Shadow," she hissed quietly. "Lord without power. You can no longer even claim the rights of a clansman, can you?"

Morgin ignored her, stepped around her and elbowed his way back into the throng of observers. She'd have to make a scene if she wanted to stop him.

The debate between Tarare and AnnaRail had grown more heated, and Tarare snarled something at her. Morgin's unease grew, his stomach churned, and the Errin-Castle situation seemed a distant problem.

Olivia stepped down to the floor and didn't wait to be recognized by the Council. "If Lord Tarare et Penda feels so strongly about peace, we of Elhiyne will not fault him if he chooses to lay his arms aside when his enemies plunder his lands."

The crowd buzzed momentarily at the open insult, but the old witch outclassed the Penda lord and he knew it, so he wisely chose not to strike back with an insult of his own. "But my enemies have not plundered my lands, most gracious lady. It is your lands that have suffered. It is your fight, and a wise man does not champion another without careful consideration."

Olivia smiled that stone-hard, straight-lipped smile of hers. "Be careful, Tarare, that you are not too careful, for you might find your lands have already been plundered before you finish your consideration."

BlakeDown stepped down from the periphery and moved to join his kinsman. "Is that a threat, Olivia?"

AnnaRail started to speak, but BlakeDown cut her off. "Silence, woman," he shouted. His magic flared for an instant, but he brought it under control quickly.

AnnaRail's eyes grew livid, though she held herself in check. Morgin sensed her anger as if it were his own. His magic flared within his soul, a magic he thought he no longer possessed; it washed slowly over him, crawled up the back of his spine like a living creature from beyond life. He sensed something growing within the Hall, something wrong, something evil. For a moment he thought only *he* sensed it, but in the midst of the argument raging about her he saw AnnaRail perk up and cock her head, and slowly she turned her eyes toward the back of the Hall.

Morgin was close to the end of the Hall where the weapons had been placed. She was at the other end, and even from that distance he saw the fear in her eyes. She began walking toward him, slowly at first, then more rapidly. Just as she approached him she veered away, and as she walked past him he realized her goal was the back of the Hall.

There came a clattering of steel from the weapons there. No one stood near enough to them to have caused such a disturbance. AnnaRail hesitated, blocking Morgin's view of the weapons. She tensed, and the sudden sound of steel sliding clear of a sheath reached everyone's ears. A harsh, red light flared near the amassed weapons, and raw, uncontrolled power filled the Hall with a note of anger and rage.

Knowing only that AnnaRail stood between him and his sword, he charged at her as if she were an opponent in battle. He hit her from behind, slammed her protectively to the floor and hurtled over the top of her. He caught a glimpse of the angry red power as it arced up from the pile of weapons over his head. He tried to convert his forward momentum into a leap, stretched his muscles to the limit to intercept it and caught something in his outstretched hand that felt like the hilt of a sword. Its momentum jerked him back in midair, pulled him toward the center of the Hall where he crashed painfully to the stone floor in a tumbling sprawl.

There was an instant of stunned silence as he lay there with one hand wrapped about the hilt of his sword, all eyes in the Hall upon him. He sensed what was coming, and there was no time to explain or cry out a warning, so he brought his free hand around to join the other in a two handed death-grip. The sword screamed at him to re-lease it, to free it to taste blood and sate its desire. He was still lying on his back as the sword jerked and bucked in his grip, swinging from side to side and cutting chips of stone from the floor. In his soul he sensed the carnage it would lay upon the land if he released it, and he vowed to hold it, even if it pulled him into the depths of the Ninth Hell.

Suddenly it stopped jerking about and shot upward, lifting him off his feet and well into the air. Then just as suddenly it let go and he crashed to the floor. It started pulling him down the length of the Hall, dragging him on his back toward the lone figure of BlakeDown, who stood at the far end eyes wide with fear. Morgin swung his legs about, got his feet in front of him and dug his heels in. It pulled him to his feet, then crashed through the table of councilmen, upending the heavy plank table and sending them all sprawling.

Desperately Morgin wrapped both legs around a table leg and locked his ankles, try-ing to use it as an anchor. The sword jerked and pulled in his hands, slowly dragging both him and the massive table forward. He'd slowed it, and that enraged it. It growled its hatred and turned on him, cutting spasmodically at his own throat while he struggled to hold it at bay. He fought it with only the strength in his arms, sensing that it would choose him over any other victim. But when the sword couldn't have him it turned outward, and to his surprise it sought Rhianne. "Nooooo!" he screamed, and a momentary flood of power crashed through his soul.

It changed tactics, chopped toward the table and bit deeply into the wooden planks, sending a shower of splinters in all directions. Blistering waves of black-hot hatred washed over him, igniting the splinters and scorching his tunic. With a dozen blows the blade dismembered the table into four large pieces, and with the size of its anchor now diminished it began dragging Morgin again in spasmodic jerks across the floor.

At the far end of the Hall BlakeDown backed fearfully up the steps to the periphery as Morgin unlocked his legs and released the last remnant of the table. The sword pulled him in a long skid the length of the Hall, but at the last moment he swung his legs in front of him, got them beneath the sword so that he slid on his heels and butt, and caught his heels on the lowest of the steps beneath BlakeDown. He put his back into it, pulled with all his might, brought the sword to a momentary halt.

He was on his back with his heels locked against the lowest step, stretched to his full length. The sword slowly started lifting him off his back, like a rigid timber. Gritting his teeth, trembling with strain, he looked down the length of the blade at BlakeDown, whose eyes were filled with stark terror. Only then did he realize the Penda leader was the sword's intended prey, and that he could no longer restrain it. Morgin gave one last effort, knowing he could only delay the blade, and through his gritted teeth he growled at BlakeDown, "I . . . can't . . . hold it . . . I have . . . no . . . power."

BlakeDown's eyes widened with fear, then a strange mixture of triumph and gladness appeared on his face, and in an instant he backed through the heavy plank door at the end of the Hall, slammed it shut and threw the bolt loudly into place. Morgin's strength finally reached its limit; the sword tore from his grip, dropping him on his back, and it buried itself to the hilt in the planking of the door. The blade hesitated for an instant, then pulled itself half way from the door, and slammed back into it with such force the door's hinges groaned.

Morgin scrambled to his feet, shot up the steps, locked his fingers about the hilt. It shot backwards, slamming the hilt into his stomach, knocking the wind from him and driving him out into the center of the Hall where it dropped him painfully on his back. It turned on him, and he screamed as he struggled against it. Then it picked him up, swung him from side to side, tossed him about like a tassel hanging from its hilt, and like the time it had cut the Kulls to pieces he could only hold on, and hope his strength would not fail him.

Soon his battle narrowed to the grip he had upon the hilt, and as the world about him receded he saw only the sword, and the chasm of power it had opened before him.

3

Betrayal

RHIANNE ALMOST FAINTED when the storm of power hit the castle. It flooded her soul as if the ground beneath her had split and a volcano of malevolent power had erupted within the castle, a power with a conscious will of its own, conscious of her and Morgin. For a single moment it tried to attack her, but Morgin held it back. She leaned heavily on a vanity and tried to reassure herself the attack would not come again. And then she realized she was safe only because Morgin held the monster back by taking the brunt of its assault.

She reached the Hall of Wills just as the massed nobility of four clans were pouring from every exit. The power she sensed was like a scar on her soul, and deep within she knew she was probably the only person who could help Morgin. But the panic of the crowd was a current she could not oppose, and they nearly trampled her as they swept past her. Then Olivia appeared, took Rhianne by an arm and stood her ground like a granite monolith on the shore of an ocean storm. "Seal the Hall," she commanded. "We must seal the Hall, and Ward it against the possibility he may fail. We cannot allow whatever it is he has unleashed in there to turn upon the land. It would devastate the countryside."

"Let me go," Rhianne shouted. "Let me go. I have to help him."

The old woman's hand arced out of nowhere and resounded loudly against Rhianne's cheek, stunning her momentarily. "There is nothing you can do, girl. At least not at this time." She pointed to the barred doors of the Hall. "That battle he must fight alone."

As if in answer to the old woman's words Rhianne heard Morgin's voice raised in a terrified scream, followed quickly by an inhuman growl of hatred as vast waves of power crashed outward from the Hall. A large crack raced down the stone of a nearby wall, as if the power trapped with Morgin in the Hall would escape by tearing down the castle itself.

Olivia cursed, turned upon the crack and cast her power at it like a spear. The stone was once again whole, and again the old woman stood rock still against the forces that reached out against them. Rhianne looked on as the old woman called her power forth. It coalesced about her like a shield, then she fed it into the stone walls of the Hall. Olivia turned on Rhianne; her eyes burned with the power in her soul. "Help me, you foolish girl. You're a grown woman. Don't just stand there like a child."

Rhianne obeyed without question, casting first a small spell to calm her reeling thoughts, then moving up to the more demanding task of imitating the old woman. As she concentrated she sensed others who were far ahead of her—BlakeDown, AnnaRail, JohnEngine, NickoLot, Brandon—already lending their power to the aged stone of the Hall. She joined them carefully, and as she touched her power to the veil they had constructed, she sensed again the special affinity the malevolence within held for her. She did not retreat, and with the others she settled down to a long and exhausting vigil.

••••

"There's a horse waiting for you near the man-gate," DaNoel told Valso. But then DaNoel hesitated, for he had no recollection of how he'd come to be standing with Valso in the Decouix's tower prison. He shook his head to clear it, careful not to mention his lapse to the prince. The pandemonium in the Hall of Wills was a muffled roar in the distance.

DaNoel tried to reconstruct his memory of recent events: Morgin's fantastic struggle with the talisman he had unleashed, and his open admission to BlakeDown, within everyone's hearing, that he had no power. Thinking of that moment in the Hall, DaNoel bit back a shout of triumph. "He never did have any power, did he? It was all in that talisman, wasn't it?"

Valso, in the midst of sorting and packing the few belongings he wished to keep, looked up and shrugged indifferently. "Does it matter now?"

"No," DaNoel said. "He's discredited himself to such an extent that even if he does survive the talisman, some clansman will kill him soon enough."

DaNoel had a sudden thought. He looked carefully at Valso. "Were you responsible for unleashing that talisman, and at the worst possible time, and in the worst possible place?"

The Decouix prince didn't answer, but the corners of his mouth curved upward in a satisfied smile, answer enough for DaNoel.

"I assume you've provisioned the horse properly?" Valso asked.

"Twelve days' trail rations. I'd give you better, but trail rations weigh little and they go far. And once the cry is raised you'll need to move with all possible haste."

"Well enough," Valso said. "I've lived on worse." He finished packing, turned abruptly and walked out of the room. DaNoel followed him down the stairway to Olivia's veil of containment. The old witch's spell, so complex and powerful before, was failing quickly as she concentrated more and more of her strength on the struggle to contain the talisman within the Hall. The veil was now tattered and rent in a dozen places, though Valso still needed the help of someone with Elhiyne blood to escape without alerting the old witch.

DaNoel chose a weak spot in the veil and enlarged it carefully. He stepped through and Valso followed without hesitation. As DaNoel closed the veil, the Decouix turned to the guard dozing under DaNoel's spell and took the man's sword.

"What are you doing?" DaNoel demanded.

"I need a weapon," Valso said as he pulled the sword from its sheath and looked it over. "This isn't much of a blade, but it'll do until I find better."

The guard groaned and opened his eyes. He looked at DaNoel, then at Valso, and his hand shot instinctively to his side, but his sword was in Valso's hands.

DaNoel reacted instantly, smothering the man's consciousness with a hastily constructed spell. "You did that," DaNoel hissed. "You woke him on purpose."

The Decouix shrugged. "You can handle one minor clansman, can't you?"

"But if I tamper with his memories Olivia will surely sense it, and she'll trace it to me."

"Then kill him."

DaNoel stepped back. "I didn't agree to murder."

Valso shook his head sadly. "Treason is acceptable, eh, but not murder?" The prince turned his back on DaNoel, pulled the tower door open just a crack and looked carefully outside. He turned back to DaNoel. "I'd really like to stay and discuss your strange code of honor, but I'm afraid I don't have the time. We'll meet again, Elhiyne." And with those words Valso slipped through the door and was gone.

DaNoel turned toward the guard. He struggled to find some other way of handling the man: a bribe perhaps. But Olivia had chosen her guards for their personal loyalty. Reluctantly, DaNoel pulled his dagger, hesitated for an instant, then drove it between the man's ribs into his heart, though even then it took some moments for the guard's spirit to depart fully.

DaNoel cleaned his dagger carefully on the man's tunic and returned it to its sheath, then checked the man one last time to be certain he was truly dead. Satisfied, he stood, turned to leave, but his heart almost stopped at the sight of NickoLot standing in the tower door, looking at him oddly.

"What's going on here?" she demanded, her eyes narrowing.

He said, "The Decouix escaped. Killed this guard on his way out."

NickoLot's eyes narrowed further. "You're lying."

DaNoel looked at her carefully. "Lying about what?"

"I don't know, but I do know you're lying."

"And what did you see with your own eyes, little sister?"

"I didn't have to see it with my eyes. You're tainted with the scent of the Decouix's power. What have you done here?"

DaNoel reached out and gripped her viciously by the throat. "I've done nothing. I'll deny any accusation you make, and since you can't prove it, you'll only hurt mother and father if you speak out."

He threw her to the floor in a heap of petticoats. "Little girls should not interfere in the affairs of men," he said, then walked quickly out of the tower to raise the alarm for the Decouix. He'd better do everything he could to appear innocent just in case the little bitch did speak up.

••••

With experience Morgin had become quite adept at recognizing the texture of his dreams, knowing almost instantly when he had awakened in one. But this was different, for memories of a past from within this dream clouded his mind with hatred, pain and exhaustion, as if he had been part of it for years. For quite some time he walked down a muddy, dirt road beneath a dark, gray sky. He carried an unsheathed sword in his right hand, concentrated on his footsteps only enough to avoid the muddiest of the potholes, and thought instead of the small Benesh'ere village in which he'd been born. He recalled the days he'd spent helping his mother Eisla at the forges as she shaped the finest of Benesh'ere steel, and of the warm nights when his father Binth taught him the notes of the pipes, while Eisla looked happily on . . .

Morgin stopped in the middle of the road in mud up to his ankles. He shook his head and shouted, "No!" He looked up at the dark clouds above him. "I am not Benesh'ere, and I was not born in a village named Indwallin. My mother was not named Eisla and she did not pound steel at the forges, and my father was not Binth and he did not play the pipes."

He was shaking with fury, so he took a deep breath and tried to calm himself. He looked quickly at his sword—it was his sword—and at the hand holding it—but not his hand. He looked carefully at both hands, for they were rough, scarred hands that had seen long days of hard fighting, and long nights of swinging a hammer at the forges. Dirt had ground its way deep into the skin about the nails, and in places untended blisters had finally grown over into hard, knobby calluses. But the thing that made them most obviously not his hands was the color of the skin beneath the dirt and grime, a white so pale it reminded him of bones long bleached in a hot desert sun, the white skin of the Benesh'ere. He shook his head to clear it, and became aware of shoulder length, coal black hair that had not been washed in days.

He took hold of himself, acknowledged that he was dreaming again, though this dream had not the misty and dreamlike sense of unreality of his past dreams, but seemed very real, too real. And in it he haunted the soul of a Benesh'ere warrior named Morddon, though it was the whiteface warrior who commanded this body, while Morgin seemed to be only a passenger along for the ride.

He looked about, found that this dream had deposited him standing alone in the middle of a long and narrow road. It wound its way through a hilly and green countryside before disappearing over the next hill. The strange memories that swirled through his thoughts told him that in this dream he had been walking for some days now. His muscles ached and he knew he had covered many leagues with little rest.

His stomach growled, but he tried not to think of food. He had no cloak, and the clouds above looked as if they might burst at any moment. His only possessions were the begrimed tunic on his back, the dingy leather jerkin about his shoulders, a pair of loose fitting breeches made of a coarse material, an old, scuffed pair of calf-high brown boots, and the unsheathed sword in his hand, but no sheath. A dozen cuts and bruises brought back memories of the confusion of a large battle, and a gray and dingy bandage high on his left arm was marked by a reddish-brown stain some days old. His memories told him a sword cut had recently opened a fresh wound there, and he was lucky it had been a glancing blow; otherwise it would have taken off his arm.

He looked again at the sword, and there was no doubt it was the sword he knew, though wholly unlike the sword he remembered. Plain and functionally unadorned, it would never be a pretty blade. But it lacked the centuries of tarnish that couldn't be wiped away in Morgin's time, and it lacked many of the scars of battle he remembered, the nicks and scratches he knew so well. It might now be only a few years old. But he knew this blade for a certainty, for in this dream he had an awareness of the steel that defied understanding, as if the steel were a living thing, an old friend that spoke to him of a place called Indwallin, a woman called Eisla the SteelMistress, and a man called Binth the Pipist. Both names touched his heart with longing and sorrow. "No!" he shouted. "Those are lies." Still, he could not refute the pale whiteness of his skin, or the black cascade of hair that streamed over his shoulders.

He shrugged. At least he had the sword, and that gave him some small feeling of confidence, though that also frightened him. It didn't appear the dream was going to end in the next instant. Just standing there waiting for it to end seemed ridiculous, so he resumed walking, though he had no idea what lay at the end of this road.

Later that day it began to rain, a steady drizzle that continued through the afternoon and into the approaching night. It plastered his hair down against his shoulders, soaked his clothing to the skin and chilled him to the bone. But luck was with him, for just as the last of the gloomy day turned into an even gloomier night, he spotted an old animal shelter some distance off the road.

Someone had tended the surrounding fields at one time, but the shelter had been abandoned long ago and was now riddled with leaks. He managed to find a dry corner and there he curled into a tight ball. He didn't expect to sleep well, for his clothes were wet through and through; there was no hope of lighting a fire, and the chill of the rain reached into his soul. But the constant roar of the rain pounding on the roof of the shelter pulled him toward sleep, and he drifted slowly into a light doze, still half-conscious of his surroundings.

A faint movement—just a flicker of motion—in one corner of the shelter brought him to full wakefulness. His Benesh'ere reflexes startled Morgin, for like a cat he rose from a tightly curled ball on the floor to a full upright stance in one fluid motion. He stood in a crouch and faced the corner where he'd sensed the movement, though he couldn't have seen it in the dark interior of the shelter on such a black, stormy night.

The Benesh'ere warrior in him tensed, ready for a fight, but recognizing the being in the corner as a shadowwraith Morgin tried to reassure him with his memories. Facing it, the being's name came to him. "Soann'Daeth'Daeye," he whispered. "Why do you haunt my dreams?"

The being spoke, but its words touched his ears as if no more than the sigh of a gentle wind. *Beware, oh King of Dreams*, the wind sighed. *Beware of what comes from beyond these walls.* And then the being was gone, and Morgin's senses told him he was alone in the shelter.

By touch he examined the corner where the being had crouched, and while he was doing so its words finally registered on his consciousness. He stood erect for a moment, waited and listened, but heard nothing beyond the pounding of the rain on the roof. Conscious of the warning, he crossed the floor of the shed and slipped out through the door into the open field, fearing that the shelter might become a trap. He pressed his back against a nearby tree, tried to become part of its nighttime silhouette, and waited, though not for long.

Three shadows appeared out of the night, slogging through the wet grass of the field, creeping stealthily up to the shed. They listened for a moment, and one asked the other, "Is he in there?"

"Must be. He come this way."

"Think maybe he's asleep?"

"He ain't makin' no noise. Either he's asleep or he ain't in there. Let's move quiet like, kill 'im fast."

The three thieves melted through the door into the shed. Morgin would have run the other way, but Morddon stepped quietly into the shed behind them.

"Guess he ain't in here."

"Guess I am," Morddon said in a gravelly voice.

Startled, all three figures jumped, hesitated for a moment, then moved quickly to attack. Again, the Benesh'ere reflexes left Morgin's thoughts behind, and the thieves lay dead on the floor of the shed before he realized the action was over.

He searched them quickly, took the best cloak they had among them, and a small purse of coins one had tied to his waist. Then, with the cloak to keep him a little warm, he returned to his corner and curled up for the night.

4

The Child of Indwallin

THE NEXT MORNING the dream had not ended, and that disappointed Morgin, though at least the rain had stopped and the sun had come out. Morddon returned to the road and began walking again in the same direction as the previous day. After two more days of walking the weather became warm and dry, and the countryside about him turned quite flat and featureless, though by no means barren for he passed tilled and carefully tended fields bearing grain of an unfamiliar type. He watched for a farmstead, but only after some time did he spot one a good distance off the road at the end of an arrow-straight cart track. He thought of food and his stomach growled, so he turned toward the farmhouse.

The farmer met him in the middle of the cart track where it opened out into the farmyard. He held a pitch fork in both hands across his chest like a soldier carrying a pike, and while he did not level it at Morddon, he was clearly prepared to defend himself if need be. The man was short of stature, far shorter than Morddon, and he was quite terrified, though he stood his ground bravely.

"Who are you?" the farmer demanded. "What do you want? And why would a whiteface come to my farm?"

Only then did Morgin realize the man was not unusually short; Morddon was unusually tall, for he inhabited the towering, spindly body of a Benesh'ere, and by that he stood head and shoulders above ordinary men. "I'm just a soldier," Morddon said. "As you can see I'm a bit down on my luck, but I mean you no harm."

"What do you want here?"

Morgin followed Morddon's thoughts as he gave up the idea of food. "Just a drink of water."

The farmer pointed at an animal trough with his pitchfork. "Drink your fill. Then be gone."

Morddon gulped at the water mechanically for a few seconds, then left the farmstead quickly.

As he walked down the road he saw more farms to either side, and an occasional horseman rode past him in one direction or the other. Soon the traffic on the road increased, and he passed several crossroads where other, smaller paths joined the main road. He descended into a dryer, browner landscape, and in the distance caught his first sight of a strange and beautiful walled city of tall glasslike spires that glistened in the sun. Morddon knew the city to be Kathbeyanne, the city of the gods, but Morgin scoffed at such a notion.

Like most large, walled cities, the great majority of Kathbeyanne's inhabitants lived outside its walls. In fact many of the most interesting and lively markets were located there. The road he traveled appeared, from a distance, to lead straight to the city's main gates. But as it entered the sprawl of shops and booths at the base of the wall it widened and split and separated. The traffic became so heavy—mostly foot and cart traffic—he found it impossible to determine exactly where the road led. He soon became lost among the vendors, though most people made way quickly for the filthy Benesh'ere carrying a naked blade.

He stopped at a weapons maker's shop, feeling a strange affinity with the various tools of death on display. But this was no true weapons maker, for the steel in the shop called out to him, and the flaws in it grated at his nerves. His eye caught the motion of his own reflection in the face of a polished brass shield. He stopped and looked into it carefully, and he saw Morgin's face reflected there, though reshaped to conform to the long, narrow lines of a Benesh'ere.

"Would yer lordship be interested in tryin' the shield out?"

Morddon turned slowly to face the shop owner, but the man stepped back a pace, seeing for the first time the naked sword in his hand and noticing now his unwashed and road-weary appearance. "You've no need to fear me," Morddon said. To Morgin it felt odd to speak, because it was Morddon who chose the words. "I carry the sword this way because I have no sheath for it."

"Ah!" the shop owner said, turning and sweeping a hand toward the center of his stall. "If it's a sheath you want then step this way."

Morddon followed him, but the flawed steel about him bothered him, so he chose a sheath quickly, paid for it, and buckled it on. "Are you sure you don't want the shield?" the shop owner asked him. "It's a good shield, finely crafted."

"I don't want a shield," Morddon said. "But I do want directions. Aethon's hiring mercenaries. I want to know where, and how I get there."

A small boy appeared at Morddon's feet. "I can show you the way, whiteface, and for no more than the price of a small copper."

"He's my customer," the shop owner growled at the boy.

Morddon turned carefully to the shop owner and spoke with deliberate malice. "But it's the boy's wares I choose to buy." The shop owner wisely chose not to argue with a Benesh'ere warrior.

The boy led Morddon through the gates at the wall and into the city itself. Kathbey-anne was far bigger than any city in Morgin's experience, and each time they walked from one section to the next he was forced to revise his estimate of its size. They passed through a thieves quarter much like that in any city, but scaled up with the size of Kath-beyanne, then a merchant's quarter where families of wealth and worldly power lived in luxury, and an oddly small clan quarter where the aristocrats of otherworldly power lived in arcane mystery. Ultimately the boy led Morddon to the heart of the city, and for the first time his eyes fell upon the palace of the Shahotma King. Morgin knew he would never forget that first sight, spires that reached toward the heavens, balconies and balustrades that soared high above the city, with level upon level of parapets and bat-tlements.

There was a large open parade ground in front of the palace, and after demanding his copper coin, the boy left Morddon there to seek his own fate. At the far end of the parade ground, close to the gates of the palace, there were a number of contestants practicing their weapons skills. Most were in pairs refining their swordsmanship, and the almost dance-like cadence of the ring of their swords was hypnotic. The constant activi-ty raised a hint of dust in the dry afternoon air that gave an eerie quality to the entire scene.

To one side of the parade ground stood several large barracks, and in front of each, with one exception, stood two smartly-dressed, well-armed guards with their backs ar-row straight and their eyes keen and piercing to any who might pass by. Also, with one exception, the stone of each barracks had been scrubbed clean. Above each barracks door fluttered the banner of the company of warriors occupying it. The exception, however, had no banner, had not been scrubbed or cleaned in any way in a long time, and no guards stood at its entrance. Close to the door they'd placed a plain wooden ta-ble behind which sat three rather hard and unsavory looking warriors of unknown rank. A long line of hard looking men snaked out from the table far across the parade ground. Morddon took a place at the end of that line.

Several men nearby in the line looked at him oddly, and Morgin noticed that he was the only Benesh'ere there. He stood head and shoulders above the tallest of the rest, and he also remembered his image in the shield, was probably the most unsavory of the bunch, so he settled down to a long wait. Slowly, one step at a time, the hours passed while he moved closer to the plain wooden table with the three men seated behind it.

He lost track of the time, and in the warm afternoon sun, with the cadence of the swords ringing in the distance, he slipped into the depths of his own thoughts. Morgin now understood that he and Morddon jointly inhabited this Benesh'ere body. Where there might have been strife in this relationship, he and the Benesh'ere were so alike they were almost indistinguishable. Yet when it came to reflexes and instincts, the body always moved with the reactions of its Benesh'ere soul, and Morgin understood well which of them was dominant.

Morgin started as a sharp, unpleasant sound cut at his nerves, like that of a badly tuned harp. The men in the line stepped fearfully away from him.

The sound came again, an unpleasant, harsh ring cutting through the dry afternoon air. Morgin, or maybe it was Morddon, recognized the sound of flawed steel, though muffled enough by the distance to be bearable. But the wrongness of it commanded his attention and his eyes unerringly picked out the blade and its owner. And even though they were at the extreme limit of the parade ground, he knew somehow, having once heard the flaw in the steel, he would recognize that blade instantly if he ever met it again.

The line moved forward; Morddon moved with it.

He glanced upward and noticed a large black speck against the bright blue of the afternoon sky, some sort of bird gliding on a warm, dry thermal. He kept an eye on it as it circled the parade ground in a slow descent, drifting ever closer until finally Morgin heard the beat of giant wings and saw that the shape of this bird was wrong. But not until it settled to the ground in front of one of the distant barracks did he comprehend the enormity of this animal. Part eagle and part lion, an odd misshapen creature larger than any horse, coal black from head to foot, it turned its head and looked Morgin's way with blood red eyes that pierced the distance and cut into his soul. Morddon knew it as a griffin.

A dozen Benesh'ere poured out of the barracks where the griffin had landed. Among them came a warrior who wore only black, and walked with a grace and surety of step beyond that of any mortal man. Even at that distance Morgin recognized Metadan.

All of the Benesh'ere but one bowed deeply in the presence of the griffin. That one, and Metadan, bowed courteously, but only as equals. Then all, including the griffin, entered the Benesh'ere barracks.

The line moved forward; Morddon moved with it.

Sometime later a horse-drawn carriage left the palace through its main gates at the far end of the parade ground. It raised a cloud of dust as it crossed to the Benesh'ere barracks and came to a halt there. A tall Benesh'ere woman wearing robes of wealth and power stepped out of the carriage. Again, Metadan and a dozen Benesh'ere warriors emerged from the barracks to greet her. Again, all but one of the Benesh'ere bowed deeply to her, while Metadan and that one bowed courteously to her as equals. Then they escorted her into the barracks and the carriage pulled down an alley to wait.

The line moved forward; Morddon moved with it, and eventually arrived at the table facing three surely mercenaries. One of them looked him up and down and asked, "What can we do for you, whiteface?"

Morddon answered, "You're hiring mercenaries. I'm here to be hired."

The mercenary rubbed the stubble on his chin. "Hmmm! I never hired a whiteface before. What's yer name?"

"Morddon," he answered. "And you won't do better."

"Aye, I don't doubt that," the mercenary said. "Never met a whiteface wasn't worth two ordinary men in a fight. What's yer price?"

"What do you pay these other men?"

"One copper a day. A bonus of twelve at the end of each month if they're still alive."

Morddon nodded. "Then you'll pay me twelve coppers a day and a bonus of one silver at the end of the month, if I'm still alive."

The mercenary's brow wrinkled. "Are you worth that much?"

"And then some," Morddon said flatly.

The mercenary captain rubbed his chin and considered Morddon. While doing so one of the men seated next to him leaned toward him and whispered in his ear. The captain frowned and nodded unhappily. "Hadn't thought of that," he said, then looked up at Morddon. "Sorry whiteface. Deal's off. Won't be hiring none o' yer kind here."

This time Morgin saw it coming and managed to keep up with the speed of Morddon's actions. While his right hand tore his sword from its sheath, his left reached across the table, closed in a vise-like grip about the mercenary captain's throat, lifted him out of his chair and well off his feet. He slammed the choking mercenary on his back on the table and raised his sword high in the air in preparation for decapitating the man then and there. The other two jumped up and stepped back. "What made you change your mind?" Morddon growled in the captain's face, relaxing his grip on the man's throat a bit so he could talk.

"Not by choice," the mercenary coughed out. "Gilguard wouldn't like it."

"Who's Gilguard?"

The man choked out, "Warmaster of the Benesh'ere."

"What does Gilguard have to say about who you hire?"

"Ordinarily nothing. But he'd spit me and roast me alive if I hired one of his precious whitefaces."

Morddon nodded, knowing well the pride of the Benesh'ere. "Well then. Let's go talk to Gilguard."

Again he picked the mercenary up by his throat, and dragging him on his heels like a piece of baggage he marched toward the Benesh'ere barracks, trailing a crowd of curious mercenaries behind him. As he passed the other two barracks he noticed the guards in front of one were ordinary human men, while angels guarded the other.

At the Benesh'ere barracks the two guards eyed him curiously, and one grinned at the sight of the poor mercenary captain slowly turning blue in Morddon's grip. But when Morddon tried to walk past them they crossed their halberds in front of him, and one of them demanded, "I don't recognize you. What do you want here?"

"I have business with Gilguard."

The guard looked Morddon up and down, made no attempt to hide his contempt for the obviously low caste of the Benesh'ere who stood before him. "You need a bath," he said.

Morgin sensed Morddon's anger building, and he couldn't understand why the Benesh'ere seemed bent on picking a fight with everyone he met. "I'm not here to see Gilguard about a bath," Morddon said.

The guard shook his head. "Well I don't think you'll be seeing the warmaster about anything."

Morgin felt Morddon tense. "Are you going to tell him I'm here?"

"Gilguard's too busy to be bothered with the likes of you. And if you're smart, whiteface, you'll get yourself—"

The term whiteface was a common enough reference to the skin color of a Benesh'ere, and the Benesh'ere tolerated its use by ordinary men. But no Benesh'ere would use it in that tone of voice except as the most derogatory insult. Morddon kicked the talkative guard in the crotch and simultaneously slammed the hilt of his sword into his partner's chin. The first doubled over groaning and clutched his groin while the other went down with a crash. Morddon then hit the one groaning in the back of the head and walked over the top of him through the high double doors of the barracks.

Just inside he met a wall of Benesh'ere warriors with swords and lances leveled at him. He halted, dropped the poor mercenary captain on the floor, gripped his sword in both hands, and at the possibility that he might now die, Morgin sensed in him joyous anticipation.

"What's going on here?" a voice called out. The warriors facing Morddon parted, and the Benesh'ere who had bowed to the griffin and the lady as equals filled the gap. A moment later Metadan joined him, and with an ungainly shuffle the black winged griffin, towering over them, took a place behind them.

"You're Gilguard," Morddon said. "I've come to see you about keeping me from gainful employment."

The Benesh'ere warmaster frowned, so Morddon kicked the mercenary captain in the ribs. The poor fellow coughed and spluttered and rolled over. Morddon picked him up by his tunic and threw him at Gilguard's feet. "He won't hire me because he says you wouldn't like it."

Gilguard looked at the mercenary at his feet, then at Morddon, then at the mercenary again. He frowned and shook his head. "But of course he can't hire you. And you wouldn't want to work for him. He's a mercenary."

"I know," Morddon said, "So am I."

A female voice said, "No! That cannot be!"

To Morgin it sounded like Rhianne's voice, but he was careful not to react in any way. He saw in a dozen pairs of Benesh'ere eyes he'd be spitted on a dozen lances were Morddon to move quickly.

"Let me through!" the woman demanded. The warriors facing Morddon parted again, and the tall Benesh'ere woman from the carriage stepped confidently into the open gap. She was unlike any of the Benesh'ere women Morgin had seen in his own time, who had all worn breeches like a man. This woman wore a gown that would be proper in any king's court, and in the bone white skin of her face he saw Rhianne's features, but like his own that face was reshaped to conform to the long, narrow lines of a Benesh'ere.

"Pardon, my lady?" Morddon asked. "What cannot be?"

She looked at Morddon and her eyes narrowed with distaste. "No Benesh'ere would draw his sword for a few coins of gold."

Morddon bowed. "You are quite right, my lady. I draw my sword only for *many* coins of gold."

Her eyes flashed hot and angry. "Well you'll find no employment here."

Morddon frowned. "But I am a mercenary and Aethon is hiring mercenaries."

"But not the likes of you," she spat.

"And why not me?" Morddon asked. "I've never fought for the Goath."

"Since when is a mercenary so particular about the choice of his employer?"

"And since when is an employer so particular about the choice of her mercenaries? Perhaps you yourself would like to employ me, my lady? I'm also good in the bedroom."

At that insult the warriors Morddon faced tensed angrily, but Gilguard stopped them with a shout, "Hold!"

"Ah ha!" the griffin laughed. "A mercenary Benesh'ere is rare indeed. But a Benesh'ere with a sense of humor? Now that is an even rarer bird."

Gilguard, however, was not impressed with Morddon's wit. He carefully drew his sword, leaned forward and put the tip of it beneath Morddon's chin. "Benesh'ere or not. No vagabond speaks to her ladyship that way."

Gilguard was leaning forward in an awkward stance, his arm fully extended. There would be an instant before he could thrust effectively with his sword, so the sword tip at Morddon's chin was not an immediate threat. And too, Morddon believed Morgin would help him in some way against the steel of the other soldiers. Then, for the first time, Morddon acknowledged Morgin's presence. *Whatever you are that haunts my soul, do not act to hinder me, or we will both die.*

Morddon looked into Gilguard's eyes, and smiling viciously he said, "If you and your men choose to kill me, you may perhaps succeed. But many of you will die with me, and to die for nothing but a few unimportant words would be a shame."

"Enough of this," the griffin said. "Put your sword away, warmaster. I command it."

Gilguard looked at the griffin angrily. "But he—"

"But nothing," the griffin said. "He is certainly rude, and he has a loose tongue, and the gods know he stinks to the Ninth Hell, but he has done nothing that gives you the right to kill him."

Gilguard bowed his head. "Yes, my lord," he said, and withdrew the tip of his sword from Morddon's chin, though he did not sheath it.

The griffin looked at Morddon, and if the beak of an eagle could be said to smile, it seemed this one did. "I myself may choose to hire you."

"But how can you trust him?" the woman demanded.

Morgin sensed the shift in Morddon's emotions, and the words that came from his lips were bitter and harsh. "I am a mercenary, my lady. I trust no one, and no one trusts me."

"Ahhh!" the griffin said sorrowfully. "Such bitterness in one so young. But then I see you are young only in years, mercenary, and not in battles, eh?"

The woman persisted. "How do we know he doesn't bring some nameless evil with him?"

The griffin shook his head. "No, AnneRhianne. There is no evil in this one's heart, only sorrow. Tell me mercenary," he said to Morddon. "What fills your heart with such sorrow?"

Morgin sensed the sorrow the griffin spoke of, but Morddon only laughed. "The only sorrow in my heart, half bird, is for the lack of coins jingling in my purse."

The griffin nodded as if he knew the truth behind such a lie. "We shall see, mercenary."

Metadan, silent and unmoving until that moment, stepped forward to stand almost chin to chin with Morddon, though his chin was quite a bit lower. "What is your name?" he asked.

"Morddon."

"And how old are you?"

"I have seen two twelves of summers," Morddon said. "And why do you ask all these questions?"

"Because I might hire you myself."

"No!" the woman said, but Metadan ignored her.

"How much fighting experience do you have?"

Morddon shrugged, considered the question carefully, and a kaleidoscope of horror and death flashed through his thoughts. "I first fought the Goath hordes with Karre on the Sangee Plain, and I've been fighting them ever since."

"That was twelve years ago. Do you mean to tell me you've been a soldier since you were a boy?"

Again Morddon shrugged. "Believe me. I was never a boy."

"And where have you fought most recently?"

"I fought with Elish at Mount Tadour"—someone gasped—"but on the way here I heard you've all started calling it Grim Dying Hill." Memories of the carnage there flooded through Morddon's soul. He threw his head back and laughed maniacally. "A good name that. We did do a lot of dying there, didn't we? But a bit confusing there at the end. Tell me, how many of us are left alive?"

Metadan's eyes were steel hard. "Not twelve twelves."

Morddon grimaced.

"But that was only twelve days ago," Metadan said. "How did you get here?"

"I walked."

"Impossible," Gilguard said. "You'd have to walk day and night."

Morddon looked at the warmaster angrily. "Not exactly. I slept for a few hours one night."

"And why did you come here to Kathbeyanne?" Metadan asked.

"Because here is where you're hiring mercenaries."

Metadan nodded. "I've heard of you. Elish told me about you a few years ago. He said you were the most bloodthirsty man he'd ever met, the most bitter, and the saddest. He told me when other men tire of fighting, you go forth to fight the Goath alone, if necessary."

"Elish is dead," Morddon said. "Are you going to hire me? If not I'll find someone else."

"I'll hire you," Metadan said calmly. "How much do you want?"

"One gold each month," Morddon said, then added the customary phrase that ended every mercenary contract, "if I'm alive to collect it."

"Agreed," Metadan said, extending his hand. "And for a period of one year neither of us may break this contract without the consent of the other."

Morddon sheathed his sword and shook the archangel's hand. "Agreed. Now when do we go to battle?"

The archangel shook his head. "We don't. The First Legion is commanded to remain in the city as His Majesty's guard."

"Then the deal's off," Morddon said. "Our contract is for fighting."

"The deal is not off," Metadan stated flatly. "For I do not give my consent. You are my man for a period of one year. You will obey the orders I give you. And you will stop shouting at everyone."

"You tricked me."

"No. You tricked yourself. Now report to the legion barracks and tell the archangel Ellowyn you are now part of the First Legion. And take a bath." Metadan turned away from Morddon, and the crowd of Benesh'ere parted as he walked through them.

The woman AnneRhianne joined his side. "I'll be glad to be away from him," she said angrily. "The stink of his body offends me not half as much as the stink of his soul." She looked at the griffin. "Are you coming Lord TarnThane?"

"In a moment," the half bird answered her. He looked at Morddon. "You are a curiosity to me. Perhaps some time we can speak of the battles you've fought."

Morddon shrugged. "I'll speak of anything you wish, if you have the price to buy my time."

The griffin laughed, and turned to follow AnneRhianne and Metadan. "Come, Warmaster Gilguard. We still have much to discuss."

Morddon turned unhappily and stormed out of the Benesh'ere barracks, but as he stepped outside the harsh ring of that flawed blade struck at Morgin's soul again. No longer able to ignore it, he walked the length of the parade ground and approached the two men whom he'd seen earlier, and who were still practicing beneath the wall of the palace. "You there," he said to the man with the flawed blade. "Your blade is flawed. It will fail on you some day."

The two men, both obviously noblemen, halted their practice and looked at Morddon curiously. "What did you say?" the man asked.

Morddon pointed at the blade. "That blade's flawed."

The nobleman looked at his sword, then at Morddon, then he frowned angrily. "This steel was forged by the finest armorer in all of Kathbeyanne. Now go away before I call the palace guard and have you flogged."

Morddon persisted. "But the blade—"

"I said go away."

By now the scene had attracted the attention of a small crowd. "Ah, to the Ninth Hell with you!" Morddon said, and turned away. But as he did so he caught sight of a young man standing on a balcony in the palace high above them and observing the incident curiously. Morddon didn't recognize the young man, but Morgin remembered Aethon from another dream.

5

The Power of the Blade

RHIANNE, ALONE IN her boudoir, sensed the ebb of the power in Morgin's sword. She withdrew from the netherworld enough to concentrate on the worldly matters of her mortal soul, though she dare not withdraw completely. She had dismissed her servants two days ago when Morgin's ordeal had first begun, latched the door to her apartments from the inside, and set the most powerful Wards she could conjure. Then lying upon her bed she entered the netherworld to help Morgin with his lonely battle, and by virtue of the pandemonium in the Hall she had remained undisturbed. But during those two days she had only been able to glimpse Morgin's soul from a nether distance, as if some power far greater than her own was determined to keep her from his side. Nevertheless, she sensed she had a role to play in this game, and she understood now that her part had only just begun.

She recalled her servants, and they were unusually quiet for they sensed the strangeness that hung about her. She had them bathe, perfume and dress her, prepare and apply her makeup, curl and shape her hair high atop her head. To help Morgin she must confront the old woman first, and there her appearance would be all-important. If she showed the slightest weakness in any way, the old woman would surely oppose her, so she must appear fresh, ready, powerful; to the old woman, and to all those around her. But at the last moment, as she stood at the threshold of her suite with her hand upon the door's latch, her own doubts threatened to overwhelm her.

She threw the latch, stepped out into the corridor, and had to race to stay ahead of her fears, though she forced herself to an outward calm she did not feel. She marched down the stairs to the main floor of the castle, leaving a retinue of nervous handmaidens behind. She sensed her own power building within her, much as she sensed the sword weakening under Morgin's constant onslaught, and that gave her the confidence to move through the castle as if she were Olivia and no one would dare refuse her access to any part of it. She knew she succeeded when wide-eyed clansmen stood aside to let her pass.

There were a dozen men guarding the main entrance to the Hall of Wills, though Rhianne was relieved to see they were all clansmen of lesser power. Now that the flow of power from the sword appeared to be waning, the highest caste had gone to rest, having exhausted themselves maintaining Wards to seal Morgin and the sword within. Not one of them, Rhianne thought bitterly, had thought to aid him, only to trap him inside with the sword so they might save their own souls.

One guard, probably their leader, stepped in front of Rhianne, blocking her path to the doors of the Hall. Rhianne did not allow the man time to speak. "Stand aside," she barked at him.

The man was smart enough to sense her power, and to fear it. "I'm sorry, my lady," he said. "But the Lady Olivia has left strict instructions no one may enter the Hall, and that I will answer to her if I—"

"Stand aside now!" Rhianne snapped at him. "Or you'll answer to me this moment."

The man cringed, stepped back but not aside. He appeared to waver for a moment, then seeing something or someone behind Rhianne, his confidence returned and he stood his ground.

Olivia's voice crackled in Rhianne's ear. "What is this?"

Rhianne did not turn to face the old woman, but instead remained facing the guard and the doors of the Hall behind him. "She wishes to enter the Hall," the guard said.

"Face me, girl," Olivia demanded.

Rhianne refused to turn away from her goal. There was a moment of silence, during which she sensed Olivia's power probing at her own, and then the old woman walked carefully around her and stepped in front of her. Rhianne sensed others entering the room behind her, among them Roland, AnnaRail, JohnEngine, the swordsman France, BlakeDown, PaulStaff and Wylow. A crowd was the last thing she wanted.

Olivia looked into her eyes and smiled like a cat about to make a leisurely meal of a small, helpless mouse. "What are you about, girl?"

Rhianne tried to imitate the cold and disapproving look she'd seen the old woman use to cow clansmen. She said, "I think the term *girl* no longer applies, not since the night I had to endure the brutality of two twelves of Valso's halfmen, endured because I tried to defend Elhiyne."

There, she'd said it, out in the open. They'd all heard the rumors, but no one had openly acknowledged the brutal gang rape she'd suffered.

Olivia nodded acquiescence. "Very well, woman, what are you about?"

"I have to bring my husband back from the netherlife."

"Why you?" Olivia asked, her eyes narrowing. "Why not me?"

"Because you could not resist the temptation of that power in there, and to defend itself that blade would awaken again. You cannot defeat it, and in his present condition

Morgin can't defeat it a second time. It would devour him, and you, and the countryside about us. Only the gods know when it would finally be sated, if it would be sated at all."

AnnaRail appeared at Rhianne's side, though Rhianne did not turn from the doors of the Hall to look at her. "Then I will go," AnnaRail said softly.

Rhianne, still looking directly into Olivia's eyes, tried to reply as softly. "No. You mustn't. Your kindness would be as honey to a bear, and that sword would come forth to devour you as readily for its own pleasure, as for its own defense. The result would be the same."

The old witch looked at Rhianne for a moment, her eyes afire with godlight and boring into the depths of Rhianne's soul. "You have told us why we should not enter. Now tell us why you should."

Rhianne held her back straight and refused to flinch away from the old woman's gaze. "I don't know why. I only know it is what I am meant to do."

Olivia's eyes narrowed even further, and Rhianne sensed the old woman's power dancing about her like a wild animal pulling mindlessly at its leash. But then the old witch smiled, and with a predatory laugh said, "You are much like your husband, Rhianne esk et Elhiyne. Much like him indeed."

Olivia turned with lightning speed to the guard. "Let her pass. Either she will bring him out to us, or together they will both perish within."

The guard bowed and turned toward the two massive wooden doors that sealed Morgin and his sword within the Hall of Wills. Rhianne was expecting to see the doors thrown open quickly now that she had passed the test of Olivia's scrutiny, but instead she had to wait while the guard and two of his subordinates began prying away a patchwork of timbers that had been hastily added to the planks of the doors, and only then did she take notice of their condition. Beneath the added timbers the doors, once so massive Rhianne alone would have found it difficult to move them on their hinges, were now splintered and pitted with holes where Morgin's sword had punched through them time and again.

The guards were careful to remove only the timbers needed to allow her access. They propped one of the doors open slightly and held it there, waiting for her, and she noticed they took great care to avoid looking through the gap into the Hall itself.

Rhianne had still not turned away from her destination, though somehow she knew France was standing in the crowd behind her. "Swordsman," she said softly.

France stepped carefully into her field of view, though he remained to one side as if reluctant to stand between her and the Hall. "I'm here," he said flatly.

"Do you know the measure of that blade in there?"

He shrugged. "When it's just a blade, I do."

"Then please find me a sheath within which it will find comfort."

"Aye, my lady," he said, then disappeared from sight. She heard movement in the crowd behind her, then the swordsman said to someone, "Give me your sheath." She heard a sword being drawn, then more movement within the crowd, and France appeared again at her side. He held before her an empty sheath.

Rhianne's confidence began to falter, so without further ado she took the sheath in one hand, crossed the space to the gap in the doors, and entered the Hall with all of her defenses up, as if she were entering the Ninth Hell itself. The guards closed the gap quickly, and immediately began pounding the extra timbers back in place.

As Rhianne's eyes took in the interior of the Hall her heart raced with fear. A haze of white dust drifted on the air, made the sunlight visible as rays splashing across the Hall from a high window near the ceiling. The dust filled her lungs and eyes and mouth, covering the floor, the walls, and the remnants of the table where the council had sat. Then, as if by instinct, her eyes pierced the haze and settled on the shape of a stone pillar, one of many that lined the edge of the Hall to support the high vaulted ceiling. As wide as two men standing back to back, the blade had nearly cut it in two, and about its base lay a pile of stone chips. Deeper into the haze she saw other pillars in even worse condition, and at her feet the stone steps that led down to the central floor of the Hall were chipped and broken; the floor pitted and scarred to the point where it would be easy to turn an ankle when walking across it. She wanted to turn and run, but something pulled her toward the center of the Hall where she saw a dark and still form huddled close to the floor.

She walked down the three steps carefully, then started slowly across the floor toward the dark shape, her heart threatening to pound its way out of her chest, squinting to make out the form of the thing on the floor. His face was hidden by hunched shoulders and a bowed head. He was resting on his knees, sitting back on his heels, arms extended forward and down, hands gripped together about something on the floor.

She stopped at a point that would be just out of the sword's reach, and facing him she lowered herself slowly to her knees. She tried to relax, closed her eyes, let her magic expand outward carefully. Morgin's hands gripped the hilt of the sword, and he had buried the blade itself deep within the stone of the floor. For the moment it lay quiescent and still, though it filled the entire room with its power.

Too late, she realized her mistake. The power of the blade did fill the room, and now that she had entered its trap it would consume her with its hatred. It flared angrily, and with a shower of stone chips it lifted out of the floor, flooding her soul with wave after wave of torment, allowing her to glimpse for a moment the vastness of its power and the malevolence of its desire. Then another power arose behind it, equally as vast and equally as malevolent. It met the power of the blade, surrounded it, squashed it, compressed it smaller and smaller, both powers coalescing into white-hot sparks that receded into the depths of Morgin's soul, farther and deeper, until Rhianne could no longer sense them.

The Hall became again quiet, though Rhianne's thoughts shouted with the revelation of the vision she had seen. Morgin had not lost his power, not as he believed. He had used his power to control and imprison that of the blade, and equally matched, both had become compressed and tightened until they were locked away in some deep recess of his soul unknown even to him. Now that Rhianne knew what to look for, she saw the constant struggle within him, and knew that she must help him at any cost.

••••

Morgin awoke to a fierce headache and a churning stomach. His mouth tasted like last night's ale and the air about him smelled of old urine and stale vomit, and even before he opened his eyes he understood he was dreaming from within Morddon's soul again. "Damn!" he growled through Morddon's lips.

When he did open his eyes he was lying on filthy straw in a dark, musty dungeon, and the previous night's memories flooded into his mind with merciless clarity: drinking alone in an inn near the center of Kathbeyanne, waiting day-in and day-out to go back to the wars and the battles and the bloodletting. He had practiced his sword skills with the strange, enigmatic angels by day, and each night tried to drink himself into oblivion. The other Benesh'ere hated him openly—one of their own who sold his sword to the highest bidder. Last night, sitting alone, pouring one tankard of ale after another down his throat, trying not to think of the hatred that drove him, their taunts and insults had become intolerable.

The bolt on the door to his cell slammed back loudly and the door crashed open, spilling a cascade of light onto the straw. A guard with a loaded crossbow stepped warily into the cell, keeping his back to the wall and his eyes on Morddon. The dungeon master followed close on his heels and said, "Up with you, scum. On your feet for your betters."

Morddon pulled himself slowly to his feet. Gilguard and Metadan entered the cell. Metadan's anger was almost palpable, but Gilguard looked at him with a calm, cold hatred, though when he spoke his voice came out almost a whisper. "Why?" he asked simply.

Morddon shrugged. "They started it. I finished it. Besides, it was seven to one."

The Benesh'ere warmaster nodded slowly and for a long moment considered Morddon's answer. "I've spoken to the innkeeper, and he confirms that my warriors did start it, and they did outnumber you seven to one, otherwise I would kill you myself."

Morddon tensed. "Would you like to try? I'd like to see you try, but you'd better have more than seven of your comrades to help you."

The guard with the crossbow tensed. Metadan looked at him and shook his head.

Gilguard shook his head at Morddon. "No, I don't want to try to kill you, and not just because I probably couldn't win. I just want to know why you take your hatred out on your brothers."

"I don't have any brothers," Morddon said.

"Two of them are dead," Gilguard continued as if Morddon had said nothing. "Another lost an arm last night, and another a leg this morning, and the other three: broken arms, legs, ribs, noses, jaws, skulls. Do you feel no remorse?"

Again Morddon shrugged. "They picked a fight, and I know of only one way to fight."

"Is it that simple?" Gilguard asked. "From what I've seen you're the best fighting man I've ever come across, though to look at you one would not know it—you look rather scrawny and underfed—but single-handed you take on seven of my best warriors, kill two and nearly kill the rest, and to you it's just a brawl. Do you fight anyone you can, any place, any time, for any reason? Is it really that simple?"

Morddon shook his head. "Nothing's that simple."

"Then explain it to me."

"I don't care to." Morddon looked at Metadan. "You've questioned the innkeeper? You know I was minding my own business, and it was not I who picked the fight?"

Metadan nodded without expression.

"Then I'm free to go?"

"You're free to go," Metadan said. "But go straight to the legion's barracks. Tomorrow, at dawn, we leave for the wars."

Morddon threw back his head and laughed. "Finally! Now I can have some peace." And with that he brushed Gilguard aside and walked out of the cell.

Gilguard frowned, looked carefully at Metadan. "Going to war will bring him peace?" he asked, and his frown deepened.

Metadan nodded, though as always there was no expression on his face. "That one's soul is a curiosity to me. And each time I meet him, my curiosity deepens."

••••

The voice, soft and gentle, was the only thing in Morgin's universe, and even though exhaustion and fatigue threatened to devour him, he struggled onward, following it blindly in the vain hope of a respite from the constant battle within his heart.

"Morgin . . . Morgin . . . Morgin . . ."

Cautiously he opened his eyes, parted his lips and tried to swallow, but a coarse, gritty dust caked his mouth and throat. The sword!

As if his thoughts were a trigger the sword flared in his hands, lifted itself high over his head and screamed its hatred at him. He pulled at it with weary muscles, threw his own hatred at it and forced it to the floor where it bit into the stone and raised another shower of chips. Again it grew silent.

Fatigue clouded his mind. He was on his knees in the center of the Hall, with the sword gripped in both hands before him, trying to control it with no power. *How long?* he wondered. *How long have I held it so?*

"Two days and nights," Rhianne said softly.

He was glad for the sight of her, even if she was a hallucination.

She shook her head. "No. I am real."

I'm sorry, he thought, thinking of all the years of pain he had given her. He struggled constantly just to hold onto consciousness.

Rhianne shrugged. "We were both stupid, and for that we must both bear the blame."

The words meant nothing to Morgin, and for some moments this beautiful girl kneeling before him was a stranger. The sword demanded too much of him. If his diligence failed for only an instant . . .

•••

"Morgin . . . Morgin."

Morgin opened his eyes again, looked again at the beautiful hallucination kneeling before him. In her right hand she held an empty sheath extended toward him. "Here," she said. "It will be easier if you cage the beast."

She was right. But how was he going to take hold of the sheath when he needed both hands to hold the sword's hatred in check?

The beautiful hallucination turned the open end of the sheath toward him. "I will hold the sheath, but I'll not touch that blade."

Morgin looked down at the tip of the sword where it rested in the last gouge it had cut from the floor, then he looked at the distance between it and the open end of the sheath. It might as well have been the distance between heaven and hell, for all it mattered.

"You must do it now," the hallucination said, "while you still have the strength."

Morgin nodded, lifted the blade slowly from the floor, sensed the evil within it tensing for a struggle, but with his will he clamped down on it mercilessly and it subsided. He held the tip out toward the sheath, though it wavered unsteadily before him. But just when he could go no further the beautiful hallucination moved with lightning speed and slammed the open end of the sheath down over the blade with a loud metallic crash, and suddenly Morgin felt free again. He felt as if he had been carrying a great weight for many leagues, then someone had taken the weight from his shoulders, and now nothing mattered but sleep.

He let his shoulders slump toward the floor, prepared to curl up right there and sleep for a century, but a hand arced out of the midnight surrounding his soul and struck his face with enough force to rock him back on his heels. His thoughts were as slow as winter honey, but the hand struck again, and again, and each time it stung more, until finally he saw Rhianne raise her hand to strike him a fourth time, and he raised his own hand to block the blow.

Rhianne hesitated, withheld the blow, looked at Morgin carefully. "Good. You're lucid. You must stay that way. When you leave this Hall every major clansman in the Lesser Clans will be watching you, and you must appear to be in control."

Morgin nodded. He understood her somewhat, but the fatigue was far too demanding. "Keep talking," he said. "Don't stop. It helps me stay anchored to this world. And let's don't waste any time."

"Then get on your feet. Now." Rhianne jumped to her feet, stood over him, helped him struggle to a standing position, though he staggered against her. "You'll have to stand straight, walk straight, look straight."

"You sound like Olivia."

Rhianne laughed as they started toward the doors of the Hall. "And you sound like me."

They waited while the extra timbers were again removed from the doors, then one door creaked open no more than a miserable crack. Morgin thought of Morddon, and decided the angry Benesh'ere's harshness might act to his advantage here. So with the last bit of strength he possessed he put a shoulder to the door, pushed hard, and at the same time growled, "Out of my way before I lose my temper." He shoved the door wide and stepped out among the waiting clansmen, who in turn stepped fearfully away from him. He looked at them carefully, as they all looked at him suspiciously. "Well?" he demanded. "What are you looking at?"

All of them but Olivia stepped back a pace, while she stood her ground and looked through him as if she understood well the game he played. At least she did not interfere.

"Of course I look like hell," he said, and like sheep they stepped back again. "I haven't had any food or sleep for two days, a situation which I intend to remedy shortly."

He walked with long, great strides, approaching the impenetrable wall of the crowd as if he would walk right over any who stood in his way, and the crowd parted fearfully. All the way to his apartments he did not look back, though he knew Rhianne was close behind him and in his heart he thanked her for that again and again. Just before he reached his rooms his legs gave way beneath him. Rhianne stepped around him quickly, and pretending to be an obedient cow of a wife, she opened the door and held it for him, saying only, "My lord."

He walked past her on trembling legs, and barely managed to get to his bed before passing out.

6

The Hire Sword

MORDDON AWOKE LONG before dawn on the morning of his departure from Kathbeyanne, though with the exception of a single angel sitting on the cot next to his, he was alone in the barracks of the First Legion. He often wondered if any of the damn angels ever slept, which reminded Morgin of his own thoughts concerning Ellowyn that seemed so long ago. From the perspective of this dream that was actually still in the distant future. As he wiped the sleep from his eyes the angel sitting on the cot nearby said, "You are to follow me, Benesh'ere."

Morddon nodded, reached under his cot and retrieved a long, thin, gray canvas sack, about the length of an ordinary man, though considerably shorter than his Benesh'ere frame. Beneath the stiff canvas his hands recognized the shape of the most powerful of the Benesh'ere weapons: the longbow. Fashioning the bow had been the only worthwhile thing he'd done during his weeks in Kathbeyanne, and it and his sword were now his only permanent possessions.

The angel led him to a large staging area well outside the walls of the city where thousands of men, horses and hundreds of supply wagons were gathered. They went directly to a temporary corral in which several hundred horses had been penned. "Choose your own mount," the angel said, and without another word he turned and walked away.

Morddon leaned on one of the beams of the corral and shook his head sadly. "Damn angels!" he muttered, closing his eyes and running his fingers through his knotted and unkempt hair. He opened his eyes just in time to see a tall mare separate herself from the jostling mass of beasts in the corral and trot his way. She was coal black, without a single feature to mark her coat, and as she approached Morgin instantly recognized Mortiss. She trotted up to him, snorted derisively as if to remind him what a fool he could be, and waited impatiently for him to saddle and ride her.

That first morning out of Kathbeyanne, riding with the First Legion of Angels, Morddon's heart soared with joy like a prisoner freed after many years in a dark and deep dungeon. It turned Morgin's stomach to see the Benesh'ere ride so joyfully to war, and to feel that joy himself. But the joyful sense of freedom died in the choking dust of several thousand horses, and as the leagues passed beneath Mortiss's hooves Morgin noticed that the closer Morddon got to the wars the more he managed to relax, to put the tension and the hatred behind him, and to view life without the harsh edges of his bitterness. Morgin, plagued with Morddon's memories of many years of slaughter, and his own memories of Csairne Glen, grew morose and fearful of the days to come.

He was part of a combined force of the first four legions of angels, two full companies of Benesh'ere, one company of mercenaries, and a flight of about one hundred of the black, winged griffins. As a common soldier Morddon's only responsibilities were to take care of his horse and weapons, and to keep up with the general pace of the march. And since his riding companions were angels of the First Legion, all of whom he found inhumanly boring, he was left to himself for the most part, which suited him nicely.

On the eighth day out of Kathbeyanne he awoke at sunrise, used a small portion of his water ration to shave and wash—as they approached the wars he was beginning to pay attention to his personal appearance again. He rolled up his kit, and to kill time before his breakfast ration he left the camp, found a small, clear hillock some distance from the outer perimeter. There, he began a series of stretching exercises he used when a real workout was not possible. With his sword drawn, and his eyes closed, he concentrated on each muscle carefully, extending it, then contracting it, until he felt the knots and tension relax. He must now prepare his body for the battles and the warring that would soon come, and he drifted slowly into a mild state of self-hypnosis at the pleasure that came with Morddon's knowledge and control of his body.

"Harrumph! Um . . . excuse me."

At the sound of the voice Morddon froze, then after many seconds opened his eyes. A young Benesh'ere lad stood cautiously in front of him. Morddon spoke softly, "What do you want, boy?"

The boy frowned, obviously thinking of the stories he'd heard of the maniac that towered over him. "You're Lord Morddon, are you not?"

"I am Morddon, but I'm no lord. And who are you?"

"I am WindHollow," the boy said.

Morddon nodded. "A powerful name that. What do you want with me, Wind-Hollow?"

"I was told by the warmasters Metadan and Gilguard to bring you to them." The boy stood uncertainly, as if Morddon might burst into a murderous rage at any moment.

Morddon tried not to smile, but failed. He sheathed his sword. "Then lead the way."

Near the tents at the center of camp several men, angels and one woman were leaning over a table full of maps, while not far to one side two of the black griffins sat quietly on their haunches. Even from a distance Morddon recognized one as TarnThane himself, the Griffin Lord, for the strange winged beasts were massive towers of taloned might. Closer yet, he saw gathered about the table Gilguard and two of his lieutenants, the Benesh'ere princess AnneRhianne, Metadan and two archangels whom Morddon did not recognize, plus Ellowyn. Weeks earlier Morgin had learned she didn't recognize him.

Morddon and WindHollow stopped near the group at the map table and waited silently for the ongoing conversation to cease. TarnThane was giving a scouting report: "...Most of the countryside is unoccupied. We saw no sign of the Goath, but we caught an occasional glimpse of a hound."

Several of them started at that. "In large numbers?" Metadan asked.

TarnThane shook his head. "No. Just a few. Probably scouts."

Metadan considered that carefully. "I wonder if WolfDane himself is considering some action against the Goath."

Morddon had heard of the hellhounds, and their king WolfDane, but he himself had never seen one. They were reputed to be giant hounds as large as a horse, with jaws that could snap a man in two. Legend had it they had escaped from the netherhells when Beayaegoath was first exiled there, and had never stopped fighting against the hordes he commanded. They shunned man and all things of mankind, and they fought their own battles against the Goath, refusing to work in any way with the mortal forces fighting their common enemy. Morddon had heard a story that Metadan had once saved WolfDane's life, but no one knew if there was any truth to it.

"If the hounds intend to attack the Goath," Gilguard said thoughtfully, "I would dearly like to know where and when." He looked at Metadan. "Is there any chance you could get them to work with us. If they trust any of us, it would be you."

Metadan shook his head. "It's not a matter of trust. Their ways are just too different from ours. We'll have to depend on our griffin friends here."

TarnThane threw his head back. "And we need someone working with us from the ground."

At that Metadan turned to Morddon, nodded for him to come forward. He did so, and politely greeted the group assembled at the map table, and as a formality he apologized for being absent when they needed him.

"Polite words?" AnneRhianne asked sarcastically. "And an apology? And all in the space of a single sentence! And he's shaved, and washed! I begin to believe you, Metadan, when you say he is a changed man."

Morddon stifled an angry retort.

"Now I want no arguments here," Metadan said carefully, looking at each of them, "unless you're arguing the business at hand. This is a council of war, and we have decisions to make."

"Why am I here?" Morddon asked, "A common soldier among such hallowed company?"

The griffin TarnThane spoke with a hearty laugh. "Because you're not that common, my sad Benesh'ere friend."

Morddon kept his eyes on Metadan. "What does he mean by that?"

Metadan answered with a question. "How long have you been fighting in the wars?"

Morddon shrugged. "Better than twelve years."

"And how old are you?"

"I've seen twenty-four summers. But we've been through this before so what's the point?"

"From childhood to manhood," the griffin cried sorrowfully, "with no boyhood between. Ahhh! A hard life indeed!"

"No breaks?" Metadan asked. "Fighting for twelve years without rest?"

Morddon shook his head and wondered at all the questions. "A day or two here and there. Sometimes more. This last stretch in Kathbeyanne was the longest I've ever been away. Why?"

Metadan nodded. "As near as we can tell, you have more experience out here than anyone among us. When I question the more experienced commanders, and jog their memories a little, not one of them can remember a time when you weren't out here, though they remember you only because of your longevity and not because of any great deeds. And AuelThane there"—Metadan indicated with his hand the griffin perched next to TarnThane—"tells us you scout these hills with such stealth not even the griffins can spot you from the air, even if they know you're down there somewhere."

Morddon nodded, remembering the other griffin now from battles past, and how he'd used Morgin's shadowmagic through the years to conceal his position from his enemies, and apparently from his allies too. Sharing such memories reminded Morgin he'd always been a part of this dream, and that, he did not like. "What do you want of me?" Morddon asked the archangel.

"Your knowledge of these hills," Metadan said, stabbing a finger into the map on the table. "I could use a scout with your abilities. Would that suit you?"

Morddon nodded. "I like working alone."

"I thought you might."

"What is this?" AnneRhianne demanded. "A mercenary accepting extra duties without demanding additional pay? I don't believe my ears."

Gilguard grinned, though he turned his face aside to conceal it. But Morddon could not hide his own anger as he looked at the tall Benesh'ere princess. Morgin kept wanting to call her Rhi. "I hadn't really thought of it that way, Your Highness," Morddon said to her, then grinned. "But now that you mention it I should be paid more."

"Fine," Metadan said. "You can have whatever you want. I really don't care about the gold."

"No," Morddon said flatly. "I won't hire out to you as a scout. Our agreement was for one year of my services as a common soldier, nothing more."

Metadan actually frowned, the first expression Morddon had ever seen on the angel's face. Metadan shook his head. "But I thought you said—"

Morddon interrupted him, pointed at AnneRhianne, "If you want me as a scout then she must hire me, and she must pay me, with coins from her own purse, and by her own hand."

If there were any color in the white of a Benesh'ere face, it disappeared from AnneRhianne's in that moment. "Never," she said.

TarnThane crowed with laughter. "You thought he had no pride, my princess."

"Shut your beak," she said, though even Gilguard saw the irony in Morddon's demand and his grin widened. "Wipe that grin off your face," she said to him.

"If you won't pay me," Morddon said, "then your sharp tongue has cost this army the best scout it could have had, for there are no other circumstances under which I will accept."

AnneRhianne was ready to explode, but with visible effort she controlled herself. She looked at Morddon closely, and when she realized he would not yield, she said, "Very well, what's your price, mercenary? Another gold coin for your purse?"

Morddon shook his head. "No. One small copper coin, to be paid to me each day, and by your own hand. And when I am out of the camp, and unavailable, you will hold the coins for my return. But remember, it is you who must seek me out, and you who must pay me."

Her eyes narrowed further at the added insult of such a small price. "It appears I have no choice," she said. "I agree. And now that we have a bargain, mercenary, never doubt that I will keep my end of it. Just see that you keep yours." She looked at Metadan. "Am I required further, my lord?"

Metadan shook his head. "You may go."

She looked once more at Morddon, and the hatred he saw in her eyes saddened him.

••••

AnnaRail's attention drifted away from the heated debate raging in the center of the Hall of Wills, and settled on the scarred and pitted walls that surrounded them all. The Hall had received only a cursory cleaning for this unprecedented extended session of the Lesser Council, and as yet no real repairs had been attempted. The magnitude of the destruction drew her eyes again and again away from the debate. It struck a cold shaft of fear into her heart, and served as a constant reminder to them of the topic of discussion.

Olivia and BlakeDown had argued through the afternoon and well into the night, though AnnaRail knew they'd soon settle the issue. But even though Morgin's life hung in the balance, she stayed far back in the crowd and was careful to avoid participating in any way, for nothing she said would serve in his favor. Instead she waited quietly near an exit, ready to leave the instant she determined the battle was lost.

"He has endangered us all," BlakeDown said, speaking loud enough for everyone to hear. "Each and every one of us, our families, and our kinsmen far from here, for he cannot control that beast he has brought into this world, and who can say what will stop it when it begins devouring the countryside? Certainly not I, and you all know I am a sorcerer of more than trifling power."

BlakeDown paced back and forth in the middle of the Hall as he spoke, stopping occasionally to look fearfully at one of the stone pillars Morgin's sword had whittled down to a splinter of rock. "All of us here have sensed the magnitude of its evil. We stood outside for two days while he fought it, and I grant you it was a valiant fight. But it was through his own stupidity such a power was allowed access to this world, and by his own admission he has lost his power. He lays now in a stupor of exhaustion with no remaining strength for the next battle we all know will come. So I can have no pity for the man. He has brought this fate upon himself, and now he must bear the responsibility for his actions."

BlakeDown paused and looked at Olivia, who stood with him in the center of the Hall. Under normal circumstances the old woman would have spoken out long ago, but the odds had been stacked against Morgin all afternoon, so she was moving carefully lest she incite public opinion even further against him. AnnaRail sensed within the old witch that the battle was lost, that she could not sway the Council sufficiently to save Morgin. Believing his life was the only thing that held the power of the talisman within this world, the Lesser Council would soon place him under sentence of death, then move speedily to carry out the sentence while he lay unconscious and defenseless. As Olivia spoke AnnaRail slipped quietly out of the Hall.

She kept her pace to a calm, even walk, knowing any appearance of haste might alert Morgin's enemies to her purpose. When she knocked softly on the door to Morgin's suite the answer that came to her ears was a muffled, "Who's there?"

She said nothing, but touched the door with the palm of her hand and knew all those of power within were satisfied. She heard muffled words behind the door, then the sound of heavy furniture being moved aside, then the door opened a crack.

France peered out, looked up and down the hall, then, holding a bare sword in one hand, he opened the door to admit her. Within, Morgin lay on his bed in a stupor, one hand unconsciously gripping the hilt of his sword, the other gripping the sheath. Rhianne sat beside him trying to comfort him with her power, and JohnEngine, Brandon, Roland, the Surriot and the Balenda stood nervously ready with swords of their own. AnnaRail was surprised to find DaNoel absent, and NickoLot present. Nicki seemed much older. "What are you doing here?" AnnaRail asked her.

Nicki's eyes hardened. "No one is going to murder my brother, not without a fight from me."

"It won't be murder," AnnaRail said flatly. "It will be a proper execution carried out under a legal sentence of death."

"Call it what you like," the young girl said. "I'm going to fight."

There came no rousing chorus of cheers from the others, but their eyes held the same determination as Nicki's.

"Are they really going to kill him?" Nicki asked.

AnnaRail nodded. "Yes. We don't have much time."

"Then we fight," JohnEngine said flatly.

"No we don't," AnnaRail snapped angrily, shaking her head. In that moment she saw in the eyes of the swordsman that he, at least, understood the futility of such a battle.

JohnEngine's eyes widened. "But—"

"Be silent and listen," AnnaRail barked at him more harshly than she intended. "If you make a stand here you'll die, and then he'll die too, and you'll have gained nothing."

"I won't abandon my brother."

AnnaRail found it difficult to hold her temper in check. "And you believe I will?"

JohnEngine shook his head and lowered his eyes. "No. Of course not."

"Then be silent and listen, for I intend to keep him alive, and all of us with him."

"How?" JohnEngine demanded.

"Shortly the Council will declare him an outlaw, and then not even we can legally help him without starting a full scale war. So he must leave. Now." She looked at France; he nodded his agreement. "But it's obvious he cannot travel on his own so someone will have to go with him." Still looking at France, she asked, "Will you go?"

France nodded, though he said nothing.

"I'll go with you," the Surriot said without emotion.

"And I," the Balenda added flatly.

"I'll go too," JohnEngine said.

AnnaRail shook her head. "No. House Elhiyne must stay out of this. Besides, you're going to be our diversion."

7

The Outlaw

ALL OF MORGIN'S instincts pulled him urgently toward consciousness, but his body remained locked within a sea of lethargy. In the background of his soul he sensed Rhianne and AnnaRail feeding him strength with their own power, but when he peeled open his eyes his lids hung heavy with exhaustion, and it required a constant effort to remain conscious. The sound of heavy rain pounding on the roof of the castle dominated his thoughts, a constant, numbing roar that threatened to lull him back to sleep.

"You must stand," AnnaRail told him, "And you must move on your own. If you lean on us someone will surely notice and alert the Council. And by the name of the Unnamed King keep a tight rein on that sword!"

Morgin wanted to ask a hundred questions, but the urgency in AnnaRail's voice drove him to obey in silence. He shook his head to clear it and sat up, stood unsteadily, and asked, "What's going on?"

Rhianne answered. "This moment the Council is declaring you an outlaw, and within the hour they'll come for your blood. There's no time to explain further. We've prepared an escape, but you must move quickly. A second's delay might mean your life."

Fear helped sober Morgin. "What do I do?"

AnnaRail handed him a dark, hooded, sleeved cloak, said, "Put this on, and make sure the hood shields your face."

Morgin noticed then that both women were wearing similar garments. He pushed his arms into the sleeves, pulled the hood over his head, fumbled at the cloak's clasp for a moment before securing it.

AnnaRail adjusted her own hood, burying her face in shadows. "Now follow me. We're going to the stables. If someone tries to stop us, Rhianne and I will take care of them, but you must not stop. Keep your face turned away from the light, and keep walking, but do not run, for that will certainly attract attention."

Rhianne opened the door a crack, peered out into the hallway, then opened the door fully and stepped out. Morgin followed her, with AnnaRail close behind.

The castle was unusually dark and badly lit, and it occurred to Morgin that AnnaRail had probably seen to that. Out in the hallway the roar of the rain was even louder, and while it would be miserable outside, he couldn't have hoped for better if he must become a hunted fugitive.

They moved cautiously down the large stairway at the center of the castle. Once on the main floor he heard raised voices coming from the Hall, punctuated occasionally by the growl of an angry crowd. AnnaRail quickened her pace, but they had barely reached the castle's front entrance when the doors of the Hall burst open and the growl became a roar, and with only an instant to spare they slipped out into the night. A driving wind slanted the rain horizontally into their faces.

AnnaRail shouted above the wind, "We have only a few moments before they reach your room and find you've gone." She turned, and with Rhianne following close behind, she started across the castle yard toward the stables. Morgin followed, splashing through mud up to his ankles, knowing he would make an easy target for an ambitious bowman. When they reached the stables AnnaRail raised a hand to pound on the stable doors, but before she could do so one of them creaked open.

Inside, the stable boy Erlin held a hooded lamp with one hand, and with the other slammed the door shut. Someone grabbed Morgin and pushed him toward Mortiss, who was saddled and ready. He climbed up into her saddle, marveling that he had the strength to do so. JohnEngine mounted a horse nearby, and by the dim light of Erlin's lamp Morgin noticed four more horses behind JohnEngine's, all saddled, and each with a sack of grain tied in its saddle and a hooded cloak tied about the sack. JohnEngine grinned at him. "The cloaks were my idea," he said proudly. "Makes 'em look just a little more like riders crouching low in the saddle, eh? The night and the rain'll have to do the rest."

Rhianne gripped Morgin's left hand tightly. "Ride out of the stable alone," she said, "And keep your horse at a walk. The guards opened the gates earlier for Val, and with a few small spells we've managed to keep them that way. Try to get out of the castle unnoticed, and as soon as you reach the woodland between here and the village, cut off the road to the right. Val and Cort and France are waiting there for you. Go southwest, to Aud. Aiergain would not allow the clans to hunt you there."

It occurred to Morgin that in many ways his life was coming to an end. He was no longer a wizard, nor a clansman, nor an Elhiyne. They had given it all to him when he didn't want it, and now they were taking it away when he did. His soul and heart filled with bitterness, and he asked, "But they'll hunt me tonight, eh?"

Rhianne shook her head. "No. When the mob comes looking for you JohnEngine and his sacks-of-grain are going to lead them in the opposite direction. They'll hunt him, not you."

She threw her hood back and her eyes filled with tears. Morgin had so many things to tell her, but all he said was, "I love you."

She clutched at his hand, tears now streaming freely down her cheeks. "And I you."

"You must go," AnnaRail hissed sharply. "Now."

Erlin shielded his lamp and pulled the stable door open, again only a crack. Morgin touched his spurs to Mortiss's flanks and she trotted forward at an easy pace that should arouse no suspicion, though the very fact of a rider going out in this weather would not go unnoticed.

The rain was pouring down even harder now, cutting his visibility to almost nothing and pounding with a roar into the mud of the castle yard. Yet at the same time the yard was possessed of an eerie quiet, as if the castle and MichaelOff's ghost were waiting for something.

As Morgin approached the open castle gates they loomed out of the blackness of the night like the jaws of some enormous beast. There were always crossbowmen and archers on the battlements above, and with the gates jammed open they would be uneasy and watchful, so he fought the growing urge to spur Mortiss into a charge. He watched the gates grow larger before him as she trotted forward, all going well, but then at the last instant, only a stone's throw from freedom, a voice called out from above, "Halt! Identify yourself."

Morgin tugged gently on Mortiss's reins and brought her to a stop. He couldn't answer them. He was too well known. His voice would be recognized.

"Identify yourself," the voice called again. "Speak now, or we'll drop you and your horse where you stand."

In that instant an angry mob burst out of the castle and began spilling into the yard. The next instant JohnEngine and his sack-of-grain riders charged out of the stables heading straight for the gates and Morgin. At the same time a cloaked figure—whom Morgin later realized was Rhianne—pointed at JohnEngine and shouted above the rain, "It's the outlaw wizard!"

Morgin heard the twang of a crossbow, waited through an eternity of an instant for the bolt to punch its way through his chest, but saw it bury itself instead in one of the sacks of grain as JohnEngine and his horses raced past him. On foot the mob charged chaotically across the yard to the gates, so Morgin pulled his sword, waved it above his head, pointed it through the gates at the fleeing figure of JohnEngine and shouted, "It's the outlaw wizard. I'll get him." Then he spurred Mortiss into a charge, slapped her flank with the flat of his sword, and raced through the open castle gates.

He had to trust Mortiss to sense her own footing, for the rain and the gloom of the night blinded him completely, and at full charge the drops stung his face like grains of sand in a high wind. He kept low in the saddle, waiting for an arrow to pierce his back, or for Mortiss—like poor SarahGirl before her—to collapse beneath him. But no arrow came out of the night, and then he reached the edge of the forest, and there JohnEngine waited.

"Turn off here," JohnEngine said. "Stay close to the edge of the forest and ride hard. Don't try to find Val; let him find you, and by the gods don't hide in your shadows or he never will."

JohnEngine looked sharply toward the castle. "They're coming," he said. He nudged his horse next to Mortiss, reached out, gripped Morgin's forearm tightly. "We'll meet again, brother. I swear that now before you, and next time we'll stand and fight, eh?" And with both of them seated atop horses, he leaned over and tried unsuccessfully to kiss Morgin, but gave up as their two horses jostled beneath them. JohnEngine spun his horse about, and with his horses and sacks of grain charged off into the night.

Morgin spurred Mortiss off the road, but on the uneven ground there he was forced to keep her pace to a slow trot, and after what seemed only seconds his ears caught the sound of the mob on the road behind him: the thunder of many hooves and the shouts of angry riders. Quickly he pulled Mortiss just within the edge of the forest and waited breathlessly. The cries and hoof beats approached, then dwindled slowly into the distance, but even after they were gone some instinct told him to wait longer.

While he waited the rain slackened, and after what seemed an eternity he heard the creak of saddle leather, a horse moving at a slow walk. Then out of the darkness a lone rider appeared and pulled his horse to a stop at the point where Morgin had entered the forest. Morgin moved his hand carefully to the hilt of his sword.

"Elhiyne," the rider called out. Morgin recognized ErrinCastle's voice. "I know you're there. But unlike my father I'm not here to hunt you. Not that I have any great liking or admiration for you, but I owe you a debt, and I am here to repay it. My conduct toward your wife was unforgivable. I know now that I was enspelled by the Decouix, but to use him as an excuse would be as dishonorable as my previous actions were unforgivable. I therefore grant you your freedom, and I give you my word I will do nothing to hinder your escape. This makes us even, Elhiyne. The next time we meet, I will kill you for the outlaw you are." And with that, ErrinCastle yanked his horse's reins toward the road, and disappeared into the night.

Morgin waited a few moments more, then continued on. As he rode through the driving rain the trees of the small forest beside him were almost invisible in the darkness of the night's gloom, and just to keep them in sight he stayed uncomfortably close to them. He traveled for a good distance, following the curve of the forest as it turned away from Elhiyne, and began to wonder if he'd missed his friends. But then three mounted riders loomed out of the darkness before him with swords drawn.

There came no greeting. France merely said, "Let's ride, now, fast and hard, before that mob finds out who they're really chasing."

••••

An odd silence descended on the castle yard as the last of the mob raced through the gates on hastily saddled mounts, and AnnaRail breathed a sigh of relief. She crossed the yard quickly to get in out of the rain, but she met Tulellcoe standing just inside the main entrance, and at the look on his face her heart almost came to a stop.

"What have you done?" he demanded coldly.

She ignored him, tried to walk past him, but he grabbed her arm and spun her to face him. "What have you done?"

She yanked her arm out of his grip. "No more than any mother would do."

"You're a fool!" he said, then turned away.

She reached out desperately and caught his arm, but he refused to be stopped and pulled her along beside him. "Where are you going?" she pleaded.

He halted, turned to face her. "I'm going to find him myself, and carry out the Council's sentence." He hesitated, looked in her eyes, and, as if reading her thoughts, added, "And you can believe I'll not be foolish enough to follow horses ridden by sacks of grain."

She reacted without thought. Her magic came upon her unbidden, coalesced into a black, hot spark of hatred cupped within the palm of her hand. She swung it at him like a club, realizing she had lost control and might well kill him. But his hand shot out instinctively and caught her wrist in an iron grip, stopping it only inches from his face. They stood that way for several seconds, facing each other silently while she fought for control, and slowly the power she had called forth faded, though not until she had released it completely did he release her hand. Shamefully she dropped it to her side.

Tulellcoe's face could have been chiseled from stone for all the expression it held. His eyes cut into her soul like white-hot steel. "As much as I hate that damn Council, I have to admit they're right."

"You don't know that," she said.

"And you don't know they're wrong."

Roland, speaking softly, startled them both. "I do."

Tulellcoe turned to face him. "What did you say?"

"I said I know the council is wrong."

"You know nothing."

Roland shook his head sadly. "The only thing I don't know, is how I know what I do know. But I do know the Council is wrong, as only I can know such things."

Tulellcoe shook his head, though while outwardly he scoffed, AnnaRail saw that Roland's words had stung him. She understood then that he was forcing himself to do what he thought was right, even while he hated the doing of it.

"Use your own judgment," she said to him. "Don't follow the dictates of the Council blindly."

He frowned uncertainly, then looked at Roland, and the silence between them grew heavy and stilted. He turned about, threw the doors of the castle open, and walked out into the stormy night.

Olivia stepped out of a shadow near the base of the stairs. "Well done, Roland. You may have just saved Morgin's life."

AnnaRail exploded. "What do you mean well done? You betrayed my son to that pack of wolves and now you speak of saving his life."

The old woman threw her head back and laughed. "Oh you foolish woman! Do you think there is anything you do within these walls that I do not know about long before the doing of it? If I had wanted those jackals to have him, they would have had him. Do you believe for an instant you could have spirited him away without my help? Who do you think instructed the guards to open the gates for the swordsman and the twonames? Had it not been for me those gates would have never been opened in the first place."

Speechless, AnnaRail spluttered, "But—"

"But nothing!" the old woman said. "Your greatest danger was Tulellcoe, and you didn't even realize it. He feels responsible for Morgin. He knew about this talisman even before Csairne Glen, but he failed to help Morgin then, and he failed to help him during the intervening months. He blames himself that Morgin is under sentence of death, and he would rather kill Morgin himself, kill him cleanly, than let those jackals have him."

"But why didn't you stop him?" AnnaRail demanded.

Olivia shook her head. "The only way to stop Tulellcoe when his mind is made up is to kill him, and not even Morgin is worth that. Tulellcoe can be as stubborn as Morgin, and as uncontrollable when his mind is set. The two of them are alike in so many ways, if I didn't know Tulellcoe better I'd wonder if he didn't do a little whoring about nine months before Morgin was born. The only way to stop Tulellcoe is to convince him to stop himself, and Roland began that process by introducing doubt with his intuition. But you had to lose control like a stupid young girl, and in doing so you hurt Morgin's cause in Tulellcoe's mind. We can only hope the doubt Roland introduced will grow, for Tulellcoe will find the whoreson, and if that doubt fades between now and then, then Morgin will die. It is that simple."

8

To Sense the Sword

RHIANNE STUMBLED UP to her room, conscious only of the sword and its power. A part of her knew she should feel some triumph at Morgin's escape, but the talisman demanded too much of her for her to feel anything beyond a need to find a place where she would not be disturbed.

Her handmaidens were waiting for her, and immediately they began a flood of gossipy twittering that threatened to overwhelm her. She silenced them with a single, angry bark, and when they finally took notice of the magic in her eyes they understood what was required of them. In silence they helped her out of her wet clothing, wrapped her in a dry nightgown and put her to bed. She was barely conscious of these things, for all of her power was devoted to the sword, to holding it at bay during the first critical hours of Morgin's escape so he could concentrate on the world about him.

She shut out the world around her, thought only of Morgin and the blade, placed her own magic between his power and that of the sword, and let the hours pass without rest or comfort. She had never done anything so terrifying, for as she penetrated deeper into the depths of the talisman's magic, a malign intelligence hovered there, an unwholesome consciousness that, until then, had been aware only of Morgin. But now, with her interference, it had grown aware of her, and never again would she be able to lower her defenses fully and rest.

••••

Morddon brought Mortiss to a sudden halt and eyed the trail suspiciously. All about him the soft roar of a slow drizzling rain spattered on the leaves of the forest. It made him uneasy to have his sense of hearing so encumbered when on the trail of his enemy, not to mention the discomfort of the damp cold that penetrated to his soul. For the hundredth time he looked at the sky; blanketed by low, gray clouds, it gave no hope the rain would end soon.

He climbed wearily out of Mortiss's saddle, squatted in the middle of the trail and stared for a long time at the hoof prints, undeniably a group of seven Kulls. Without Morgin's memories to guide him, Morddon would not have known what a Kull was, for they were foreign to this time and this dream.

The spoor was fresh, not more than a few hours old, the signs were there for even the most inexperienced tracker to read: seven Kulls; not six, not eight, but exactly seven. And yet only that morning he had been following just three. Something strange was going on; of that he had no doubt.

He got back into the saddle and started up the trail again, moving with more caution than before. He was well behind his own lines, and there should not be groups of Kulls roving about here. Possibly his enemy might have begun using Kulls, and a small number of halfmen might have become separated from their main column, and through the fortunes of war find themselves behind the lines of their enemy. But this was the second group Morddon had come across, and like the first, after tracking it for some time, it had met and joined forces with another group. He continued tracking them in the steady drizzle of the rain-soaked forest.

Morddon had been scouting the Goath hordes for Metadan for more than a month, and during that time Metadan's forces had met the enemy in full-scale engagements twice. Both times they had been victorious, though not without losses of their own. Morddon knew that he—and the intelligence he'd gathered—had been partly responsible for those victories, and that gave him almost as much satisfaction as doing the killing himself, though he'd managed to do his own share of killing on his scouting expeditions. Then six days ago the clouds set in and the rain began; it had stopped only occasionally, poured heavily for brief periods, but mostly it just rained a constant, steady drizzle, without wind, thunder or lightning.

The weather ended any plans for real battles, so he decided to come in and get a well-deserved hot meal since he'd been out on the trail for more than twelve days. But on his way in, after crossing into what was friendly territory, he'd come across the trail of that first group of Kulls: two of them. He followed them, and the next day they joined up with four more that had come from a different direction. That night he killed them all in their sleep.

It had bothered him at the time; two separate groups of Kulls well behind enemy lines meeting and joining forces. But then, stranger things had happened in war. And then late yesterday he'd come across the trail of three more. Of course he took up the trail, intending to catch up and kill them in their sleep like the others. Of course it troubled him that there were three such groups of halfmen wandering through these hills; but for the third group to join up with a fourth . . . Morddon didn't need magic to know that something was up.

About midday the rain stopped, though the clouds hung close and gray. Without the constant patter of raindrops on the forest leaves, Morddon's ability to hear danger improved. Several hours later he caught a hint of sound, pulled Mortiss to a stop and waited. After many seconds it came again: a faint, distant cry of death.

He dismounted and led Mortiss off the trail, while Morgin pulled a cloak of shadow about both man and horse. He found it difficult moving through the undergrowth of the forest, but earlier he'd spotted a high ridge from where he should be able to see a good distance through the mist shrouded hills, and a direct route appeared to be the only means of gaining access to it. The climb was difficult, but as he approached the ridge his ears picked up certain sounds with increasing clarity: a shout, the clash of a sword, silence for a long time, the whinny of a frightened horse, the hoof beats of a charging animal on a muddy road.

At the summit of the climb he left Mortiss to graze, then dropped to his hands and knees and crawled to the lip of the ridge. Far below, in the middle of a long strip of road that wound its way through the misty hills of the forest, a coach lay on its side. The coachman, two attendants, and two guards lay sprawled and lifeless in the road, while nine Kulls swarmed over and about the coach. He reasoned that the seven he was following had met up with another two, then, as a group, had stumbled across an unlucky traveler on the road below.

While Morddon looked on the Kulls pried open the door of the overturned coach. Three of them dropped down into the body of the coach, and moments later lifted the unconscious form of a woman from its interior. Though the distance was too great to distinguish any detail, Morddon caught a momentary flash of bone white skin and knew she must be AnneRhianne.

The Kulls moved quickly, tying her to the bottom of the coach between its axles in an upright position with both arms and legs spread wide, which meant she was still alive. The Kulls were probably going to have a little fun, and since Morgin understood all too well what the Kulls considered fun, Morddon started hastily down the slope leading Mortiss on foot.

With the Kulls concentrating on looting the coach, and their minds preoccupied in anticipation of torture and rape, Morddon took the chance of depending almost wholly on Morgin's shadowmagic and his own sure footing. The Kulls would wait for AnneRhianne to regain consciousness before beginning, so he had only a little time to spare. A deep ravine in the side of the hill forced him to veer far to one side, and by the time he reached the road the overturned coach was hidden around a sharp bend far in the distance.

Leading Mortiss he trotted up the road, and at the bend he pulled her into the forest and started to tie her reins to a nearby tree. But she shook her head wildly and refused to let him do so, though she was careful to avoid making any noise by snorting, and seeing the intelligence in her eyes, he changed his mind. "Have it your way then," he whispered, tying her reins loosely to the saddle horn. "But stay here until you're needed."

He untied the bow case from the saddle, unwrapped the canvas and strung the bow quickly. The bow pleased him. He'd made it from the best ash, spent hours shaping and treating the wood. It could punch one of the steel tipped, arm-length shafts he'd fashioned straight through a man, or pierce full plate armor. He worried momentarily about the string so recently fashioned of stretched gut and not properly aged, and now exposed to the damp. He forced that thought from his mind, strapped his sheathed sword over his back to keep it out of the way, slung his quiver of arrows over his shoulder, and slipped quietly into the forest and one of Morgin's shadows.

The coach came into sight as soon as he rounded the bend. He didn't go deep into the forest, but stayed close to the edge of the road, slipping in and out of the shadows there as he worked his way toward the coach, trying to keep it in sight at all times. AnneRhianne had regained consciousness, and was pulling quite actively at her bonds, shouting angrily at her captors, though with no hint of hysteria in her voice. With the coach turned on its side, the Kulls had tied her to its underbelly, torn her clothing away down to her waist, and two of them were busily groping at her breasts and crotch. A third Kull was on his knees in the middle of the road much closer to Morddon and facing him, busily rifling the body of the coachman; his back to his comrades and the coach. Morddon kept a close eye on him since he might look up at any moment. Then one of the two groping at AnneRhianne leaned back and slapped her with a blow that resounded loudly through the damp mountain air. "Bitch!" he shouted.

Morddon froze as the Kull in the middle of the road looked up and back toward the coach. "You monsters!" AnneRhianne cried. One of the Kulls jammed a torn piece of her gown into her mouth to silence her, then the two went back to their groping. Their comrade in the middle of the road laughed and returned to his scavenging.

They were just within bowshot, but still too far for good accuracy, and he still didn't know where the other six Kulls where, though he saw their horses tethered on the far side of the coach. As he worked his way closer he caught glimpses of four more behind it, but even after he'd reached a reasonable range he had yet to locate the last two. Tentatively he drew an arrow, nocked it, edged closer a few more steps, still wondering where the last two Kulls might be.

"Blast you!" one of the two Kulls groping at AnneRhianne cried. He cuffed her hard with a closed fist, gripped her chin and slammed her head against the coach's floorboards two or three times. Her eyes fluttered near the edge of consciousness. This time the Kull in the road scavenging the dead coachman did not look up. The overturned coach rocked and one of the missing Kulls hoisted himself up out of its interior. He climbed up onto the side of the coach and looked down at his two comrades.

One more left, Morddon thought. *Just one more.*

The Kull standing on the coach said to his comrades, "If you can't handle that bitch any better than that I'll take her for myself."

The one who'd cuffed AnneRhianne displayed a large, ugly knife and snarled, "If you try you'll get nothing but steel."

Morddon tensed, turned slightly to one side to get a better aim and pull on the bow, stood up straight and flexed it once. He'd rather be closer, and he still wanted to know where that last Kull was.

The halfman standing above shook his head and turned his back on them, bent to look into the interior of the coach again. AnneRhianne spit the gag from her mouth; her head shot forward, her teeth flashed and she bit into the ear of the halfman holding the knife.

"You whore," he shouted. He hit her with the butt of the knife but she refused to let go of his ear. He flailed wildly at her while his comrade cuffed her again and again. When they finally pulled her away the Kull's blood dripped freely from her mouth, and with a triumphant gleam in her eyes she spit his ear in his face.

"Ahhh!" he raged, grabbed a fist full of hair, forced her head back and raised his knife to cut her throat.

Morddon's bow rose into position almost with a will of its own, and his muscles strained against the pull of it. He sighted down the arrow toward the back of the Kull's head, a part of him conscious of the shaft's fletching tickling his cheek. But at the last moment he realized the shaft would pass straight through the Kull's head and into AnneRhianne without stopping. In the flash of an instant he changed his aim to the outstretched arm holding the knife, corrected upward for distance and slightly to one side, leading the arm already striking inward toward her throat. Then he relaxed the fingers clutching the string.

••••

AnneRhianne understood instantly she had pushed her tormentor too far, though she experienced a moment of triumph in the realization she would die now, rather than being raped first by these monsters, then killed afterwards. As the blade rose high above her head and paused against the gray the afternoon sky, she thought of WindHollow, and of the likelihood he would not die so cleanly, and in that moment the blade began its descent toward her throat.

She heard, but took no notice of, the familiar hiss that always reminded her of water on white hot steel. Then a loud thud and a sharp vibration pounded the coach's floorboards. The knife, still glinting high above her exposed throat, jerked to a sudden, unexpected stop.

The monster holding the knife frowned angrily, looked toward his arm to see what had prevented him from delivering the death he so wanted to see in the Benesh'ere woman's eyes. Both she and he saw it at the same instant: a steel-tipped, Benesh'ere war arrow, glistening with the blood of his arm, pinning it to the coach. The monster looked down at her, his face wholly ignorant of pain, stretched into a grimace of hatred. He turned with a growl, moving awkwardly because of the arm still pinned to the coach, tried to look over his shoulder to locate the source of this affront.

The hiss came again, the second arrow punched into the ear she had bit off, out through the temple on the other side of his head, thudded into the coach's floorboards, and the monster stood with his head spitted like a gobbet of meat and pinned to the coach beside his arm. He twitched, but could not fall.

9

Rescue

MORDDON TRIED NOT to hurry as he nocked another arrow, took careful aim, paused for just one instant. The dead Kull's comrade was busy biting one of AnneRhianne's breasts, and again any shot now would kill her as well as him. But then the monster looked up, saw the fate of his comrade, turned to look down the road, and Morddon's third arrow caught him squarely in the center of his chest, thunked into the floorboards of the coach and pinned him upright.

"You bastards," AnneRhianne cried. "Stop that! Take your hands off me."

Morddon hesitated, then realized she was buying him time, certainly not knowing who he was, but knowing a sudden silence would draw the attention of the other Kulls, all of whom were still ignorant of the fate of their two dead comrades. He nocked another arrow, waited for the Kull standing on top of the coach and bending over the open door to rise to an upright position. Then he shot the arrow cleanly through the back of the halfman's head, though it didn't stop there, but arced well out over the forest beyond. The Kull twitched, leaned heavily to one side, then toppled off the coach with a crash.

Still kneeling in the middle of the road, the Kull scavenging the dead coachman looked up at the sound and turned to look over his shoulder. Morddon nocked another arrow, raised his bow, shot the shaft square into the middle of the halfman's chest. He toppled backward off his knees and lay face up in the road.

Morddon drew another arrow, nocked it, jumped out onto the road and started sprinting toward the coach, wishing he'd been able to get closer before shooting the first arrow. He was still a good distance from the coach when a Kull stepped from behind it into view, and though the halfman was unprepared to see such carnage and his reaction was slow, Morddon was at a full sprint and wasted precious moments coming to a screeching halt before raising his bow. The Kull stepped aside just as Morddon released the arrow; it hissed past his ear, buried itself in one of the Kull horses on the far side of the coach. The animal screamed, toppled over with a crash as the halfman shouted a warning and disappeared behind the coach. Almost instantly another Kull appeared with a crossbow in hand.

Morddon dove desperately to one side, narrowly escaped the crossbow bolt as it tore a chunk of flesh from his shoulder. He rose quickly to his knees, pulled, nocked, shot an arrow at a flicker of movement near the side of the coach, pulled, nocked and released two more in rapid succession. A hint of movement; another arrow, then five arrows in rapid succession as the Kulls behind the coach tried to get a glimpse at him. A Kull head appeared above the door of the coach, a single halfman still trapped inside. Morddon heard the thunder of Mortiss's hooves pounding up the road behind him. He put his last arrow into the face above the door of the coach, tossed the bow and quiver aside, drew his sword and jumped into the middle of the road.

A crossbow bolt cut the air beside him as Mortiss bore down on him at full charge, her nostrils flaring with exertion, her eyes burning with the lust for battle. He broke into a run toward the coach, trying to match her speed in some slight degree, managed to catch the saddle horn as she tore past him and wrenched him painfully into her saddle.

He almost toppled off the other side, though a Kull arrow pierced the air where he would have been if he'd mounted cleanly. He got his feet into the stirrups and leaned forward, low in the saddle.

He saw the crossbow bolt quite clearly an instant before it struck: straight ahead, seeming to hover in the air in the middle of the road directly before Mortiss's heaving breast. Then the moment ended and it hissed toward her, and without a sound she collapsed beneath him like SarahGirl had done beneath Morgin so long ago.

Morddon had the presence of mind to dive forward out of the stirrups, though he landed hard in the middle of the road and bounced and skidded for a good distance. He came up slowly, dazed and without his sword, just as a Kull saber hissed past his face, and with the road swaying heavily beneath his feet he charged blindly beneath the halfman's guard. He caught a momentary glimpse of the Kull's three remaining comrades mounting their horses and escaping up the road, then he gripped the halfman's throat in one fist, the wrist of his sword arm in the other. His ears filled with a strange metallic voice, speaking as if from a great distance, warning him to beware of the Kull's free hand and the steel gripped within it.

AnneRhianne shouted a warning; Morddon's back lit up with fire, but the blade refused to stab deeply no matter how hard the Kull tried, though it cut into his back painfully. Morddon's grip tightened about the halfman's throat with a spasmodic jerk. The Kull's neck snapped, and he slumped to the ground at Morddon's feet.

Morddon staggered, almost tripped over the dead Kull crumpled about his ankles, and turned back down the road thinking only of Mortiss. He found her laying quite still and peaceful in the middle of the road, her neck at an odd angle, her eyes glassed over in death.

"Unbind me," AnneRhianne called. "Unbind me now."

He turned about to face her. She was a grizzly sight tied to the underbelly of the coach with her two assailants pinned by arrows beside her, stripped to the waist and more, blood from the Kull's ear covering the lower half of her face, still drizzling down the front of her throat and across her bare breasts.

He swayed unsteadily, thought for a moment he saw concern in her eyes, then staggered toward her. Half way there he found his sword laying in the road, picked it up, picked up the knife the Kull had used. AnneRhianne shouted something at him, but his head swam and his ears were filled with a muffled roar. He cut the rope tying one of her hands and handed her the knife, then turned away from her to retrieve his bow and quiver and gather his arrows.

Oddly enough, he found them all, even the shaft that had gone through the back of the Kull's head and disappeared into the forest beyond. He had the strangest feeling he found it because the steel in the barbed war point called to him, but he scoffed at such a ridiculous notion.

As he returned to the coach with his quiver full he heard voices, all like that strange metallic voice he had heard when the Kull had tried to stab him, and he had a compulsion to take the sword from the dead Kull's hand and hold it in his own.

His legs buckled and he dropped to his knees beside the Kull. He pried open the halfman's tightly gripped hand and removed the sword. The instant his fingers touched its steel the voices grew stronger, though there were so many of them speaking at once he could understand none of them clearly, only a name: SheelThane.

". . . Morddon . . . Morddon . . ."

A hand shook him gently. He opened his eyes, was still kneeling beside the Kull, though the voices were gone and his head had cleared. AnneRhianne knelt in front of him, looking at him oddly. She had found a ragged wrap of some kind to cover her breasts, and this time he did see concern in her eyes, and too, a frown on her lips. "My nephew?" she asked. "Where is my nephew?"

Morddon shook his head. "I didn't know you had a nephew."

"But you've met him," she said angrily. "Back at Metadan's camp, WindHollow."

"Ah!" Morddon said. "The boy."

"Yes," she said. "The boy. Those monsters carried him away and I'm going after them."

She started to rise. Morddon reached out and gripped her shoulder, forced her back to her knees in front of him. "You're going back to Metadan; I'll go after the boy."

"Then I'm going with you."

"No you're not. You'll only slow me."

"I can ride with the best, and I'm as good with a bow as any man."

Morddon shook his head. "You have no bow, no riding clothes, no equipment. And can you track those Kulls through the darkness of the night, and slip into their camp and slit their throats while they sleep?"

She frowned, started to say something but he cut her off, "Who or what is SheelThane?"

She hesitated, looked at him oddly and he regretted the question. She asked, "Are you a sorcerer?"

He ignored her question, demanded, "Answer my question."

"A strange question," she said.

"Nevertheless, a question that deserves an answer."

She flinched at his tone, and he flinched inwardly for he hadn't meant to speak so sharply. She asked, "And does your question deserve an answer more than mine?"

If there had been any empathy between them, he had banished it with his bitterness. "Just answer my question, woman. I saved your life, you owe me that."

"Very well," she said angrily. "SheelThane was the last Queen of the House of the Thane. The last griffin Queen. She was imprisoned by Beayaegoath twelve centuries ago, and to this day no one knows her fate, though all of griffindom mourns her. What does she have to do with all of this?"

"I don't know," he snarled.

She looked at one of the dead Kulls lying in the road. "What kind of demon is this that is a man, and not a man?"

"You don't know the truth of your own words," he told her. "They are called half-men, or Kulls." With Morgin's memories he described the magic that created a Kull from a demon and a man, and her mouth opened slowly in utter horror.

"No man would willingly go to such a fate."

"For power," he said, "men have been known to do many things."

"You're speaking of sorcery again. Are you a sorcerer?"

"I'm speaking of power," he said as he pulled himself slowly to his feet, looked up the road and was pleased to see two of the riderless Kull horses still milling about. "I need a horse. Hope those Kull mounts are worth the meat they're made of."

"Why not ride your own?"

He looked at her angrily, about to growl that Mortiss was dead, and noticed her looking over his shoulder down the road. He turned to look that way. In the middle of the road Mortiss trotted toward them, quite unharmed. When she reached them she snorted at Morddon, as if to remind him of what a fool he was. "A horse for you," he lied. "We need a horse for you."

She turned away from him and walked toward the Kull horses, checked the two animals carefully, chose one and walked it back to the coach. She tethered it there, then took the Kull's knife and split the skirt of her gown up to her waist. While she was at that he dug into his saddlebags and pulled out a leather pouch he kept full of healing unguents and herbs, quickly prepared a poultice and pressed it into his shoulder where the crossbow bolt had nicked him. He put together another larger poultice and struggled unsuccessfully for some seconds to press it into the stab wounds in his back.

"Here," AnneRhianne said. "Give me that." She tore the poultice out of his hand, pushed him forward against Mortiss's side, lifted the back of his tunic. "These are nasty. You're lucky they aren't deeper."

He closed his eyes as she pressed the poultice into each wound, gritted his teeth and refused to cry out. She tore strips of material from her gown and used it to secure the poultices on his shoulder and back. "You'd better have a healer look at those as soon as possible."

When she was done he unstrung his bow, returned it to the canvas case and tied it carefully to Mortiss's saddle. He started giving AnneRhianne instructions on finding her way back to Metadan, but she interrupted him. "I can find my own way, thank you."

"Good," he said, turned abruptly and climbed up into Mortiss's saddle.

AnneRhianne took hold of Mortiss's reins to keep her still, stroked the horse's long black mane and looked up at Morddon. "A real mercenary would not have risked his life for me the way you did." She looked so like Rhianne Morgin could not believe his eyes, and on impulse he cast a spell of shadow over her, one that would stay for many hours after they parted, one she would not herself be aware of. "And a true mercenary would not so risk his life now."

Morddon frowned. "You're talking like a foolish woman."

The hint of a smile touched the corners of her lips. "Well now, I am always a woman, but only sometimes a fool. Don't you think we all have the right to be a fool upon occasion?"

She stepped away from Mortiss. "Ride well, brother," she said. "And safely."

"Watch out for more Kulls," Morddon said, then tugged on Mortiss's reins and started up the road.

••••

"Rhianne!"

Rhianne heard the sound of her name shouted angrily, followed by the sound of a loud slap.

"Rhianne!"

Again the sound of the slap.

"Come out of it, girl."

Until then the sounds had been remote, as if she were disconnected from it all. But this time the slap was accompanied by pain, a stinging, smoldering burn than ran up the side of her face.

"Let go, girl. Morgin has to control that sword himself."

Three more slaps in rapid succession and she was awake and conscious of the pain. She opened her eyes, found that she was being held upright by her handmaidens while AnnaRail raised her hand to slap her again. "No," she groaned. "No more."

She tried to retreat back to the source of such exquisite power, but another slap brought her back. And then another severed the contact completely.

"Put her in a chair." Olivia's voice; Rhianne had no recollection of seeing the old witch in the room. "She mustn't sleep. Not until we're sure the connection is fully severed."

They made her drink something. She took a large gulp—brandy—and it burned more than any of the slaps. She coughed, choked and gasped.

AnnaRail and Olivia stood over her. AnnaRail looked concerned, while Olivia looked satisfied. The old witch spoke: "It appears that, like her husband, she is more than we thought."

Rhianne had trouble speaking. "Is he safe?"

AnnaRail shrugged. "For the moment. It's taken them two days to catch up with JohnEngine, so he has that much of a head start. Now he's on his own, and you have to leave him that way. You cannot take on the burden of that talisman for him."

"But someone has to help him."

AnnaRail touched her shoulder gently. "And you have, far more than you know. But you've exhausted yourself and have no more left to give. You'll do him no good by killing yourself now." She turned to Olivia. "I sense no further contact with the sword." It was half question and half statement.

The old witch agreed, "Nor I."

Before Rhianne stood two of the most powerful witches in the Lesser Clans, yet somehow they didn't sense the contact that was undeniably there. She sensed the sword hovering about the edges of her magic, coveting her power, waiting, biding its time. Yet these two sorceresses, whose power far exceeded her own, were totally unaware of that contact. Rhianne now understood that, like Morgin, she was on her own.

10

Fugitive

FRANCE LEANED OVER Morgin and demanded angrily, "Didn't you hear anything I just said?"

Morgin rubbed his eyes, tried to take in the scene about him without appearing totally lost. He was seated in front of a low, smoldering fire in a clearing on a hill overlooking the river Bohl. France stood over him, with Val seated to one side, the horses tethered nearby, and as France walked back and forth before the fire the mists of early morning swirled about his ankles. Morgin shook his head, gave up trying to fool them. "No. Not a word."

"What's wrong, boy? Is it that sword again?"

It could be the sword, though he doubted that. There was no way he could explain the dreams to France, so the sword was a nice, simple excuse that required no further explanation. Morgin nodded.

France shook his head. "You still ain't learned how to lie."

Morgin grimaced. "I'm sorry."

"That's all right, lad. I'd rather you didn't tell me anyway. I probably wouldn't understand, and I have enough to worry about. We're being followed, you know?"

Morgin asked, "A posse?"

France shook his head. "No. A single rider. Cort says he has power, plenty of yer damn power, and he's tracking us. Don't you remember anything?"

Morgin shook his head. "No. Nothing. I've been . . . elsewhere."

France squinted at him. "I'll bet you have. Well we can't shake this fella, probably 'cause of his power. Anistigh ain't far from here, so we're thinking maybe we can lose him in the crowds."

"I can't think of anything better," Morgin said. He rubbed his chin thoughtfully, found several days of stubble there, an odd measure of the time that had passed since they'd left Elhiyne. "It'll be nice to bathe and shave again."

France shook his head. "No shaving for you. It's best you grow a beard; make you that much harder to recognize."

"Are we really in that much danger?"

"Listen to me, lad." France's face turned serious. "I know you got all sorts of magical things on yer mind, but yer going to have to start paying more attention here. Yer slowing us down. We've already lost a lot of the lead we started with, and we can't afford to lose more. You gotta remember, lad, if we get caught, the rest of us hang with you."

Morgin nodded, stood up, stretched, yawned. "All right. Let's get going. I'll keep up, and if you see me start to doze, give me a good kick."

Val winked and said, "With pleasure."

"Get a move on," Cort shouted from a good distance down the trail. "He's gaining on us."

For the next two days they traveled from dawn to dusk, pushing their horses hard, then pacing them carefully to get the most out of them. But no matter how hard they rode, the man on their trail kept up with them easily. In the middle of the third day the countryside leveled off into flat, sparsely forested land. They were approaching Anistigh and in another few hours would start passing through outlying hamlets and villages. They stopped in a small copse of trees to rest the horses and consider their situation. Val closed his eyes for a moment; the rest held their silence while he concentrated. When he opened his eyes he announced, "He's still there."

"I don't like it," France grumbled. "I ain't riding into Anistigh with that fella on our trail. Let's wait here and see what he has to say for himself."

"And what if he is tracking us?" Val asked. "What will you do then, kill him? I tell you I'll be no party to murder, for then we'll be the outlaws they've branded us."

France shook his head. "Who said anything about killing? We don't have to kill him. We can maybe take his horse from him, or any number of things to slow him down. As it is he's not an hour behind us."

Cort grinned deviously. "So it's horse stealing, is it?"

"We won't steal it," France argued with a big grin on his face. "We'll just borrow it fer a while, then swat it on its way back to him when we reach the edge of the city."

Morgin stopped listening to their argument, walked to the edge of the trees and looked out on the untended land that stretched back to Elhiyne, an ocean of yellow-brown grasses and low rolling hills, with the Worshipers sitting majestically on the horizon. He wondered if he would ever see this land again, if he was going to be a hunted man for the rest of his life; for that matter he wondered if he would ever see his magic again. But while he stood there considering forlorn thoughts, a small black speck appeared at the base of the foothills in the distance. The air was clear, the visibility good. He watched the speck for a time as it approached, watched as it drew nearer and he could make out the bounce of a rider on a horse at a moderately fast trot, a nice steady pace that would cover a lot of ground without overtaxing the animal. He called back to his friends, "France. Val. Your argument is now moot." He pointed into the distance. "Our friend approaches."

The others gathered around him quickly. France's eyes narrowed for a moment, then he said, "Well I ain't facing him on foot." He was in his saddle in an instant; the others followed suit, though Morgin hesitated for a moment. There was something about the approaching rider that tickled at Morgin's soul, something familiar, something dangerous. "Come on, lad!"

Morgin climbed into Mortiss's saddle, and with his friends he waited just within the shadows offered by the small grove of trees. As he watched the rider approach the tickle in the back of his soul grew unbearable, until finally he felt a stirring at his side as his sword attempted to slide out of its sheath on its own. He moved quickly, caught its hilt, gripped it hard with his will as well as his hand, but still it came free of the sheath.

Val looked at him unhappily, misunderstood his actions. "Is that really necessary?"

Morgin didn't feel like trying to explain so he just shrugged, and at that moment France made the connection that was bothering him. "By damn, I think it's Tulellcoe!"

Morgin saw it now, the way Tulellcoe sat his horse, the way he rode, a hundred undefined nuances that hinted at the familiar. He relaxed, sheathed his sword, released a breath he didn't know he'd been holding and touched his spurs to Mortiss's flanks. She trotted out into the sunlight gladly, broke into a gallop and put the wind in his face.

Until that moment he hadn't realized how much he missed Elhiyne. Of course, he was glad his friends had chosen to come with him, but Tulellcoe, as mad as he was rumored to be, was still family, and in his veins flowed the same blood as Roland and JohnEngine.

Tulellcoe brought his horse to a stop and let Morgin approach him, though the set of Tulellcoe's shoulders gave Morgin the feeling they were two enemies meeting on a field of battle to discuss terms. Morgin brought Mortiss to a stop, halting just beyond the reach of Tulellcoe's sword. "Nephew," Tulellcoe said by way of greeting, and his lips parted in a smile, but there was no smile in his eyes, only fear and sorrow. Then Tulellcoe blinked, the moment passed, and nothing remained in his eyes but steel-hard determination.

"Uncle," Morgin said, and just then his friends rode up in a cloud of dust.

"It's good to have you with us," France said. "But if you join us, you may not be able to go back."

Val shook Tulellcoe's hand joyfully, but Cort held back as if she sensed something amiss.

Tulellcoe shrugged. "I can't go back anyway, not once I've done what must be done." Morgin wanted to ask him what he meant, but before he could speak Tulellcoe's shoulders straightened, and the fear and sorrow Morgin had seen a moment earlier disappeared. He smiled again, this time a genuine smile. "At least out here I won't have the old witch reminding me daily of the madness that flows in my veins."

Morgin laughed at that. "Well you're quite mad if you choose to ride with us."

Tulellcoe threw back his head and laughed. Morgin had never before seen him laugh so openly. "Well now I'd say I'm riding in good company." But then the humor left him, and he was again the Tulellcoe Morgin knew. "And it's riding we'd better be doing now. The four of you have been moving at a snail's pace. By now BlakeDown is well aware of JohnEngine's ruse, and he's got a small army headed this way looking for you."

"My fault," Morgin said sheepishly, but when Tulellcoe looked at him for an explanation he said no more.

Tulellcoe's eyes darted down to the sword at Morgin's side, the skin around them tightened, and again for just an instant Morgin saw fear and sorrow hidden deep within them. Then Tulellcoe pulled his horse toward Anistigh, and as he spurred the animal he shouted over his shoulder, "Let's ride."

••••

By late midafternoon they were only a few leagues out of Anistigh so they knew they'd be well inside the city before nightfall. As they rode at a steady gallop they carefully planned out their identities. Val and Cort were definitely twonames, and Tulellcoe's obvious power labeled him as either a twoname or a clansman, so they decided the identity of a twoname would be best. He took the names Vergis Caladan while Val changed his to Seurrak Aldwith and Cort became Thenda Sa. Morgin had no idea if there was any meaning in the names.

Since he and France had no power, they would take the identities of simple swordsmen. "Rindal, you can call me," France declared as they rode past the first of the outlying hamlets.

"Take care, my friend," Val said. "You've gone by many names before, so pick a new one, rather than an old one that might get us all hung."

"It's a new name, me friend, unused and untried. But I'll likely get us all hung anyway, so what does it matter? And if asked, remember we're wandering mercenaries."

They entered the city without mishap just as the sun was touching the horizon. France led them straight to the Thieves Quarter and a sleazy little inn that promised unwholesome fare. Out in front of the inn Morgin climbed tiredly out of Mortiss's saddle, and like the others took a moment to brush some of the dust from his clothing. Tulellcoe called them all into a quick huddle. "You haven't chosen a name," he demanded of Morgin.

"Aye, lad," France said. "We have to have a name for you."

Morgin had chosen his new name far back on the trail, but hesitated both then and now to speak it in this world. "Call me Morddon."

"Right you are," France said, and turned toward the inn, but Val and Cort and Tulellcoe hesitated. Tulellcoe's eyes narrowed unhappily; he reached out and took Morgin's arm in a painful grip. "Where did you get that name?" he demanded.

"In a dream. Why? What's it to you? Have you heard it before?"

"No," Tulellcoe said, "I've not heard the name before. But it stinks of ancient and dead magics, so stop playing your damn games, boy."

Morgin was tired of hiding everything from everyone. He looked Tulellcoe in the eyes and did not flinch from the madness he saw there. "But I'm not the game player, dear uncle," he said. "I'm merely one of the pawns on the board. I don't even know the game, let alone the players. But I'd dearly love to learn, so if you ever find out please let me know." He started to turn away, but his anger forced him to hesitate, to turn back. "One more thing," he said. "The next time someone calls me boy, one of us will die." And with that, he pulled his arm angrily out of Tulellcoe's grip and turned toward the inn.

He ducked low to get through the heavy plank door into the inn's common room. Just within the entrance he stepped to one side to avoid giving anyone a silhouette to target. He paused to let his eyes adjust to the hazy interior: a single shuttered window next to the door throwing a dim excuse for light across the room, a fireplace at the far end, tables and chairs strewn haphazardly about, some occupied by a most unsavory clientele, and the smell of sooty candles, stale urine, old beer and greasy meat.

At the far end of the room France leaned against the bar with a mug of beer in one hand, talking to a man that looked to be the innkeeper. Morgin started toward him as he heard Val and Tulellcoe coming through the door behind him.

"Morddon, me old friend," France greeted him. "The innkeeper here tells me we'll have no trouble hiring on as guards on a caravan."

Morgin looked at the innkeeper carefully, a large man with a big gut hanging over a rope belt holding up patched and tattered pants. "Anything going south?" Morgin asked, "To Aud?"

The innkeeper nodded, "Every few days or so. Why Aud? Why the City of Thieves?"

The innkeeper's comments reminded Morgin that Aiergain, the Mistress of Aud, was called the Queen of Thieves. Apparently, Aud had been founded by pirates and thieves several centuries ago, though he'd heard that the lawlessness of the past was no longer tolerated in Aud.

France shrugged. "It's as good a place as any. How 'bout a drink fer me friend, me good man?" France threw a few coppers on the bar as Cort and Val and Tulellcoe joined them. "And a couple more fer me other friends too."

The innkeeper eyed Tulellcoe, Val, and Cort suspiciously, then stepped into a back room and started shouting at someone. While he was gone Tulellcoe quietly asked, "Did you get us a room?"

"Aye," France answered him softly. "Paid extra fer a window too. I always like to have a quick out if I need one."

A barmaid shot out of the back room, headed for the front entrance splashing the contents of a mug of beer in her wake. The innkeeper returned with a large clay pitcher, put four metal tankards on the bar and slopped a brown, foamy liquid into them. Morgin was just thirsty enough to drink the stuff. It tasted strongly of Elhiyne wheat, though hard and bitter, but it nevertheless washed the trail dust down the back of his throat.

The innkeeper kept glancing out of the corners of his eyes at the three twonames, until Tulellcoe finally asked, "Is something bothering you?"

The innkeeper shrugged. "Don't know. You three got the smell of magic about you, like maybe twonames, eh?"

"And if we are, is that a problem?"

Morgin tensed, tried to note the location of every man in the room and judge if they might be armed, but the innkeeper shook his head. "Not if you mind yer own business. In fact, what with this outlaw wizard coming out of Elhiyne, should make it easier to hire on with a merchant."

"What's this?" France asked. "An outlaw wizard?"

"Aye, man. Where you been?"

"Just got in from Penda," France lied. "Ain't heard nothing fer days."

The innkeeper leaned forward on the bar, looked about furtively and spoke in a half whisper. "It's this ShadowLord we been hearing about. They say he did some magic scared the piss out of the rest of the clans—beggin' yer pardon, me lady," he nodded at Cort. "And now they want his head to protect their own butts. Even his own family's after him . . . they say."

France's eyes narrowed and he rubbed his chin, and when he spoke his voice was filled with obvious greed. "They offering a reward? I mean me an' me friends here just might be interested if there's enough money in it."

"Big reward," the innkeeper said. "Hundred gold coins."

Even Morgin tried to get into the act, widened his eyes and tried to look greedy.

"Won't do you no good though," the innkeeper continued. "They say he went east from Elhiyne. By now he's days from here."

"Damn!" France swore. "Been a long time since me purse was that fat." He slapped his mug down on the bar with a clang. "Fill us up again, and tell me about these caravans to Aud, and how some good swordsmen might hire on."

Morgin's mug was still half-full of the heavy brown beer and he had no desire for more. While the innkeeper poured the next round for his friends he picked up his mug and turned away from the bar, found an empty table in a dark corner, pulled up a chair and dropped into it with his back to the stone wall. Thankfully, no one paid him any attention; unwashed and covered with leagues of trail dust, he was not at all out of place among the inn's customers. And he was pleased none of his friends chose to join him. He wanted to be alone with no questions to answer, no decisions to make.

The brown, bitter beer turned out to be quite strong, especially on an empty stomach with road weary muscles. His eyelids grew heavy, so he leaned his chair back against the wall, rested his head against the rough stones and tried not to drift into sleep. His last conscious act was a precautionary one. Beneath the table where no one could see, he slid his sword out of its sheath and laid it across his knees with his hand resting on the hilt.

11

Beware the Self-Forged Blade

ALMOST AS SOON as Morddon left AnneRhianne at the overturned coach the rain began again with renewed vigor. It poured heavily through that day and well into the night, and not until sunrise of the following morning did it return to the slow steady drizzle he'd grown used to. By then the trail had cooled and his tracking slowed to a crawl. For the next four days he descended tenaciously upon every broken twig along the track, each hoof print, any spoor his eyes or nose or soul could detect. The course the Kulls followed meandered through the hilly forest, taking them further each day from the fields of battle that drew Morddon. Each day they met and joined other small groups of halfmen; their numbers swelled, and when finally he did catch up with them there were too many to be dealt with by simply slitting their throats under the cover of darkness. He followed them closely for a while.

Morgin grew uneasy on the trail of the Kulls, though he found it difficult to clearly identify the sensation, but the discomfort grew slowly through the day, until finally he could not deny that something strongly arcane was afoot. When the Kulls made camp that night Morddon decided to investigate, though because of their numbers he was heavily dependent upon the constant roar of the rain on the leaves of the forest to hide any sounds he might make, and Morgin's shadowmagic to shield him from any alert Kull eyes.

As was Mortiss's want—her demand actually—he left her untethered to wander at her will, though his intuition told him to leave her saddled. He could unsaddle her later if he discovered nothing unusual in the Kull camp.

Moving carefully on his feet, and still a good distance off, he noticed that the half-men were unusually quiet. Closer yet, to his surprise no perimeter guards had been posted, nor did he see their string of horses, which should have been easily visible at that distance. Moving with extreme caution he entered the camp itself, and found it deserted.

"Damn!" he swore quietly. How could he have been so stupid as to let them slip away from him?

He circled the edge of the camp looking for any telltale signs to indicate the direction they'd taken, but with all his skill as a tracker he found nothing. He circled the camp a second time, and again found nothing, no broken twigs or branches, no horse manure, no hoof prints. There had been at least twenty Kulls in the group, and that number could not slip away without leaving some sign of their departure. Twenty Kulls didn't just simply vanish.

On impulse he turned for the first time to cross through the middle of the camp, but as he did so Morgin's arcane senses rang one alarm after another. The closer he came to the heart of the camp the more his soul recoiled from something that awaited him there unseen, until to preserve his own sanity he was forced to stop well short of the camp's center. He could go no further, and at that distance his reaction was so strong he needed to back up several paces before he could even breathe again.

Mortiss spluttered out a whinny, letting him know she stood in the shadows at the edge of the camp. She trotted forward, stopped beside him, made it quite clear she wanted to get out of there as soon as possible. For once they were in complete accord, so he took her reins and climbed quickly into the saddle, thinking he would return at sunrise to investigate further. But before he could turn her about she leapt forward, charging straight toward whatever lay at the center of the camp. He had a single instant to shout, "No!" then his senses twisted inside out, and a moment later his stomach followed, pain lanced through his head as if someone had driven a spike there and he passed out.

••••

Morddon regained consciousness lying face down on the forest trail, sweating in the sticky, sultry, hot air. He rolled over, found Mortiss standing over him. "You damn stupid pile of bones and meat," he said as he struggled to his feet.

The rain had finally come to an end, though now a flood of sweat bathed him from head to foot. The sky had shifted to a deep orange red, streaked with wisps of gray black clouds; and the sun, through some trick of the atmosphere, had taken on a slight purplish tint. Everything seemed wrong.

He rubbed his temples, tried to recall what he'd felt just before passing out, remembered only the sensation of a shifting, changing power swirling all about him, and then it all slipped into place and his heart almost skipped a beat. "You idiot!" he snarled at Mortiss. "This is the netherworld. I'm not just walking through it with my soul, you've actually dragged my body here as well. How can I find my way back without my body in the Mortal Plane to anchor me?"

She looked at him, snorted, turned her backside toward him and started walking up the trail. Trying to contain his anger he pulled himself to his feet, but his attention was drawn to the brush at the side of the trail, the horse momentarily forgotten. His eyes locked onto a freshly broken branch, and then another nearby. He'd found the Kulls' trail.

Mortiss snorted at him.

"All right," he said. "You found it, not me. I just hope you can find your way back."

Morddon picked up the trail again. He moved with extreme caution because much of the forest growth was foreign to him. He quickly lost any sensation of time. The sun never moved from its spot in the sky, and he was forced to resort to the needs of his stomach, eating trail rations when it growled at him hungrily, resting for short periods when his eyes refused to remain open. By that clock he estimated he followed the Kulls for another two days, and during that time he saw not one living creature in this nether forest of his dreams, though often he glimpsed something following him at the edge of his senses, something there and yet not there. There were several of them, and they swirled about him like the wind. Morgin identified them for him: shadowwraiths.

The morning of the third day in the netherworld the small forest trail joined a much larger trail, almost a road. He turned up the road, still following the Kulls, staying close to the edge of the forest, ready to duck into its shadows at the first hint of movement on the road.

He first became aware of the scent in the air on a subconscious level. As the day progressed his stomach fluttered and his abdomen tightened up with fear. He became almost physically ill, though the scent on the air was not an obnoxious or evil smell, just the smell of a particular kind of animal that for some unknown reason produced within him an overwhelming dread. Eventually he became so preoccupied with the growing strength of the scent, and trying to keep the food in his stomach, he almost missed the sound of distant hoof beats on the road; Mortiss did not. She froze in the shadows at the edge of the forest, and instinctively Morgin drew a cloak of shadow about them.

The patrol that passed by was made up of a large party of mounted soldiers, a mixture of Kulls and another kind of beast, the sight of which struck him like a physical blow and raised the hackles on the back of his neck. They were much like dogs, these beasts that rode on the backs of horses. Their bodies had been warped into a grotesque imitation of man, the better to carry lances, shields and swords, and to wear the armor and raiments of war. As Morddon watched them pass his gut twisted with fear and his mind filled with visions of Binth, his face split by a war ax, and Eisla, pinned to a cross by these grotesque imitations of men, beings who rode with Kulls as equals. Involuntarily he whispered a single word: jackal.

He soon found it necessary to duck regularly into the forest to avoid one patrol after another. A large encampment must be just over the next hill, and following the road, or even staying close to it, might bring disaster. He left the road completely, and though the going was difficult he avoided even the game trails in the forest, returning to them only after he had left the road far behind. He circled the hill, trying to approach the encampment from the other side, hoping the uninterrupted forest there would not be well guarded. He also hoped that this deep within the netherworld the jackal hordes would not think to keep watch for marauding mortals.

His first glimpse of the camp was from a distant hill. Near its center a cluster of luxurious tents had been erected, and the single banner fluttering over them instantly drew his eyes. At the sight of that banner the horrifying death visions of Binth and Eisla arose again within his soul, and a name came to him from a distant past—Magwa, the Jackal Queen. The little boy in him wanted to run screaming into the forest, while the man within him fought to control the blind rage that threatened to tear his soul apart.

The camp contained about two hundred of the jackal warriors, with fifty or more Kulls among them. They'd cleared a large patch of ground near the pavilions at the center, then, like an arena, ringed it with logs to mark its boundaries. A post the size of a tree had been staked in the center of the empty arena. Nearer to the pavilions, though well outside the arena, there were a dozen more posts staked into the ground at regular intervals, and what appeared to be prisoners of some kind tied to them, though at that distance he couldn't make out any details. Leaving Mortiss behind, he took his bow and quiver of arrows and moved in closer, hoping WindHollow would be among the prisoners.

Some sort of ruckus arose as he approached the edge of the encampment so he settled into a comfortable shadow to watch and wait. He'd managed to circle the camp completely, was now directly opposite the point where the road skirted the edge of the camp. A large crowd of jackals and Kulls were gathering near the road. Morddon finally got an unobstructed view of the prisoners staked to the posts outside the makeshift arena, and to his relief WindHollow was among them, his head bowed in shame, his shoulders slumped in defeat, his clothing torn and begrimed. Morddon watched him closely for some moments until he felt certain the boy was unhurt. And he wondered how he would ever get him out of there in broad daylight, since the sun never set in this netherlife where he now dreamed.

A chorus of horns blared, announcing the arrival of someone important. Morddon turned his attention back to the crowd near the road, noticed a cloud of dust rising from the far side of the crowd in the vicinity of the road. From amidst the cloud of dust a banner emerged, bobbing up and down, clearly carried by a mounted soldier, though because of the crowd Morddon could see little of the rider himself. As the banner approached the crowd parted, and the jackal warriors howled out a cheer that broke up into choruses of yipping and barking. Then Morddon saw her: Magwa, riding into the midst of her warriors, wearing the revered royal collar of the jackal court, brandishing a feather the size of a sword as if it were the standard of her vanquished enemy.

Riding immediately behind her were her generals, old jackals with slumping backs and graying muzzles. Behind them came her kennel of consorts, young sleek warriors to warm the jackal queen's nights. Next came attendants, ladies-in-waiting, handmaidens, servants, her warrior escort, and finally a gang of slaves pulling a large, wooden, flat-bed cart.

Morddon stopped breathing for a moment, for a griffin had been chained upon the flat boards of the cart. By her smaller size she was probably female, though each of her talons was easily the length of his arm, and she was small only in comparison to TarnThane and the other male griffins. A chain attached to the cart circled her neck, shortened enough so it forced her into a constantly undignified squat.

As the slaves pulled the cart through the crowd to the edge of the arena the jackal warriors spat on the griffin and threw rocks and mud at her. Clearly she had long suffered such abuse. Small cuts and gashes marred her flesh, and in spots her feathers had been ripped away. The fur of her lower body, the lioness part of her, was mottled and discolored with grime and mange, and Morddon felt great pity for her.

The abuse of the griffin ended quickly, the jackals probably tiring of the familiar exercise. Magwa took up residence in the pavilion flying her banner, and the camp filled with the smells of cooking food drifting in the air. After a few hours the activity slowed, then a retainer appeared outside the queen's tent and hissed warnings at those nearby to be silent. Morddon huddled within one of Morgin's shadows, and watched closely as the camp took on the aspects of night, with guards posted at the perimeter, and most of the warriors dozing near campfires, though the orange sun remained hot and high in the sky.

Morddon strung his bow, and carrying it in his left hand, and a knife in his right, he relaxed and let Morgin's instincts guide him through the shadows within the camp. Morgin was tense, for while the harsh, orange sun cast sharp and deep shadows, they did not flicker or move like those of a candle flame, and to dance among them required every bit of stealth he commanded. Not until he finally stepped into the shadow of the griffin's cart did he stop to rest.

"It is a curious thing," the griffin whispered softly, confirming with the tone of her voice that she was female, "when shadows move of themselves. A curious thing indeed!"

Morddon froze while Morgin deepened the shadow about him. The griffin did not move so much as a single feather, but her eyes held Morddon as if they were lances of light. For the first time Morddon thought there might be some truth in a legend. He whispered a single question, "SheelThane?"

"You have the advantage of me," the griffin whispered, though again she was careful not to move. "The centuries have been long, my white faced friend, and recently I had begun to doubt you would ever come."

"You knew I was coming?" Morddon asked.

"Of course. You were sent to free me."

Morddon shook his head. "I came to free the boy. The Benesh'ere. He's small enough I can sneak him out of here, and get a good distance away before his absence is noticed. But you! There's no sneaking you anywhere."

A slave sleeping near the cart sat up rubbing the sleep from his eyes. "Shut up, bird," he growled softly. "We're trying to get some sleep here." And then to emphasize his point he threw a stone the size of a man's fist at the griffin. It struck her above her left eye, opening a small wound that began to bleed.

She flinched, but uttered no cry, and her eyes bored deeper into Morddon's soul. "All you need do, my Benesh'ere friend, is unlock these chains that bind me, and then I will do what I have longed to do for twelve centuries. With these talons I'll gut the royal bitch of the jackal court from womb to chin, and dine upon her entrails myself."

"But her warriors will kill you."

SheelThane shrugged. "What matters that? I'll at least die free, and the bitch-queen will die before me."

Morddon shook his head. "No. I can't let you die." Then he looked at the massive locks and chains binding her talons and neck. "And besides. Those locks. I don't have the key."

The griffin's eyes brightened. "You have always had the keys, my white faced friend."

Morddon started to ask her what she meant, but at that moment a jackal howl rose from the queen's tent.

"Quickly!" the griffin hissed. "The bitch is awakening. You must go, without delay."

Morddon hesitated, feeling that he'd missed something in the conversation, driven by a sudden need to help the griffin in some way. But he had trained himself for many years to harden his heart against such suffering, and he wondered now if she weren't enspelling him.

"You will help me when the time is right," the griffin said. "Now go. Quickly."

The camp was beginning to wake around him. He turned his back on the griffin without a word—though that was one of the hardest things he had ever done—and he moved quickly toward the safety of the forest at the edge of the encampment. He found a comfortable shadow there out of the harsh, orange sun and sat within it to rest, understanding now that even in this perpetual daylight a camp of soldiers would have its own rhythm of activity and rest. His eyes grew heavy, though he fought the urge to sleep, but the demands of his body were stronger than those of his will, and he slipped easily into slumber, wondering in whose soul he would awaken this time.

••••

Morgin started awake at the touch of a hand on his arm, felt the sword across his lap come to life beneath the table. He crushed it back into quiescence, though in doing so he touched the blade with his other hand and the steel filled his mind with the whispers of a thousand souls. He gasped, let go of the bare steel and the whispering ended as suddenly as it had begun.

The twoname Val stood over him. "You've slept most of the evening away Morgin. We knew you needed the rest so we let you be."

Morgin shook his head, trying to clear it of his dreams.

Val pulled up a chair, sat down across the table. The common room of the inn was almost empty, filled only with dark shadows cast by a low smoldering fire in a large hearth. Under the table Morgin quietly slipped his sword back into its sheath.

"You know, Morgin," Val said carefully, "you should try to appear less dangerous."

Morgin wiped the sleep from his eyes. "I'm a man running for my life, and I'm afraid."

Val frowned, shook his head. "I'm not speaking of fear. A little fear tells those you meet that you're merely a cautious man. But too much fear, while you're on the run like this, will brand you a hunted man and bring the jackals down upon you. No, it's not fear that those around you sense. It's danger, plain and simple. You're a dangerous man who sits by himself in the shadows with an unsheathed sword in his lap beneath the table. You look like a dangerous man, and even those without power sense it. And that is not good."

Morgin shrugged, and for the first time he looked at Val carefully. The twoname was not an imposing man, and in fact seemed quite ordinary. "Why did you come with me?" Morgin asked. "Why become a hunted man for me?"

Val considered the question carefully. "I didn't do it for you. I have a questioning nature, and I'm curious to see what is going to happen to you."

"Oh I can tell you the answer to that," Morgin said bitterly. "I'll probably end up hanging by my neck from some gallows, and no doubt my friends will hang with me, but my dear family will remain quite safe."

Val leaned forward and his eyes were sharp points flickering in the shadows of the fire. "Did you dream that in your dreams, Morgin?"

"How do you know about my dreams?"

"I don't. But I can see they bother you."

Val leaned back in his chair and considered Morgin for a long moment. "You know Cort and I lived with the Benesh'ere for a time, and they have some mighty strange legends. They revere steel in an odd way, and of course their worst efforts at forging the stuff are far better than our best. Did you know they believe that before the gods came the world was ruled by the men and women who shaped the best steel? They were called SteelMasters and SteelMistresses, though they didn't really rule as much as they guided and educated. Have you heard of them?"

Morgin shook his head, trying to ignore the chill running down his spine at Val's words. Val shrugged. "I'm not surprised. The Benesh'ere don't speak of such things lightly. In fact I'd been among them for three years before I heard the first mention of a SteelMaster. According to legend these men and women shaped steel of a quality that surpasses even the greatest of today's Benesh'ere steel. But don't think of them as merely talented smiths, for though the legends are a bit obscure on this point, they apparently had some strange powers over steel that were far from natural. The legends say the steel spoke to them, and they spoke to it, commanded it in fact, for they were reputed to rule the steel."

Val's words struck chords in Morgin's soul he did not want to hear. "If you're trying to make a point," Morgin said abruptly, "then make it."

Again Val considered him for a long moment, then continued speaking as if Morgin had said nothing. "Of course, the steel of the Masters was used only for the finest of weapons, and because of that the SteelMasters had a saying, supposedly the most fundamental tenet of their craft. They maintained that the greatest weapon you will ever face, is the blade you yourself have forged." Val stopped talking as if he had made his point.

"I've never forged a blade," Morgin said.

Val shook his head. "This very moment, and for many months now, you have been forging a blade of bitterness and hatred, and that kind of weapon will always turn against you. It can only turn against you."

Val stood up. "Come on up to the room. If you sleep here alone you might not wake up in the morning."

Morgin stood slowly, followed the Surriot to their room on the second floor of the inn. That night as he lay on a pile of blankets on the floor, he tried again and again to fathom the meaning of the twoname's words. As always it eluded him, until his eyes became heavy, and without the will to resist he returned to Morddon's world of dreams.

••••

"I will not!" Rhianne shouted. Her eyes glowed with anger as she planted her fists on her hips defiantly. Then she spun about and stormed out of Olivia's audience chamber.

AnnaRail watched her leave, then turned to the old woman and said, "You shouldn't goad her that way."

"Goad her?" Olivia asked innocently. "But I like her. Why would I goad her?"

"For the same reason you like her. Because she is willful, and she has power, and the brains to use it."

Olivia shook her head. "But not the brains to use it properly."

AnnaRail disagreed. "Oh she has the brains, but not the training. I make the distinction because we can't correct a lack of brains."

"But we can correct a lack of training, eh?"

"Yes. And it would help if you'd stop baiting her."

Again Olivia shook her head. "Steel must be forged with fire."

"But she is not steel," AnnaRail said. "Your grandson is steel, and his wife is the sheath to contain that steel. If you try to make of her what she is not, you'll only destroy her."

Olivia turned upon AnnaRail. "And what would you make of her?"

AnnaRail shrugged. "I don't know yet. I must first determine the substance of her. Is she the ash from which we make a bow, or the oak from which we make an arrow. She is not steel, so I cannot make of her a blade. Patience is required here, and you have never been the one for patience."

Olivia laughed. "No, I haven't, have I? But look at you. I shaped you, and you turned out all right."

AnnaRail nodded. "And now I'll shape her, but you'll have to give me room."

"Very well," Olivia said. "You shall have what you need."

AnnaRail bowed her head. "Thank you, mother. I will shape her properly." She did not add, *But I'll not shape her with the same lack of love you thrust upon me and your sons.*

12

The Jackal Hordes

MORDDON AWOKE, AND as he had learned long ago, remained completely still for a moment, listening for any nearby threat. He sensed Mortiss nearby, knew she wouldn't stand there complacently if he were in danger. He opened his eyes and stood, splashed a few drops of water on his face, ate a quick meal of jerky and hardtack, then crept up to the edge of Magwa's camp.

There were quite a few jackals up and about, but all moved quietly and carefully. Morddon suspected they feared waking the bitch-queen prematurely, so he sat down to wait. WindHollow didn't seem to be in any imminent danger, and before making a move he needed to understand the pulse of the camp, the timing of changes in guards, the location of sentries. He decided to watch through at least one cycle of activity and rest.

A sudden chorus of howls, shouts and yipping drew his attention to Magwa's pavilion. She stood just outside the entrance, berating one of her guards on his knees in front of her. Morddon couldn't make out all her words, but apparently she'd appeared suddenly and found him dozing on watch. Morddon got the impression she liked to do this regularly.

Two of the unfortunate guard's comrades hauled him to his feet, his paws pinned behind his back. Magwa issued orders, pointing at the guard, then at the griffin. Slaves rushed to the griffin's cart, then grunting and sweating they pulled it over to the logged-in arena. A dozen jackal warriors surrounded the griffin with long, deadly pikes, forced her to remain docile while the slaves transferred her steel collar to a chain on the pole at the center of the arena. The chain was just long enough for her to reach the edge of the arena.

Surrounded by the entire camp yelling and howling, they marched the unfortunate guard to the edge of the arena, his bonds were cut, then they kicked him into the ring of logs. He stumbled and fell down on all four paws, looked back at Magwa and howled plaintively. Another guard tossed a sword onto the ground near him.

Magwa raised her paws and the camp went silent.

"Please," the poor guard howled. "Please, it was an accident."

Magwa yipped and laughed. "You know how it works," she said. "It's kill or be killed. If you can kill the griffin, then you get to live."

The guard looked at her for a moment, his shoulders hunched, but she said no more. He stood, picked up the sword and turned toward SheelThane. He dropped into a crouch and walked one, cautious step at a time toward her.

The griffin didn't react, just watched him silently as he approached, nothing but her eyes moving to track him. About ten paces from her, the guard edged slowly to one side, and still she didn't react. As he moved farther to the side and just a bit behind her, one eye tracked him carefully.

He charged, sprinting toward the body of the lion, probably hoping for a thrust to her heart, and still she didn't move. But when he was only a single pace from her, his sword raised for a thrust, she swept a fore-claw out to the side with lightning speed, and four, razor-sharp talons the length of a man's arm sliced through the guard, eviscerating him. His head flew to one side, half his torso to another, stringy lengths of guts and sinew flying through the air, and it was over.

SheelThane's head turned slowly to look down upon Magwa, and Morgin now understood why the bitch-queen hated the griffin queen so much. Filthy, begrimed and mistreated, SheelThane stood proud, regal and majestic, and Magwa's royalty paled in comparison.

After the slaves returned SheelThane to the cart and chained her neck and talons, Magwa climbed up onto it with her. She dropped to all fours, climbed up onto the griffin's back, and to the jeers of her followers urinated on her crown feathers. Then she called one of her consorts forth from the kennels, and to the cheers of her jackal horde, she copulated with him in the middle of the camp.

Morddon watched all of this from the edge of the forest, while the shadowwraiths that danced at the edge of his senses watched him. He tried to formulate a plan to free the griffin as well as WindHollow, but every strategy centered on the chains and locks binding her, and the keys Magwa carried hanging from a chain about her own neck. He noticed she never released them to anyone for more than a few moments, so his only chance would be to sneak into her tent during one of the sleep periods. But she was so heavily guarded he abandoned that idea almost as soon as it occurred to him, admitting finally that he would have to be content with rescuing WindHollow, and leaving the griffin behind.

While he waited he also noticed large, ghost-like shapes moving stealthily through the forest about him. They were about the size of a small horse, and while he often heard the panting of a large beast, they stayed too well hidden for him to see them clearly. His nose caught the scent of hound, and he took no action because they seemed uninterested in him.

At the next rest period he strung his bow, and cloaked in one of Morgin's shadows he moved quickly toward WindHollow. The boy had not yet suffered any great hardship, though he had been beaten a few times and fed poorly for the past days. But he was young and strong, and obviously more frightened than harmed.

They had tied him to a tall post that produced only the thinnest of shadows behind him. Morddon stepped uneasily out of the last shadow that gave him any real concealment, moved quickly to that all too small shadow behind the post, hoping no one would notice it had grown larger. The prisoner tied at the post next to the boy—a barbaric, beast-like man—looked up for an instant with a dull-witted stare, then appeared to convince himself he'd seen nothing and let his head drop again. Morddon waited for several moments, allowing time for the barbarian's suspicions to recede, and too, time to calm his own heart. Then slowly he leaned close to the boy's ear and whispered, "Wind-Hollow."

The boy tensed.

"Don't move so much as a hair," Morddon hissed at him. "You're a Benesh'ere warrior so act like one. Think, don't react. Keep your head down, change nothing in the way you stand, and speak only in the softest whisper."

WindHollow obeyed. "But I'm no warrior," he pleaded, close to tears. "I'm not of age."

"Well you've just come of age, boy. You're a warrior now, or you're a dead man."

"Who are you?" the boy whispered.

"I'm the madman," Morddon told him, and the boy tensed again. "Now I'm going to cut your bonds. Keep your hands behind the post as if you're still bound to it, and don't move until I tell you."

Under the circumstances stealth was far more important than speed, so Morddon cut methodically at the ropes binding the boy's hands and feet, and during those few moments he glanced toward the griffin. The short chain that bound her neck to the floorboards of the cart forced her to lay flat on her breast, with her chin thrust forward and her wings splayed awkwardly to either side. Her eyes were open and staring straight at Morddon as if she saw through any shadow Morgin cast. Those large, silent eyes bore into him with a sadness that touched his soul, and he could not leave without speaking to her one last time.

Morddon directed WindHollow's attention to the closest patch of open forest at the edge of the camp. "When we go we'll make for that large boulder to your left, but first I have to speak to the griffin. You wait here, act like you're still tied to the post, and if anything goes wrong just run for your life. You'll find a coal-black mare waiting on the other side of that boulder—" Somehow Morddon knew Mortiss would be there. "Mount her, and don't try to guide her. Let her carry you where she will. Do you understand?"

"I understand," WindHollow whispered.

Morddon pressed the hilt of the knife into WindHollow's hand. "You might need this, warrior," he said.

He left the shadow behind WindHollow's post, picked his way through the shadows in the camp toward the cart bearing the captive griffin, finally stopping between the wheels beneath the cart. He swung carefully up onto the floorboards of the cart beside the griffin, then hunched into the shadow cast by her massive bulk. The chain prevented her from turning her head toward him, but he saw her eyes straining in his direction.

"Will you free me now?" she whispered.

"I'm sorry," Morddon said. "I can't. I told you I don't have the keys."

Once again that remark appeared to amuse her. "And I say again you have always had the keys, though I doubt you can use them until you realize they are yours to use. But won't you at least try?"

Morddon shook his head. "You don't understand. I tell you I don't have the keys."

"But it is you who do not understand, my white faced friend. Come. Step closer. Touch the steel of the locks and then tell me you don't have the keys. Humor me, if nothing more."

Morddon edged closer to the lock binding one of her taloned feet, and though he knew nothing of lock mechanisms, a quick examination would cost him no time, and it seemed that in some way it would comfort the griffin. As he reached out to touch it something in Morgin shouted a warning, and for the first time he and the Benesh'ere were truly at odds. In a panic Morgin threw his will into resisting the movement of the Benesh'ere's hand as it edged toward the steel, and he tried to scream into his soul to stop, to run, to flee into the forest, but Morddon ignored him, even fought him, until his fingers brushed the icy hardness of the steel lock.

Morgin tried not to listen, but a hundred voices told of a thousand sorrows and a million joys: the point of a blade piercing a man's heart, stealing the last breath of life from his soul; the blade of a plow slicing cleanly through rich soil, bringing life to a bountiful harvest. And without warning the lock fell away from the chain about the griffin's foot.

Morgin staggered back from the steel, now fully in control of Morddon's body, shaking with fear but driven nevertheless toward the lock on the other foot. He struggled to turn away but could not as something within his own heart fought against him. His fingers touched the lock and again the voices came to him as if plucked from time itself. They spoke of the majesty of steel, and too they spoke of the heartache and sorrow it could bring . . .

There was shouting somewhere. Morddon shook his head, came out of a daze sitting stupidly on the floorboards of the cart next to the griffin. The locks on the chains binding her had fallen away, though she did not yet flee, but lay quietly beneath the chains as if still bound. "The boy is in trouble," she said flatly.

The harsh growl of a Kull voice raised in laughter finally cut through Morddon's stupor, and protected by one of Morgin's shadows he staggered to his feet. Wind-Hollow's cut bonds had been discovered by a Kull officer, who had quickly aroused a mixed group of Kulls and jackal warriors. The group had formed a ring around the boy, cutting off any chance of escape, and making it rather clear they intended to have a little fun. The Kull officer joined WindHollow in the center of the ring, drew a knife from his belt and tested the sharpness of its edge. And though the Kull was twice his size, the boy stood his ground and faced him with the knife Morddon had given him.

Morddon hissed at the griffin, "You are free. I make no claim upon you," then he jumped off the cart and sprinted toward the royal tents, praying Morgin's shadows alone would be enough to conceal him. He found what he wanted: a smoldering cooking fire not far from one of the tents. He grabbed a cooking pot, scooped it full of hot embers, crossed the short distance to the tent, poured the coals in a pile at the base of the canvas. He repeated that three more times, while in the distance he heard the rising noise of the cheering crowd.

Breathing heavily he sprinted back to the cart, climbed up beside the griffin, drew an arrow from his quiver. He'd counted on the fact that the Kull would prolong the contest with WindHollow and not kill him out of hand, though by now the boy was bleeding from several shallow cuts. Morddon let the Kull continue to torment the boy until a well-defined column of smoke rose from the vicinity of the royal tents. Then he shouted, "Fire! The queen's tent is on fire!"

Every eye in the camp turned toward the smoke and for an instant utter stillness descended upon them all, then pandemonium erupted as the jackal warriors, thinking only of their queen's rescue, forgot the contest and turned into a mindless pack of howling dogs. But the Kull facing WindHollow hesitated. He glanced once at the fire, then turned back to the boy with the obvious intention of finishing the fight quickly.

Morddon raised his bow and released the first arrow. It arced high over the heads of the panic-stricken jackals and caught the Kull just under the left eye; he toppled backward into the dust.

WindHollow took his cue, lowered his head and sprinted toward the boulder Morddon had pointed out earlier. The jackals were all too busy rushing to their queen's aid to pay him any mind, but the few Kulls present cared nothing for the bitch-queen and moved to intercept the Benesh'ere boy.

Morddon ignored all but the most immediate threats and picked his targets carefully—an arrow for the first Kull to get within sword's reach of the boy; another for a halfman sighting his crossbow. Morddon placed his confidence in the safety of Morgin's shadows and released his arrows one after another, but he learned all too quickly such confidence could cost him his life.

"Beware, whiteface!" the griffin hissed.

Morddon, already sighting down the length of one of his shafts, released the arrow before looking away. He caught a momentary glimpse of a Kull standing beside the cart, looking up at him with a frown of indecision. But in that instant the frown disappeared as the halfman realized the meaning of the strangely shaped shadow that stood over him.

The Kull's sword was out in an instant, slicing through the air toward Morddon's ankles. Morddon jumped frantically over the blade, but he came down off balance and toppled from the cart. In desperation he swung the heavy wood of his bow like a club, connected with the halfman's unprotected skull and heard both his bow and the Kull's head crack loudly.

Morddon hit the ground beside the cart in a roll as the Kull, his head crushed, crumpled behind him. He came up with his sword drawn, and almost stepped into a Kull saber as another halfman joined the fight. His momentum nearly carried him into the Kull's blade, and he barely deflected it as it cut a line of fiery pain across his ribs. He threw a forearm up, caught the Kull under the chin and slammed into the halfman with his full Benesh'ere weight. They went down with Morddon on top, and he threw all his weight into his forearm, crushing the Kull's throat.

Morddon jumped to his feet and sprinted toward WindHollow. The bitch-queen's warriors were like a river of bodies flowing in the opposite direction, all rushing to Magwa's aid, and though they were unaware of him because of Morgin's shadows, they were still a strong current against which he struggled, and through which he saw nothing. When the mob thinned he saw WindHollow lying on the ground clutching his side, a Kull officer standing over him with a blooded saber. The Kull nodded his satisfaction, then raised his saber high over his head to finish the boy, and Morddon hit him like a warhorse at full charge.

They both tumbled into the dust. Morddon was up quickly, while the stunned Kull crawled to his feet slowly, so Morddon kicked him in the face to make sure he stayed down. Another Kull slammed into Morddon shouting something about shadows, and they both sprawled onto the dirt. The wound in his side was taking its toll and this time Morddon only made it to his hands and knees before the Kull kicked him in the ribs.

He saw a saber flashing toward him, rolled desperately away just as it cut a furrow in the dirt near his head. Another Kull boot swung out of the dust toward his face. He caught the boot in his left hand, twisted and continued his roll, pulling the Kull down with him. He tried to get to his feet, but the hilt of a Kull saber crashed into his temple, and he hit the ground in a sprawl with his head spinning wildly. Then massive wings darkened the sky above him, beating and pummeling at the Kull's heads, with the hind claws of a lioness tearing at their eyes. The razor-sharp, arm-length talons saved the moment, slicing about them like an army of airborne swordsmen. In those few seconds Morddon saw close at hand how the talons of an adult griffin could truly cut men and halfmen to pieces. And yet only an instant later those same talons descended upon WindHollow and delicately lifted the injured boy into the air.

Morddon struggled to his feet clutching his sword with one hand and his wounded side with the other. He crouched low as he ran after the griffin, tried to keep the halfbird in sight and follow her, but lost her as she turned to one side and dipped dangerously close to the ground.

Staying within the clouds of dust raised by the battle, he heard the howl of jackals and the shouts of Kulls all about him, so he had little hope of getting out of the camp without another fight, and in his present condition it would be his last. Then a horse cried out somewhere in front of him, though not the sound of a poor, frightened animal but rather the netherscream of an arcane warhorse sounding its anger and its battle lust. His soul caught the scent of dangerous magic as the ground shook with the thunder of pounding hooves. Out of the clouds of dust Mortiss reared above him, and when she came down and disappeared into the dust again Morddon heard a jackal die horribly.

An instant later she was beside him. He clutched desperately at her saddle horn, managed to pull himself into the saddle, got his feet in the stirrups and slapped her rump with the flat of his sword. She trampled two Kulls and four jackals to death trying to get out of the camp, but was quickly surrounded by pike carrying jackal warriors cutting off all escape. In that instant between life and death a sound rose above the noise of battle, a wolf howl that bore such hatred it gave even the Kulls pause. The howl was answered by another, then another, and the jackals panicked, yipping and yelling with fear as giant loping shapes bounded among them.

Morddon could see almost nothing because of the clouds of smoke from the burning tents and dust stirred up by the battle, and so he was never quite sure of what he saw. But he caught a glimpse of an enormous hound-like beast with a jackal in its teeth. It shook the jackal, snapping its spine and tossing it over one shoulder, then it disappeared into the smoke leaving behind a strong scent of magic. Morgin felt it flooding through him, inundating him, carrying him and Morddon and Mortiss with it, and for just that instant something opened within his soul, as if a doorway locked for millennia had burst under the pressure of a tidal wave of magic. For that single moment he felt he understood it all, as if all the questions of his life had been answered. Then he was through the door, and it slammed shut behind him, as he struggled to hold on to the horse, his sword, and consciousness. Soon the shadow of night settled about him, Mortiss lengthened her stride and put the wind in his face.

13

The House of the Thane

MORTISS HAD RETURNED Morddon to the Mortal Plane, and he wondered about poor WindHollow and the griffin. Mortiss had carried him barely a league when she charged into a small clearing and came to an abrupt halt. By the light of a full moon he saw the griffin waiting there, standing guard over WindHollow who lay curled upon the ground near her taloned claws.

Morddon dismounted, sheathed his sword, leaned over the boy to check his wound, though by the dim moonlight his examination was more by touch than sight. The wound was a puncture just above the boy's right hip. Morddon's own wound, on the other hand, was nothing more than a shallow slice along his rib cage; painful, and dangerous if it festered, but nothing to fear beyond that.

A jackal howl in the distance told him the pursuit had begun. He looked at the griffin, and only then did he see the arrow protruding from the joint of her right wing. He tried to smile as he said, "We're a sorry lot, aren't we?"

The griffin threw her head back and laughed. "But not half as sorry as the bitch-queen's warriors, I'll wager you. It felt good to fight again without chains hindering me. If only I could have gotten my talons into that slut of a she-dog!"

Morddon looked closely at the arrow in the griffin's wing. "Well the opportunity is past. Now we run. I'll remove the arrow. Will you be able to fly?"

The griffin shook her head. "If we can get to the top of a hill I might glide for a good distance, but flying is out of the question. If I hadn't already gained good altitude before I caught this I wouldn't have gotten this far. But I can run, faster than you might think, especially if the dark one there"—she nodded toward Mortiss—"can carry you and the boy."

Morddon looked at Mortiss and nodded. "She can usually do far more than I would have thought possible." He cut the shaft of the arrow in two with a knife, then removed the shaft carefully.

The griffin's wound bled very little, but WindHollow was not so lucky. There was no time to do more than apply a quick bandage, then with the half-conscious boy seated in front of him on Mortiss's saddle, they moved out at a quick pace that kept them well ahead of the jackal pack.

In a few hours they could no longer hear the pack behind them, and by mutual consent they traveled on. After several more hours the griffin was exhausted, and even Mortiss had begun to struggle. The sky was showing the first hints of the coming day, so they stopped and Morddon set about properly treating their wounds; Wind-Hollow first, then the griffin, and finally himself. He was thinking about a meal, and maybe some rest, when far in the distance a jackal howl broke the stillness of the forest dawn.

"They have our scent," the griffin said, "and with that they can track us for days. The jackal pack is relentless when their prey is at hand."

"Then we'll have to keep going," Morddon said. "Maybe they'll tire eventually."

The griffin shook her head. "They won't tire, not before they catch us. We need to reach help before then."

They continued on as the sun rose in front of them, a right and proper sun. Morddon felt better knowing they'd left the netherworld behind, but they were still traveling when the sun set behind them and a cold night descended upon the forest. They hadn't heard the jackals for some time so they stopped to rest.

Morddon wrapped WindHollow in a blanket and tried to lay him in a comfortable position, then set Mortiss to graze, knowing she wouldn't go far. For himself he sat on the ground with his back to a tree and tried to sleep sitting up, knowing Mortiss would rouse him if the jackals came near. After a short period of fitful dozing the wind woke him with the sound of a jackal howl, and again they fled on.

All through that night, and the next day, and the following night, they repeated that same scenario again and again: racing ahead of the packs until they could go no further, then resting for what few moments they had until the next jackal howl told them they must move on. On the morning of the third day they found they could not gain enough distance to rid their ears of the howls of the packs, and there was no rest.

They were gaining altitude now, climbing into a range of low mountains, and through that day their pace slowed ever more as the howls of the packs grew closer with each passing league. By midday they moved their exhausted bodies at little more than a fast walk. The jackals were so close there was no stopping, and through the afternoon the howls of the various packs blended into a single, snarling entity. He guessed the packs behind them were converging in anticipation of the kill. The forest before them thinned out as their flight carried them above the tree line, and Morddon quickened their pace until in desperation they were running in headlong flight up a barren, rocky slope with no knowledge of what lay before them. Mortiss strained under the combined weight of Morddon and the young boy, while the griffin struggled along in front of them. But suddenly the griffin skidded to a halt, and when Morddon caught up with her he found that the trail before them ended in a sheer wall of stone that dropped unbroken into a mist shrouded valley far below.

Morddon looked right and left. If they tried to run parallel to the ridge in either direction the jackals would quickly intercept them, so he turned to the griffin. "You said you couldn't fly, but if we reached a high hill you might glide for a good distance. Is this high enough, and can you carry a passenger or two?"

The griffin looked out over the valley. "It's high enough, but I can't carry both you and the boy."

"Can you carry the boy alone?"

"Yes, but I won't leave you behind."

Morddon shook his head. "If you stay I die. And if you leave I die. But if you leave I've at least accomplished something, and if you stay your life is wasted, and the boy's too." Morddon leaned out over the edge of the cliff and looked down. It wasn't truly vertical, and there were hand and foot holds. "Besides," he added, "I can climb a lot better than those jackals."

The griffin looked down the rock face and shook her head, then she looked at Mortiss. "And what of the dark one?"

Mortiss snorted at her derisively, as if to say she could take care of herself. It gave Morddon a twinge of satisfaction to learn her derision was not reserved exclusively for him. The braying of the jackal pack changed as it sensed its prey close at hand.

Morddon slid off Mortiss's back, took the unconscious WindHollow in his arms and laid him at the griffin's feet, turned back to Mortiss to tell her she was on her own. But the horse had vanished without waiting for word from him.

"You will be remembered for this," the griffin said.

Morddon spun back toward her. "No!" he said. "Speak of this to no one. Keep my name out of it. You owe me that much."

"If that is your wish?"

"You're damn right that's my wish."

The griffin nodded. "Very well, my white faced friend, but then you must bear this," and as she spoke she reared back on the hind legs of the lioness part of her body. The talons of one fore leg shot up with lightning speed, and before Morddon could react the tip of one talon nicked his left cheek just below the eye.

He staggered backward, clutching at the wound on his face, blood flowing freely between his fingers. "Why did you do that, you crazy halfbird? Why?"

The griffin ignored him for a moment, looked out over the valley, balanced her weight on her lioness hind legs and one taloned foot, lifted WindHollow gently with the other. She looked back at Morddon and said quickly, "Now you bear the mark of the House of the Thane. I am sorry I must repay you with such a heavy burden. In your ignorance you left me no choice." And with that she launched herself over the edge of the cliff, dropped without flight for a desperate heartbeat, then unfolded her mighty wings and soared out away from the rocky face.

The din of the pack behind him reminded him he had no time to waste. He turned his back on the cliff, dropped to his hands and knees and learned in that moment just how badly his side had stiffened without care. He resolved to ignore the pain and started edging his way backward down the cliff. He moved downward with an almost careless abandon, taking chances he would not have considered under ordinary circumstances, knowing that if he didn't put some distance between him and the top of the cliff by the time the jackals arrived, he'd be dangling at their mercy.

There was no time to plan his descent, no time to survey the face of the cliff and choose the safest or fastest route to the bottom, no time to test the next hand or foothold before putting his weight upon it, only time to choose and take his chances. He lost all concept of distance as he became fully absorbed in the frantic descent, sometimes groping blindly for purchase, twice almost falling as an outcrop of rock gave beneath his weight. Not until the first rock—easily the size of his head—crashed against the cliff face only an arm's length from him, did he realize the jackal packs had arrived. He stopped moving, hugged the wall of rock tightly, looked up carefully to see how far he'd gotten.

The face of the cliff was slightly rounded, something not obvious from above, and from below he could no longer see the top. The jackals knew he was below them, and a steady rain of dirt clumps and small rocks dropped around him. It also told him there were few large rocks above, that the jackals had already used them up in their haste to dislodge him. He remained still and after a time the rain of debris ended, and in the silence that followed he heard Magwa shouting something he couldn't make out.

Occasionally a rock bounded past him, so he started down again, but this time with more care. He reached a point where the cliff face angled outward, losing some of its steepness but taking him out into view of his enemies above. He never saw the rock that hit him as it clipped the side of his head. There came an instant of vertigo during which he flailed wildly for anything to grasp, then he hit something hard, felt and heard several ribs crack, bounced and slid for a good distance until he came to an abrupt halt with his arm wedged between two rocks. Bent at an odd angle, it hurt like netherhell.

An arrow chinged against a nearby rock. He struggled to dislodge his arm, and almost lost consciousness as each movement brought a sharp, stabbing pain in his chest. When he finally freed his arm he realized he could go no further. He huddled on a small ledge, curled up into a fetal position and waited to die.

Somewhere he thought he heard Mortiss laughing at him, then massive wings obscured the sun, and he heard shouts and screaming high above. He saw the body of a jackal warrior tumble past him, and then talons the size of a man's arm surrounded him. They closed about him, lifted him gently, and he passed out.

••••

He came to, lying on the ground beside a road. When he opened his eyes he found a giant beak only inches from his nose, and the night-black eyes above the beak stared at him curiously, examining him. The griffin standing over him backed away a step, and Morddon managed to prop himself up on one elbow.

"Where did you get that mark on your face?" the griffin demanded.

Morddon touched the scar where the female griffin had nicked him with her talon. From the position of the sun in the sky she had cut him less than an hour ago, but in that time it had healed fully. "None of your damn business," he growled at the halfbird, then struggled painfully to his feet, clutching his broken left arm to his side, trying to ignore his broken ribs.

A Benesh'ere war party burst from a copse of nearby trees, charged across a small glen to the road, then up the road toward Morddon and the griffin. The war party came to a halt in front of the griffin. Their leader opened his mouth to say something to the griffin but glanced for a moment at Morddon. His face turned into a mask of rage, he drew his saber and spurred his horse into a charge at Morddon. As he passed the griffin the halfbird swept a wing out and knocked the warrior from his mount into a dusty sprawl. The warrior jumped to his feet, saber in hand, and demanded of the griffin, "Why the hell did you do that? That's the madman, don't you see? He abandoned the Princess AnneRhianne in the middle of an empty road. He deserves to die."

"Perhaps," the griffin said. "But he is under the protection of the House of the Thane. So if you would kill him you must kill me first."

Morddon snarled, "To netherhell with you, halfbird!" But the effort started him coughing, rewarding him with a mouthful of blood. Between coughs he managed to grunt, "If this fool thinks he can kill me, let him try." Angrily Morddon reached for the hilt of his sword, drew it in a single motion, but unendurable pain shot through his side as he did so, and again he passed out.

••••

Rhianne had trouble sleeping. She rolled out of bed, guessed sunrise was still several hours off, threw on a heavy robe and slippers, and walked through the castle. She found a high terrace off an upstairs sitting room, and there she found peace and calm in the stars above her and the darkness that surrounded her.

She stood there for quite some time, until the rustle of someone moving behind her startled her out of her thoughts. She flinched, thinking the old woman had come for her, but then she sensed the calm of AnnaRail and she relaxed.

"It is a lovely night," AnnaRail said softly.

Rhianne nodded. "Yes. It's quiet."

"It's more than quiet. It's . . . It's the kind of night when one can be at peace with everything and everyone."

Rhianne thought of the old woman. "Not everyone."

AnnaRail chuckled softly. "You know, Morgin had the same trouble with her. Oh, you and he are very different people, but both of you have the traits that entice the old woman's avarice. You both have power, though for some reason we only saw hints of it until now. You are both smart enough to learn to use it properly, and more than anything you are both willful enough to fight her, though you fight her more directly than Morgin, but with less danger. Oddly enough she likes that in both of you. She likes someone who'll give her a good fight; someone whom she considers a worthy opponent."

Rhianne considered the offhand compliment, but it didn't help any and she could contain herself no longer. "I just . . ." She struggled to hold back the tears, but her chin betrayed her with a tremble. "All I want to do . . . I don't know what I want to do . . ." She started sobbing and felt foolish. "I just wish I knew how to do it."

AnnaRail came toward her and wrapped her arms around her. "Only you can determine what your talents are, and how you can best use them."

"But I don't know how, especially when I'm pushed."

"Ah!" AnnaRail nodded. "The old woman."

Rhianne shook her head. "No. Yes, the old woman too. But that's not what I meant. Something else is pushing me."

AnnaRail nodded thoughtfully. "I begin to believe we are all pieces on a giant gaming board, and we all have a role to play in this. Some, like my son—your husband—and perhaps you yourself—have a greater role to play than the rest of us, and some have very minor roles. But we all have our place, and in the end only you can determine what your place will be. You must be patient. Don't push yourself beyond your limits, and don't allow the old woman to push you either. When your time is at hand, you will know it. Believe me."

Rhianne let her tears flow, and she held tightly to AnnaRail while the sun rose slowly over the mountains in the east. She felt better for it; she had an ally in her husband's mother, a friend and a source of knowledge. For that she was infinitely grateful.

14

The Seven Deeds

MORGIN AWOKE FROM troubled sleep, sitting on the floor where he'd slept twisted uncomfortably in a pile of blankets. He was alone in a dark, cramped, musty room. Bright slashes of sunlight cut past the edges of a shuttered window, telling him that morning was well advanced, though it took a moment to remember which morning. In his dreams he'd been haunting Morddon's soul for several days, when in reality no more than a few hours had passed since he'd left the inn's common room.

He untangled his legs from the blankets, stood and crossed the room to the window, threw open the shutters to let the morning in. A washbasin rested on a stand in one corner, a pitcher of moderately clean water next to it. He filled the washbasin, leaned over and splashed water on his face. As he stood up with water dripping through his beard he caught a glimpse of his image in a polished brass mirror on the wall. He ran wet hands through his hair in the hope of taming it somewhat, and looked at the young, bearded stranger staring back at him. He stepped closer, impressed with how much his new beard had changed his appearance, and then he noticed the scar.

The mark of the House of the Thane, SheelThane had called it, a small scar, just below his left eye at the boundary between beard and skin, not a deep or well-defined scar. It might not be visible at all were it not for the beard, for no hair had grown within the line of the scar. He might never have noticed it, but for the beard and his dreams. Perhaps it had been there all this time, and perhaps his dreams were just that: dreams. He wanted so much to deny the reality of those damn dreams.

Down below in the common room he found Cort waiting for him at one of the tables. As he sat down she asked, "Did you sleep well? You needed the rest so we let you sleep in."

He shrugged. "I slept adequately."

She ordered breakfast for him: bread and meat and cheese and that black, foamy beer. Morgin ate more out of a sense of duty than any real appetite.

"You look tired," she said. "Not like a man who's slept the morning away. The dreams again?"

"Aye," Morgin nodded. "Always the dreams. Where are the others?"

"They're off looking for employment. We were thinking you and Val and France could hire on as guards in one of the caravans. And after we know which one, Tulellcoe and I can buy passage as husband and wife. Female twonames are not at all common so it will be best if I travel as a clanswoman with her husband."

Morgin ate in silence, washed a few bites of bread and meat down with some beer. He looked carefully at Cort, remembered that she too had spent some time with the Benesh'ere. "Val said you and he spent time with the Benesh'ere."

"Yes we did. Why?"

Morgin shrugged. "I don't know. Last night Val said something about SteelMasters, and SteelMistresses. Tell me about them."

She considered that carefully, then said, "Well now. There isn't much to tell. The whitefaces themselves can't come to agreement about the SteelMasters. Some of them think they were some sort of kings and queens who ruled before the gods came. Others—and this is what I think bears the most fact—think they were just wise ones who disdained the actual leadership of the Benesh'ere, but were looked to for sage council. But they do agree on a few things, especially the fact that the SteelMasters could do incredible things with steel. I mean the best steel we know of today is Benesh'ere steel, and the Benesh'ere smiths all agree the SteelMasters made steel that puts their own efforts to shame. In fact . . ." Cort frowned and squinted, ". . . they apparently did something quite magical with steel, though no one seems to know what."

Morgin thought of the sword he carried strapped to his side, old Benesh'ere steel. And with the knowledge of his dreams he now understood the true age of this steel.

"Something else those whitefaces can agree on is the Seven Deeds, which they sometimes call the Seven Wrongs."

Morgin asked around a mouth full of food, "Seven Deeds?"

Cort nodded. "It's one of their most important legends. Apparently the last Steel-Master is going to come back from the dead, or from hiding, or from somewhere, and perform the Seven Deeds, and in doing so he'll right the Seven Wrongs. All Benesh'ere children can recite the Seven Deeds from memory almost as soon as they learn to talk."

"Can you?" Morgin asked.

Cort looked at the ceiling of the inn thoughtfully. "Let me see now. I think I can. The first thing this SteelMaster is going to do is restore the House of the Thane."

Morgin almost choked on a piece of bread, but he caught himself and took a deep draught of the brown beer.

"Now no one knows what the House of the Thane is, but that's what this SteelMaster's going to do first. Second, he'll free the hand of the thief. Your guess is as good as anyone's on that one. Third, he'll free the daughter of the wind. I can't even speculate on that one. Fourth, he'll free the Dane King. I've never heard of any Dane King, and I've done quite a bit of traveling. Fifth, he'll free the spirit of the sands. That's got to have something to do with the Munjarro, but no one has the least idea what. Sixth, he'll free the soul of the Fallen One."

Cort didn't comment on the sixth deed, she just shrugged and shook her head, but Morgin remembered that Ellowyn had referred to Metadan as the Fallen One. "And seventh," Cort continued, "he'll free the heart of the Benesh'ere. Now that's an easy one, and that's the one the Benesh'ere are waiting for. Somehow he's going to free them from their exile, and they believe he'll do it at Gilguard's Ford where the Gods Road crosses the river Ulbb. That's why the whitefaces call it the Road of the Seventh Deed. But there's a riddle here no one's ever solved. It says the Benesh'ere will not be free until they stand north of the Ulbb, but the Benesh'ere cannot cross the Ulbb until they are free. Now since their exile means they must live forever south of the Ulbb, solve that riddle, my friend, and you could live like a king among the Benesh'ere for the rest of your days."

At that moment the front door of the inn opened and a shaft of sunlight splashed across the room through the sooty, smoky atmosphere. Everyone turned suspiciously to watch Tulellcoe and France enter, close the door and cross the room to Cort and Morgin. When they pulled up stools and sat down, and everyone understood there would be no trouble, the inn's patrons turned their attention elsewhere.

France spoke softly. "We've got work in a big caravan, but the guardmaster's a twoname, real cautious sort, wants to meet you before he'll commit himself. He ain't a real pleasant fellow, but he's got a good business guarding caravans so he's probably honest."

"When's this caravan leaving?" Morgin asked.

"First light tomorrow," France said. "Which is a good thing. There's Penda armsmen in the city askin' about us. And there's more arriving each hour. By morning the city'll be full of 'em, and you'd best not be around." France looked at Cort. "Or you either. They're askin' after the female twoname. You stand out easily."

Cort nodded, looked at Tulellcoe. "Give me an hour and I won't look like a twoname."

Tulellcoe said, "That's why Val is staying with the caravan until it leaves. He won't be coming back into the city." Tulellcoe looked at Morgin. "And you'd better join him as soon as possible. That beard won't hide you for long."

Morgin lifted his empty hands above the table. "I've got everything I own on me. I can leave right now. All I need is my horse."

"We left orders with the stable master to saddle her."

Morgin looked at France. The swordsman seemed to be enjoying this, as if danger made life worth the trouble. "Let's go then, eh?"

"You won't see Cort and me again," Tulellcoe said. "Not until we join the caravan as passengers. And remember you don't know us; you've never met us before."

••••

Outside the street was full of people going about their business, and a few children playing in the gutters. There were clouds high overhead, but they didn't have the look of rain, and the sky was otherwise clear.

France led Morgin to the stable and their horses, and once mounted they followed a well-traveled road out the southwest side of the city. They found Val waiting by a large staging area near the river where several small merchant caravans had joined a much larger one.

"Guardmaster wants to meet you," Val said to Morgin.

"What's his name?" Morgin asked.

"He goes by the name Chiren Tesha."

Morgin shrugged. "Let's get this over with."

The Tesha was a big man, tall, broad shouldered, and trim of waist. He wore a simple, leather doublet over a plain linen blouse, and loose fitting breeches tucked into knee high boots, the kind of attire Morgin himself found most comfortable.

"You're a swordsman?" the Tesha asked Morgin. He was seated on a stump of wood sewing up a hole in an old cloak.

"Not for dueling," Morgin said. "But I can fight."

"How well?"

"Well enough to keep myself alive."

The Tesha considered him carefully. The staging area for the caravans was a noisy hive of activity swirling about them. Morgin tried to ignore the distraction.

"You're hiding something," the Tesha said flatly. He stood up and towered over Morgin. "You've got a chip on your shoulder, you're hiding something, and I'm not sure if I can trust you."

Morgin shrugged. "What man here does not have something to hide? I have my own private thoughts and I will keep them. You need swordsmen. Well I am a swordsman, and an honest one."

"I sense the truth in you, swordsman, but I sense you are close to a lie. Very close. Speak your name."

"Morddon."

The Tesha's eyes narrowed. "My magic tells me if someone speaks the truth or not, and it tells me that name is a lie, but only half a lie."

Morgin got angry. "Then listen to the truth in these words," he said. "I have no intention of harming anyone in this caravan or stealing its goods. I'm a decent swordsman in a fight and I will do my best to live up to the terms of any contract I make. If I have to defend myself I will do so against anyone, contract or not." Morgin then looked the twoname in the eyes. "Beyond that, any secrets I have are mine to keep, unless of course the Tesha would like to try to pry them from me with the point of his sword. Then one of us will die . . . needlessly."

The Tesha stared at him for a long moment. Then he nodded and said, "Very well. I'll pay you two coppers a month like the rest, plus meals and beer. I don't pay more to a first hire. You'll take orders from me and stay with the caravan until we reach Aud. After that, if I'm happy with you, and you want to stay, I'll pay more, though not much."

"Fair enough," Morgin said, and they shook hands.

The Tesha split up Morgin, France and Val, gave them separate assignments, probably a precaution until he knew them better. He assigned Morgin to a group of twelve men who were responsible for scouting the road ahead of the caravan, which suited him nicely. Better that than eating dust all day long.

The leader of the scouts was a small, wiry man named Katha. He had a distrustful nature about him, and that first day before the caravan left he and Morgin and the scouts rode several leagues down the road. That close to Anistigh there were no real dangers to be concerned with. Morgin knew Katha was watching him closely, testing him, so he paid close attention to everything Katha told him, kept his mouth shut, and resolved to do his job and stay out of trouble.

"The road to Aud is too well traveled," Katha told him, "for us to do much worryin' about bandits. But keep yer eyes open. It happens every now and then, though most bandits ain't stupid enough to attack a caravan this well manned. And the Tesha's been known to go out of his way to hunt down those that do. He likes to bring 'em back alive, so he can hang 'em in front of everyone."

"Well then what are we out here for?" Morgin asked.

"Chiren just likes to know what's up ahead. There might be a swollen river, or a tree down over the road, or a wash-out somewheres. And now there's that outlaw wizard out there too."

Morgin looked sideways at Katha, tried to detect any underlying suspicion in his last statement, but apparently the scout was merely making conversation.

Katha scanned the horizon. "I don't like wizards. Makes me skin crawl."

"But the Tesha's a wizard," Morgin said.

"Yah," Katha said with a long sigh. "Poor fella. It's a shame too, 'cause he's a good man. But every man's got his own problems, eh?"

That night Morgin slept peacefully, and awoke the next morning without strong memories of Kathbeyanne, though he had dreamed of the ancient city, and of Morddon, angels and griffins. Those memories were vague and indistinct, as dreams should be.

The caravan left Anistigh at daybreak. Morgin had learned over beer and dinner the night before that the Tesha was an independent contractor who hired his men out to protect traveling merchants. He had a good reputation, and Katha warned Morgin to help him keep it. Morgin also learned that because of the *outlaw wizard* three smaller merchants had banded with a larger one for their mutual protection.

It took half the morning for the caravan to stretch out and get up to speed, but once under way they made good time. Katha kept Morgin close by because Morgin was an unknown. He divided the twelve scouts into six groups of two, and they rode well ahead of the caravan investigating just about anything and everything. Katha was thorough; he or one of his scouts stopped at every farm and manor and chatted politely with the head of the household. Clearly, he'd made this trip many times before. When they found a few peasants camped near the road they investigated. Katha was kind, never pushy or arrogant. He questioned the peasants until he was satisfied they were just that.

That night, with the caravan camped in a long line along the road, Morgin learned that the Tesha's men's duties were more that of police than guards. They had to break up the occasional fight, settle a petty dispute here and there. Morgin was lucky. He was assigned to a three hour watch in the middle of the night, and with the camp asleep and quiet there was little for him to do beyond walk up and down the length of the caravan, keep his eyes open, and whisper a soft greeting to the other guards as he passed them in the night.

Morgin saw almost nothing of his companions during the days that followed, but with the caution of a hunted man he noted where they placed their blankets each night. He never did see Tulellcoe or Cort, though France assured him they were somewhere in the caravan. He actually enjoyed himself, working for the Tesha, good, honest work, sometimes rather strenuous, but nothing demanded of him beyond his capabilities. He was just Morddon, a simple guard, and no longer the great sorcerer known as the ShadowLord.

It all came to an end on the sixth night out of Anistigh. A hand awakened Morgin shaking him harshly. When he opened his eyes another hand clamped over his mouth. In the darkness the man standing over him was just a shadow against the moonlit sky, but Morgin recognized France's voice lowered to a whisper. "Penda armsmen. Just come into camp. They're talking to the Tesha now and it won't take them long to figure out who you are. Tulellcoe and Cort are fine where they are, but the rest of us have to get out now. Get the horses. I'll rouse Val and we'll meet you at the west end of the caravan."

Morgin rolled up his blanket, gathered up his few belongings and slipped into the shadows of the camp, moving cautiously toward the string of horses. He moved quickly and efficiently, but it took an eternity to saddle three horses. He'd just finished when he felt the cold steel of the tip of a sword touch the back of his neck. Katha spoke behind him. "I thought I could trust you."

"You can," Morgin whispered. "But I have my enemies, though I do not count you or the Tesha among them. Just let me go and say nothing of it."

"I can't just let you sneak out. The Tesha'll have me hide."

"Better to face the Tesha," Morgin whispered, "than the House of Elhiyne."

Katha hissed, sucked air through his teeth. "What do you mean by that?"

Morgin turned slowly to face him, though Katha kept his sword at Morgin's throat. "I am a son of the House of Elhiyne," Morgin said. "The one they call the Shadow-Lord."

"The outlaw wizard?"

"Yes," Morgin answered flatly. "The outlaw wizard. And if you stop me, then you'll be siding with our enemies, and I know full well you'll not enjoy facing my grandmother." Morgin was hoping Katha didn't know he was being hunted by his own family as well as the Pendas.

Katha's upper lip curled into a snarl. "If I let you go then I'm siding with you, and the Pendas won't be kind either."

"No," Morgin said. "They won't." He thought quickly. "You could attempt to stop me and I could knock you unconscious. My grandmother would not blame you for the attempt, as long as you failed, and the Pendas would not blame you for the failure, as long as you made the attempt."

Katha considered him for a moment, then slowly lowered his sword and turned his back on Morgin. He waited there, standing patiently in the moonlight. He tensed when he heard Morgin draw his sword, perhaps wondering how traitorous Morgin might be. But Morgin didn't let him wonder for long. He hit him in the back of the head with the hilt of his sword, though he softened the blow considerably. Katha didn't need to be unconscious, just have an appropriate bump to back up his story.

As Morgin led the three horses to the front of the caravan, one of the night guards stopped him. "What's this?" the man asked. Luckily Morgin knew the man enough to be recognized.

"Damned if I know," Morgin said in a whisper. "Katha kicks me out of me blanket and he's mad as hell about something. Tells me to bring meself and three horses and meet him up front of the caravan. I've already stood me watch. I should be sleepin'."

"Got any idea what's up?" the guard asked.

"Na," Morgin said. "Katha didn't say. But I'll bet it's somethin' to do with them Pendas. I best be movin' on quickly. Katha's mad enough as it is without me bein' late."

The guard nodded. "Move on," he said, then he turned and went about his business.

Morgin found France and Val waiting for him at the appointed place. They led their horses on foot, hoping to gain some distance before mounting up. But they'd only gone a few hundred paces when an outcry arose from the camp.

"Well that's it," France said. "Let's get the netherhell out of here."

15

The Queen of Thieves

THEY RODE HARD through the rest of the night, stopping only to walk the horses for brief periods. Sometime past dawn Val reined his horse to a stop on a small rise and turned to look back down the road. The countryside about them had flattened out as they approached the port city of Aud, and from the low hillock they could see for a good distance. Not far behind them, they saw the Penda posse riding fast and hard in their wake.

"I've been hearing rumors about trouble in Aud," France said as they watched the Pendas for a moment. "I was thinkin' we might skirt the city altogether. But we got no choice now. Aud's our only hope for refuge."

Morgin asked, "What'll stop them from following us into Aud?"

"Oh they can follow us into Aud," France said. "And they'll be as welcome as we are. But if they try to impose the authority of the Lesser Council, or that of any clan, Aiergain will have their heads."

"How far?" Val asked.

France looked up at the sun. "At this pace, if our horses hold up, dawn tomorrow."

The next morning their horses were exhausted, even the indomitable Mortiss. The animals struggled just to maintain a reasonable gallop, though the Pendas, who were now only minutes behind them, seemed to be in no better shape. As the three of them rounded a sharp bend in the road, they found themselves facing a company of two twelves of armed and mounted warriors, with long, deadly lances leveled at them.

Morgin and his companions reined their horses in and came to a stop just beyond the points of the lances. Another two twelves of armed warriors coalesced out of the thin forest and took up positions behind them.

Nothing happened for a long moment, though in the distance Morgin heard the thundering hooves of the Penda posse pounding down the road toward them. France slowly and carefully dismounted, making every effort to keep his hands clearly visible. He handed the reins of his horse to Morgin and he stepped forward to face the warriors in front of them.

One of the warriors, a young man only a few years older than Morgin, obviously the captain of these men, also dismounted, and stepped cautiously forward to face France. He frowned at France and squinted, as if trying to peer through a hazy fog. He stopped a few paces short of France, and France said, "It's good to see you again, Pandorin. You've grown quite a bit since we last met."

The young man's eyes opened wide, and in an instant he dropped to one knee before France, bowed his head. "My lord," he said. "How may we serve you?"

"Well first you can stand and face me, friend Pandorin." The young man did so. "And then there's a bunch of Pendas right behind us that mean us no good. You might see to it they don't get into the city, but as a favor to me try not to kill any of them, eh."

"Yes, my lord."

Pandorin jumped to obey. He blocked the road with his four twelves of men, while Morgin and his companions waited behind them. A few moments later the Pendas rounded the same bend in the road and came face to face with Pandorin and his warriors. Pandorin's four twelves outnumbered the Pendas, and the soldiers from Aud were rested and fresh while the Pendas and their horses swayed with exhaustion.

"What is this?" the Penda captain demanded. It saddened Morgin to see a few Elhiynes among the Pendas.

"This is the border into Aud," Pandorin said flatly. "And you're not welcome here."

"Are you telling me Aud will protect the outlaw wizard, the renegade?"

"That is for the Mistress of Aud to decide," Pandorin answered. "I know only that these men are not outlaws in Aud, and it is up to the Queen of Thieves to decide their fate. Now turn back. As I have already said, you are not welcome here."

The Pendas turned back with angry shouts. Val looked carefully at France, then at Morgin, and he said, "I should have known France would be a prince among thieves."

France turned on him angrily. "I ain't no prince."

••••

Pandorin sent one of his armsmen ahead as a messenger to tell the Queen of Thieves "Lord France has returned." Then he left one of his lieutenants in charge and decided to personally escort them into the city. There was something amiss in Aud. Morgin had never been there before, but he sensed the unnatural pall that hung over the city, as if its inhabitants were in mourning.

"What's wrong here?" France demanded of Pandorin as they dismounted their horses in the palace yard at the center of the city. "I'd heard rumors of trouble, but I hadn't thought it would be this bad. What is it, man?"

Pandorin's eyes pinched with pain as he spoke, and lines of strain crossed his face. "Aiergain is dying. It is some illness of the mind that's slowly eating away her sanity.

We're all powerless to help her. The whole city is just watching, and grieving, as every day she deteriorates even further. It hurts us all to watch her suffer so."

Pandorin looked carefully at Morgin and Val. "I take it one of you is the outlaw wizard?"

Morgin said flatly. "I am."

Pandorin looked him over for a second, then shrugged and turned to France. "Her Majesty wants to see you right away, and you are to bring your friends."

Pandorin led them into the depths of the palace, a grand place, with high vaulted ceilings. There were large windows everywhere that let in the sun and brightened the halls. Somewhere Morgin had heard it was called the Palace of Lights. But as they approached a particular hall he heard a woman shouting, and when they brushed past uneasy servants and entered the hall the shouts grew louder, then stopped.

"France," the woman's voice cried joyfully, and Morgin got his first glimpse of Aiergain as the crowd surrounding her parted. He guessed her to be in her early thirties, still young and beautiful, and there was an air of confidence about her, though her face was marked with strain and fear. "My dear friend France," she cried as she strode across the room to greet the swordsman, her arms extended, a happy smile on her face.

France tried to bow and drop to one knee, but she lifted him and hugged him, and Morgin saw tears in her eyes as she rested her chin on the swordsman's shoulder. She looked past France at Morgin, and she looked through him as if he weren't there, a very noble snubbing. Then she looked at Val, her eyes darkened and her smile turned to a look of anger. She stepped away from France and pointed at Val. "Is this your companion?" she demanded angrily.

France looked at her uncertainly and nodded. "Yes. They're friends of mine."

She turned on France viciously. "You too?" she asked, shaking with fear. Morgin caught a momentary glimpse of uncontrolled magic as it swirled around her shoulders. "Even you betray me? You bring magicians into my midst, sorcerers, practitioners of evil. I thought I could trust you. At least you!"

She started sobbing and turned her back on France, raised her chin and shouted hysterically at the ceiling, "Guards! Seize them."

She spun back toward them. Morgin saw power buried behind her eyes and he sensed it with his soul. She pointed a finger at France. "You betray me like all the rest. Seize him. Bind him. Kill him. Now."

Pandorin stood like a man who'd just received a horrible blow to the stomach, his mouth open, his eyes wide, tears streaming down his face. "But Your Majesty! It's Lord France! He's always—"

"Seize them, I tell you," she said, "or I'll have your head too."

The guards moved slowly, for their hearts were not in the task. They seized France and Val. Aiergain shouted orders about executing the two men, and for the moment

Morgin was ignored, so he grabbed Pandorin's arm and pulled him behind a few on-lookers. Morgin asked one question. "Has the queen ever shown signs of magic be-fore?"

Pandorin frowned, looked at him stupidly. "Of course not. She's no witch."

"Oh yes she is, my friend," Morgin said. "And she doesn't know it, and that's what's killing her."

Morgin was probably the only person in the room who could truly understand growing up without magic, then having it thrust upon you unprepared, unbidden, with-out control. He shook Pandorin, "Listen to me. I'm going to try to save your queen's life, and that of my friends. But you'll have to back me, even if it means defying her. Just remember it's for her own good."

Pandorin looked at Morgin carefully. "You can save her?"

"Maybe," Morgin hissed. "Maybe not. But I'm willing to try. Will you back me?"

"Of course," Pandorin said. "Any man here would die for her."

"Well you may have to," Morgin said. "Now just follow my lead."

Aiergain was still ranting. France and Val were on their knees before her, their hands bound behind their backs, their heads forced down to the floor by unhappy guards. "Bring me a sword," Aiergain shouted. "I want to see their heads roll now."

They hesitated and an instant of silence followed. Morgin said, "Hold." His com-mand had the desired effect. Aiergain froze into an angry stillness and the crowd in front of Morgin parted to get out of her way. She looked at Morgin for one instant, then said to the guards, "There's another one of them. Seize him too."

"No," Pandorin said, and his behavior stunned even Aiergain.

"You're all turning against me," she said. "Even my most trusted men. You're probably all wizards and witches."

"No," Morgin said, and he pointed a finger at her. "It is you who are the witch, and you don't know it, and you don't know how to deal with it, and that's why you're sick."

"I'm not sick." She looked at the guards. "Kill him. Now."

"If you do that," Morgin said calmly, "then you'll lose the one thing you want more dearly than anything else in this world."

"I want for nothing."

"Ah, but you do, and like your magic you don't know what you want, nor even that you want it."

"Well then," she said. "If you're so smart, tell me what I want so dearly."

Morgin closed his eyes, remembered when his magic had first come upon him fully, and how, untrained for it, he had been tormented for days and nights on end. There had been just one thing he had wanted, and he'd felt that if he got that one thing, then he would have the strength to handle all the rest. He spoke softly, and carefully. "You want a decent night's sleep."

Aiergain gasped, stepped back as if she'd been slapped.

"You want rest, release from the strain and pressure that's forever pulling at your soul. And I can tell you how to get it."

She looked at him angrily but said nothing, waiting for him to speak further.

"Do what I say," he said softly. "Speak the words I want you to speak, think the thoughts I want you to think, do that for just one minute, and I'll give you the first decent night's sleep you've had in months."

Aiergain shook for a moment, and a dark cloud of hatred passed behind her eyes. But then she calmed. "Very well. I'll do what you want, for just one minute." She extended her hand out toward him with her palm open, then slowly closed her fingers as if crushing his heart in her fist. "But if you're lying, if you're deceiving me, you will die the slowest and most painful death I can devise."

Morgin had them clear the hall, though Aiergain instructed her guards to burst in if they heard her cry out. Morgin then sat cross-legged on the floor in the middle of the large hall and instructed her to sit likewise opposite him. Reluctantly she did so.

"Now," Morgin said. "Give me your hands." He extended his and she unhappily took them.

"Close your eyes and try to empty your mind." Morgin thought of AnnaRail, and how she'd done exactly the same thing with him. He tried to remember every word she'd said, every action she'd made, and he tried to imitate her. "Now repeat after me."

He dug deep within his soul to find the word, a word completely incomprehensible to him, a word that only took on meaning when his magic came upon him, and so a word he would never again understand. He searched his memory hard, and he did find the word, and he spoke it, and then it left him as if it had never been uttered.

Aiergain repeated the word, but on her lips it rang a bell of meaning and pleasure.

Morgin struggled to find the next word, brought it forth, spoke it, listened to Aiergain repeat it. If Aiergain responded as he had, she'd be well into the spell before she realized what was happening to her. One by one he brought forth the words of the spell and asked Aiergain to speak them, and from a distance he saw the spell building about her. Then at the right moment he had her speak the final phrase.

She collapsed, would have fallen backward had he not been holding her hands. He lowered her gently to the floor, then stood and lifted her in his arms. He pounded on the doors of the hall with his foot. The guards opened them instantly and their eyes filled with fear.

"She's just sleeping," Morgin said. "Lead me to her apartments."

Her ladies wanted Morgin to leave her so they could dress her properly for bed, but Morgin wouldn't let them touch her. He laid her on top of the bed, still dressed in her gowns. He called for a blanket, placed it over her, tucked it tightly about her.

Her eyes opened into slits, and he saw she was still caught within the spell. "Thank you," she said.

He smiled at her, but as he did so something within her eyes changed and he saw a darkness from deep within her soul come boiling forth. A sudden pain stabbed at his soul. Something lifted him off his feet, slammed him against a wall high up near the ceiling with his feet dangling well off the floor. Powerless to defend himself against her magic, he lost consciousness.

••••

Aiergain ran in a panic stricken rush through a horrifying forest of death and decay. She heard the howl of a pack of large beasts she was certain were hunting her, and they were catching her, and soon they would devour her. Her skirts were heavy with mud, and tangled about her ankles they hindered her constantly.

She caught a glimpse of motion far to one side, retained an image of something large and hairy. She saw another, then another, and now they no longer tried to hide themselves, but rushed at her, all fangs and muscle.

They suddenly stopped and froze in their tracks. Large, hairy, man-like beasts, they raised their muzzles in the air and sniffed. One of them let out a yelp, a frightened, terrified yip. They hesitated for a moment, then turned away from her and ran, leaving her behind just when she was theirs for the taking.

She heard a rustle in the dank undergrowth, looked fearfully toward it, wondering what horrible thing could have frightened away an entire pack of such monsters. What stepped out of the brush was a small, decrepit child, dressed in torn rags, with terrible, oozing sores on his face. The child dragged an old sheathed sword behind him, a sword too big to lift, and almost too big to drag.

He looked at Aiergain and croaked, "Close your eyes and we'll leave this place."

"Where will we go?" she asked.

"A place you'll like much better than this. We're going to go see Erithnae and the Unnamed King. You'll like them. I do."

16

The Hand of the Thief

MORDDON RETURNED TO Kathbeyanne on a stretcher. He had a broken arm and several broken ribs, a serious concussion and a number of bad cuts and bruises. He was part of a train of carts and wagons carrying wounded back to the city, and they were still a few days out of Kathbeyanne when a messenger arrived with joyful news. SheelThane, the griffin queen, had escaped from captivity in the *netherworld*. After twelve hundred years the House of the Thane was again whole, and the entire city rejoiced, though the man had no information on how she'd escaped. It was rumored she refused to speak of the matter entirely.

The griffin that found Morddon at the base of the cliff stayed curiously close to him. His name was TearThane, and Morddon often found him staring silently at the scar on his cheek. Then at the oddest of moments TearThane would ask, "Where did you get that scar?"

Morddon would growl, "I don't remember. Now leave me alone." By the time they reached Kathbeyanne it had become a strange kind of ritual.

They put Morddon in a large, overcrowded hospital ward. His wounds had begun to heal on the trip back to Kathbeyanne and he was anxious to return to his duties. Almost immediately Gilguard and AnneRhianne came to see him. "Is there anything we can bring you?" AnneRhianne asked.

"Yes," Morddon said. "Some peace and quiet, and some privacy. Now go away."

Gilguard flinched angrily, but AnneRhianne stayed his hand. "Don't take offense," she said to the warmaster. "That's just his way. You must understand he feels guilty when he's not out fighting the Goath, and it makes him surly."

Morddon said, "Don't try to understand me, woman."

She ignored him, continued speaking to Gilguard. "And he did save my life, and I saw a glimpse of his true nature then, a glimpse of the man he hides from us all."

Gilguard nodded. "I owe you an apology," he said to Morddon. "I'm told one of my warriors tried to kill you, thinking you had abandoned the Lady

AnneRhianne. You must understand that facts can become garbled out there with all the fighting."

Morddon opened his mouth with an unpleasant retort on his lips, but he forced his anger down. "Apology accepted."

"There," AnneRhianne said. "You see? He can be civil."

"Bah!" Morddon growled.

AnneRhianne said, "And I owe you my thanks for saving my nephew's life."

Morddon didn't want the attention that would come if they knew he had rescued SheelThane, and since WindHollow was intimately connected to that story, he denied it. "I didn't save him. I never found him. I ran into those Kulls before I could track him down."

"That's not what he says, though he was sorely wounded and remembers little of what happened. But he does remember *the madman*. And he remembers the griffin Queen."

"If he was wounded then he must have been delirious."

AnneRhianne shook her head sadly. "Isn't it odd that you were there when she and he were both rescued?"

"I had nothing to do with it."

AnneRhianne chuckled. "Of course. Have it your way, my angry, bitter friend."

AnneRhianne wanted to have him moved into the palace where she could care for him personally, but he would have nothing of it. She and Gilguard left him alone and he hoped he might now return to the anonymity of a common soldier. Through the rest of that day he was nagged by doubt, wanted to mend the angry rift between him and Gilguard, and he wanted to see AnneRhianne again. *It's you*, he thought to Morgin, who was buried deep within his soul. *Your damn soft-hearted kindness is changing me.*

The next morning Morddon dressed, retrieved his sword and left the hospital to report back to the barracks. "Are you well?" Metadan asked him.

"Well enough to fight," Morddon said.

Metadan nodded. "SheelThane has been asking after you," he said without elaborating further, then turned back to the business he'd been about when Morddon interrupted him. Metadan didn't take offense just because a man chose to speak his mind, and Morddon liked that about him.

That afternoon he coaxed an angel into a workout. They went out onto the large parade ground in front of the barracks and Morddon quickly discovered he was still in no shape for swinging a sword. He decided to limit himself to a few exercises and some stretching, and even that was painful.

A messenger arrived from the palace. "Her Majesty's compliments," the messenger said to Morddon. "The queen of the House of the Thane requests your presence at your convenience."

Morddon looked at the messenger and snarled, "Go away. I'm busy."

"But Her Majesty—"

With almost inhuman speed Morddon put the tip of his sword at the man's throat. "I said go away."

The man bowed politely and left.

The next day Morddon returned to the parade ground, and while exercising and stretching found that the effort of the day before had done him some good. A messenger approached him with a slight smirk on his face. "His Majesty's compliments," the messenger said. "The king of the House of the Thane commands your presence now."

Morddon stopped exercising and glared at the man. The fellow's self-satisfied smirk slowly disappeared. "I don't want to see any of them halfbirds," Morddon said. "And I don't want to see any more of you. Now go away."

The messenger gulped and hurried away.

Morddon went back to his exercises, thought he might even find that angel again and try a little sword practice. But while still stretching, bent deeply over and trying to work the kinks out of the backs of his legs, he caught one glimpse of a shadow sweeping across the ground toward him, and with the instincts of a man who'd survived many a battle, he dropped flat to the ground. He barely missed being gutted by steel tipped talons that sliced past him only a hair's breadth above his back.

He jumped to his feet, spun about in time to see the back of a black griffin as it arced upward at the end of its dive, banked to one side and turned for another deadly pass. Morddon bent quickly and grabbed a hand full of dust from the ground. He waited, watching the griffin steady itself in its dive toward him, held his position until the last instant, then as the griffin swept past him he jumped to one side and tossed the hand full of dust into its face.

Morddon hit the dirt in a roll, bounded to his feet in time to see the blinded griffin touch a wing tip to the ground. The halfbird crashed in a spectacular roll of feathers and wings and claws. Before it stopped tumbling Morddon sprinted after it, bounded onto its back just as it picked itself up, wrapped an arm around its neck and slammed the hilt of his sword into the back of its head. The griffin arched its back, flopped down onto its side and rolled over. As the weight of the halfbird pressed into his damaged ribs Morddon cried out, almost lost consciousness. Then the halfbird was on top of him, pinning his sword arm to the ground with one set of talons while lifting the other to rip his throat out. "Now you will pay for your insolence to the queen of the House of the Thane," the griffin said, and its steel tipped talons descended toward his face.

Something within Morgin cried out to the steel to hold, and the halfbird froze, its talons only inches from Morddon's throat. The sudden reprieve startled Morgin, and he wondered if his silent command to the steel had actually stopped the death strike of the griffin's talons. Both he and Morddon noticed the look in the griffin's face, a look of incredulous surprise and disbelief. The griffin arched its neck forward until Morddon could smell the breath panting out of its beak. It hesitated for a moment, then asked, "Where did you get that mark on your face?"

Morddon heard other wings slicing through the air as a flock of griffins landed in a circle about them. "Hold!" TarnThane cried angrily at the griffin on top of Morddon. "Do not harm that man. I command you to stand aside."

The griffin moved slowly, retracted its talons and stepped back. AnneRhianne and Gilguard stepped in and helped Morddon to his feet. Clutching his ribs he looked about carefully. He was ringed by a strange assemblage of beings: Metadan, Ellowyn, AnneRhianne and Gilguard and several other Benesh'ere men and women. But commanding the attention of everyone were the griffins: TarnThane, AuelThane, TearThane, and foremost among them SheelThane.

Gilguard grabbed Morddon's arm unkindly, whispered into his ear, "She's come to see you. The queen of the House of the Thane has deigned to come to you. Why she didn't let that griffin gut you, I don't know. But she's here, so curb that angry tongue of yours."

Morddon yanked his arm out of Gilguard's grasp, and bowed carefully to SheelThane. "I am honored."

SheelThane said, "No. It is I who am honored." Everyone but the griffins gasped. "Well now, whiteface," she said. "You managed to stay alive after all."

"It's a habit I picked up a long time ago, and one I find difficult to break."

"You see, my queen?" TarnThane laughed. "He does have a sense of humor, and though somewhat barbed, a rarity among the whitefaces."

AuelThane stepped forward, looked closely at Morddon's face, eyed the small scar on his cheek with the same curiosity as TearThane. It clearly give him some sort of satisfaction, then he stepped back and remained silent.

SheelThane looked about carefully at each of the griffins, then she looked at Morddon. "No griffin will ever again harm you, unless in self-defense." Then she nodded at the griffin that had attacked Morddon. "And this one will be punished."

Morddon shook his head and said, "Ah don't bother. He did a poor job of killin' me, and I hold that against him more than the tryin'."

••••

Morgin drifted slowly out of his dreams, and when he opened his eyes he was resting in the soft, billowing blankets of a large bed, in a spacious and extravagantly appointed room. Nearby a young woman sat in a chair. She was about Morgin's age, dressed in the finery of a courtier, and had apparently been waiting for him to awaken. She had dozed off into a light sleep, her head bowed at an uncomfortable angle.

Morgin reached up and touched his face, found they had shaved his beard. He tried to prop himself up on one elbow, succeeded, but learned in the doing that every muscle and bone in his body ached, especially his ribs. At his efforts the young woman's head snapped up and her eyes widened. "Where am I?" Morgin asked, found it difficult to speak since the left side of his mouth was swollen and tender. "What happened to me?"

The young woman shot out of her chair, knelt beside Morgin's bed, took one of his hands and kissed it tenderly. "Oh my lord!" she cried. "You were so close to death, and we were all frightened for you."

Morgin decided this was one of his dreams because she kept kissing his hand and calling him things like "Your Highness," and "my most gracious lord." But then his skin color was that of Morgin, not Morddon, and this didn't have the taste of a dream.

The young woman jumped to her feet. "Oh my goodness!" she cried, put her hands fearfully to her mouth. "The queen must be told, and her physicians." She spun about and shot out of the room in a flurry of petticoats.

"The queen?" Morgin thought. He didn't want to have anything to do with that crazy woman. He was too fond of staying alive, and he wasn't going to wait around passively for them to carry out her execution order.

He threw the covers back, noticed then that his ribs were wrapped in some sort of bandage, and he was badly bruised everywhere. He sat up, threw his legs off the bed, got to his feet, found that while just about everything hurt he could still get around. One ankle had been badly sprained and he limped a bit, though that too was bearable. But exhaustion pulled at him, and he struggled just to hold his head up straight.

Someone had dressed him in a long, linen bed gown so he searched for his clothes, ripped through several drawers before he found them in a large closet. He was pleased to find that his sword lay sheathed among them. He picked up his clothes and boots and sword, carried them across to the bed, dumped them there in a pile, sorted through them and found his breeches. All of his clothing had been badly torn, as if he'd been in a nasty brawl.

"Well now," a voice said from behind him.

He dropped his breeches, ripped his sword from its sheath and spun about. An old man stood just within the entrance to the room and Morgin put the tip of his sword at the fellow's throat.

The old man frowned. "Now, now, young man. Be careful—"

"Shut up," Morgin said. Keeping his sword at the old fellow's throat he limped around him and kicked the door shut.

The old man wore long, elegant, expensive robes, and stood with an air of authority about him, masked a bit by the scent of fear. Morgin used the point of his sword to nudge the old fellow toward the chair the young woman had been sitting in, then he pricked the old man in the chest and forced him to sit down with a certain loss of dignity.

The old man said, "You're making a mistake."

"Shut up, I said," Morgin said. "My mistake was getting anywhere near that queen of yours."

The old man shrugged unhappily. "We're all sorry about that."

"Keep your voice down. In fact, don't say anything." Morgin pressed the tip of his sword beneath the old man's chin. "I'm getting the netherhell out of here. But first I've got to find my friends, and you're going to help me." Morgin longed for his shadow-magic, then he could dump the old man and find them himself. He turned back to the bed, and keeping one eye on the old man he put the unsheathed sword down next to his clothes and reached for his breeches again.

This time a woman's voice interrupted him. "It's good to see you up and looking so well, Morgin."

He dropped the breeches and again grabbed his sword, spun about, thought at first the young woman had returned. But this woman was older, though still young and quite beautiful, and she wore a gown of a different color, and spoke in a different voice, more self-assured, more mature, and somehow familiar. And then slowly, as he looked at her, his eyes penetrated the courtly manners, and the gown, and the hair elegantly prepared, and the delicate touches of makeup applied here and there.

"Cort?" Morgin asked. "Is that you?"

The Balenda threw her head back and laughed heartily. "Morgin, you should see the look on your face."

The old man rose slowly from his chair, regained his dignity and bowed with a flourish to Cort. "Lady Cortien. It appears you've rescued me from being abducted by this young ruffian, then forced to help him find you and the rest of his companions so you might all escape our hospitality."

Cort laughed again. "The day I need to be rescued by you, Sacress, is the day all thieves become honest men."

Morgin lowered his sword, sat down on the edge of the enormous bed and shook his head. "You two know each other?"

"It appears," Sacress said, "that the young man remembers nothing of his ordeal."

Morgin looked at the old man. "Who are you?"

"I'm Sacress, the queen's physician."

Cort crossed the room carefully, taking a wide berth around the naked blade in Morgin's hand. She picked his sheath off the bed, held it out to him. "Put that away. You won't need it here."

Morgin took the sheath, slid the sword into it. Both Cort and Sacress relaxed visibly, and the old man crossed the room to stand over Morgin. He began probing at

Morgin's ribs. "You appear to be doing quite nicely, though for a time you gave us quite a fright. How are the ribs? Tell me if this hurts."

It felt as if someone poked Morgin's with a dagger. "Owe!" Morgin cried. "You're damn right it hurts."

The old man nodded. "Still got some healing to do, but you're doing better than expected. Now back into bed with you." The old man and Cort forced him back into the sheets.

The door opened again and France stepped into the room. "Morgin, me boy. Just passed a young lady in the hall said you was up. Yer lookin' fit."

A small crowd gathered in the hall behind France and for a moment it appeared they would all enter the room. Cort intervened, stepped in the way and spoke to a large man dressed in the livery of the palace guard. "You may tell everyone His Highness has regained consciousness, and that he is doing well. But for the moment he needs his rest. So, with the exception of the queen herself, Sacress and his assistants, and of course His Highness's traveling companions, let no one pass. And send someone down to the kitchens for food. His Highness needs sustenance."

"Yes, Your Ladyship," the guard said in a deep voice. He closed the door.

Morgin demanded, "Will someone tell me what in netherhell is going on here?"

France grinned. "Yer a hero, lad."

While Sacress probed at every joint and muscle in Morgin's body, Cort asked, "What do you remember?"

Morgin closed his eyes, recalled an image of the hatred in Aiergain's eyes. "Only that just when I thought I had her under control, she went berserk."

Cort nodded. "Yes. She did. Don't blame her; she wasn't exactly sane at the time."

France said, "She bounced you around perty bad. Picked you up without touchin' you and slammed you against the ceiling and every wall in the room. No one could help you, not even Cort and Tulellcoe when they arrived. She bounced you around for about two days, then she dropped you to the floor like you was an old rag, and it all ended. After that she rested comfortably, though she kept murmuring something about rats and the god-queen Erithnae. She slept for more than a day and a night, and when she awoke she was her old self again, though you were in pretty bad shape."

Morgin shrugged, touched his ribs. "I'm sore, but I don't feel that bad."

"Physically," Sacress said, "the worst damage is three broken ribs and a badly sprained ankle. What almost killed you was the injury to your soul."

Morgin heard bells tolling throughout the city, hundreds of bells. "What's that?"

Cort slapped Morgin on the back. "Well now, four days ago when Aiergain first regained consciousness they rang all of the bells in the city to celebrate, and since then the whole city has been worried about you, the man who saved the life of their beloved queen. The bells are ringing again to let everyone know you too are well."

France grinned evilly, leaned close to Morgin's ear. "You know, lad, all the young ladies have been anxious to meet you, and I think you'll be findin' 'em real receptive, if yer so inclined. Do yer old friend France a favor, will ya? If you find you got more than you need, throw a couple me way, eh?"

There was a knock at the door. Cort opened it and admitted a large, round woman, apparently the palace's chief cook. She had several servants in tow, each carrying a large platter of food; among them they'd managed to bring enough to feed a platoon of soldiers. Morgin was not terribly hungry, though it had apparently been days since he'd eaten. He ate what he could, and with his stomach full his eyelids grew heavy. When he tried to get them to take the food away Cort and Sacress insisted he eat more. He put down a few bites, was starting to doze off before he finished that. Sacress chased everyone out of the room, and Morgin was asleep before they were gone.

17

Of Magic Learned

MORGIN AWOKE TO someone shaking him violently. "Wake up, Your Highness."

A lone candle lit the room, casting a flickering army of shadows on the wall. Morgin could just make out two guards standing near the door, while someone stood over him shaking him. "Wake up."

Morgin recognized the voice of the young guard captain. "I'm awake, Pandorin. Stop shaking me."

"The queen needs you. Desperately!"

Morgin sat up and ran his hands through his hair, then rubbed his eyes. "Why does she need me in the middle of the night?"

"She's ill again."

Morgin shivered. He did not want to face the insanity of Aiergain's magic again, but he doubted Pandorin and the two burly guards would let him ignore her plight. He crawled out of bed. "Get my clothes."

They argued briefly about the need for haste, but Morgin refused to go wandering about the palace in a bed gown. Pandorin and his guards helped him crawl into his torn and battered clothing. "All right. Lead the way."

Pandorin led, but his guards followed close behind Morgin. Still well before dawn, the palace halls were dark. There were people moving hurriedly everywhere, and after several turns they approached an open doorway from which a shaft of light splashed out into the hall. Within Morgin found a large, well lit sitting room that was a hive of activity and excited voices. Sacress leaned over a man lying still and prone on the floor; the physician shook his head sadly. Tulellcoe sat on the floor against one wall; blood running out his nose and dripping off his chin. Cort and Val knelt beside him, trying to stem the flow of blood. They all looked up at Morgin as he entered the room, and those of Aud looked at him expectantly, as if he would fix everything now. "What happened?" he asked.

Tulellcoe groaned, shook his head to clear it, spattered Cort and Val with blood. "Ahhh! She had a nightmare, so I came to help her. I've been trying to help her since I arrived. I don't understand. I just don't understand."

"Of course you don't," Morgin said flatly. "You were born with magic, and as you grew up every facet of your life was steeped in magic. You've been trained since the cradle to use magic, and you make assumptions about it that I've never been able to understand. You can't know what it's like to suddenly have it thrust upon you."

Morgin looked at Pandorin. "Where is she?"

With a nod Pandorin indicated another door that led from the sitting room. "That's her bedchamber."

Morgin nodded, crossed the room and put his hand on the latch, but he hesitated for an instant and turned to Pandorin. "Post a guard outside this door, and keep everyone—I mean everyone—out of this room until I, or the queen, come out. I don't care what you hear from within."

Pandorin nodded.

Morgin opened the door slowly, pushed it inward but didn't follow, and except for the shaft of light spilling past him the bedchamber was dark. He took one step forward, then another, and another. When he was past the open door a hand touched it and closed it softly behind him, and the room went completely black. Aiergain spoke softly into the darkness, "I'm told you relish shadows, ShadowLord." There was a hint of hysteria in her voice.

Morgin closed his eyes, tried to pretend the darkness in the room was a shadow, hoped he needed magic only to make shadows and not to see through them. It didn't work, but he still felt comfortable in the dark, in shadow. "I like shadow," he said.

"I'm also told you can see through shadows."

"I could once, but my magic is gone now and like everyone else I'm blind in the dark."

"I'd give you my magic if I could." Her hysteria bubbled to the surface. "I'd give anything to be rid of this."

"I once felt the same," Morgin said. "Like you I was born without magic, and like you it came to me unbidden, and like you I found it a burden. But my wish came true, and my magic is gone now, and I feel like a man who's had his eyes gouged out, and his ear drums punctured, and his tongue cut from his throat. I feel empty."

She answered him with a long silence, then finally asked, "Would you like a light?"

"Yes. May I call for one?"

"No," she snapped. "Make it yourself. I don't want them in here."

"I don't have a flint and striker with me," Morgin said, thinking desperately. He had to get her out of the dark, so she could face herself. "Do you have a candle?"

"There's one on the table by the bed." Her hysteria was now a palpable thing. "But don't let anyone in here."

"I won't," Morgin said. He felt his way to the bed, then to the table near it. He found no candle, but intuition told him to check the floor. He dropped slowly to his hands and knees and found it after only a short search. It had been knocked there during all the excitement.

"Please come here," he said. "I need your help."

He heard the rustling of her bed gown as she felt her way across the room, then blindly her hand gripped his arm. She gasped and jumped back, and he did the same. There was a moment of silence, and then she started laughing softly. "I do believe you're as frightened of me as I am of you." She hesitated, and he heard fear in her voice. "Will you help me? Please. Help me like you did before."

Morgin nodded, a useless gesture in the dark. "All right. But I can't help you unless you do what I say."

"I will. I promise I will."

Morgin thought carefully about a time when he'd gone through a crisis much like this. He'd been a lot younger then, but what AnnaRail had done with him would still be appropriate for this young queen. "Sit down on the floor," he said, improvising and modifying AnnaRail's approach to fit the situation. "Sit with your back to the bed and cross your legs."

He heard her moving to do so and he sat on the floor facing her. "Now, I'm going to teach you a spell of confidence. It will help with what will follow. But first you must clear your mind of all turmoil. Think of yourself sitting in a cart bouncing down a road full of ruts and potholes. You're being jostled from side to side; you're uncomfortable and tense. But then you reach a stretch of road that's less bumpy, and while the jostling is still there it's bearable. It's now no more than a light rocking from side to side. In fact you're almost comfortable, like a babe rocking in her cradle. The tension seems to leave you, and like the smoke emanating from a peasant's hut it drifts away slowly on the wind."

Morgin sat in silence for a moment, rocking side to side; he heard her doing likewise. "Now the road levels off, and is straight and plain and simple, as smooth as glass. There's no more rocking or swaying or jostling, and you could almost fall asleep."

Morgin concentrated, trying to remember the spell of confidence. "Now think of yourself looking up that road. It's so straight it seems to end in a sharp point on the horizon. Focus on that point; concentrate on it and repeat after me."

He brought forth the first word of the spell of confidence and he spoke it, and it meant nothing to him, but she repeated it, and as he spoke each succeeding word she repeated that too, and when the spell was complete he heard her breathe a sigh of relief. It had worked. He needed such a spell for himself, but of course he no longer had the power to create it.

"Now let's have a little fun," he said softly. He held the candle out between them. "I'm holding the candle in front of you. Reach out and touch it."

She reached out and her hand touched his elbow first. This time she did not flinch away from him. Her hand hesitated for a moment as if she were curious, then it slid down his arm toward the candle, but when it reached his hand it lingered again for a moment of curiosity before sliding to the candle. "You have a nice hand," she said.

He ignored her. "Touch the wick on the candle. Form a picture of it in your mind and then let go of it. But keep that picture in your mind and think constantly of the location of that particular wick. And please don't think of me, because I really wouldn't like it if you lit me on fire."

"Me?"

"Yes you. You're going to do a fire spell."

Again Morgin reached into his memory for the spell, and he spoke the words, and they meant nothing to him, and she repeated them, and the spell worked. A faint glow formed on the tip of the candle's wick and it grew until it became a flame. Aiergain let out a soft, little chirp of delight. "Did I do that?"

"Yes you did," Morgin said as he tipped the candle to one side, dripped some wax on the floor and stuck the candle there.

She said, "The maid is not going to like that."

"I'll worry about the maid later."

He had her repeat the spell of confidence on her own, helping her only when she faltered. They then tried several other minor spells, simple things for everyday living: a spell to heal a small cut, a spell to mend a broken rope—in their case they used a short piece of twine. Among them he slipped in the spell to banish fear, and several times he returned to the spell of confidence until satisfied she could repeat it on her own without any help from him. At one point the candle had burned so low they needed another. She let him go to the door, open it a crack, and have a guard give him several more.

Much later, when she'd gained considerable confidence, not the kind brought forth by spells but natural confidence, he let her try something more difficult: a wind spell. He got her to approach it as an adventure, a challenge, and he didn't let her know elementals could be extremely dangerous. The spell got away from her a bit, literally trashed her bedchamber before she got it back under control. But then she hugged him excitedly and let out a healthy laugh.

Shortly before dawn all of the energy she was using finally caught up with her, and slowly she drifted off into sleep sitting on the floor leaning in the corner made by the edge of the bed and the wall. Morgin moved over to sit beside her, decided not to leave the room in case she awoke and needed him. He fell asleep there, with his head leaning against the bedpost.

••••

Morgin awoke close to midday, alone in Aiergain's bedchamber. He climbed to his feet, staggered groggily to the door and opened it, and was mobbed by a crowd of retainers and servants and courtiers all of whom had been waiting for him. Several tried to kiss his hand and they all called him, "Your Highness." Looking at these elegantly dressed people he grew conscious of the tattered nature of his clothing. Then Aiergain entered the room and the pandemonium ended. France, Tulellcoe, Cort and Val accompanied her.

Morgin looked at Aiergain closely. The madness was gone from her eyes, the lines of strain gone from her face, and now she was very much a queen, a young and beautiful queen.

Pandorin had followed her into the room. He dropped to one knee in front of Morgin, took one of Morgin's hands and kissed it. "We can never repay you the debt we owe you, Your Highness."

Morgin was embarrassed, and he was tired of people kissing his hand. "What is this *Your Highness* stuff?"

"By my decree," Aiergain said, "You are a prince of this city, and you will be treated as such by all her subjects."

A somewhat older man—Morgin guessed by his dress and manner he was one of the lords of the city—dropped to one knee beside Pandorin. "For the man who saved Her Majesty's life no such decree is required," he said as he tried to kiss Morgin's hand. "Is there anything you lack; anything you want? Name it, and we will grant it."

Morgin thought carefully, and in the silence that followed his stomach growled loud enough for everyone to hear. They all laughed openly and France said, "Now that's a request well spoken."

Morgin frowned. "There are a few things I would like."

Aiergain looked at him expectantly. "Name them."

"Well," Morgin said uncomfortably. "I mean no disrespect, but I'd be a lot happier if everyone just called me Morgin, not 'Your Highness.' And maybe I don't need to have my hand kissed anymore."

Aiergain looked at Cort. "You warned me he would be uncomfortable with titles and attention." She turned back to Morgin. "Very well. Anyone whom you wish may call you by your name without incurring my wrath. But you must understand my people will show you what's in their hearts, and if they are a bit joyous and freely giving of their gratitude, then so be it. I will not command them to withhold their joy."

Morgin was given a manservant named Terrikle. Morgin had never had a manservant before and didn't know what to do with him. Terrikle was much older than Morgin, and very stiff and formal, much like Avis during the most formal of situations. But unlike Avis, Terrikle never dropped the formalities when they were alone.

Terrikle quizzed Morgin carefully on his preferences, learned Morgin did not like clothing that set him apart. Then the manservant called in the palace tailor to see that Morgin was properly attired. Terrikle dealt with the tailor himself, refused to let Morgin even speak to the man, and the conversation between the three of them was an odd one. The tailor might ask Terrikle, "Would His Highness like the cuffs long or short?"

Morgin didn't know what he wanted, so he looked at Terrikle and shrugged helplessly. Terrikle nodded and answered, "His Highness would like the sleeves fashionably sized, though be certain to keep the effect sedate and understated." After the measurements were complete Terrikle picked out several bolts of cloth, conferred at some length with the tailor while Morgin waited restlessly for them to finish. Terrikle's final instructions to the tailor were, "His Highness will be waiting for you. Please have an afternoon suit ready within the hour. And we'll expect the rest by dinner."

After the tailor departed, Morgin asked, "Weren't you a bit hard on him?"

Terrikle looked offended, and his demeanor broke for an instant. "You saved our queen," he said. "Any man in the kingdom would have died for her, but we were helpless until you came. If that tailor cannot have you properly clothed within the hour, then his business will be ruined. He came here knowing that. He also knows that if he succeeds, his business will thrive beyond his wildest dreams."

After the tailor left, servants brought in a feast. Of course France showed up with the food, and he and Morgin dined on pheasant and beer and bread and cheese and fruits. It appeared that Terrikle's new purpose in life was to provide whatever Morgin wanted as soon as possible.

After the meal the tailor returned with a fully completed suit of clothes. Morgin tried it on, and it needed a few minor adjustments. The tailor sat down right there and did them, and when he finished Terrikle asked, "Does that suit Your Highness?"

Morgin looked in a large mirror. The suit pleased him, not flashy or loud, but still expensive looking. "It's very nice," Morgin said, though he wasn't sure when he'd have the need to wear something so dressy. When Terrikle wasn't looking he turned to France and whispered conspiratorially, "Go out to a plain old shop and get me some plain ordinary clothes, will you?"

France winked and nodded. "Leave it to me, lad."

18

Of Gratitude Misplaced

MORGIN BOUNDED UP a long flight of stairs in the Palace of Lights. Caked with dust from the practice yard, his tunic soaked with sweat, carrying his sheathed sword in one hand, he took the steps three at a time and at the top turned right and got quickly lost.

During the last month he'd forced himself to exercise almost daily. France and Val usually joined him, and sometimes Cort, Tulellcoe and Pandorin. They always drew a crowd of onlookers; at first Morgin had assumed they were curious about the female twoname: a woman dressed in the breeches of a man, and swinging a sword like a man. An hour later she might show up in a gown, with the manners of a lady of the court. But even without Cort the crowd gathered to watch, and Morgin realized their curiosity was for the outlaw wizard, the ShadowLord fallen from grace, the man with no power of his own who was tutoring their beloved queen in the dark arts.

Morgin had to ask directions from a servant to find his way back to the wing where he'd been given an entire suite of rooms high up in the palace. Terrikle was waiting for him with a disapproving look on his face. "I know I'm late," Morgin said. "But I accidentally knocked poor Pandorin unconscious, and then I lost my way in this palace."

"I know, Your Highness. But you have plenty of time before your meeting with Her Majesty."

Morgin shook his head sadly. Terrikle's job was Morgin, and he took that job so seriously he often seemed to know what Morgin was thinking before Morgin thought it. "Shall I draw your bath?"

Morgin nodded. "Sure."

Terrikle bowed and left.

A private bath all his own! At Elhiyne only Olivia, AnnaRail, Marjinell and selected guests had their own private baths. And he had a sitting room with a balcony. He liked the view of the ocean from there.

He pulled off his tunic, stepped out onto the balcony. From high in the palace he looked out at the ocean that rested so serenely on the horizon. He tossed his tunic over his shoulder, stood there in the warm sun, and leaned against the iron rail, taking in the sight of that vast body of water.

Between him and the water lay the western half of the city of Aud, and from his vantage Morgin noted that the palace was not a castle. It had no battlements, no parapets or murder holes, nor had it been constructed with any eye to defense. It was an incredible mixture of turrets and balconies and high walkways lined with balustrades. The palace itself was constructed at the top of a gentle slope, with the city beneath it slanting down toward the ocean, though the city had been terraced into hundreds of randomly spaced districts that formed a giant staircase down to the docks. There were several large, busy avenues, but Morgin was intrigued most by the little staircase alleys that connected the various levels of Aud, each with its own environment of businesses and shops and inns.

At the bottom of the city, wedged tightly between the city and the ocean, the docks were the busiest district in Aud. The masts of dozens of ships pointed to the sky, though the docks and warehouses obscured Morgin's view of the ships. Out beyond the docks ships at anchor bobbed in the sheltered bay formed by a large spit of land that extended out into the ocean. Perhaps they were waiting for a berth, or their crews had unloaded their cargo and were enjoying themselves for a few days while their captains negotiated for outgoing tonnage.

Morgin thought it might be fun to explore the docks, and some of the inns and taverns down there. But he'd have to be discreet, for he was quite a celebrity now and could no longer escape the public eye. He'd spent the last month tutoring Aiergain in the ways of magic, and she was becoming quite proficient, though most importantly she was gaining control and learning confidence.

He'd already toured most of the city, though always in an entourage, and often accompanied by Aiergain herself and a large crowd of onlookers. He liked her company, but that wasn't really his style; there was so much more to see when one was free of all the attention. He decided to visit the haunts in and around the docks in less formal company, thinking he'd have to choose his companions well: France and Val, and maybe Pandorin. The young guard captain had proven to be a sympathetic ally, once Morgin had broken him of the need to kiss his hand. And in the right company Pandorin no longer called him "Your Highness."

Terrikle interrupted his thoughts. "Lord Tulellcoe and Lady Cortien wish to see you."

"Sure," Morgin threw over his shoulder. "Send them in."

A few moments later Cort stepped out onto the balcony beside him, leaned against the rail and followed his gaze out over the ocean. "It's beautiful, isn't it?"

"Yes. You mean the ocean, don't you?"

"That, and the city, and the way the two fit so nicely together, almost as if such a sprawl were natural."

Morgin stepped back from the rail, looked carefully at the twoname. She was wearing her lady-of-the-court persona.

"We missed you at practice today," he said. "Whenever I get a little overconfident, it helps to be bested by a woman with a sword."

Cort threw her head back and laughed. "But I've never had to fight your shadows."

Tulellcoe joined them on the balcony, asked bluntly, "How is your tutelage of Her Majesty progressing?"

He and Morgin had argued repeatedly about this. Tulellcoe was concerned Morgin might teach the young queen improperly. Morgin looked at his uncle, tried to see if there was some extra meaning hidden within his eyes, saw only distrust. "She's a very apt pupil, and she's old enough to have good concentration; she's older than I. I just wish I was a better instructor. Can't one of you help her?"

Both Cort and Tulellcoe shook their heads. Cort said, "She won't let anyone but you speak to her of magic."

Tulellcoe rubbed the side of his face as if remembering the night he'd tried to help Aiergain. To have struck Tulellcoe down that way meant she was very powerful. "She's becoming attached to you," Tulellcoe said. "Too much so."

Morgin nodded unhappily. "I know."

Tulellcoe demanded, "Then why weren't you more careful?"

Morgin frowned, felt the same kind of anger rising within him that came when he faced Olivia. "Be more careful? What in netherhell was I supposed to do, let her execute us? Or maybe I should have let you try again. How many bloody noses could you take before you lost your temper, and got one of us killed?"

Tulellcoe looked much like Olivia. "Don't talk to me that way, b—"

He'd almost said it. He'd almost said "boy." And if he had Morgin would have had to decide if he was willing to carry out his earlier threat and try to kill him. Morgin said, "I left my grandmother behind me at Elhiyne, so don't try to take her place."

Cort intervened. "Now stop this—both of you."

Morgin brushed past Tulellcoe, walked back into the sitting room. Terrikle was waiting for him. "Your bath is ready, Your Highness."

"Good," Morgin said. "See my uncle and the Balenda out."

"Yes, Your Highness."

The hot bath relaxed Morgin somewhat, and by the time he was dry he regretted having been so harsh with Tulellcoe. Terrikle had laid out riding clothes for him. "What's this?" he asked.

"While you were bathing Her Majesty sent word she is canceling her daily lesson, and would instead like you to take her riding."

••••

As the royal barge touched the dock, the deck on which Morgin stood lurched slightly. Aiergain looked out over the water, while at the other end of the barge Pandorin and several soldiers waited as the gang plank was lowered to the river dock, then he and his men led the horses down and waited there for Morgin and their queen. The horses' hooves knocked loudly on the heavy wooden planks of the dock as Morgin extended his arm. Aiergain took it gaily, and he escorted her down the gang plank.

The city of Aud controlled the entire Bohl delta, but not until now did Morgin appreciate what that meant. Aud had little land beyond the city itself, but where the Bohl met the sea the river divided and split again and again, forming a system of islands nestled amidst the lazily flowing tributaries of the great river. Many were tiny, but some, like this one, were leagues across and one could ride for quite a distance without reaching the other side.

"This island is called Dass," Aiergain told Morgin as she swept a hand from horizon to horizon. "It is one of the three largest islands in the delta, the three sisters we call them: Dass, Dess, and Diss." She looked at Morgin and winked. "It is said the three sisters are identical triplets, and if you can speak their names quickly, again and again, and not make a mistake, then they will come to you in your dreams. They are reputed to be quite beautiful."

Morgin shook his head. "My dreams are complicated enough, Your Majesty."

"I know," Aiergain said sympathetically. "Cort told me your dreams haunt you, though she doesn't know what they're about." She looked down at the sword strapped to his side. "Is that the talisman I've heard of?"

She was in an inquisitive mood, and he wasn't sure how far she might press him. "Yes," he said flatly.

"Aren't you afraid of it?"

"Yes." He didn't add anything to that simple answer and the silence became thick for a moment.

"Come," she said. "It's a beautiful day. Let's put the wind in our faces, and we'll put magic and talismans and dreams behind us."

They rode down the island toward the sea. The sun shone down from a clear blue sky. They had dressed warmly because the sea air had a cool bite to it. Pandorin and his men remained at a polite distance, though one of his men was always within sight of their queen. Aiergain stopped frequently and showed Morgin little coves and inlets she had explored on previous rides. In one cove that was deep and enclosed by steep rock walls she dismounted, stood on the beach and looked out over the water. Morgin dismounted and stood beside her. "I love these islands," she said. "You know when the tide is high these waters are salty. And then when it's low they're fresh again. But the changing tides can make the currents of the river quite treacherous, and that's what forms these little coves all up and down these islands."

She turned about and faced inland, facing Morgin. She scanned the cliffs above them, as if looking to see if Pandorin or any of his men were in sight, and for a moment Morgin thought she might try to kiss him. He turned away from her, tried to do it casually, didn't want to appear to be avoiding her. "What is it you see?" he asked, looking up the cliffs.

There was a moment of silence. "Oh nothing," she said. "Nothing."

Farther down the coast they stopped in a little fishing village. At the sight of Aiergain everyone dropped what they were doing, formed a tight crowd about her, and she forgot Morgin. Pandorin and his men caught up with them but seemed unconcerned, so Morgin joined the soldiers to water the horses. "She always picks a different island to ride on," Pandorin said as he and Morgin watched her from a distance walking among the people of the village. "I would venture to guess in the course of a year she manages to visit every village on every island in the delta. She takes her duties very seriously, our queen."

Clearly, more than just a duty for Aiergain, she enjoyed the ride, and she enjoyed her people.

They rode farther down the coast, eventually reached the tip of the island and started back up the other side. They picnicked on a high bluff overlooking the ocean, stopped in more villages and explored more coves, though Morgin was careful to avoid dismounting and standing close to her if they were out of sight of Pandorin and his men. As dusk approached they turned inland, and Morgin learned that carefully tended fields covered the center of the island almost completely. They reached the barge just as the sun touched the horizon and the air was beginning to chill.

For the return crossing Aiergain stood at the rail at the bow of the barge, and since the air was calm, the weather good, and the river currents steady and even, the barge captain didn't object too strongly. He gave them both heavy furs, and steaming mugs of heated, spiced wine, and Aiergain took Morgin's arm and nestled close to him for warmth. "This has been the most wonderful day of my life," she whispered softly as the barge lurched out into the river current. "The most wonderful."

Pandorin and his men had gathered around a stove near the back of the barge, warming their hands and talking softly. The night descended rapidly, though the surface of the river was alive with the running lights of other craft. Aiergain nestled closer to him, pressed her cheek against his. The scent of her perfume drifted about him, and the hot, spiced wine was a warm glow in his stomach. It would have been a perfect night, if only Rhianne were there, if only she nestled against him. It would have been wonderful.

Aiergain's lips touched his cheek softly, but he leaned carefully away from her. "Why are you avoiding me?" she whispered. "You know I love you."

"No you don't," he said. "You've just come through a terrifying time in your life, and I helped you through it, and now you feel indebted to me. You're just confusing gratitude with love."

"Perhaps," she said. "But right now it feels like love, and you're avoiding me. Why are you avoiding me?"

He tried to think of a way of saying it without hurting her. "I could fall in love with you, but I already have a wife, and I love her very much."

Aiergain said nothing in reply but stood there letting a long silence draw out between them, and now the night seemed cold and biting. Then she slid her hand out of the crook of his arm and stepped softly away from him. And saying nothing she left him alone at the bow of the barge.

19

A Kiss in a Dream

THE BARMAID SLAMMED the mugs down on the table, splashing ale across a litter of cards and coins. "Arrr," France bellowed merrily, his eyes settling on the maid's jiggling breasts. "You've ruined our game. You must be punished." He reached out and threw an arm around her waist, pulled her into his lap. "Fer yer crimes yer sentenced to a kiss."

"Oh my lord," she squealed. "Have mercy." Then she kissed him, and she did so with less resistance and more ardor than he had anticipated. Sitting next to Morgin, Val merely laughed. A group of sailors at the next table began timing the length of the kiss by slapping their fists on the table top in unison.

The maid ended the kiss, whispered something in France's ear and his eyes lit up with delight. Val handed her several coins, and she walked away with France's eyes locked on the sway of her hips.

Morgin's head swam with the effects of the ale; he was close to his limit and he knew he'd better slow down.

He'd done a little conspiring to get away from the palace like this: dressed in simple clothes, without a retinue, and with no horns blaring to announce his coming. Terrikle had actually caught him out, discovered him only moments before he was about to sneak out dressed in what the servant considered rags. And of course Terrikle had been livid with the impropriety of the situation. Morgin had tried to explain, but Terrikle had only shook his head sadly and turned to leave, though half way through the door he'd paused, looked back at Morgin and grinned. "If you're questioned later please remember I didn't see you." Then he winked, closed the door and was gone.

A fight started in a far corner of the tavern, though it seemed to be just an overly rough form of play. France leaned across the table and spoke. "When you come into one of these dockside places, you gotta sense the mood of the place. Most times, like tonight, it's a little rough but friendly. No one will get killed, just a few bruises. But when you first walk in, if the mood's bad, don't stay. Just get out."

Morgin slid his chair back, stood up. "I need to make room for more ale. Where's the privy."

France grinned. "Ain't no privy here, lad. There's a door near the back. Just step out into the alley."

Morgin worked his way slowly toward the back of the crowded tavern. He was a little unsteady on his feet, and he had no desire to bump into some large sailor and get into a friendly brawl. There were three doors at the back of the tavern and at first he wasn't sure which to choose, not wanting to intrude into some private office, or perhaps the bedroom where the barmaid conducted most of her business. But then one of the doors swung open and two men stepped through it, one still lacing his breeches.

An ungodly stench assaulted Morgin's nose as he stepped into the alley. The faint glow of a quarter moon gave enough light to avoid stumbling into the next man, or stepping into the gutter full of urine. At the moment three sailors were making use of its facilities, standing shoulder to shoulder facing an alley wall. They talked of wenches and whores, trying to decide the best place to spend their money.

Morgin took a place beside them, unlaced his breeches and relieved himself. While he was at it two more men stepped out into the alley, took their places in line against the alley wall between Morgin and the door to the tavern. But something about the newcomers struck Morgin as familiar: both were dressed in hooded cloaks with the hoods up over their heads, their faces hidden. He thought he might have noticed them earlier in the tavern, drinking mugs of ale but not really joining into the spirit of the place. His mind was a little cloudy with drink, but he remembered seeing three or four similar figures in another tavern they'd stopped in previously.

The three sailors finished, stepped away from the wall tying up their breeches and returned to the tavern. As they stepped through the door a very drunken sailor stepped out, staggered against the opposite wall of the alley, nearly fell into the gutter full of urine, barely managed to keep out of it.

Morgin finished, stepped away from the wall and started lacing up his breeches.

The drunken sailor staggered against one of the two hooded figures who were between Morgin and the door. "Arrr!" he said as he breathed heavily into the man's face. "Tish a fair night," he slurred.

The hooded figure elbowed him away harshly. Again he almost fell into the gutter, and again he miraculously managed to stay on his feet, though they wobbled unsteadily beneath him. He turned and leaned heavily against the wall with one arm, fumbled at his breeches with his free hand, though it didn't look as if he'd be successful at handling the laces there.

Morgin finished lacing up his own breeches, started walking up the alley toward the two hooded figures and the door to the tavern. The two men finished at that same moment. They peeled away from the wall and blocked the narrow alley, but oddly they spent no time tying up their breeches. Morgin hesitated, but the figures parted to let him pass, one against each wall of the alley, and one of them spoke in a deep voice. "After you," he said politely, indicating with his hand Morgin should pass between them.

Morgin stopped, and with the instincts of a wanted man checked his distance to be certain he was beyond a quick thrust of a sword, felt the comforting weight of his own sword resting against his hip. "No," he said politely. "After you."

They stood that way for a moment, the two hooded figures waiting for Morgin to move, and Morgin waiting for them. Then one of the figures shifted position slightly and his cloak parted for an instant, and by the faint light of the moon Morgin caught a glimpse of a long sliver of steel hidden beneath his cloak.

France had told him again and again, "The best defense you'll ever have, lad, is yer feet. You'll live a lot longer if you just turn tail and run when you can."

Morgin faced the two figures squarely, drew his sword as if he was going to stand and fight. The two men reached for their swords, and while they were doing so Morgin spun and took to his heels. His fake had gained him an instant of surprise and a little distance, but he heard the two men behind him quickly take up the chase.

The alley wasn't long, and sprinting like a madman Morgin shot down its length. The street beyond was better lit, and the end of the alley appeared as a square frame of light in the near distance. But as he approached it three more cloaked men stepped from the street to block his way, all holding swords.

Morgin dug in his heels and came to a grinding stop, looked back over his shoulder at the two men bearing down on him. A door opened in the alley wall beside him and a sailor stepped out fumbling at the laces of his breeches. Evidently several establishments used the alley for the same purpose.

Morgin elbowed the sailor aside, shot through the door into the building, slammed the door behind him just as he heard his pursuers crash into it. There was no latch so he turned and ran down a short hall into a large room full of whores and sailors in various stages of undress. Seeing Morgin shoot into the room carrying a naked sword, one of the women screamed. A large, heavy-set bouncer appeared from behind a curtain and swung a club at Morgin's head. Morgin ducked beneath the blow and back stepped up a flight of stairs.

One of the hooded men stepped out of the hall on the bouncer's right. The bouncer turned away from Morgin and swung in a single motion, caught the man squarely in the side of the head. As he slumped to the floor one of his companions cut past him with his sword at the bouncer. Now all the whores started screaming, and the sailors with them began pulling at their breeches and searching for their swords.

The hooded man faced the bouncer squarely, unaware Morgin hid in the shadows a few steps above and behind him. Morgin kicked out, buried his heel in the man's ribs, knocking him to the floor with his companion. As he tried to get up the bouncer finished him with his club, then turned and faced Morgin angrily.

"I've no quarrel with you," Morgin said. "I'm just trying to escape these cutthroats."

"Then get out," the bouncer said, and hooked a thumb toward the front door.

"Right," Morgin said. He vaulted down the stairs, past the whores and their clients, into an entrance way at the front door, and there he met three more cloaked men carrying unsheathed blades.

He swung out, met one of their swords with a crash, parried a stroke, ducked beneath another, back stepped back into the room full of whores. From the other end of the room he heard the clang of two blades meeting, caught a glimpse of the bouncer slumping to the floor clutching his side, two more cloaked figures swinging their swords at a sailor who desperately tried to fend them off. For some reason the sailor seemed familiar.

Badly outnumbered, Morgin and the sailor had the same thought and backed toward each other, swinging wildly at their opponents. "Keep yer back to me, man," the sailor called as he cut out at one of the hooded figures. Why he had chosen to take Morgin's side, Morgin could not guess.

Morgin's hands tingled with heat and power, and his ears caught the hint of a familiar, evil sound: a deep, resonant hum building toward a berserk eruption of power. His sword was coming alive in his hands, and if it came fully to power it would slaughter everyone in the room and many beyond.

It sliced out, cut one of the cloaked figures down, met another's sword with such force it knocked him several steps back creating an opening. Both Morgin and the sailor shot through it, out of the room, through the front entrance and out into the street. Their pursuers followed them, and they took up the fight there, though Morgin was more preoccupied now with controlling the talisman's thirst for blood.

The street suddenly filled with mounted riders, men wearing the livery of the queen's guard and swinging their swords with deadly accuracy. They surrounded Morgin and the sailor, cut them off protectively from their opponents. Pandorin appeared above them, spurred his horse into a charge at the sailor who'd helped Morgin, sliced down at the sailor as he charged past him. The sailor parried the blow, staggered back as Pandorin brought his horse about for another charge.

Morgin sheathed his sword, quenching its power, and jumped to the sailor's side, waved his hands at Pandorin and shouted, "No! No! He was helping me."

Pandorin hesitated, nudged his horse toward the sailor warily, demanded angrily, "Why would a ruffian like this be helping you?"

"I don't know," Morgin shouted above the pandemonium in the street. "But he was."

At that moment the fighting and noise ended abruptly as the last of the cutthroats was either killed or taken into custody.

Pandorin pointed at the sailor with his sword. "Why would you choose to help His Highness. From the look of you, you'd be more likely to steal his purse."

The sailor looked about slowly at the queen's guardsmen surrounding him, then carefully sheathed his sword. He bowed politely at the young captain. "Well now I got me vices, but murder ain't one of 'em. And I didn't know he was a Highness."

Just then Morgin realized why the sailor seemed familiar. "You were the drunk in the alley. But you don't look drunk now. You were following me, weren't you?"

Pandorin spurred his horse closer to the sailor. "Why were you following His Highness?"

The sailor looked at Pandorin belligerently and turned to Morgin. "Them thieves tried to hire me to pick a fight with you. Me! Bakart, first mate of the *Far Wind*. I told 'em where they could put their blood money, and they roughed me up a bit, so I figured if I stayed close I might even the score some."

••••

Rhianne shot awake, for the sword had come to life somewhere, and she could feel Morgin struggling desperately to contain it. There was no time to place Wards so she'd have to take her chances. She closed her eyes, concentrated on her magic, brought it forth and muttered a quick spell of confidence.

She sensed the power of the sword as if it was there in the room with her, and she had the sensation her hands were locked about the hilt, fighting its constant struggle to be released; an odd sensation since they were strong male hands, callused and rough. She was standing in the middle of a street somewhere fighting for her life while waves of heat washed over her hands and arms and chest and face. And slowly, the power of the sword opened like the petals of a flower in sunlight, a vast chasm of hatred that threatened to consume her. She refused to be daunted by it, and she bent her will to stop it.

She had only the faintest glimpse of Morgin's power, but what opened before her was a chasm equally as vast and frightening. She felt sorry for poor Morgin that he had to bear such a burden. Then her own power opened, and it frightened her far more than the power of the sword, for she was not meant to control such forces.

The struggle ended abruptly; Morgin and the sword were gone, her own magic was gone, and she felt as if a great weight had been lifted from her shoulders.

Her nightgown and sheets were bathed in sweat, as if she'd been fighting a fever for hours. And she sensed the Wards, four of them: Sextus, Septimus, Octavus, and Nonus. She opened her eyes just as Nonus winked out of existence, and by the light of the three remaining Wards, she caught a glimpse of Olivia and AnnaRail standing on either side of her bed. The other Wards disappeared and the power in the room dissipated.

Rhianne sat up as Olivia spoke, "Child, you choose a strange hour and a strange place to practice the arts."

AnnaRail touched the old woman's arm, a respectful gesture, but still one few people would attempt. "Mother, I don't believe she did the choosing."

Olivia shook her head. "No. Nor do I."

The old woman stepped closer to Rhianne, reached out and took her chin in one hand. There was no light in the room, but Rhianne saw the old witch's face as if lit by a dozen lamps. The old woman's eyes bored into her soul, and Rhianne suspected that she had done the same to Morgin many a time. Then the old witch's face lit up with an unpleasant, avaricious smile. "This one has power," the old witch said happily. "More than we thought. Much more."

····

"The sailor's story checks out," Pandorin said. "He's the first mate on a fairly reputable ship, though I use the word reputable rather loosely."

"Then who were the cutthroats?" Morgin demanded. "And why were they after me?"

Pandorin sighed deeply, turned and looked out the window of Morgin's apartments at the city below. France got up unsteadily from the couch and poured another tankard of ale.

Val asked him, "Haven't you had enough?"

France said, "I should be with that wench, instead of back here in the palace."

Morgin ignored them, looked at Pandorin who was still looking out the window. "You haven't answered my question, Pandorin. Who were the cutthroats?"

Pandorin shrugged. "Bounty hunters."

France sat up straight, seemed far less drunk.

"Bounty hunters!" Morgin asked. "Looking for me?"

Pandorin nodded slowly, turned to face Morgin. "Yes. The Lesser Council has increased the price on your head to a thousand gold coins. And they'll pay the price only if you're dead."

"Whew!" France sucked air through his teeth. "Fer that kind of money even I might decide to cut yer throat, lad."

"Exactly," Pandorin said. "Every rogue and cutthroat and malcontent in the land has come to Aud. We've already stopped five assassination attempts. And three men who fit your description have been murdered in cases of mistaken identity."

"Well lad," France said. "Me thinks we've over stayed our welcome. Where do we go from here?"

Morgin shook his head. "I don't know. But wherever we go we'd better go there soon."

Val stood, stretched like a cat. "Yes. That's obvious. Let's sleep on it. I'm sure Captain Pandorin can keep you alive for one more night."

••••

Tulellcoe sat in the dark and fingered his dagger unhappily, contemplating the gloom in his soul. He told himself again and again he was a fool; twice a fool; thrice a fool. He'd sensed the evil in Morgin's talisman long before Csairne Glen, and yet he'd ignored it. If only he'd opened his eyes back then, listened to his soul and recognized the sword for the danger it would become. He might have been able to help the lad, but he'd failed to do so, and he could only blame himself for the consequences.

He knew what he had to do. He'd known all along, and the knowledge of his responsibility filled his heart with sorrow. He tried to deny it, hoped that if he only gave it time a better solution would come to hand. He'd been living under that idiotic pretense ever since they'd entered Aud. Morgin was helping Aiergain immeasurably, and surely that meant he had achieved some form of control.

"Bah!" Tulellcoe growled into the darkness. "I'm a damn fool."

Cort stirred, rolled over in bed, mumbled something about him returning to the sheets. Then her breathing returned to that slow, steady rhythm that signaled a deep and restful sleep.

Tulellcoe tried to look at her in the darkness, tried to see some hint of her face. She was such a strong woman during the day, and yet when asleep her mouth opened and her face took on the aspect of childish innocence. That was the part of her she hid from everyone, even him, but a part of her he cherished.

"Will you understand?" he asked her in a whisper. "Will you still love me when I have done what I must do? Or will you hate me? Will you think me a traitor, for certainly everyone else will?"

He stood, resolved to do what he must, and crossed the room to the door. He put his hand on the latch and hesitated. He didn't want to kill Morgin, but it must be done, and better he than some rat of a Tosk or Penda. He recalled the evil he'd sensed in the blade. It had come alive that night somewhere in Aud, even if only for an instant. He didn't know the circumstances but he had sensed it, sensed the depths of evil within it, the chasm of hatred that struggled to be released. Morgin had just barely been able to contain it, and he knew that when it did break free, the land would run red with blood.

Tulellcoe understood it was up to him to prevent that. At least he would make some effort to make Morgin's death an easy one. He dressed quickly, turned the latch on the door and stepped out into the hall.

••••

Morgin enjoyed this dream. He walked through a vibrant forest in a proper dream: a little indistinct around the edges, a bit surreal. And then he saw the one thing that could make it even better: Rhianne. She appeared without warning, smiled at him, opened her arms and held them out to him.

He stepped into them, kissed her long and sweet. "I'm sorry I misunderstood you," he said.

"That is the past and we can put it behind us now."

He leaned forward to kiss her again, but she leaned away from him and gently covered his lips with her hand. "No. There isn't time."

"But this is a dream," he pleaded. "We have all the time in the world."

She shook her head. "No. We don't. You're in danger."

"Not here," he said, looking about at the forest.

"Of course not here," she agreed. "Not in the Kingdom of Dreams. But it's not in your dreams that you're in danger. You must go back, now."

"No," he said angrily. "I don't want to." But even as he spoke his hands passed right through her, and she and the forest and everything about him dissipated slowly on a nether wind.

"You must go back," she called after him. "You must go back."

20

The Pipist

TULELLCOE PUT HIS hand on the latch on the door to Morgin's room. He was about to turn it when something tugged at his sleeve. He looked down, found a small child dressed in filthy, tattered rags. "No," the child hissed softly. "You are wrong. He must live."

••••

Morgin awoke with a start and sat up in bed. The lights of the city threw enough illumination through his open window to see tolerably well. No assassin stood over him or lurked in the shadows with the intention of slitting his throat. But he sensed something undefined and indistinct, though not yet of any danger to him.

Curious, he climbed out of bed, threw on a robe and crossed the room to the door. He put his hand on the latch, hesitated as he tried to sense what might await him beyond, but no image came to mind. He knew only that it awaited him there.

He turned the latch and slowly opened the door, saw a man standing there as if waiting for him, though the hallway was much darker than his room and he saw nothing of the man's face. The man looked down and to one side, and he whispered, "Rat?" more a question than a statement.

Recognizing Tulellcoe, Morgin breathed a sigh of relief.

"Uncle," Morgin asked groggily. "What brings you here this time of night?"

Tulellcoe shivered visibly, still looking at the floor beside him. He looked up into Morgin's face. "May I come in?" he asked.

"Certainly." Morgin stepped aside and admitted the older man to the room. As Tulellcoe stepped past him Morgin's eye caught the glint of some metallic object in his hand. But the room was too dark to see what the object might be.

Morgin lit a lamp, but after the room filled with light he noticed Tulellcoe's hands were empty. "What can I do for you, uncle? It is rather late."

Tulellcoe walked to the balcony doors, looked out at the city below, spoke with his back to Morgin. "Where will you go now?"

"How do you know I'm going to go anywhere?"

Tulellcoe shrugged. "You don't have much choice."

Morgin sat down on the edge of the bed and ran his hands through his hair. "Well I think I'm no longer welcome here."

Tulellcoe turned and looked at him for the first time, and Morgin was struck by the despair in his eyes. "What do you mean by that?"

Morgin told him about the day he and Aiergain had gone riding, and how he'd rejected her on their return. "I tried to be kind, but I'm afraid I still hurt her. Since then I haven't seen her, not even to tutor her in magic. Besides, I couldn't stay here even if I were still welcome, not with every cutthroat and assassin in the land coming into the city to slit my throat. I'm just a target, living publicly like this. I need to disappear, blend into the population again, into the countryside somewhere. I've been thinking I might take passage on a ship, travel north up the coast a ways, maybe spend some time in Drapolis."

Tulellcoe wasn't paying attention and was clearly preoccupied with something else. "What's on your mind, uncle? You have something to ask or say, so why don't you just spit it out?"

Tulellcoe considered Morgin for an instant, then blurted out, "The talisman. The sword. How did you acquire it?"

Morgin flinched, told a half truth. "I bought it in a weapons maker's shop in Anistigh. You know that."

"Yes I do. But I also know there has to be more to it than that."

Morgin hesitated, considered Tulellcoe carefully, wondered at his motives and desires. But he wanted to tell someone, for he'd never told anyone the truth of the matter. "It came to me in a dream."

Tulellcoe frowned. "You told me that once before. What do you mean?"

So Morgin told him the story. They all knew the story of how he'd snuck back into the castle after Valso and his Kulls had killed SarahGirl in the road, but now he told Tulellcoe of how he'd been struck on the head in the corridor, and dreamed he'd been shot through the heart with a crossbow bolt. He told him of the magic alcove, and how it had come to him so often as a child, and how it came to him then as he lay dying in a corridor in Elhiyne. He told of how he crawled into it to die, and dreamed of a giant burial chamber connected to the alcove, and of the skeleton king that had returned to life to heal his horrible wound, then, as an afterthought, had given Morgin the sword.

"The Alcove was real," Morgin added. "That's where I awoke. But the rest was all just a dream. The sword was the sword I bought in Anistigh. France says it's very old Benesh'ere steel."

Tulellcoe seemed entranced by the story. He asked, "You say the king took the sword from a dead warrior sprawled at the foot of his throne? But when the king returned to life, the warrior remained a skeleton while everything else seemed new. What else was different about this warrior?"

Morgin closed his eyes and tried to picture the scene again. "Well, the decayed rags he wore were common, not the kind of thing to find in the burial chamber of a king, or even on the back of a king's guard."

"And why do you say this warrior came to his death long after the king?"

Again Morgin tried to picture the scene. "Before the king came back to life, and after he returned to being a skeleton, when everything was old and decayed, there was a thick layer of dust on the floor, as if it had been settling there for millennia. The warrior had left a trail in the dust where he'd crawled before dying. But still that was just a dream."

Morgin continued his story, told Tulellcoe of his battle in the sanctum with the Kulls, of how the magic in the sanctum's walls had come to him, and of how the sword had taken over and butchered the Kulls, dragging Morgin along behind it.

Tulellcoe frowned deeply. "The magic in the sanctum should not have come to you in that way, not so readily. And without one of us there to moderate it, it should have destroyed you. Only someone of Elhiyne blood could have handled that power that way, only someone directly of House Elhiyne."

Morgin's heart wanted to pound its way out of his chest at the import of Tulellcoe's words.

"Perhaps Malka!" Tulellcoe continued. "He was always one for whoring when we were in Anistigh. And his penchant for raw power would explain your penchant for raw power." Tulellcoe shook his head. "No. Impossible. It can't be."

"What do you mean by that?" Morgin demanded. "Does it really bother you that we might share the same blood?"

Tulellcoe shook his head. "No. It's not that."

"Yes it is," Morgin said. "You're just like all the rest, aren't you? Don't want the taint of the whoreson's blood. Well I need some sleep so please leave?"

Tulellcoe turned and looked at Morgin for a long moment, his anger easily visible. Morgin noticed his hand had slipped into his tunic as if reaching for something. "As you wish," he said flatly, then turned and left the room.

Morgin extinguished the lamp and returned to bed, but he lay there for a long time before returning to sleep.

••••

Morgin awoke, took one look at his hands, sat up in his cot and swore with Morddon's voice, "Damn! Will these dreams never end?"

There were several angels in the barracks and they all looked his way. One of them, sitting on a nearby cot sharpening his sword, asked, "Did you dream badly, whiteface?"

"This is the dream, you damn fool," Morddon said. But then he hesitated, looked at his hands once more, understood Morgin's anger was mixing with Morddon's guilt to form a deadly combination. Morgin concentrated on calming down while Morddon said to the angel, "Sorry. Guess I didn't wake up well."

The angel frowned, perhaps more at the apology than anything else, then went back to sharpening his sword.

Morddon swung his feet off the cot and looked about groggily. His afternoon nap had lasted longer than expected and evening was now upon him. He staggered to the bathhouse at the back of the barracks, washed carefully. Since returning to Kathbeyanne he'd taken up what for him was the unusual habit of bathing regularly, and he was drinking less. Glistening with moisture he threw his long, black hair back over his shoulders and returned to his cot. While he was dressing Metadan approached him and said, "You are to dine in the palace tonight."

He almost said, *I don't want to*, but thought better of it and said merely, "Why?"

"The Lady AnneRhianne requests your presence. And she specifically said it was to be presented to you as a request, not an order. But from me, it is an order."

Morddon curled his lips back into a snarlish grin. "I almost like you, angel."

That evening AnneRhianne sent a palace guard to guide him through the labyrinthine corridors of the grand palace of the Shahotma King. Corridor upon corridor led off to unknown destinations, with people moving about everywhere; most refused to meet Morddon's eyes. That saddened him, for he knew he'd gained an unpleasant reputation, but not until that moment did he realize how far it had gone.

The guard led him to a large sitting room where at least a dozen people had already gathered. They were mostly Benesh'ere, though there were other races present. They stood in small groups chatting politely, while servants walked among them with trays of delicacies and cool summer wine. They all wore elegant, expensive garments that made Morddon's plain, simple clothing seem even shabbier by comparison. He snagged a goblet of chilled wine, was careful to sip at it rather than gulp it down.

He spied AnneRhianne across the room at about the same moment she saw him. She started toward him immediately, followed closely by two young, pretty Benesh'ere girls, but Morddon had eyes only for AnneRhianne. In her Morgin saw only Rhianne, and she was more beautiful than he had ever imagined

"Morddon," she said happily. "I'm glad you could come."

"I wasn't sure what to expect."

One of the young girls harrumphed loudly. AnneRhianne looked at her. "Of course. How rude of me." She introduced the two young ladies, but Morddon was so preoccupied with AnneRhianne he forgot their names almost immediately.

"That was a very brave thing you did," the youngest of the two said, dripping with admiration.

"What thing are you talking about?" Morddon asked.

"Why! Rescuing WindHollow and SheelThane that way."

"That wasn't me," Morddon lied. "Must have been someone else."

AnneRhianne winked at the young girl. "He still denies it, I think because he's shy. And SheelThane will neither confirm nor deny it, because I'm certain he swore her to secrecy."

Morddon felt an angry, bitter retort climbing up his throat, but he suppressed it. "I really don't know anything about it."

AnneRhianne took him under her wing for the rest of the evening. She piloted him through the crowd, saw to it he met everyone, and filled in those unpleasant moments when the conversation took a bad turn or died away. He had no experience at small talk. After what seemed an eternity they sat down to dinner. The table was carefully arranged, and the number of guests had been chosen to make everything perfect. Morddon looked at the array of utensils placed around his plate and cringed inwardly. AnneRhianne, seated next to him, managed to coach him in their proper use without seeming to do so, and for that he was grateful.

After dinner they adjourned to a large garden court, an atrium in the center of the palace—apparently there were many such—with private little, tree lined pathways that opened out into small, carefully tended garden clearings. Lamps hung overhead illuminated the pathways, and in the dim lighting Morddon caught glimpses of fountains, flowers and places to sit in private little groups amidst the beauty.

He heard pipes ever so faintly, a sound that hadn't touched his ears in centuries. But the pipist fumbled for his notes, unsure of himself, trying to play a tune that wasn't coming easily. "Who's the pipist?" Morddon asked AnneRhianne.

She shrugged and shook her head. "I don't know."

They began a search through the pathways of the garden, pausing, listening for the next sequence of notes, then following whatever path led in that direction. The pathways wound and curved endlessly, frustrating their efforts to find the pipist, but Morddon refused to relent, and eventually found Metadan and Ellowyn seated on a stone bench in a small clearing. Metadan hesitantly picked out the notes of his tune, while Ellowyn looked on with the eyes of a lover. Morgin was dumbfounded, for to his ears Metadan had piped the most beautiful tunes with true mastery of his instrument, and yet now he seemed the unsure novice.

As Morddon and AnneRhianne joined the two archangels, Metadan took the instrument from his lips, looked at it forlornly and sighed. "Ah! A folly I picked up recently. But I have no teacher, and the skill of this thing escapes me."

Morddon sat down next to him, his fingers itching to touch the instrument. "But it's not skill that's required for piping. It's the feeling, the sense, the emotion. Learn those, and the skill will follow."

AnneRhianne looked at him queerly. "You speak as if you know the pipes with more than your ears."

Morddon nodded. "My father was a pipist." He tried to hide his excitement at having such an instrument close at hand.

Metadan considered him carefully. "And no doubt your father taught you some of that feeling. Can you play?"

Morddon closed his eyes, tried to recall Indwallin. Working at the forges with Eisla had been a pleasant task, a chore joyful for the physical exercise and time spent with his mother, but the pipes had come naturally to him and they were his first love. He and Binth had filled their village nightly with the magic of their sounds. "I can play," Morddon said. "A little."

Metadan offered him the instrument. "Then please, show me."

Morddon's hands almost shook as he caressed the pipes carefully, felt the grain in the wood, sensed the music buried within it. He put the instrument to his lips, blew a tentative note, blew another, tested its range and depth. It needed proper tuning, but with a small knife, and a few hours, and a great deal of care, he could correct that.

He had to play something, anything, but he could remember none of the tunes he and Binth and Eisla had loved so much. And then Morgin's memories flooded into him, memories of Metadan sitting in a clearing in the forest near Csairne Glen at the top of Sa'umbra, and Metadan's sad tune came back to him.

He touched the pipes to his lips, played the first note of the tune, and the next, and soon he was deep into it. He played a sad tune that fit his mood, and so it flowed out of him as if he had played it time and again for centuries. He played Metadan's tune from Morgin's memories, and did so with considerably different style. When Metadan had piped the tune it had been more of a dirge, while Morddon piped a sweet, sad song of loving memories from a joyous time never to be retrieved. His fingers crawled up and down the length of the instrument, and the tune flowed from his heart, while tears flowed from his eyes.

When the tune ended he pulled the instrument from his lips slowly, looked at it for a long, solemn moment, then looked up, and for the first time noticed he'd gathered a large crowd about him. AnneRhianne too had tears streaming down her face, as did most of the women in the crowd, and many of the men. There were also griffins among them, though because of their size the griffins were limited to only the most open spaces of the garden.

"That was very beautiful," AnneRhianne said in a choked whisper.

TarnThane stood nearby, and for once, when he spoke, his voice lacked its usual boisterous confidence. "The madman has shown us a hint of the beauty he hides within his soul."

Morddon wanted to snarl a reply, but the mood of the tune was still upon him, and his voice came out without its usual bitterness and sharp edges. "Be quiet, half bird."

"Your father was a pipist?" AnneRhianne asked him.

Morddon looked at the instrument as he answered. "Yes. His name was Binth, and he was the pipist in our village. I liked working with my mother Eisla during the day at her forges, but I loved the pipes most, and Binth and I played endlessly through the evenings."

AnneRhianne's sharp intake of breath startled Morddon. He looked at her carefully, saw that her eyes had narrowed and her face had hardened. He'd said something wrong, and he sensed anger from her now, and he sensed anger within the crowd about him too. She spoke carefully, and she asked him one question: "And the name of this village?"

Morddon frowned and answered her. "A small village, a simple village of which you've probably never heard. It was named Indwallin."

AnneRhianne shot out of her seat and stood over him. Her hand arced out, and her palm crashed into his cheek with a loud whip-crack. She lifted her hand again to slap him, and it startled him so he didn't even attempt to defend himself while twice more she struck him with such force his head rocked back and he gripped the stone bench to keep his seat.

"You blasphemous bastard!" she cried. "What evil lies within your heart that you must always turn us against you? I could forgive your constant mockery, but you choose to mock us with the Abomination, and for that I can only hate you."

She turned away from him and stormed out of the clearing, leaving him in the midst of a stunned silence. The crowd about him grumbled angrily, then slowly dispersed, though one young Benesh'ere warrior stopped for a moment to spit on him before following the rest.

Morddon sat in the empty silence that followed, unable to comprehend what had just happened. "What did I do?" he asked of no one.

TarnThane answered him. "You truly do not know, do you?"

Morddon shook his head. "Know what?"

TarnThane shook his head sadly. "You chose the wrong lie, my friend Morddon, for among your people the name Indwallin is never spoken. It is instead referred to as the Abomination, for at Beayaegoath's command the village was sacked by Magwa the jackal queen, and while it's inhabitants were tortured to death, their children were made to watch."

TarnThane's words struck at Morddon's heart, and were more painful than AnneRhianne's blows, for they released long forgotten memories hidden within Morddon's soul. He sobbed, remembering a night filled with torches and soldiers and hatred, a young boy tied to a stake with his young friends, while they watched their parents slowly crucified. He would never again forget the sound of their cries. And then . . .

Morddon nodded at TarnThane's words. "I remember now. And after they crucified our parents, they tortured the other children, and made me watch."

TarnThane shook his head again, though with less confidence. "That cannot be. Indwallin was desecrated twelve hundred years ago at the very beginning of these wars. The SteelMistress Eisla was the greatest of the SteelMasters, and the first to be murdered. Since then Beayaegoath has systematically sought out and murdered each Steel-Master, until now there are no more."

Morddon handed the pipes to Metadan, looked at the calluses on his hands and recalled hauntingly vague memories of swinging a hammer at the forges. But Eisla was not part of those memories for they were not Eisla's forges. Eisla was long dead and the fires of those forges were stoked by hatred, and malice, and the lust for power. Those forges had never been meant for good steel: the steel of a plowshare to till the soil and bring new life to the earth; the steel of a surgeon's knife to cut away death and make room for life. Those forges had been used only for the steel of death, the steel of hatred, the steel of one single blade, a blade twelve hundred years in the making.

Morddon looked wonderingly at the sword strapped to his side, then at his callused hands. A year in such slavery would seem no different than a century. He looked at his calluses and whispered, "And so the blade was born. What have I created?"

21

The Isle of Simpa

MORGIN STOOD ON the stern castle of the ship *Far Wind*, watched the hurried activity down on the dock as the *Far Wind's* crew made last minute preparations. Just past dawn on a gray day, low clouds blanketed the sky, with a light breeze coming in off the ocean to put a chill in the air. Morgin pulled the hood of his cloak forward and hunched tightly within its folds. It shielded him from the nip in the air, but most importantly it hid his identity.

Bakart, the sailor who'd saved Morgin's life three nights ago, and first mate of the *Far Wind*, sprinted across the ship's foredeck and vaulted agilely up onto the stern castle. He leaned insanely out over the rail near Morgin and shouted down to someone on the dock, "Belay that, you idiot." He climbed up onto the rail, jumped out into midair and caught the ropes of a nearby crane, then slid down the rope easily to the dock. He sprinted across the dock to a longshoreman, stopped with his nose only inches from the man's face, and bellowed something Morgin couldn't hear.

The *Far Wind* was making a trade run up the coast to Toblekan at the mouth of the Dahaun river, then on to Drapolis near Castle Tosk. France and Val had arranged for passage for their small company all the way to Drapolis. Penda was only a short distance up the Dahaun from Toblekan, and too close to Aud anyway, so Morgin would stay hidden on ship during the two days the *Far Wind* laid over there. After that he'd breathe more easily. Drapolis was quite remote, and reputed to be a bit primitive for a city.

He was leaving Aud quickly, and in secret. Terrikle had arranged the deceit with his usual attention to detail. During the last three days he'd made sure Morgin was seen regularly both in the city and within the palace. Later this morning, as the palace awoke, Morgin would not come down at his usual time. Terrikle would spread the word that His Highness was not feeling well and call in Sacress the physician. The physician would then announce that Morgin had taken on a slight fever, nothing to be alarmed about, but it would be best if he remained in isolation. They would continue the ruse indefinitely, hoping to give Morgin several days before the bounty hunters in the city realized they'd been deceived. And by that time Pandorin would have started several conflicting rumors about the direction Morgin had gone. Besides Morgin and his companions, only Terrikle, Sacress and Pandorin were aware of the plan, and only Pandorin knew Morgin's destination and mode of travel. Of the ship's crew, only Bakart and her captain, Darma, were aware of Morgin's true identity, and they'd taken him on as a passenger only because the palace had made it clear they'd have trouble doing any trade in Aud again if they didn't. Morgin's only regret was that he'd not been given the chance to say goodbye to Aiergain. She'd refused to see him since the day they'd gone riding together, and that saddened him.

Down on the dock Morgin noticed the *Far Wind* had apparently taken on another passenger. A young man was helping an old matron up the gang plank, though both young man and old woman were hidden against the chill within their cloaks. The old woman, however, was bent with age over a knobbed cane, and for a moment it seemed she might not be able to handle the slight slope of the gang plank. The ship's captain, a man Morgin had yet to meet, stepped in to help, but the old woman brushed him away angrily and he backed off.

The old woman managed the gang plank, then disappeared into one of the few cabins below. Morgin continued to watch the activity on the dock until some minutes later France joined him on the stern castle. "Morddon, me friend," he said, using Morgin's assumed name. "Come below for a moment. We need some private talkin'."

The *Far Wind* had four private cabins. The captain had his own; the first mate Bakart and another of the ship's officers shared the second, and the third and fourth were used for the occasional passenger. In this case Cort and Tulellcoe would occupy one, while France and Morgin and Val shared the cramped confines of the other. Morgin wondered where the old matron would stay.

France led him to Cort's cabin, said, "Go on in, lad. I'll be there in a minute."

Morgin knocked, heard a muffled "Come in," opened the door and found the old matron waiting there in the tight confines of the cabin, standing with her back to him. He half entered the cabin, hesitated, said, "I'm sorry. There must be a mistake."

"Come in and close the door," she croaked.

Morgin hesitated for a moment at the open door, then did so cautiously. Bent in a crouch, the matron turned toward him. She straightened and threw the hood back from her face. "Ah!" Aiergain said. "It's a relief to stand up again, and croaking like that makes my throat sore."

Morgin lowered himself to one knee. "Your Majesty."

"Oh stand up, Morgin," she said. "There's no need for that kind of formality between us."

He stood cautiously.

"You're hesitating, aren't you?" She took the one step necessary to cross the length of the small cabin, took his hands in hers. "I'm sorry, Morgin. You were right, and I was just confused. I do love you, but as a friend who was there when I needed you, not as a lover. And like everything else between us, you were wise to reject me."

"I'm sorry," he said.

"No! Don't be sorry. We will always be friends, you and I. I realize that now. Perhaps someday I can help you when you are in need."

Morgin now felt better about leaving Aud. The grayness of the day and the chill in the air no longer mattered.

"Where will you go," she asked.

He shrugged. "Drapolis."

"I mean after that."

He shrugged again. "I don't know. I have no plans beyond Drapolis. Maybe I can stay there long enough to make some plans. Maybe I can just find a place to disappear."

She frowned sadly. "Not a very good life the clans have given you, is it? Tell me, why do they fear you so?"

Morgin touched the sword at his side. "The talisman."

She shook her head. "No. That's not enough. They may believe that's the reason, but there has to be more."

A loud knock on the door interrupted them, and a voice on the other side shouted, "All visitors ashore."

Aiergain leaned forward and kissed him on the cheek, on the stubble of the beard he'd begun growing again. "I must go. We told the captain I was your aged mother, come to wish you a safe journey. Remember you will always be welcome in Aud."

She knocked softly on the door. It opened and Pandorin stepped in. He shook Morgin's hand, then hugged him tightly. "Fare you well, friend," he said.

Aiergain resumed the guise of the aged matron and Morgin and Pandorin escorted her back up on deck. Morgin stood at the ship's rail watching her coach disappear into the streets of Aud. France leaned on the rail next to him, said, "You done a good thing, lad."

Confused, Morgin asked. "What? Done what?"

France looked at him. "You freed the Hand of the Thief."

Morgin staggered backward, remembering Cort's recitation of the Seven Deeds. "What's that mean?"

France nodded toward Aiergain's coach. "Among us rogues she's called the Hand of the Thief, though not often."

••••

Once the *Far Wind* cleared Aud's harbor, they stayed close to the coast line. The first two days out from Aud were slow going for the *Far Wind*. The weather continued gray and cloudy, and the light sea breeze that put a chill in the air never grew beyond a whisper. On the afternoon of the second day France and Morgin were standing in the bow of the ship when Bakart joined them and commented, "I don't like this."

"Aye," France agreed. "We should be makin' better time."

Bakart shook his head. "It ain't that. A sailor's got nothing to complain about if he's got wind in his sails, even if it's a poor wind. We could be drifting in a dead calm, you know, and then we'd have no control if the tide carried us onto the rocks."

Morgin asked, "Then what's wrong?"

Bakart wrinkled his nose as one might for a bad smell, and he looked up into the sky. "This weather's just wrong." He licked a finger, stuck it in the air. "Notice the wind has shifted? She's coming from off the coast now, blowing out to sea. That's rare, and when she does blow that way, she should blow the clouds away, clear the skies for us. I don't like it."

France asked, "When do we reach Toblekan?"

"Maybe noon tomorrow, at this rate."

That evening as the sun set the wind picked up. Bakart told them a short blow near sunset was not uncommon. But after sunset the wind continued to gain intensity. By the time Morgin was told to go below, waves were just beginning to break over the bow.

Down in the cramped confines of the little cabin Morgin found France and Val ready to wait out the storm. France sat on his bunk with his head buried in a bucket, while Val tried vainly to cast a spell to ease his churning stomach. The lamp overhead swayed constantly back and forth, and Morgin wondered if that might not be the cause of France's ailment.

A short time later Tulellcoe and Cort joined them. With all five of them there the cabin felt extremely cramped. With Cort and Tulellcoe assisting Val, they managed to ease France's vomiting. They could all hear the storm growing in intensity. There was a tempo and a flavor to the creaking of the ship's timbers that sounded a counterpoint to the swing of the lamp overhead and the sway of the deck beneath their feet. The wind outside had grown to a howl that whistled constantly through their thoughts. As the storm grew worse, all the sights and sounds of the cramped cabin changed with it. The deck no longer swayed but lurched beneath them; the lamp jumped and rattled on its hook; the timbers creaked and shuddered, and the wind grew to a howl.

They all heard and felt it when it happened: a loud snap that reverberated through the hull, and the *Far Wind* listed to one side. Then a few minutes later the door of their cabin burst open and a dripping wet sailor lurched into the room. "The captain needs help," he said fearfully. "We got a broken timber, and if the bulkhead she supports goes we'll sink. Can't shore her up properly 'cause there's too much pressure on her now.

Captain wonders if magic might help, and if any of you what knows it would come and lend a hand."

Val and Cort and Tulellcoe left with the sailor. Without their help France returned to his bucket. Morgin wondered how the horses were taking the storm down in the hold. But there was nothing he could do for them, or for the ship, or for himself, so he retrieved a bottle of brandy from his gear, and decided to get a little drunk.

••••

Morgin was thankful for the warm sunshine as he stood on the bow of the *Far Wind* and tried to catch a glimpse of the land one of the sailors had spotted from high up in the sails. They'd managed to shore up the weakened bulkhead the night before, but the storm had driven them quite a distance out to sea before blowing itself out. They'd all been grateful for the clear day that greeted them that morning. Now they limped toward the nearest land, hoping to find a sheltered cove where it would be safe to send divers over the side and assess the damage.

Bakart shook his head worriedly, shouted up to the sailors in the rigging. "Well? She be the coast or not?"

One of the sailors shouted back. "Still can't tell. Too far."

Bakart continued to shake his head. "It can't be the coast. But there ain't no islands out here, not that big."

Morgin's companions joined him at the rail, while any sailor who didn't have specific duties at the moment climbed up into the rigging to help the lookouts. They all waited patiently for the *Far Wind* to get close enough to determine what form of land they'd spotted, until one of the sailors shouted, "It's Simpa, captain! By damn it's Simpa!"

Bakart's eyes widened and he shot up into the rigging. For some reason every member of the crew waited breathlessly for the first mate to confirm the sighting. And he did with a shout, "Aye, captain, it be Simpa all right."

Darma gave orders to steer the ship away from the island and the crew broke into frantic activity. As Bakart dropped out of the rigging Morgin grabbed his arm. "What's going on?"

Bakart angrily yanked his arm free of Morgin's grip. "That's the Isle of Simpa. It's phantom land, enchanted, bewitched. If we get anywhere near it we'll all die."

Bakart strode off hurriedly to consult with Darma. They were northwest of the island so they tried to take a wide berth past its northern coast and then hope they could make it to the mainland. But as they neared it the wind picked up again, this time blowing south as if it would force them into the rocks of Simpa's jagged shore. And as they passed the island the wind blew harder still, shifted again, then grew in intensity until it reached gale force, blowing now southwest directly into their faces. Oddly the day remained clear, and showed no symptoms of another storm.

Morgin and his companions retreated to the stern castle as waves broke over the bow. Darma tacked into the wind and the ship struggled against a sea that seemed bent on turning them about. After an hour he said angrily, "We can't take much more of this. We'll break up soon enough if the wind doesn't let up."

Tulellcoe looked behind the ship at the Isle of Simpa. "This is an enchanted wind," he said. "And the enchanter apparently wants us on that island."

"No!" Darma shouted above the wind. "Never."

Tulellcoe shook his head. "I don't believe you have a choice."

It took a great deal of persuasion to convince Darma to turn toward the island, though what apparently convinced him most was the fact that Tulellcoe, Val and Cort were all practitioners of magic. He had some hope they could combat the evil the sailors believed awaited them on Simpa.

As soon as Darma turned the *Far Wind* toward the island, the wind dropped back to a steady but unthreatening breeze and the sea calmed. They found a small cove near the north end of the island. It offered the sheltered water they needed to send divers over the side, so they dropped anchor in the middle of the cove well away from shore and went to work.

Darma's two best swimmers went over the side, while some of the crew kept watch for sharks, and the rest looked nervously at the supposedly enchanted shoreline. Morgin found an empty stretch of rail up on the stern castle and leaned against it to watch the work. While the divers were over the side Darma had a crew below working on the damaged bulkhead. At one point he said something about sending a crew ashore to cut fresh timbers, but none looked happy at the thought so he let it go.

Later in the afternoon Bakart leaned against the rail near Morgin. He puffed on a foul smelling pipe, and unlike his captain the proximity of Simpa didn't seem to bother him. He looked up at the sky. "Weather sure has cleared up, ain't it?"

Morgin followed his gaze. The sky had turned from the angry gray of the day before to a pale blue. The sun hung in the sky with no clouds to speak of, and a gentle, steady breeze ruffled his hair. "How bad is the damage?" Morgin asked.

Bakart shook his head. "It ain't good. We can't make it to Drapolis, nor back to Aud. If this weather holds maybe we can make a run for Toblekan. They don't have much of a shipyard, but we can get a better look at the damage and decide what to do then."

Bakart narrowed his eyes to a squint, looked out over the water to the shore. "Now what's that?"

Morgin looked toward the shore, saw some movement near the edge of the water, couldn't make out much detail. A small boat edged out into the water. It had no sail, but was powered by the backs of several oarsmen.

One of the other sailors spotted the small boat, and raised the cry. Darma called in the divers and the ship broke into a furor as the crewmen rushed to arm themselves. Only Bakart remained relatively calm.

Morgin kept his position in the stern castle and watched the small boat draw nearer. The crew took up defensive positions on the deck while Morgin's friends joined him up in the stern castle. Bakart joined the crew on the main deck while Darma took his customary position in the stern castle. As the small boat drew near Morgin could make out six oarsmen and one passenger. They were all well hidden beneath hooded cloaks, though those of the oarsmen were a light blue in color while that of the passenger was a simple, dark black.

Tulellcoe lifted his chin as if sniffing the air like a hound. "There's magic in this."

Darma looked at him unhappily.

Cort nodded her agreement. "Yes. Quite a bit of it. Captain Darma, I think it would be unwise to attack whoever is in that skiff."

Darma spun on her angrily. "And what am I supposed to do? Sit back and watch while they cast some plague on me ship?"

Cort shook her head. "I doubt that's her intention. Keep in mind whoever can control the wind and sea that way, has no need to come here to destroy this ship."

Darma considered that for a moment, then shouted down to Bakart and his men. "Stay your swords until I give the word. Any man acts without my command, I'll have his hide for sail cloth."

Cort's words bothered Morgin and he asked, "You said her. Is this a sorceress we face?"

Cort frowned. "I did say that, didn't I? But I have no more information than you. I suppose this just feels like a woman's touch."

The small boat pulled up alongside the *Far Wind* and one of the oarsmen climbed the rigging up to the main deck, hopped over the rail and landed lightly on the deck. The hood of his cloak still hid his face, but then he reached up with a rather delicate looking hand and threw the hood back to reveal a woman, a most beautiful, young woman. The sailors backed away from her fearfully, mumbling and making superstitious signs to ward off evil. She looked up to the stern castle and for an instant her eyes locked on Morgin, but then she looked to Darma and spoke. "Captain. My mistress is too old to climb the rigging. Please lower a chair for her."

Darma shook his head. "I ain't lettin' no witch on me ship."

The young woman smiled unpleasantly. "Then she will turn you and your crew into toads and let the fish feed upon you. Or, the sorceress of Simpa can guarantee you safe passage to Toblekan, with a calm sea and a steady wind at your back. It's your choice."

Reluctantly Darma had his men lower a chair for the old woman. She stood on deck bent with age, hobbled with a cane on unsteady legs as her beautiful young companion helped her below deck. They didn't ask for permission, or to have a cabin assigned to them. And while the sorceress was bent with age, Morgin had the impression if she could stand straight she'd tower over most men.

The boat that brought her, and the oarsmen—or perhaps oarswomen—literally vanished. No one was looking that way when it disappeared, and so no one saw it vanish. But when they did look there was no boat to be seen in the water between the *Far Wind* and the shore, and there had not been enough time for it to traverse the distance.

She commandeered the cabin France, Val and Morgin were sharing, though the only notice they received was their gear piled up outside the cabin door. Darma and his crew finished the temporary repairs to the ship's hull, and before sundown that night they left Simpa behind.

22

The Daughter of the Wind

MORDDON MOVED SOFTLY through the underbrush of the forest. In the mist shrouded mountains to the far north of Kathbeyanne the faintest sound might carry for leagues. With the Goath about, a wise man moved carefully with every step.

He'd been tracking a mixed group of Kulls, jackal warriors and human Goath, and for two days now they'd been moving fast, as if desperate to make some rendezvous. But now for the first time they'd come to a stop and posted guards. Morddon's curiosity got the best of him and he decided to investigate further. He left Mortiss back in the forest, slipped into the undergrowth, and wrapped in one of Morgin's shadows he edged closer to the enemy camp.

He almost stumbled into the first perimeter guard, an idiotic and potentially lethal mistake. But his nose caught the scent of jackal only moments before he did, and he froze into stillness not ten paces from the deformed beast that stood before him.

They'd set their perimeter much larger than normal, with the guards much too tightly spaced, as if they were aware a shadow might try to slip between them, and were willing to use every warrior they had in an effort to prevent that.

Morddon sat very still for a few moments and listened. The guards were disciplined and silent, and the forest itself possessed an unnatural calm. As he waited and the silence grew, his ears picked up the sound of voices carried on the mist from the center of the camp. They were faint, and muffled by the distance, and he understood none of what was said; his curiosity grew.

Morddon backed off to a more comfortable distance and circled the perimeter slowly, hoping to find a gap in the sentries. The forest was thick, and he found it impossible to get a straight view of the center of the camp without some branch or bush in his way. And whenever he did catch a glimpse of the figures clustered there, the mist in the air wrapped them in a hazy cloud of anonymity.

A Kull, a jackal warrior, and someone not easily visible through the ever-swirling mist, were discussing something in hushed tones. At first he thought the third, unidentified fellow was one of the human Goath, one of the many traitors who'd given his soul to the nethergod. His stature and girth pointed to that conclusion, but when he moved or gestured, the grace and poise of his actions hinted at the unthinkable: an angel meeting secretly with a Kull and a jackal in the middle of the forest.

Morddon refused to believe it. No angel would betray Aethon that way. But Morgin dredged up the memory of Ellowyn telling the story of the dark angel, the Fallen One.

A sharp cry broke the silence of the forest, then Morddon heard the sound of a single horse riding off into the distance. The perimeter guards closed in on the center of the camp. Morddon moved in with them, keeping a safe distance but still anxious to know more. Then the Kulls and jackals and human Goath all mounted up and rode out, following the single rider.

"Damn!" Morddon swore. He no longer cared about the Goath; he wanted that single rider, but the larger troop of Goath had obscured the trail and it took him more than an hour to find it. Even then he wasn't sure he'd found the right one. He followed the track through that day and into the next, and as he'd suspected it led in the general direction of the First Legion's camp. He tried to push himself, to catch up with the rider, but in his haste he lost the track several times and had to back track. And then late in the second day, just as he thought he might be closing the gap with his quarry, it began to rain; only a light drizzle, but enough to destroy the track completely.

Morddon gave up and started back to the First Legion. He didn't have far to travel since the track he'd followed had led in that direction. He found the camp early the next morning of a bright, sunny day, and was surprised to learn that the legion had been joined by Gilguard and a company of Benesh'ere. As always, he rode straight to Metadan's tent to give his report, but as he approached it he noticed a groom nearby brushing down a horse that had recently been ridden. Morddon dismounted, gave Mortiss's reins to a guard, but instead of entering the tent he approached the groom.

Morddon looked at the horse the groom was rubbing down. A cloud of steam rose from its back and shoulders. It had clearly been ridden long and hard. "A beautiful animal," Morddon commented. "Whose is it?"

The groom paused and looked at him with the vacant stare so typical of the damn angels. "It is the warmaster's horse," he said flatly.

"Gilguard's?" Morddon asked.

"No."

"Metadan's been out then?"

"Yes."

"Scouting?"

"Yes."

"How long's he been out?"

"Several days."

"Hmmm! I wonder if our paths crossed. I'd like to compare reports with him. Do you know where his scouting took him?"

"No."

Morddon could get nothing more out of the groom; the flat and unembellished conversation was typical of his interactions with the angels. He wondered if, among themselves, they spoke with more life in their words.

••••

Morgin stood in the bow of the *Far Wind* and looked at the moon glow reflected off the dark waters of the nighttime sea. Standing next to him, Val spoke casually, "Bakart says the weather is perfect. We're making good time, and having no problems with the damage. Should make Toblekan tomorrow sometime."

The sea was dark, silent, and glassy smooth as the *Far Wind* sliced through the water with a barely audible hiss. Morgin didn't really hear Val's words, for the sorceress of Simpa occupied his every waking thought. Ever since she'd come aboard he could sense her presence, like he sensed Olivia when she was near, though she was far different from Olivia, with none of the steel, ice and anger that drove the old Elhiyne witch. In fact the old woman from the isle seemed oddly familiar.

"And you are familiar to me," an old, old voice croaked.

Both Val and Morgin started, turned about quickly, found the old witch standing behind them, a gray-black shadow barely distinguishable from the darkness of the night. She stood horribly bent with age, barely able to support herself, her young companion hovering close at hand. Again Morgin had the impression that if the old witch could stand erect she would stand taller than most men. Slowly, with her companion's help, the old woman lowered herself to the deck and sat on the planks with her legs crossed. Her companion remained standing behind her. "Sit," the old woman commanded, and she extended a hand to indicate that Val and Morgin should sit on the deck facing her. For just an instant Morgin saw the moonlight reflected off the skin of her hand as it passed in front of him, and he thought it had the bone white cast of a Benesh'ere hand.

Morgin and Val sat down facing her. The hood of her cloak hid her face in moon shadow, though the moonlight penetrated the shadow just enough to cast a reflection from her eyes: two bright, hot sparks that cut to the depths of Morgin's soul. "Come closer," she said to him.

The old woman drew Morgin like a moth to a flame, and without hesitation he stood up, crossed the few feet between them and sat down again. She extended her hands, and in the moonlight Morgin confirmed they were the hands of a Benesh'ere woman.

Morgin reached out to take her hands in his, and as their skin touched his mind filled with images of Kathbeyanne in all its glory, and the palace of the Shahotma. "Who are you?" he asked.

She shook her head. "I am no one and nothing. I am what's left of the end of the old, and I am here to see the beginning of the new." Her words were sad, but there was joy in her voice.

Morgin reached up to her face, touched the folds of her cloak and slid the hood back off her head onto her shoulders. His heart pounded in his chest with such force he thought it might burst at any moment, for the face the moonlight revealed was a face from his dreams. And though withered and wrinkled by centuries of age, he would never forget AnneRhianne.

She looked at him with centuries of longing in her eyes. "You said you would come back, and so I've waited through the centuries. As you taught me I've listened to the netherwind, and when you freed the Hand of the Thief, I knew you were coming." She lifted one of his hands to her face and kissed it gently.

"You've waited all this time?" he asked.

She didn't answer, but pressed his hand against her cheek and closed her eyes. "I am content now," she said, "and my waiting is done. At long last I am free." As Morgin looked on she dissipated into the night, melted into the shadows of the moon and drifted away on the sea air. The small circle of deck where she'd sat was empty. Nor was there any sign of her companion.

••••

Morgin awoke with the dawn, wrapped in his blanket and laying on a bunk in the crew deck of the *Far Wind*. Nearby France still slept in his blanket, though Val was already sitting up, rubbing the sleep from his eyes.

Morgin shook his head, said to Val, "I had the strangest dream last night."

Val ran his fingers tiredly through his hair, arched his back and stretched. "It was no dream."

Morgin looked at the twoname carefully. "What do you remember?"

Val blinked and shook his head. "I remember she said you had freed the Hand of the Thief, and now I see the connection to Aud, and Aiergain, the Queen of Thieves."

Morgin climbed angrily out of his bunk, leaned over Val and said, "Don't start vomiting those superstitions at me."

Val nodded thoughtfully. "I'm curious. Before you freed the Hand of the Thief, you had to have restored the House of the Thane. What does that mean?"

Morgin gripped Val's tunic angrily, pressed him back against the bulkhead behind his bunk. "I don't ever want to hear those words again."

The twoname didn't resist him, but shrugged and said, "She's gone, you know?"

"Who's gone?"

"The old witch. I heard two of the crew talking a little earlier. They found the door to her cabin wide open this morning, and she was gone. They've searched the entire ship and found no sign of her or her companion. Like she said, her waiting is done."

••••

The *Far Wind* put into port late that afternoon. Toblekan was a bustling seaport on the mouth of the river Dahaun, and while quite small, still a dangerous place for Morgin. Castle Penda was less than a day's ride up the river, and BlakeDown maintained a large and well equipped garrison in the middle of the city. There were too many Penda armsmen about for an outlaw wizard to feel comfortable.

Tulellcoe wanted news, so as soon as the *Far Wind* docked he and Morgin's other companions hustled ashore. With his beard now full Morgin considered going ashore with them. But if all went well the needed repairs would be minor, and they'd be on their way to Drapolis sometime the next day, so he decided not to press his luck.

Darma and Bakart put the crew to work almost instantly, while Morgin settled down to watch from his usual place in the stern castle. Bakart had told him they'd get a much better assessment of the damage by partially unloading the hold and stacking it on the dock; the equipment and facilities available in the shipyard helped immeasurably. But beyond a lot of grunting, sweating crewmembers, there wasn't much of interest to see. Morgin grew drowsy in the warm afternoon sun. He sat down on the deck with his back to the stern castle rail, and drifted off to sleep.

The neigh of an angry horse woke him, followed by the staccato sound of rapid hoof beats on the wooden planks of the dock. Morgin came awake in an instant, for he knew that horse well. Down on the dock they'd begun unloading the horses from the ship's hold and some poor devil was having an impossible time with Mortiss.

Morgin vaulted down to the *Far Wind's* main deck, then across the gangplank and onto the dock. His fear was not so much for Mortiss, but for the poor fool trying to handle her. It would not do much for his relations with the crew if she kicked his brains out.

Morgin took her reins from the crewman, then to everyone's surprise let them drop free, and Mortiss calmed instantly. "Lead her with a light hand," he told the crewman, "and she'll follow if she chooses. But beware if she chooses not."

The crewman looked at Morgin, then at Mortiss, and he made a sign to ward off evil. Morgin shook his head and turned back to the ship, but he noticed he and Mortiss had drawn quite a bit of attention and a lot of staring eyes.

During the afternoon they learned the damage to the *Far Wind* was worse than thought. Toblekan's shipyard could only effect temporary repairs, so Darma would have to turn back to Aud.

When Morgin's friends returned from scouting the city he told them the news and they all retired to Cort's cabin to consider their options. "Why don't we just sit tight?" Morgin proposed. "We're not in any hurry. We can take the *Far Wind* back to Aud and find another ship to take us to Drapolis."

France scowled, shook his head. "This city's too full of rumors." He turned to Morgin, "How long did Bakart say they're going to take for repairs here?"

"Four, maybe five days."

France shook his head unhappily. "Too long."

They were all tense about something. "What rumors are you talking about?"

Cort took a deep breath and answered, "Every kind of rumor you can imagine, and all about you. It's common knowledge you've disappeared from Aud, and they've got you in Drapolis, or on your way there, or headed back to Elhiyne to fight it out with Olivia. There's even one about taking a ship out into the unknown sea to spend the rest of your life exploring its vastness and hiding from the clans. But the most prevalent is that you're either here in Toblekan, or Penda, or headed this way. I hope that's just coincidence."

"In any case," Tulellcoe added, "we can't stay here. Not for four or five days. There are too many people looking for you in every shadow. They have descriptions of all of us, and they know this ship came from Aud. When these sailors get drunk I doubt they'll hold their tongues."

Morgin nodded. "Then we leave now."

Val shook his head. "If we're going to strike out across country we'll need supplies, and right now the shops are closed up tight. We'll have to wait until morning."

That night Morgin lay in his bunk and saw time and again the eyes of the strangers as they looked at him and Mortiss after the sailor made the sign to ward off evil. Eventually sleep came, a troubled and restless sleep.

23

The Greatest of the Fallen

THE FIRST LEGION and the company of Benesh'ere traveled east for some days, advancing deep into enemy territory. They came upon a large river and followed it further east looking for a place to ford. And when they found the wide shallows Morddon, through Morgin's memories, realized they were following the Ulbb, and had come upon Gilguard's Ford, though in this time and place neither the river or ford had been named.

Morgin recognized the ford only by the lay of the land, which remained unchanged. In Morgin's time the ford was in the midst of a great forest, while in Morddon's the Ulbb meandered through green rolling hills only sparsely populated by trees and clumps of bush.

Metadan decided Gilguard and his Benesh'ere should remain at the ford to keep their back trail clear in case the legion found itself in need of a hasty retreat. The legion crossed the Ford and moved on into what would someday be called Yestmark. They were only an hour or two beyond the ford when Metadan gave orders to pull the scouts in, and without outriders he chose to continue advancing the legion. Throughout that night and the next day he and his lieutenants argued about that decision repeatedly, but Metadan insisted. They obeyed, and advanced blindly.

As sunset approached on the following day they bivouacked near a small stream, and spent the night in the open without pitching tents. Early the next morning one of the perimeter guards came sprinting toward Metadan's tent. "Riders," he said. "Goath. About a dozen of them. Waving a flag of truce."

While the legion moved hastily to break camp, Metadan ordered Morddon and his lieutenants to saddle their horses quickly, so Morddon left his mess kit unpacked. He had an uneasy feeling about this, recalling Morgin's memories of Ellowyn's stories of Metadan's treachery.

The green rolling hills where they met the Goath were covered by few trees and short grass. As they approached the truce party, which waited out of bowshot on a nearby hill, they could see to the next hilltop, though not beyond. Like the group Morddon had followed, the Goath troop was a mix of Kulls, jackal warriors, and humans, with a jackal captain in charge.

Metadan halted his escort about twenty paces from the Goath truce party, and for a moment they stared at one another. Then he demanded, "What do you want with a flag of truce?"

The jackal captain's lips curled back into a snarl, exposing yellow teeth. "You have already given me what I want," he barked. "You have done well, angel. You will receive the price you demanded."

Metadan flinched. Cynaban, Metadan's senior lieutenant, looked at him innocently and asked, "What does he mean, my lord?"

Metadan frowned uncertainly, and in the silence that followed Morddon spoke calmly. "Metadan has betrayed us."

Metadan turned slowly toward Morddon. "Be silent, whiteface."

Morddon looked at the archangel, but he spoke to Cynaban, and told him of the group of Goath he'd been following, and how they'd rendezvoused with what appeared to be an angel, and how Morddon had followed that angel back to the legion to learn Metadan had arrived only minutes before him. "He has betrayed us," Morddon finished.

Cynaban shook his head. "That's impossible. What price could they pay to the foremost warmaster of the twelve legions?"

The jackal captain laughed and answered, "Power. He covets the power of the gods."

Cynaban turned to Metadan and demanded, "Deny this. I beg you to tell me you did not betray us."

"Of course I deny it," Metadan said. "I would never betray my brothers. It's not you they want, but him." He pointed at Morddon.

"Then it's him you betrayed?" Cynaban asked.

"Yes," Metadan said. "No. I betrayed no one. He belongs to the Dark Lord. He escaped and they want him back."

Cynaban frowned, and a stream of tears began pouring down his cheeks. "A slave escapes his evil master, and you would return him to his slavery, and you would do so merely for power?"

"He's not one of us," Metadan said. "He's all they want. The rest of us can go free."

"Free?" Cynaban asked as he shook his head. "My soul would never be free again. And he is one of us. He has fought beside us in many a battle, and in betraying him you have betrayed us all."

Cynaban and Metadan's lieutenants backed away from the archangel. Morddon moved with them and they left Metadan alone astride his horse. "But you'll all die with him," Metadan pleaded. Tears formed in his eyes. "I never meant for that to happen."

He nudged his horse forward to join them. "No," he said. "Let them have him. He's nothing to us."

Cynaban shook his head silently, tearfully, and he spoke one simple word: "No."

Metadan reached out to Cynaban, extending his hand. "I cannot betray you."

Cynaban struck out at the hand, slapped it away. "You already have." To emphasize the point he drew his sword and leveled it at Metadan's throat. "You betrayed one of us; you betrayed all of us."

Cynaban stared at him for a long, last moment, as if to etch the memory of that final meeting in his mind. Then he turned his back on him and signaled for Morddon and the others to follow him. They left Metadan with his new companions.

•••

"We are surrounded," the scout told Cynaban.

The new warmaster of the First Legion had not allowed Morddon to go out with the rest of the scouts. "If it's you they want," Cynaban said, "then we'll make sure it's not you they get."

He quizzed the scout. "How many?"

"We're easily outnumbered twelve to one," the scout said. "They must have closed in on us during the night. They've been waiting behind the hills around us."

Cynaban shook his head sadly. "It appears that all along they intended to betray the betrayer."

The scout said, "But Lord Metadan—"

"Never speak that name again!" Cynaban said. "He is the betrayer, the Fallen One. That is the only name he bears."

"Yes, my lord."

Cynaban thought for a moment. "There's no sense in waiting here to be butchered. We'll go on the offensive, surprise them, head southeast, make for the ford on that river we crossed two days ago."

"The river is named the Ulbb," Morddon said. "And it's called Gilguard's Ford."

"Why Gilguard?" Cynaban asked.

"I don't know."

The legion stripped down to battle gear and trail rations. They knew they were doomed, yet they went about their preparations as if their impending deaths meant nothing. These beings displayed no emotion, no fear, no uncertainty. Cynaban's anger at Metadan, and Metadan's sorrow, were the only emotions Morddon had ever seen from an angel. Watching them prepare for their own deaths was an eerie sight. They were beautiful, silent, and determined.

They took only minutes to prepare themselves, and with no word or command they mounted their horses and formed up in ranks behind Cynaban. Without requesting permission Morddon nudged Mortiss forward and joined Cynaban at the fore of the legion, and while he waited silently at Cynaban's side, it occurred to him he had never seen an angel die, not up close. Since joining the First Legion Metadan had used him exclusively as a scout, so he'd never been part of a large battle. He'd heard the stories of how, in death, an angel's mortal body withered away as its soul returned to its master. Today, he would learn firsthand if there was any truth to that.

Near midday a large force of Goath appeared on the crest of the next hill. Cynaban looked over the terrain between them. "We'll charge due south, try to cut our way through them, then turn southeast and keep moving fast."

Cynaban raised his sword above his head, then sliced it to the south and charged. Morddon spurred Mortiss, slapped her flank with the flat of his sword, and with the rest of the legion charged silently behind Cynaban.

They dropped down into the depression between the two hills, then charged up toward their enemy without a single battle cry. The Goath were only a little surprised, and turned to face them as they met. The legion had the momentum of their charge and they cut into the Goath horde like a spear. The battle turned into a free-for-all, and Morddon's old killing reflexes came out easily. The Goath outnumbered them badly, so he let Mortiss have her rein and he cut about him with his sword while Morgin protected him with a deep shadow. But to stay and fight was a mistake, for the Goath hordes covering their flanks quickly joined the battle and the odds grew steadily against them. They lost half the legion in that first battle before they broke through.

To reach Gilguard's Ford they headed southeast, but the Goath constantly intervened, forced them directly south instead. Before dark they engaged large Goath forces three more times, and by nightfall they numbered less than six hundred. The night turned into a running battle of hide and seek and kill, and when dawn broke sharp and clear Morddon was part of a troop of about one hundred warriors. He prayed there were more still alive somewhere, perhaps in isolated groups now separated, each making its own way home.

They could have hoped for bad weather to cover their trail, but the gods did not favor them that day. About midday, while traversing a small stream, a company of jackal warriors ambushed them.

Fighting in the middle of the stream Morddon cut down one jackal, turned on another and cut him down, spun about and met another's sword with his own. Their swords locked together and for an instant they fought a still, silent battle of strength.

Then Morddon reached out with his free hand and gripped the jackal by the throat, picked the deformed beast out of his saddle and snapped its neck.

Something hit him between the shoulder blades and he went down into the stream. He stood up as Mortiss struggled to her feet, neighing and spluttering with her nostrils flared and her eyes wild. He struggled into her saddle, heard an angel cry, "This way, whiteface!" and he spurred her in that direction.

That night he and about thirty angels hid in a small clump of forest. They were done for; exhausted, no food for themselves or their horses. They posted a token guard and tried to get some rest.

The next morning it appeared they'd lost their pursuers, and they rode for a while unmolested. Before noon they came across an open glen where a large battle had recently been fought. The ground was littered with dead horses and dead Goath, and many of the horse's saddles bore the emblem of the First Legion. But of angels, there were only empty bundles of clothing, no corpses.

The glen was bordered on two sides by a small woodland, the air still and silent. The small group of angels with Morddon paused for some reason over the remains of their brethren. Perhaps there was some ceremony or remembrance they practiced, so Morddon, with his curiosity aroused, dismounted to examine one of the clumps of empty clothing.

He bent down and poked at it with the tip of his sword. There were several rents in the tunic—sword cuts he guessed—but no blood, no odor, nothing of the stench of death. He did find a small white feather caught in a fold of the cloth, and he wondered if perhaps the tales were true.

A shout broke the silence about him just as something stung him in the neck. He managed to get his sword out, then his knees weakened, the ground seemed to tilt crazily, he staggered a few steps and collapsed. His head swum as a terrible lethargy overcame him, and he lay there watching arrows arc above him to cut down his companions. His vision was clouded, but after each angel went down and stopped struggling, something fluttered up from the still corpse and rose to the heavens on snow-white wings.

He tried to move but his arms and legs had gone numb, with his mind in no better shape. The ground shook with the rumble of a large company of horses riding nearby, and then a troop of jackal warriors rode into his field of view. They dispersed quickly to check the fate of his comrades. One group evidently discovered an angel still alive. Morddon saw the glint of a sword raised in the sunlight, then again he had the impression some sort of white bird rose from the corpse into the sky.

The captain of the jackal troop rode directly to Morddon with several of his warriors at his side. They circled him warily on horseback with their swords drawn, as if they feared him greatly, then cautiously dismounted and approached him. One of them nudged him with a sword, then he heard one behind him bark, "He's been well stung. The dart is still in his neck."

They relaxed and the captain sheathed his sword, leaned down and looked into Morddon's eyes. "Good," he barked. "He still lives. Her majesty would have had our heads if we'd killed him. Tie him up good, and keep any and all steel away from him."

They bound Morddon's hands and legs with heavy ropes, and though it took a dozen of them to lift him, they threw him over the back of a horse and tied him there like a sack of grain. They rode to the northwest for three days, and in late afternoon entered a sprawling encampment with large pavilions staked in the center.

Their arrival started a chorus of barking and yipping from hundreds of jackal warriors and their camp followers. They dumped Morddon on the ground. The paralyzing drug had worn off, though his arms were numb because of the way they'd been bound. They untied him and staked him out on the ground in the middle of the camp with his arms and legs spread. Then the jackal captain told an aid, "Tell Her Majesty he's ready."

The aid rushed away, and moments later a silence descended on the camp as the jackal hordes parted for Her Revered Majesty, Magwa, the jackal queen. She stood over him as deformed and unnatural as any of her warriors.

Magwa had always coveted human mortality, and for her services the Dark Lord had rewarded her with the ability to stand erect on her hind legs, though like her warriors the stance seemed unnatural and uncomfortable. She was small, and had a tendency to waddle when she walked, and at first Morddon thought her overly fat. But the robes she wore were parted down the front to the waist, and as she came closer he saw two rows of teats swollen with milk, riding on top of a bulging, protruding belly.

Her lips curled back into a smile and she leaned down, brought her muzzle close enough for him to smell her dog breath. "Well now, whiteface sword maker!" she barked. "We've waited a long time for this meeting, you and me. Though you were quite a bit younger the last time we met."

Lying on his back in a relatively comfortable position, Morddon felt the circulation returning to his arms and legs. Magwa leaned even closer to him, her muzzle only inches from his face. "Tell me, whiteface. How well do you remember Binth and Eisla after these many centuries?"

Several of the warriors about her started yipping with laughter. "I remember them well, whiteface, and I would wager I remember them the way you last saw them, their faces twisted with pain, the skin flayed from their bodies—"

At that moment Morddon snapped his head forward and head-butted her in the soft tissues of her muzzle. She jumped back and yowled as tears came to her eyes. Several of her warriors jumped on Morddon instantly, started kicking him brutally. Then one produced a large club, and Morddon saw it for an instant silhouetted against the blue sky; it came down, crashed into his ribs painfully. He cried out, saw the club rise and swing down again. This time he found it impossible to cry out, though the pain sent him close to unconsciousness.

"Stop!" Magwa barked. "Stop! I command it."

The kicking ended quickly, though one warrior hesitated for an instant and kicked Morddon in the ribs one last time. "Stop!" she barked again. "You can kill him after he tells me where he hid the second blade."

She looked scornfully at Morddon. "You will tell me where you've hidden the second blade, won't you, whiteface?"

Morddon shook his head, tried to speak but the effort brought too much pain to his chest. He guessed he had some broken ribs on one side, and all he could do was force the words out in a grimace. "I don't know what you're talking about."

"Don't pretend ignorance. We all know you forged two blades, not just the one. And the Dark God is impatient to possess both."

Morddon pulled at his bonds, found that to be a painful mistake. "I've forged not a single blade, bitch, let alone two."

Magwa dropped to all fours, squatted and urinated on Morddon's head. "You'll tell us the truth eventually," she said confidently. Then she stood again and turned to her warriors. "Tonight we celebrate," she yowled. "For tomorrow the blade maker goes back to his master."

She turned to the captain of the troop that had captured Morddon. "And for you, I have a reward." Again she dropped to all fours. She parted her robes to expose her hind quarters, with her swollen belly and teats nearly dragging on the ground. The jackal captain knew immediately what to do. He mounted her then and there, with the entire camp looking on, yowling and cheering.

The festivities continued well into the night. The celebration consisted of a lot of drinking and public fornicating, and the bitch-queen's appetite for her warriors appeared insatiable. She took them one after another in the middle of the camp, and Morddon wondered if she actually intended to screw every warrior present. They also continued the insult Magwa had begun. Whenever any of the warriors or camp followers needed relief, they stopped by Morddon and urinated on him, and by the time the celebration came to an end he lay in a large puddle of mud.

As the festivities died down and the camp grew quiet Morddon experimented with his bonds. His hands and legs were tied to wooden stakes hammered deep into the earth. But the urine had softened the ground around them, though the loosest of the four stakes was on his right side, where his broken ribs flared painfully whenever he worked at it. He tried pulling at the other stakes instead, but they were too well secured so he had no choice.

He worked at it for hours. He pulled at the rope that bound his wrist until he could bear the pain no longer, then he rested while the agony receded, and then he tried again.

He knew he was making progress when his efforts produced a slurping, sucking sound from the stake in the muddy ground, but still it refused to yield. Then he felt it give way, and in an agony of motion it slid from the ground.

With one hand and both legs still tied down he was forced to roll onto his good side in a strangely awkward position, but soon he had the other hand free, and then quickly both legs. For a moment he considered going after Magwa, sneaking into her tent and strangling her in her sleep. But his ribs were too badly damaged and he knew he'd fail. So with Morgin's shadows protecting him, he crawled into the forest and disappeared into the last hours of the night.

24

Gilguard's Last Stand

MORGIN AWOKE TO a heavy hand shaking him violently.

"Come on, ya dirt lovin' fool," Bakart swore at him. "Wake up."

Morgin pushed at the seaman, threw his legs off the edge of his bunk and sat up groggily. Still well before dawn, only a dim splash of rays from a lantern in Bakart's hand lit the cabin. "What's wrong?" Morgin asked.

"Penda armsmen. All over the dock. They've surrounded this ship, probably going to search her."

As Morgin climbed out of his bunk Bakart made sure his companions were awake. Morgin grabbed his breeches and boots, but Bakart hissed, "Don't put on the boots. You're going to have to swim for it."

Morgin and his companions hurriedly dressed as Bakart said, "The dockside's thick with 'em. But port side's wide open. You go over the side real quiet, swim down the port a couple of docks and climb ashore there. Hope they don't spot you. You can swim, can't you?"

"Sure," Morgin said. "I'm a good swimmer." He looked at his companions. "Can the rest of you swim?"

France, pulling one leg into his breeches, shook his head. "You go without us. You're the one they're looking for. If you're not with us then we're not guilty of anything. And it'll confuse them some if they find us without you. Toblekan ain't big. Make your way out the north side of town and we'll meet you on the road to Drapolis."

Morgin wrapped his boots and a fresh blouse in a tight bundle, then rolled them in his cloak and tied his sword to that. Up on deck he was thankful for the darkness of the wee hours of the morning. On the dock a Penda lieutenant, with a large group of armsmen behind him, stood facing Darma, who stood on the gangplank, speaking and gesturing angrily. Bakart whispered, "The captain'll put up a bit of argument, but then he'll give in. Anything else would look funny."

Bakart looked across the deck, bent into a low crouch and hissed, "Keep yer head down." He crouched and half crawled, half ran to a group of sailors clustered at the seaward side of the ship, all watching the argument proceed on the dock.

Morgin had lost his shadowmagic, but he still knew how to use natural shadows with almost unnatural proficiency. He followed Bakart with ease, and hidden within the group of sailors Bakart showed Morgin a rope ladder attached to the gunwale of the ship. Morgin looked over the side, saw only the first few rungs of the ladder as it disappeared into the darkness below. He couldn't see the water, though he heard it lapping softly against the side of the ship. "Try to slip easily into the water," Bakart warned him. "Don't splash around. Swim quietly down a few docks then try to find some way ashore there."

Morgin stuck his arm through the loop of rope holding his bundle together and tossed it over his shoulder, then he climbed quietly over the gunwale and stuck his foot in the first rung of the ladder. Bakart grabbed his arm and stopped him for a moment. "One more thing, wizard. Captain says don't ever ask for passage on the *Far Wind* again. We don't like having the Wind Daughter as a passenger."

"The Wind Daughter?" Morgin asked. "What are you talking about?"

"The witch of Simpa, wizard. We all know she controls the winds near Simpa."

Bakart released his arm and Morgin started down the ladder, recalling AnneRhianne's parting words. *At long last I am free.* Without even trying he had freed the daughter of the wind, and he realized more than ever he had no control over the events of his life.

In the dark he had to work his way down by searching about for each rung with his toes, and it seemed to take an eternity. He heard the sound of many pairs of heavy boots running across the deck above him. He saw slashes of light from several lanterns cutting into the darkness above him, and he wasn't sure how much farther he had to go to reach the water. All it would take would be one Penda armsman with enough curiosity to hold his lantern out over the side of the ship and look down.

Morgin kept moving, but feeling his way rung by rung he couldn't move any faster. The side of the ship had a definite curve to it, and as he got farther down it slanted away from the ladder and left him hanging in open space, and then, as he was searching for the next rung, his toes touched the icy water.

He lowered himself into it quickly, the chill forcing his breath in and out in shallow gulps. He stayed close to the ship, sliding along its barnacle coated planks, taking advantage of the curve of its side to hide him from any eyes above. He reached the ship's stern just as the beams from several lanterns shot downward to the water. He froze, held his breath, watched the beams scan back and forth for a few moments. They were thorough, but the curve of the ship's hull saved him. Then the beams of light moved on and the darkness returned with a blacker stillness.

He waited for a while to be sure they'd finished searching, then he edged his way around the rudder to the dock side. On the dock above him two lantern-carrying Pendas paced back and forth. The one nearest him seemed bored and indifferent to the whole situation. Morgin watched him pace back and forth a few times, waited for the right moment, then pushed away from the ship toward the pilings of the dock.

Underneath the dock he made better time, but his muscles ached from the chill of the water. He found a ladder up the side of an empty dock and coaxed his tired, cold muscles to pull him upward, climbing up onto its surface. He was not stupid enough to stop and rest as he dearly wanted. He ran in a crouch down the length of the dock, found a shallow, blind alley between two warehouses and stepped into it to get dressed.

The alley contained only refuse and litter, and in the darkness of the night its shadows were black and deep. He struggled to get into his soaking wet tunic. It clung to his skin, pulled and tugged and fought him all the way. His boots were in no better shape, and his cloak draped over his shoulders like a wet blanket. He knew he must escape the city before dawn.

He heard shouting in the street, so he stepped into one of the alley's darker shadows, pulled the hood of his dark cloak tightly about his face and froze.

Two Penda armsmen appeared in the mouth of the alley, swords drawn. "Think he's in here?" one of them asked, squinting in an effort to see into the shadows. Luckily, neither of them carried a lantern.

His companion stepped past him into the alley a few paces. "If he is he smells like horse shit."

"Yah. Ain't nothing here but garbage and shit."

The two turned and walked out of the alley. Morgin hadn't realized he'd been holding his breath, and he exhaled slowly.

He edged his way to the mouth of the alley, stayed hidden in a shadow and looked up and down the dimly lit street. The Pendas were sweeping the town and had moved past his hiding place, so he stepped out of the alley and walked casually in the opposite direction.

Morgin made his way out the east end of Toblekan without incident, circled cautiously around the outskirts of the town toward the north. The road to Drapolis ran parallel to the coast, and he had to move cautiously, duck behind a tree or into a clump of bushes if he spotted anyone approaching. He circled around any farm or holding that appeared occupied, and the sun was rising by the time he found the road. So he hiked a good distance off it, crawled into some bushes for concealment, curled his cloak tightly about him, and settled in to wait out the pursuit, maybe get a few miserable hours of sleep.

••••

As Morddon escaped into the forest surrounding Magwa's camp he immediately sensed something else lurking in the forest, beings with the strong scent of the nether-life about them. They paced him on all sides as he stumbled through the darkness. When he stepped into a small clearing he faced a wall of golden-yellow eyes, and he heard the steady rhythm of their breathing. The timbre of it told him these were not small animals. He turned back, only to find they'd closed in behind him. He was trapped.

Then an animal the size of a horse sauntered forward on four powerful legs. It approached to within arm's length, extended its muzzle and sniffed at him, and when it opened its mouth he saw teeth that glowed in the darkness, large, massive canines that could rip out a man's throat with a single snap. "Mortal," it growled at him, and he realized then he stood before a hellhound. "You must take a message to your king."

The hound spoke in a deep rumble. "Tell him the Dane cannot ignore their debt to the Fallen One, and so we cannot battle against him or his new master. But in honor we cannot side with them either, and so until we are released from that debt, we must remain neutral."

"I will tell him," Morddon said. He still could see only the golden-yellow eyes and the rows of glowing teeth. "But I must also tell him who sends this message."

Several of the beasts around him growled low and angry, and Morddon realized too late he'd breached some etiquette of the hellhounds. "There is power in a name," the beast growled, and in that instant Morgin knew he stood before WolfDane, the hellhound king, though how such knowledge came to him he could not guess.

"I will carry the message, Your Majesty," Morddon said, and he bowed as one should before a king.

The hellhound king growled angrily, a deep rumble in its throat. His subjects eyed Morddon for a moment, then one by one each pair of eyes winked out and disappeared. The last to leave was WolfDane himself, and Morddon marveled that such monstrous beasts could move so silently through the forest.

He dearly hoped he'd escaped without detection from Magwa's camp. Only a few hours remained before dawn touched the sky, and with his broken ribs sending stabs of pain through his chest, his progress through the forest slowed to a stagger. He needed every minute of the remaining darkness to distance him from the pursuit that would follow.

There could be no doubt they were tracking him, so he took evasive action, stopped following game trails and cut through the brush itself. But that slowed his progress even further, and too often obstacles that might have been merely difficult had become impossible with his damaged chest, while whoever tracked him was getting closer with each league. Finally, shortly before dawn, he could go no further without rest, so he chose to stop and face his enemy squarely. He searched out a small knoll where they could come at him from only one direction, then found a long branch to use as a fighting staff. It had a slight curve to it, and was a bit too light, but would have to do.

Morddon waited, wished he had his sword, wished he had good ribs so he could fight properly and take more of his enemy with him. And then just as dawn broke he saw the first of his enemies, probably their best tracker out in front of the horde. The light was still too dim and the distance too great to see more than a vague shadow moving through the forest, but like all jackal warriors it was not large, and often it dropped to all fours as it skirted a short distance of difficult terrain.

It moved furtively, hiding behind a tree for a few seconds, then scurrying through shadows to another tree. Foolishly, it appeared to be carrying a hot spark of a torch, and it flashed it about above its head in a way that defeated any attempt to conceal its presence. But the way it moved, scuttling through cover quickly, then freezing in place for a few seconds before moving on, it touched one of Morgin's memories. He was on the verge of recognition when the smell hit Morddon's nose, vile and disgusting and unfamiliar to Morddon, but all too familiar to Morgin, as familiar as the spark dancing about above the little being's head. "Rat?" Morddon called. "Laelith?"

Rat scuttled over a rocky outcrop, stopped to swat at the faerie as if she were an insect making a nuisance of herself, then, dragging something metallic behind him, he hopped and limped and stumbled toward Morddon. "I brought your sword, whiteface," he said.

He couldn't lift the heavy sword, but dragged it by the hilt, scraping the blade across the ground. Morddon bent without thought, took the hilt and lifted the sword easily. Again the stench hit Morddon's nose. "You stink."

"So do you," Rat said. Laelith dove toward him as if to reprimand him for speaking so to his master, but he disappeared behind a curtain of netherlife and she missed. She followed just as quickly, leaving Morddon alone again, with only Morgin's thoughts as company.

He stumbled through the forest for two days while Magwa and her warriors hunted him, but Morgin's shadows made it easy to elude them. His right side hurt too much to hunt or gather any real food. He ate what few berries he happened to stumble across, but that was hardly sufficient. He grew weaker, and his side stiffened with each step. At least he managed to find a gentle stream where he washed the stench of Magwa's warriors from his body. If only he could wash them from his soul.

Late in the afternoon of the third day he stopped to rest for a short while. He guessed he was about three days by horse from Gilguard's Ford; on foot at least twice that, and with his injuries at least twice that again. But then the sound of a jaymakaw startled him. He'd seen several jaymakaw's about fluttering through the air, and no one but a Benesh'ere warrior would have noticed the subtle difference between the cry Morddon had just heard and that of a true jaymakaw. But the difference was there because the cry had been purposefully altered by the throat of a Benesh'ere warrior. And the difference was a question: *Is there danger?*

Morddon tilted his head back wearily and returned the call. *No immediate danger. I need help.*

Some minutes later a Benesh'ere warrior, whom Morddon recognized as one of Gilguard's scouts, stepped into view some distance away, and approached Morddon warily. Morddon couldn't remember the man's name.

"You're the madman, aren't you?" the man asked.

Morddon scowled and shook his head. "I'm told often enough that I'm a madman. But any man who stands here in this forest today is a madman, so I welcome your company."

The scout laughed quietly. "I'm Sarker. We've been looking for you. How badly are you hurt? Can you ride?"

"Some broken ribs. And if you'll bind them properly I can probably ride, though not if we have to ride hard over rough terrain. But I don't have a horse."

Sarker threw back his head, cupped his hands to his mouth, called out like the jay-makaw again, *It's safe.* To Morddon he said, "We've got your horse for you. Found her wandering on your track just after we picked up your trail."

"Why've you been looking for me?" Morddon asked.

Sarker's eyes darkened. "Cynaban told us of Metadan's treachery."

"Then Cynaban's alive?"

Sarker shook his head. "Only for a short while. Only long enough to tell the tale, then he died of his wounds, and maybe a broken heart too. Gilguard has all the scouts out looking for survivors, but so far we've only found a few, and they're not in very good shape."

A short time later two more Benesh'ere scouts joined them, leading their own horses and Mortiss. The other two were Takit and Bendaw. Takit was an old fellow with many years behind him in the wars, and Bendaw a young boy probably still learning the ways of a scout. Old Takit bound Morddon's ribs carefully, decided to completely immobilize his right arm and bound it to his chest. Morddon managed to climb into Mortiss's saddle without help, though with his sword arm useless he would be truly helpless if it came to a fight. He ate in the saddle, the first meal he'd had in days: journeycake and jerky and water.

They were two days on horse to the ford, not three as he'd guessed. Several times they came across the site of the last stand of some remnant of the First Legion, and always they found only carnage. But early in the morning of the second day they discovered the spoor of a large jackal army in front of them. They quickened their pace, but the hard riding sent stabs of pain through Morddon's chest so they decided to split up. Sarker stayed with Morddon while old Takit and young Bendaw rode ahead as fast as they could.

That afternoon, as Sarker and Morddon warily approached the ford, they heard the cry of a Benesh'ere jaymakaw again, and they joined up with the other two in a small thicket of trees. "What is it?" Sarker asked them.

Old Takit rubbed the stubble on his chin. "You'll have to see for yourself."

Sarker tied his horse with those of Takit and Bendaw, and Morddon let Mortiss go free. The four of them left the thicket on foot, and crept silently to the top of a nearby hill that commanded a view of the ford. Magwa's army lay spread out before them, her pavilions pitched in its center.

"She's come in force," Takit whispered. "She's got us outnumbered twelve to one. Cynaban told us it's you they want, madman. She probably figures you're down there with Gilguard."

Quite a number of bodies littered the ground between the two armies. There had already been several skirmishes, and Gilguard and his company of warriors had retreated to high ground just up the river from the ford. But now surrounded, there was no further retreat to be had.

Bendaw grimaced. "We have to do something."

Takit shook his head. "There's nothing we can do but go down there and die with them. And someone has to bring the tale of Metadan's treachery back to Kathbey-anne."

"We could rush back," Bendaw said. "Get help."

Sarker shook his head. "We're at least three days from the nearest garrison, and this is going to be over before nightfall." He pointed. "Look there."

Magwa's jackals were drawing up into ranks for a charge. They were seasoned, disciplined troops, even if their leader was a wanton bitch. It took them some minutes to assemble behind one of Magwa's generals. They moved up the river, split into three columns so they could hit the Benesh'ere from three sides.

Gilguard had chosen a good place to make his last stand. Just up from the ford the river cut through a narrow defile that channeled the water into a churning roar of white water rapids. The river then spilled downhill for a good stretch where the water lost its power as it widened and leveled off into the shallow ford.

Gilguard and his men had taken the high ground near the rapids and put their backs to the river, preventing the jackals from hitting them on all four sides. Morgin remembered the place well, for by his time the river had cut down through the earth, widening the defile and turning it into the deep gorge where Morgin had placed his magical dam and later released it to wash away a company of Kulls. But that was in the distant future.

The jackal battle trumpets startled Morddon out of his thoughts, the first wave of jackals charged up the hill, and the Benesh'ere cut them down with arrows. With high ground, and the range of the Benesh'ere longbow, the jackals' bows were outranged, and they quickly retreated. The second wave of jackals fared no better, but during the third the rain of arrows diminished to a trickle, then stopped altogether. Gilguard's warriors had used their last arrows.

The fourth wave actually reached the outer perimeter before the whitefaces repelled them with pike and sword and war ax. The fifth hesitated at the perimeter for what seemed an interminably long time, and then the perimeter began to shrink. Gilguard's warriors were even more disciplined than the jackals. They held their perimeter, let it shrink rather than be broken, forced the jackals to take them one by one.

Bendaw turned away from the battle. "I can't watch," he sobbed, and he buried his face in his hands.

Takit turned away with him, threw an arm over the boy's shoulders. "Neither can I, lad."

Morddon watched, and so did Sarker. They had to watch. They had to know the end, even if they didn't want to, for someone must carry the tale of Gilguard's last stand back to Kathbeyanne.

The sixth wave pressed the perimeter back even farther, and then the seventh broke it, and washed over it like an angry storm. The Benesh'ere asked for no quarter, would have taken no quarter had it been offered. And when the battle was done the jackal army wandered about through the carnage as if disappointed, as if there had not been enough death to go around.

Morgin now knew why the ford on the river Ulbb bore the name Gilguard's Ford.

25

The Fortress at Tharsk

A NEIGH, A harrumph of a splutter, and a wet muzzle nuzzling his cheek, Morgin opened his eyes to find Mortiss standing over him. She spluttered again derisively, chiding him for laziness.

"Yah, yah," Morgin grumbled, climbing slowly to his feet. "*You* didn't have to sleep on the ground in a wet cloak." His clothing had dried for the most part, with white patches of salt crust that irritated his skin. The sun on his shoulders was a warm relief after the cold night he'd spent. He dug into his saddlebags and changed into fresh clothing. He'd have to find a stream to wash the salt out of the rest. The question remained: was he ahead or behind his friends on the road to Drapolis?

At that thought Mortiss snorted.

Morgin shook his head. "I guess I'm supposed to just let you have the reins and you'll find them?"

She snorted again.

He didn't completely release her reins, but he kept them loose and let her choose her own way. She started north up the road, moving at an easy walk. Morgin tried to remain vigilant, listening for the sound of pounding hooves on the road, anything that might give him warning of a Penda patrol. But after a few leagues of riding he learned he didn't need to. Without warning Mortiss stopped, her head turned slightly and her ears perked up. Then she turned off the road and followed a game trail into the forest. She found a thicket of heavy brush and stopped behind it. Some instinct told Morgin to dismount and he did so. Once out of the saddle he and Mortiss were both well hidden behind the thicket.

He waited in silence for a good thirty heartbeats before he too heard the faint rumble, a sound like distant thunder just barely audible above the sounds of the forest. But it grew steadily until there was no mistaking it for anything but the sound of hoof beats on the road. Because of the undergrowth of the forest he only caught a glimpse of the Penda armsmen as they shot past, and he estimated something like two twelves, riding hard.

Mortiss proved to be invaluable, for twice more that day, with some instinct or sense beyond Morgin's capabilities, she sensed approaching armsmen long before Morgin would have.

As nightfall approached she pulled off the road a fourth time, and again followed a game trail, but this time she took them much deeper into the forest. When Morgin heard muffled voices up ahead, he dismounted and moved forward carefully on foot.

He saw the dim glow of a small fire, a line of horses staked out and a couple of pack donkeys. He moved forward cautiously, but then someone pressed the point of a blade to his back and Cort said, "I could have gutted you easily."

Morgin turned to face her and she gave him a big cheesy grin.

After a quick reunion and a few pats on the back, Morgin sat down with his companions around the fire, thankful for its warmth.

France said, "We was doing a little planning, lad. Where to go next."

"And?" Morgin asked.

Tulellcoe leaned forward and stirred the coals of the fire. "We don't have much choice. We can't go south, and we don't dare go near Penda or Tosk. So that leaves only Tharsk."

France added, "When we offloaded our horses from the *Far Wind* we couldn't find hide nor hair of that nag of yers. Then you and she was spotted on the north end of town, then out on the road. So most of the rumors have you well out of Toblekan and a good ways up the road to Drapolis. That took the pressure off us, so we provisioned up." He nodded toward the two donkeys. "And that's why we cut off the road. We're going inland for a while, then cut north for Tharsk."

Morgin glanced over at Mortiss. France had said ". . . *you* and she was spotted . . ." Again, Morgin wondered who, or what, she might be. He was still thinking on that when he curled up in his blanket that night.

••••

Because of Morddon's ribs Sarker set an easy pace as they rode east from Gilguard's Ford. And with the location of the ford as a point of reference, Morgin could now correlate the countryside of Morddon's time with that of his own.

The wondrous city of Kathbeyanne lay deep in what would someday be the Great Munjarro Waste: in Morgin's time an endless sea of sand and blistering sun, but in Morddon's a land of gently rolling hills and productive farmlands. The Goath had for many years occupied the land west of the Worshipers where, in the future, there would be Elhiyne and Tosk and Penda and Anistigh and Aud and Toblekan and Drapolis. But in recent years the Goath had crossed the mountains through the pass at Methula far to the north, and were now encroaching down through Yestmark, where Morddon had spent most of his life fighting.

After two days the four scouts reached a large outpost on what would someday be the Plains of Quam. There, they met two more of Gilguard's scouts. The garrison had already been informed of Metadan's treachery, and of the disastrous events that followed. The garrison commander had sent a messenger on a fresh mount to carry the word to Kathbeyanne. Morddon and the Benesh'ere scouts paused only long enough to replenish their provisions, then started for the fabled city.

The vast metropolis waited for them in silence, like an old warrior who'd lost the will to fight. Hundreds of people lined the streets to watch the six of them ride toward the palace, and like the city they watched in silent mourning as the survivors of the massacre passed slowly by.

When they entered the parade ground outside the palace all activity came to a sudden halt. Word must have traveled ahead of them, for the eleven companies of Benesh'ere warriors that remained had gathered outside the Benesh'ere barracks. Their white faced comrades greeted Sarker and the other scouts sadly, while Morddon turned toward the barracks of the First Legion.

The building was utterly empty, and silent as a morgue. Morddon's cot remained undisturbed among those of the dead angels. He was tired beyond imagining, and lay down upon it in his clothes. And as he drifted off to sleep it occurred to him he was the only survivor of the First Legion.

••••

Morgin and his companions cut northeast through light forest. They set a steady but undemanding pace to put some distance between them and Toblekan, and late on the third day they reached a large lake into which the river Ella spilled. They were now only about a day north of Castle Penda, so they turned north and headed up the banks of the Ella, continuing until darkness made further travel impossible.

Cort found a small clearing, and as they set up camp Tulellcoe said, "I think we're far enough from Penda to set a fire and have a warm meal."

France added, "Aye, we're all tired of journeycake and jerky. And hopefully we can take it a bit easier after this."

With a warm meal in his gut Morgin had no trouble finding sleep that night.

He awoke to a bright, clear sky, with rays of sunlight slanting through early morning mists. Tulellcoe had a fire going and Morgin's stomach growled at the smell of hot porridge. Cort stood on the Ella's bank, washing her face and hands with a wet towel, while the rest remained in their blankets, though a groan or two, and the sound of smacking lips, told Morgin they were beginning to stir.

Morgin walked down to the water near Cort. "Good morning," he said as he bent and splashed water on his face. His ribs complained and he winced, more a memory of Morddon's beating at the hands of the jackals.

"Good morning," Cort said cheerily. "Did you hurt yourself?"

He shrugged. "In a dream."

"Your dreams are dangerous. I think I like my dreams just the way they are. Nothing real about them."

"Don't be too sure," Morgin scowled. "I've learned a lot about reality, recently, and I've found it is rarely what it seems."

France wandered down from the camp, rubbing the back of his neck and blinking his eyes blearily. "Me old bones hate sleepin' on the ground," he said as he sat down near them.

Morgin walked back up to the camp, retrieved his salt-encrusted clothing and returned to the riverbank. He washed the salt out of his clothes, and after Cort left he stripped down and took a quick dip in the chill water to wash the salt from his body. After that Cort trimmed his hair and beard, and they were on their way by midmorning.

Three days later, as they approached a busy ford on the River of the Serpent well upstream from Tosk and Drapolis, they split up. A merchant caravan had camped near the ford. France and Val rode down to the ford while Tulellcoe, Cort and Morgin held back. Cort changed into a riding dress to again assume the identity of Tulellcoe's wife. And when the three of them finally did venture down to the ford, France and Val were engaged in a little dicing with some of the caravan guards. The three of them pretended the two men were strangers, passed them by without acknowledgment, crossed the ford and headed up the road to Tharsk. An hour later France and Val caught up with them.

"Drapolis is alive with rumors," France said. "They've heard Morgin slipped through BlakeDown's fingers and they think he's either in Drapolis or on his way there now. And fat old PaulStaff has his armsmen making regular sweeps through the city."

Val added, "At least they got the news Morgin was separated from us in Toblekan, so they're looking for a lone rider."

The fortress at Tharsk commanded Methula, was garrisoned by Decouix regulars, and from all reports had never been taken. If they could sneak, or lie, their way past Tharsk, then the pass would let them into northern Yestmark, where they could lay low for a while.

It felt like a trap, heading for Tharsk, but hunted on all sides, they had no choice. At least they no longer needed to ride hard with a posse on their heels. They were well provisioned, and they even managed to supplement their supplies quite regularly by fishing in the river. A day and a half from Methula they came upon another lake. They took the opportunity to camp on its shore, and with no threat behind them they decided to stay through the following day and rest the animals.

That night Morgin stayed up long after the others retired. All that day he'd been trying to recall the events of his dreams. He fed the fire carefully, maintaining it as a pit of
glowing embers rather than a flickering blaze, for within the glow of the coals he found
a sort of peace, and he managed to lose himself there for long periods of thought.

He now understood that someone—perhaps more like something—manipulated
his actions regularly, and he understood too that the manipulation was not something
recently begun, but something that had gone on throughout his life. And he was beginning to suspect it had begun long before his life, and the only difference now was his
awareness of the manipulation.

Val stirred in the darkness behind him, rose from his blanket and slipped into the
bushes to relieve himself. When he returned he hesitated at his blanket, then turned to
Morgin and the fire, stepped into the glow cast by the embers and sat down. "Can't
sleep, eh?" the twoname asked in a soft whisper.

Morgin shrugged. "Not tired."

They lapsed into silence for a while. Val clearly appreciated the silent heat of the
embers and he left Morgin to his thoughts. But a question occurred to Morgin. "What
came after the wind?"

"Huh?" Val grunted.

Morgin recited what he could remember. "He's going to restore the House of the
Thane, free the hand of the thief, free the daughter of the wind . . . What comes next?"

"Oh! That."

"Yes. That."

Val considered him. "I take it you've freed the daughter of the wind?"

"That's none of your damn business. Just remind me what comes next."

Val shrugged off Morgin's short temper. "He'll free the Dane King."

Morgin nodded. "Thanks." He considered Val's words, remembered that WolfDane
had referred to the hellhounds collectively as the Dane. He thought about that while he
and the twoname sat in silence. After a time Val stood without speaking and returned to
his blanket. Morgin watched the embers of the fire for a time, but they'd lost their
meaning, so he too went to his blanket.

••••

Two days later they passed above the tree line about half a day from Tharsk. They
camped that night near a small mountain stream and made plans for how they'd approach the fortress. Val and Tulellcoe would pose as merchants, again Cort would be
Tulellcoe's wife, and Morgin and France their hired swordsmen.

After breakfast the next morning Cort set about changing Morgin's appearance. She
cast a simple spell to put streaks of gray in his hair and beard, which added about twenty

years to his apparent age, then she disappeared into the forest for a while and reappeared in an expensive looking dress. Tulellcoe and Val also put on a better cut of
clothing than their dusty trail garb, and they set out for Tharsk.

The air had a decided chill that high in the mountains. Tulellcoe told them that in
another month or so the passes would see the first heavy snows of the new season.
Morgin tried to picture the barren, rocky slopes blanketed in white, and thought it might
be a bleak existence for any animals that lived so high.

As midday approached, the trail narrowed abruptly, becoming wide enough to pass
only a single cart or small wagon, but not two abreast. The slope above them was a
steep incline of broken rock that would be difficult to climb if one were of such a mind,
and the slope below would be a long and fatal tumble for any traveler or horse careless
enough to lose footing. And then, as they rounded a sharp bend in the trail, Tharsk
towered above them, a black monolith carved from the solid granite of the mountain
face.

The trail too had been chipped out of the solid stone of the mountain. Travelers
tended to hug the uphill side away from the precipitous edge, and centuries of traffic,
the constant wear of boots and hooves and cartwheels, had worn the rock there into a
smooth and almost glassy surface, while the edge nearest the drop remained rough and
uneven. The trail skirted the base of the fortress wall for a good distance, then entered
the black shadow at the mouth of a tunnel that was part of the fortress itself. Any traveler wishing to cross the Worshipers through the Pass at Methula must either pass into
that tunnel, or climb the sheer rock of the fortress wall above it. Those in the fortress
would have an easy time dislodging such a fool.

Almost as soon as the tunnel came into sight a Kull voice challenged the small party
of travelers. "Halt," it said from Tharsk's ramparts. "Identify yourselves."

They stopped in the trail, aware that they were easy meat for an arrow or a tossed
stone. Tulellcoe rode forward a few paces, and though no one was visible above, he
looked up to the battlements at the top of the fortress wall. "I am Vergis ye Tosk. And
with me is my associate Seurrak ye Penda, my wife Thenda, and our bodyguard of two
swordsmen."

"And the names of the swordsmen?"

Tulellcoe turned in his saddle, looked back at the rest of them. "He with the mous-
tache," he said, indicating France, "is named Rindal. And he with the gray-streaked
beard is named Morddon."

"State your business."

"Lord Seurrak and I are merchants. We are traveling to Yestmark, and then on to
Durin, to renegotiate certain contracts that pertain to our business."

They waited silently through a long pause that drew out until the horses began to
splutter and fidget and stomp their hooves. Morgin grew uneasy; the air was cold

enough to see his breath, and the sky had begun to gray over with low clouds that clung to the mountaintops. If the Kulls delayed them too long a storm might catch them on the narrow mountain trail.

The voice from above spoke. "Enter the tunnel."

France turned quickly to Morgin. "We're bodyguards, so I'll ride to the fore with Lord Vergis. You take up the rear."

France spurred his horse forward while Morgin waited for the others to pass him, then he nudged Mortiss into a walk behind them. Tulellcoe and France paused at the entrance to the tunnel, for now that they were close enough they saw a heavy iron portcullis blocking the way just within the shadows. The portcullis rose with a clanking rattle of chains dragging across stone. Behind it, another portcullis began to rise slowly, and behind that another, and another, and another. One by one they all rose into the ceiling of the tunnel, but not until the noise died completely and silence descended did Tulellcoe nudge his horse forward.

They all followed slowly into the tunnel mouth, and in front of Morgin each disappeared as they entered the darkness of the shadow there. Morgin's vision cleared only a little as Mortiss stepped into the darkness, but above him he sensed the murder holes between each portcullis, while behind them the portcullises descended with the same noisy scrape of steel chains on stone.

They were guided by light from the tunnel's mouth, but the tunnel followed the curve of the mountain, and by the time they reached the center of the tunnel there was just barely enough illumination for them to see that the portcullises leading out the other side were still down. Tulellcoe waited for a few moments, then called out, "You have no cause to detain us."

Again they waited through a long silence, and then to one side a straight crack of light appeared in the rock of the tunnel wall, and with the grind of old hinges echoing in the close air, a massive stone portal slowly opened beside them. A splash of light coming from the fortress proper silhouetted France and Val and Tulellcoe. France looked at Tulellcoe with an unspoken question on his face; Tulellcoe shrugged an answer, then nudged his horse forward through the portal.

The portal let them into an empty courtyard open to the sky, circular, surrounded on all sides by high walls cut from the same black rock as the tunnel, with another portcullis on the opposite side of the courtyard. Battlements topped walls around them, manned by about two twelves of Kulls, all armed with crossbows. If the Kulls chose to kill them, there would be no escape.

One of the Kulls growled down at them, "Dismount."

Tulellcoe turned about in his saddle and nodded at the rest of them. Morgin swung his leg over Mortiss's rump and down to the ground, let go of her reins and stepped up beside Cort's mount. Ordinarily she would take insult at his offer of assistance, but

Morgin must act the hired swordsman, and she a lady who would expect such treatment. As he put his hands around her waist and helped her down out of the saddle he felt mischievous, and he whispered jokingly in her ear, "You shouldn't be so helpless, woman."

"Thank you, Morddon," she said politely, then her eyes narrowed and she whispered closely, "You'll pay for that remark, you young whelp."

Morgin stepped away from her, nodded just as politely, "You're welcome, Your Ladyship."

"Welcome to Tharsk!" someone called out, not the voice of a Kull. They all turned toward the portcullis just as it began to rise. Just beyond the grate stood four people. An older man and woman waited patiently, the woman with her hand resting in the crook of the man's arm, both wearing expensive garments. Beside them stood a younger man about Morgin's age who looked upon them with a sharp, distrusting stare. And behind them stood a Kull officer.

The older man spoke as he stepped beneath the rising portcullis, "Welcome, Lord Vergis and Lady Thenda, and of course Lord Seurrak. I am Oubba ye Rastanna. This is my wife Carri, and my son Tarkiss."

Carri let go of his arm, curtsied politely. "It's wonderful to see you Lady Thenda. You can't realize how lonely it gets up here. I have absolutely no one to talk to but my mistresses and these men."

Just as Tulellcoe had not introduced his hired men, Oubba did not introduce the Kull standing behind him. But while Oubba and his wife and son greeted Tulellcoe and Val and Cort, Morgin looked the Kull over carefully. He'd never faced one like this before, not without steel between them. And then the halfman happened to look his way and their eyes met. Expressionless inhumanity had etched itself into that face, and Morgin struggled to keep his hatred from showing in his own eyes.

The Kull grinned knowingly, and the sword at Morgin's side vibrated, something only he could feel. He rested his hand on the hilt, tried to make the action look casual and unthreatening, found it had loosened itself in the sheath ever so slightly. He pushed down on it, suppressed it, held it in check.

"You don't like Kulls, eh swordsman?"

Morgin turned to the voice, found Tarkiss standing beside him. He shrugged. "I suppose they have their uses."

Tarkiss frowned unpleasantly. "As do hired swordsmen." He looked Morgin up and down suspiciously, then he looked at France. "Only two of you seems a rather light bodyguard in these mountains."

Morgin shrugged. "I'm told Methula is well patrolled. And in any case, I'm just a hired swordsman. It's up to my master to decide how large a bodyguard he can afford. And he and his colleague are quite capable swordsmen themselves."

Tarkiss glared and his eyes narrowed. "But with this rogue wizard about . . ."

"Is he about?" France interrupted. "I'd heard he was rotting in BlakeDown's dungeon."

Everything about Tarkiss spoke of suspicion and distrust. He looked at Cort. "Why bring the woman?"

Morgin shook his head, spoke the lie they'd prepared. "I think she has family in Yestmark. And I think it's them who have the real money."

Carri and Cort had been exchanging niceties, but Carri's voice caught Morgin's attention. "Oh surely you'll stay the night."

None of them had thought to prepare for that kind of invitation. "I'd love to," Cort improvised, "but we have our schedule."

"Yes," Tulellcoe added. "They're expecting us in Yestmark in three days."

Oubba shook his head. "I won't hear of it. It's midafternoon now and a storm is brewing." He looked up at the gray sky. No one could deny it had darkened visibly in only the last hour. "You'll be caught on the trail, and these mountain storms are quite unpleasant."

No ordinary merchant would refuse such an offer. Tulellcoe nodded. "That's most gracious of you. But we'll have to insist on an early start in the morning."

Carri took Cort's arm. "Wonderful," she said as she led her away. "You'll have to bring me up to date on all the latest news. We hear nothing up here."

Oubba and Tulellcoe and Val followed the two women through the portcullis. Tarkiss and the Kull remained behind while Tarkiss instructed several servants to take care of their horses and donkeys. He turned France and Morgin over to the Kull, saying, "Brakke here will show you where you can sleep." Then he left them with the Kull.

The Kull led them through the portcullis into the fortress proper. They crossed a large terrace, walked up a flight of stairs cut into the rock of the mountain like everything else, then down a long hallway to a large room where many of the servants slept. "Throw your blankets where you choose," the Kull said. He left them to fend for themselves.

26

The Last SteelMaster

MORDDON AWOKE WITH the tip of a sword beneath his chin. He looked down the length of the steel blade to the hand gripping its hilt, and beyond that the face of Ellowyn stared at him angrily. "It's a lie," she said. "It's all a lie. Admit it. You're lying about him."

Morddon ignored the sword, sat up on his cot. He and Ellowyn were alone in the empty barracks of the First Legion. By the angle of the sunlight slanting through the windows he guessed he'd slept only an hour or two since returning to the city. "It's no lie. And in any case I'm not the one who's speaking it."

Ellowyn's eyes pinched with anger, and she clearly struggled to hold back tears. Her shoulders slumped and she lowered the sword slowly, let it hang by her side with the tip touching the floor. Her eyes emptied of all emotion and her face went blank. She stared forward at nothing for a long while before speaking again, and then her voice came out in an almost monotonic drone. "You are commanded to attend the Shahotma at his court."

"When?"

"Now, mortal."

Morddon took a few minutes to splash water on his face and run a coarse comb through his long black hair; it hung well past his shoulders now. He buckled on his sword, then followed Ellowyn as she led him out of the barracks. They walked across the parade ground to the palace in silence.

Ellowyn led him through a small side entrance, and Morddon followed her through the corridors of the palace to Aethon's court. Seeing Ellowyn in the lead, the guards at the entrance of the hall stepped aside without orders and let them pass. Morddon slowed his pace at the sight of all the people there, and he came to a complete stop as they all turned to look at him.

Morddon had come to a halt just within the entrance of an enormous hall of legendary proportions, while at the far end, on a dais raised above all else by twelve stone steps, Aethon sat in majesty on his throne. But this was not a king in a ceremonial court; today would be a working court and Aethon had dressed plainly.

Humans and angels and Benesh'ere and not a few of the Thane filled the court, though they pressed to both sides making a wide aisle up the middle to the throne. AnneRhianne stood beside Aethon on the dais, while next to her stood a Benesh'ere warrior named Jander. He had been one of Gilguard's senior lieutenants, and was probably now the new warmaster. The griffins TarnThane and SheelThane stood to one side of the dais and towered above the crowd about them. In front of the dais, but to one side, stood the Benesh'ere scouts Sarker and old Takit and young Bendaw, and the two scouts they'd joined up with at the outpost.

Ellowyn had already crossed half the distance to Aethon, but when she realized Morddon was not following she stopped and turned about. "Come forward," she said flatly.

Morddon advanced slowly, warily. He could not take his eyes off the young king, for Morgin easily recognized him as an older version of the boy in his dreams, just as he recognized AnneRhianne as the physical embodiment of both Erithnae, the god-queen, and Rhianne. It seemed to take an eternity to cross the distance between them. Ellowyn stopped at the base of the dais and Morddon stopped one pace behind her. Ellowyn curtsied carefully, then mounted the twelve steps to stand on the side of Aethon's throne opposite AnneRhianne. Morddon dropped to one knee and bowed his head.

"Arise," Aethon said. "Stand before me."

Morddon did so, and when he looked up the young king stared at him for a long moment, as if he might recognize Morgin hidden within him. The moment passed and Aethon said, "I wonder at you, warrior. You're a common soldier, a mercenary they tell me, without noble blood, without property or money. You're no warmaster, no general, no great leader of armies, and yet time and again I hear your name from the lips of those who are great and noble and wise. Why is that, whiteface?"

On anyone else's lips that would have been an insult, but Morddon knew Aethon meant no offense. He shook his head. "I don't know."

"Ah, my friend, but I think you do."

SheelThane said, "Yes, Your Majesty, he does know. But he doesn't know that he knows."

Morddon thought of WolfDane. "I have a message for you from WolfDane."

Aethon's eyebrows shot up. "How did you come to bear a message from the Dane?"

"They were waiting for me when I escaped from Magwa."

"The bitch-queen, eh?" Aethon frowned. "Of course she would be part of this story. These scouts here"—Aethon pointed at Sarker, Takit, Bendaw and the other two—"have told me what Cynaban told them of Metadan's treason. Metadan told Cynaban you belonged to the Dark Lord. That you escaped from the Dark Lord and he wants you back. That it's only you the jackals want, and the rest of the First Legion could have gone free." Aethon's frown deepened. "Why are you more important than the foremost of the legions of angels? Again, I must ask, why you, my common Benesh'ere warrior?"

"Obviously," TarnThane said, "he is not that common."

Aethon nodded, though his eyes never left Morddon. "Tell me everything. Leave nothing out."

Morddon told them of the confrontation with the jackal lieutenant in which Metadan all but admitted to treason. And he told them of the running battle that followed, and of his capture by the jackals. He passed over his questioning by Magwa, but Aethon sensed he was holding back and quizzed him meticulously, learning she had called him sword maker. As he spoke of her references to Binth and Eisla, the Benesh'ere in the hall grew visibly angry, but Aethon silenced them with a look. He made Morddon repeat Magwa's words exactly as she'd spoken them, and as he told of her description of the skin flayed from his parents' bodies, tears came again to his eyes. He told them of her claim that he had forged two blades, and the Dark Lord wanted the second blade back, and she wanted to know where he'd hidden it. He finished by saying, "But I've never forged a blade."

Aethon said only, "Continue your story."

To their horror Morddon described Magwa's debauchery and his subsequent escape. "The hellhounds were waiting for me, I think. WolfDane wanted me to tell you the Dane cannot ignore their debt to the Fallen One, and so they cannot battle against him or his new master. But he also said that in honor they cannot side with them either, and so until they are released from that debt, they must remain neutral."

Aethon thought for a moment, then asked, "And how did you know it was WolfDane himself? He would never speak his own name to you, nor would he allow you to speak it in his presence."

Morgin had known the hellhound's name without doubt, but Morddon shrugged and lied, "I guessed."

Aethon considered that and shook his head. Then he looked out over the crowd of onlookers and called out, "Perrik. Come forward."

A nobleman stepped out of the crowd, quite an ordinary nobleman, though something familiar about him struck a chord in Morgin's memory. He approached the dais, stopped next to Morddon and bowed.

Aethon held out a hand. "Give me your sword."

The nobleman walked carefully up the twelve steps, drew his sword and handed it to the king, then, bowing, he backed down the steps and returned to Morddon's side.

Aethon looked at the blade carefully, then he looked at Morddon. "You once said this blade was flawed. Well is it?"

Morddon looked at the nobleman and recognition came. His memory dredged up the incident on the day he'd first come to the city. The nobleman had been practicing his sword skills in the parade ground at the foot of the palace wall, and Morgin had recognized the blade's flaw from the ring of its steel. Morddon withdrew and allowed Morgin to control the tall, lithe body of the Benesh'ere, and he could not lie about steel. "Aye, the blade is flawed."

The nobleman shook his head angrily. "Impossible. The blade was made from the best Benesh'ere steel by the finest armorer in Kathbeyanne."

Aethon's eyes never left Morddon. "Do you still say this blade is flawed?"

Morgin shrugged Morddon's shoulders. "What does it matter?"

"It matters a great deal," Aethon snapped angrily, and for a long moment his eyes bored into Morgin's soul as if he would force him to speak. But then he nodded, leaned forward and tapped the tip of the blade on the topmost step of the stone dais. The ring of the steel filled the silence between them, and while everyone heard the simple ring of a sword blade tapped against stone, for Morgin it reverberated within his heart, reached to the depths of his soul, and he cringed visibly.

Aethon again tapped the blade on the stone of the step, but harder this time, and the wrongness of the sound rang out immediately in Morgin's heart. Aethon began tapping the blade repeatedly on the stone, harder and harder with each stroke, and the steel spoke to Morgin, cried out to him to end its torment. He closed his eyes, reached up and pressed his hands over his ears, but that did not silence the horror suffocating him.

Aethon now slapped the blade against the step with vigor, and with trembling hands Morgin threw his head back and pleaded, "Stop! I beg you, stop tormenting me."

But Aethon persisted almost maliciously and Morgin lost all control. He threw a shadow over Morddon, sprinted up the steps and ripped the blade from Aethon's grasp. At that, every guard in the hall drew his sword, and trusted bowmen in the galleries above nocked arrows. An instant later Morddon would have died, but Aethon jumped up and shouted, "Hold! I command you to hold."

Everyone froze as Morgin held the sword up away from the stone and let the ringing die, and as it did so, peace and calm washed over him. The pain stopped and once again he could breathe. He let his shoulders relax, and he held the sword out before his eyes and examined it carefully. He could almost see the flaw, though not a vision of the eyes, rather a sense of wrongness at a certain point in the steel. Something within him made him reach out with his free hand, and he snapped the nail of his middle finger against the blade. It rang out softly, a single, pure note. But within that note the flaw stood out like a cancer on a beautiful woman's face.

Morgin took hold of that note with his power, amplified it, brought it and the memories that came with it forth: his captivity in the Dark God's hands, the forced labor over the steel, the quest for the perfect blade. He remembered the days at the forges, days that turned into years, then into centuries. Such memories stunned both he and Morddon as he recalled the deception of the second blade, the laughter and scorn of a god looking upon a mere mortal without pity. The memories came back to him as the intensity of the note, fed by his power, grew to a glorious crescendo of pain. Waves of heat flooded outward from the blade; the crowd in the hall cringed away from him and even Aethon stepped back. And just when Morgin thought he could take no more, the blade melted at the point of the flaw and the note ended abruptly.

He dropped to his knees on the dais in Morddon's body, holding a sword with the tip and half its length melted away. Behind him he heard AnneRhianne mutter, "Steel-Master."

He turned to face her, shook his head. "I am the son of Eisla, but no SteelMaster, merely a pipist and a warrior, and a traitor beyond even Metadan's treason."

He dropped the half-melted blade, drew his own sword, and from his kneeling crouch he looked up at Aethon. The last of his strength had departed, and he could speak no louder than a whisper. "Beayaegoath wanted the perfect blade, but he dare not forge it himself, for rightly he feared the self-forged blade."

Aethon nodded sadly. "Speak on SteelMaster."

Morgin lowered his eyes, recalled the centuries of torment and hatred. "He took me from Indwallin and made a slave of me in a place where time has no meaning, and he forced me to forge a blade no other blade could stand against. But I was smart and cunning, or so I thought. I forged a sister to the blade he desired, but in her I placed a flaw so minute not even I can detect it now. And I intended to leave him with the flawed blade, and bring the perfect blade to you."

Morgin threw his head back, closed his eyes and cried out to the long-vanished gods, "I was such a fool." He looked Aethon in the eyes. "He knew of my deception all along, and he let me proceed. But when the time came, I could not tell the blades apart, and in the confusion that followed I escaped with only one. And now the Dark Lord has one blade, and I the other. But neither of us knows which is which, so he waits, for if he attacks, and his is the flawed blade, then he will die."

Morgin held the blade out to Aethon. "Here, it belongs in your hands."

Aethon hesitated. "But what if this is the flawed one?"

Morgin shrugged Morddon's shoulders. "Then we'll all perish with you. But you have no choice."

••••

Tulellcoe came to a decision after lying awake through many long hours of the night. He rolled off the bed quietly, tried not to disturb Cort sleeping next to him. As he pulled on his clothes he guessed dawn would be upon them in another hour, though in these high northern climates the sky began to lighten so much earlier he couldn't be certain until the sun actually appeared above the mountain peaks.

He did not buckle on his sword, but took only his dagger and slipped out of the room. In the hall beyond he paused long enough to test the dagger's edge. He'd carefully sharpened the blade to give Morgin a good, clean, fast death. Tulellcoe felt he owed Morgin at least that much.

Now, to find out where the Rastannas had quartered him.

••••

Morgin awoke slowly; lay for a time in that half world between dream and reality, then at some point crossed the threshold that brought him to full awareness. He tucked his blanket tightly about his shoulders. With only a single brazier in the middle of the room emitting a wan and colorless warmth, he was more dependent upon the heat of the dozen or so servants sleeping nearby.

He lay there with his eyes closed and he thought of Morddon and Kathbeyanne, and of course he thought of the sword. He rolled over on the thin straw mattress the Rastannas had given him, wrapped his hand around its sheath and wondered at its purpose in being. He had a sudden urge to see it in the light of day, and he sensed that dawn was close at hand, so he quietly rose from the mattress and pulled on his breeches and boots, slipped on his blouse and a leather jerkin, then over that a hip length leather coat, and finally over that his hooded cloak. He buckled on his sword, then slipped out into the hall to look for an exit.

He found a narrow stairway that led upward. The fortress appeared to be cut into the mountain on many levels, with many such stairways where, in any other place, there would be a short stretch of hallway. At the top he stepped into the scullery, found two young maids hard at work quietly pulling out pots and pans for the morning meal. Beyond the scullery he found the kitchen, and the chief cook ordering her charges around with much hand waving and harsh whispers. And beyond that another hallway and another flight of stairs. He was just beginning to think he was hopelessly trapped within the fortress when ahead he saw the dim light of the gray morning sun, and he found a passage that opened onto a small balcony. Tharsk was a rambling jumble of rooms and halls and buildings cut into the slope of the mountainside above the fortress wall, and the balcony he'd found was one of many such that protruded from the middle of it all.

Dawn had arrived gray and cloudy, with a sprinkle of snowflakes drifting down on the morning air. It didn't seem cold enough for snow, and the flakes melted as soon as they touched the ground. He guessed the trail would be muddy in spots.

Beyond the kitchen servants, it appeared he was the only person up and about, so he carefully wrapped his fingers around the hilt of his sword. Anxiously, slowly, he slid it from the sheath with the all too familiar sound of the scrape of steel against steel. He lifted the blade, held it up before his eyes and studied the runes that time had made almost invisible. They were cut into the steel in symbols unknown to him, unknown to anyone of his time, and with his free hand he reached out and touched them, touched the steel into which they'd been cut.

As they had done before, the voices came again, a great throng of them, though this time they were far in the distance and did not overwhelm him with their cries of sorrow and pain. And then one voice stood out among the rest; at first only faintly, but it grew in strength and intensity until he recognized it: his own voice. He looked more closely at the runes on the blade, and like his voice they now stood out more clearly. If he could just understand them he might control the power within the blade.

The runes took on a life of their own, shifted and swayed before his eyes like snakes in a pit. Their shape changed and he recognized the meaning of one of the symbols, and then another. He remembered the heat of the forge, and the ring of the hammer, the calluses on his tired hands and the exhaustion of the endless centuries. But just when he was on the threshold of understanding, the thread of his thoughts snapped like the string of a bow over-strained, and he staggered back to the reality of the small balcony in the cold, gray morning.

He pulled his free hand away from the steel, looked at it carefully and saw his reflection mirrored in and about the runes. "I know you now," he said softly. "I know you now as I should have known you all along. And though I cannot name you, someday I will. And when I do I will control you, and no longer will you feed at my soul like a pride of lions at the kill."

27

The Queen Emerges

RHIANNE AWOKE, CONSCIOUS that something had entered her room. It emitted a fetid, disgusting smell, as if one of the dogs had gotten loose and left a mess somewhere. But this was worse, many smells all mingled together, some stale, some fresh, but all bad.

She kept her wits about her, closed her eyes and concentrated. It took some doing, but she located the spark of netherlife slowly coalescing near the foot of her bed. She still had time so she got out of bed quickly, arranged her pillows and blankets so in the dark one might think she still lay there, then threw on a robe, and without lighting a lamp she sat down in a chair to wait for the visitation to become complete.

She'd left her window open that night, and through it the moon lit the room nicely with colorless gray shadows. As she looked on a small figure appeared before her, about waist high and covered by filthy, disgusting rags. It moved carefully, and with much stealth it climbed a bedpost and perched atop the footboard of her bed. It arched its neck, looking fearfully at the pile of blankets and pillows, and at that moment Rhianne understood she had nothing to fear from the small child. "I'm over here, Rat."

The little being nearly jumped out of its skin. It flew into the air, landed on the floor and rolled into a shadow behind her dresser. It remained silent for a moment, then she heard it sniffing the air, and she saw its nose extended ever so slightly beyond the edge of the dresser. It hissed, "Is that you, Your Majesty?" Its voice was an unpleasant snarl.

"Why do you call me that?" she asked. "I'm no queen."

"It is you!" he said, and with that it sprang out of the shadow and scurried the short distance to her. It reached out, took one of her hands and began pulling frantically. "Come with me. Please! He's in danger. You have to help."

Rhianne stood, somewhat repulsed by the touch of the filthy little child. "Who's in danger?"

"The dreamer," the child said frantically. "He who lives in shadows and knows not the name of the beast."

"Morgin?" she gasped. "How is he in danger?"

The child stopped and looked her in the face. "The one with madness hovering so near his soul."

"Tulellcoe!" Rhianne hissed. With that realization she pulled free of the child's hand. "Do not touch me again," she said, "or you will endanger us both." Then she called forth her magic, concentrated her power within her soul, and readied herself for whatever was to come. She looked down at the little being. "Lead on, Rat."

Rat sniffed at her as if he smelled the magic about her, then he turned toward the spot from which he had emerged near the foot of her bed, and there disappeared. She followed slowly, stepped carefully into the same spot, felt an odd sensation as if something was pulling at her soul. But nothing really happened, for the child could only be a guide, and to walk the *netherworld* she must do so with her own power, her own strength and knowledge.

Carefully she sought out a thin tendril of her power, connected it like a lifeline to that single point on the Mortal Plane at the foot of her bed. Then trailing the tenuous connection behind her, she stepped beyond life wondering if she would ever return.

She saw Morgin from a great distance. He stood on a balcony of a structure that had been cut from the solid, black rock of a mountainside, and though she had never seen it herself, she knew it must be Tharsk. He stood in the light of dawn, holding his sword up before his face and speaking to it as if it had ears of its own.

Oddly enough she could see through the rock if she chose, and far down in the bowels of Tharsk she spied Tulellcoe carrying a naked dagger in his hand and searching for Morgin. He stopped first in a room where several people slept, mostly servants, among them France. Tulellcoe searched quietly through a pile of empty blankets there, then stepped outside the room and closed his eyes momentarily. In her present state Rhianne saw the tendrils of his magic as they sought out Morgin on the balcony. Tulellcoe started toward him, determination written on his face, and purpose in his stride.

Rhianne stood beside Morgin on the balcony. She shouted a warning at him, but he ignored her as if she weren't there, and she had to remember she really wasn't. Tulellcoe appeared behind him, hesitated for a moment in the shadows before stepping out onto the balcony. Rhianne tried to take Morgin's shoulders in her hands and shake him, but her hands passed through him for she had brought no substance with her into the netherlife.

Tulellcoe stepped out into the gray light of morning, stood now within striking distance of Morgin's back. Rhianne had one last thing to try, a desperate, chancy venture. She stepped toward Morgin, stepped through him, made her spirit occupy the same space as his body, tried to merge with his soul, knowing if she succeeded she might very well lose herself for eternity in the netherlife.

••••

As Morgin looked at the blade in his hand and leaned against the cold stone of the balcony rail, something made him think of Rhianne. Then that same something made him think of Tulellcoe, and he knew in that moment his uncle had approached behind him. He also sensed the sorrow in Tulellcoe's heart, and knew somehow that he'd been crying. It all came together then, and he knew Tulellcoe's purpose.

Morgin lowered the sword, though he did not turn about to face Tulellcoe, and he spoke softly, "Have you come to kill me now, uncle?"

The strain in Tulellcoe's voice cut through the air like a knife. "Could I succeed if I tried?"

"No," Morgin answered flatly.

"The sword, eh?"

Morgin shook his head. "No. I doubt the sword would stop you. It comes only when it chooses, and rarely to my benefit. It is I who would stop you."

Morgin waited for a reply but none came. He waited for that faint sound he'd hear as Tulellcoe made his move, but that too did not come. He turned slowly around and found that Tulellcoe had gone and he now stood alone on the balcony.

Some instinct made him look up and to one side, and on a balcony high above he saw Tarkiss looking down at him, and he wondered how much the young Rastanna lord had seen.

••••

The whip-crack sound of a hand striking her face. The blow was brutal and hard, but Rhianne felt nothing.

"Snap out of it, girl."

Rhianne opened her eyes to find that she stood at the foot of her bed looking down at her own body where it had lain all along. Olivia and AnnaRail leaned over the bed, AnnaRail holding her body up while Olivia's hand arced high over her head, then flashed down to strike her face again with that same whip-crack sound. Her head rocked to one side, but again she felt nothing.

Blue-white bolts of lightning struck outward from her body, but the two older witches deflected it with their own power. AnnaRail looked up. "She's in the room somewhere. I can sense her."

Olivia turned, and her eyes slowly scanned the room, then settled knowingly on Rhianne standing at the foot of the bed. "You're lost, child," the old witch said impatiently. "Stop fighting us."

Rhianne wanted to give in to the old woman, but something kept pulling her back, something she could not resist.

The old witch turned back to her corporeal body lying on the bed and struck her again, and this time she felt just the faintest bit of stinging on her cheek. Olivia slapped her again, and again, and each time she felt more and more of the pain. Then she lost her balance and fell. But the fall didn't stop when she reached the floor, and she fell on and on and on. She started screaming and thrashing about. Her face burned and her head hurt, and someone held her arms pinned, preventing her from striking out. And then all of her strength left her, she could fight no longer and she collapsed.

"She'll be all right now," Olivia said.

Rhianne's face burned with a slow fire, but her head rested against her pillow. She felt AnnaRail's fingers gently brush the tangled locks of her hair out of her eyes, then AnnaRail's lips on her cheek for a short, soft kiss. "Sleep now, child. You did a very brave thing."

"Yes," Olivia barked. "And a very powerful thing too. This girl has far more potential than we'd originally thought, but I doubt that cow of a mother of hers trained her properly. We'll have to correct that."

Rhianne wanted to open her eyes and argue with the old woman about the unkind reference to her mother, but she was too weak to do even that, and sleep took her long before the two older witches left the room.

••••

Since they were nothing more than hired help, Morgin and France were served a simple breakfast of boiled wheat and honey and steaming hot tea. Warm and nutritious, it took the chill out of their bones, so they ate their fill and enjoyed it thoroughly. Half way through the meal they received word from Tulellcoe to eat quickly and prepare to leave as soon as possible. They bolted the last of their food, then asked a servant to show them to the stables.

Maintaining the pretense of hired help, they saddled their companions' horses as well as their own, then loaded the two donkeys and checked their harness. When they led the animals out into the open air of the castle yard Morgin noticed the snowfall had thickened. The flakes were large, wet, and heavy, and as they tumbled out of the sky they melted almost as soon as they touched the hood and shoulders of Morgin's cloak. A miserable day for travel, the going on the mountain trail would be difficult, though anything would be better than another night spent among so many Kulls.

While Morgin and France waited for the rest they busied themselves making last minute adjustments to the donkey packs and checking the harnesses of their horses. But while doing so Morgin caught the sound of the hooves of a large number of horses clopping on the stone ground of the fortress. He and France looked up at the same instant; their eyes met and silently they agreed to take no action, to wait and see.

The sound grew louder, and Tarkiss emerged from the fortress interior leading his horse and about four twelves of Kulls and their horses. Mortiss and the other horses grew skittish as Kulls and their mounts surrounded them, and Morgin and France struggled for some moments to calm them.

Tarkiss gave the reins of his horse to a groom and approached Morgin with a rather satisfied swagger. "Well now, Tosk," he said arrogantly. "It seems the presence of so many Kulls bothers you."

Morgin shrugged. "The presence of so many Kulls bothers most men, yer lordship."

Tarkiss nodded. "Aye. That they do. But not those of us who command them, eh?"

"And beggin' yer pardon, yer lordship," Morgin added, "but I ain't no Tosk."

"Ah yes!" Tarkiss said. "You're not a clansman." He looked Morgin up and down suspiciously. "I forgot that for a moment, didn't I?"

"And thankful I am I ain't no clansman," Morgin said enthusiastically. "No disrespect meant, yer lordship, but that magical stuff would likely be too much of a burden fer a common swordsman like meself."

Tarkiss still seemed doubtful. "But then if the burden was yours to bear, you wouldn't be that common, would you, swordsman?"

Morgin wrinkled his brow, pretended to consider the thought carefully as if such an idea were a bit beyond the simple mental capacity of a hired swordsman, and he was pleased to see a momentary flash of doubt in Tarkiss's eyes. But then Oubba and Carri diverted Tarkiss's attention as they escorted Tulellcoe, Val and Cort from the fortress proper.

Morgin didn't like the look on Tulellcoe's face, an impression that Tulellcoe confirmed a moment later when he tried to conceal his unease with an unhappy smile. He looked about at the Kulls that surrounded them and announced, "Lord Oubba has kindly provided an escort to guide us down out of the mountains."

Oubba happily added, "There are no bandit hordes in these mountains large enough to challenge four twelves of my Kulls. You should all be quite safe."

Tulellcoe and Val must have done everything possible to turn down Oubba's aid. But Tarkiss was suspicious of something, and all they could do now was hope his suspicions were a result of his general nature, and not based on something specific.

With the Rastannas and their Kulls and servants all present, he had no opportunity to discuss the matter with any of his companions. Standing in the wet snowfall they took swift leave of Oubba and Carri, and following Tarkiss they all led their horses out through the portcullis, the small courtyard beyond, and into the tunnel. The series of portcullises at the end of the tunnel were already up, and so their passage back out onto the mountain trail was much quicker than their entry the day before.

Like the trail from the west, that going east had also been cut from the solid rock of the mountain. But that lasted for less than a league, and they quickly found that the wet snow had turned the hard ground of the trail into a slippery and often treacherous track of ankle deep mud. The conditions often forced them to lead their horses on foot rather than risk a fatal fall should the animal lose its footing. The going was slow through the entire day.

The weather was not the worst of it, not when compared to Tarkiss and his Kulls. Morgin was too often forced to ride surrounded by Kulls with the nearest of his companions several positions up or down the trail. Each time they stopped for a short rest he found it impossible to speak to any of his friends in private. He watched carefully through that afternoon, and noted his companions were kept isolated in the same way. Only Tulellcoe, under the pretense that Cort was his wife, and by constant and tenacious insistence, managed to stay close to her.

The snow let up late that afternoon, but the trail was still a mess and their mood didn't improve. During the last hour of the day Morgin noticed his sword had slid a few inches out of its sheath. He pressed it back into place, assumed it had simply been jogged loose sometime during the day.

As they set camp that evening an incident occurred that bode ill for them all. Morgin had been out gathering firewood and was returning with his arms full when one of the Kulls stepped in his way and stopped him. The halfman growled, "I'll take that."

Morgin hesitated, ready to do almost anything to avoid a fight. "Beggin' yer forgiveness," he said politely to the Kull, "but this wood belongs to me master and it ain't mine to give. You'll have to ask him if you want some."

"And who's your master?" the halfman demanded.

Morgin spoke carefully. "You know who my master is. His lordship there. Lord Vergis."

The Kull let him go, but Tarkiss stood nearby, and had watched the exchange suspiciously. His lips stretched slowly into a broad, satisfied grin, and Morgin noticed that again his sword had come loose in its sheath.

That night he and France shared a makeshift lean-to. And as they crawled into their blankets Morgin whispered quietly, "They suspect something, don't they?"

"Aye, lad," France answered. "That they do. Let's do everything we can to travel together tomorrow, eh?"

Morgin nodded, a useless gesture in the dark. "Agreed," he said without further comment. He rolled over on top of his sword to sleep, not a very comfortable way to sleep, but at least the sword would go nowhere without him.

28

Pursuit

THE NEXT DAY broke clear and dry, though the air had cooled decidedly and small patches of ice now floated in puddles of water along the trail. A hard, frozen crust had formed on top of the mud; the hooves of their pack animals and horses no longer sank in so deeply and they made better time. By midday they were out of the rockiest and steepest parts of the pass, and moss, lichen and grasses bound the ground of the trail together. They grew hopeful they'd left the mud behind.

When they came across a small stream they stopped for a short rest and something to eat. Morgin sat down on a small boulder and chewed on some journeycake. He watched the Kulls eat in silence.

"Eh, lad." France nudged him out of his thoughts. Morgin looked up to find the swordsman standing over him with two water skins draped over his shoulders. "Let's go fill the water skins, eh?"

"Right." Morgin stood. France tossed him one of the skins, and the two of them walked upstream a short distance, found a stretch of calm water. They squatted down on their haunches and began filling the skins.

France looked about carefully, then looked at Morgin and spoke in a soft voice. "We have to break away from the Rastanna pup and his escort."

Morgin nodded. "I know. Even if he doesn't suspect something, I think he's looking for a fight."

"That's obvious, ain't it?"

Just then Morgin noticed three Kulls coming their way. The halfmen traipsed past them, found a spot just upstream, unlaced their breeches and began urinating in the stream. Morgin and France quickly lifted their skins out of the water. "Bloody scum!" France said.

They moved farther upstream, found another spot where they could finish filling their skins. "Tonight," France said, "just before dawn, we're going to try to sneak away. Tulellcoe and Cort are working on a spell to keep the halfmen asleep while we put some distance between us. And we—"

A commotion down in the camp interrupted the swordsman. They both heard Tulellcoe cry out, "Tarkiss, call off your dogs."

Morgin lifted the skin out of the water quickly, tapped the stopper in place and started back with France close on his heels. They arrived in time to find Cort helping Val up off the ground, a cut above his eye, and Tulellcoe facing Tarkiss angrily.

Tulellcoe stood a few finger spans taller than most men, and when angry, something in his eyes gave any man pause, even if backed by four twelves of Kulls. Tarkiss nodded arrogantly, trying to maintain his dignity, then turned toward the Kull lieutenant and barked, "Call off your men, Brakke."

The Kull barked half-intelligible orders at his halfmen and an uneasy peace settled on the camp.

"What happened?" Morgin demanded of Val.

The twoname shook his head. "One of those halfmen took affront at something."

Cort said, "For no reason at all, most likely."

Val shook his head carefully, looked around them at the Kulls now going about their own business. "No, they've got a reason. They're testing us."

Morgin asked, "Tarkiss?"

France answered him. "Aye. Tarkiss. They're operating under his order, that's for sure."

After that the five of them refused to be separated for the rest of the afternoon, though they rode in an uneasy silence. That night they also stayed close to one another, and as Morgin crawled into his blanket, France whispered, "Tulellcoe or Cort will wake us when their spell's ready."

Morgin got very little sleep, though he managed to doze fitfully. He feared he'd wake up in his dreams in Morddon's skin and spend months there before returning to this night. But his fears were unfounded, and though the night was long and restless, he still lay in his blanket in this world when Cort came for them. She wore breeches again with a sword strapped to her waist. "Get your gear together quickly," she whispered. "And be quiet about it, for the spell we've cast won't hold them in their sleep through any loud noises."

Morgin and France had unpacked only their blankets and slept under the open stars, so they were ready in moments. They found the other three rolling up the small tent they'd pitched to maintain the ruse that Cort was no twoname. "You two go on and saddle the horses," Tulellcoe whispered. "And pack up the donkeys."

Morgin followed France to the string of horses where they quickly separated out the five from their party and saddled them. They then packed one of the donkeys, and while they were at that Tulellcoe, Cort and Val arrived and began packing the other. By the time they were ready the sky had begun to lighten with the coming dawn, and there would soon be enough light to see their way easily.

Morgin took one last moment to check Mortiss's harness, and as he did so he glanced over his shoulder at the camp. In the distance the sleeping Kulls were dark lumps on the ground, with a thin morning mist swirling about them as if it would consume them. And in that silent moment, just before climbing into the saddle, he heard the scrape of a steel blade sliding slowly out of its sheath.

He ducked just as something heavy hit him from behind in the back. He went down, saw a Kull boot arcing toward his ribs, rolled to one side to avoid it, caught it, rolled and twisted, heard the halfman grunt painfully as he too went down. Blades clashed nearby, the frightened horses shuffled and whinnied and someone cried out. Then they were all over him, pinning him helplessly to the ground, and the fight ended.

They hustled him to his feet, twisted both his arms behind his back, held him that way as Tarkiss stepped out of the forest into the dawn light that now filled the camp, his teeth flashing in a nasty grin.

Tulellcoe lay on the ground clutching his side, and Morgin saw blood oozing between his fingers. Three Kulls had a struggling Cort pinned to the ground, practically sitting on top of her. Two Kulls supported Val much like Morgin, and like Morgin he grimaced each time the Kulls reminded him of his situation by twisting his arms a little tighter behind his back. France was nowhere to be seen.

"Well now," Tarkiss said arrogantly. "You were going to leave without saying goodbye. Now that's terribly impolite, don't you think?"

He looked about. "Where's the swordsman. He must have slipped away. Well he's of no matter. Without a horse we'll find him easily."

Cort stopped struggling as Tarkiss turned on Tulellcoe and leaned over the wounded man. "I'm a magician too, you know. And I'm not fool enough to let you cast such a simple spell upon me without a counter spell." Tarkiss emphasized the point by lifting his boot and kicking Tulellcoe in the ribs.

Cort began struggling again and Morgin shouted, "Leave him alone!"

Tarkiss turned toward Morgin, took two steps to stand facing him. The Kulls tightened their grip on Morgin's arms. "And why should a common, hired swordsman care so much about the fate of his employer?"

Tarkiss looked Morgin up and down and his eyes settled on Morgin's sword. "And you're still armed, I see. Well we can't have that." He reached out, gripped the hilt of Morgin's sword, pulled it from the sheath, and some instinct told Morgin this time it would come to life.

It flared in Tarkiss's hand, tore at their ears with the sound of its hatred, and with his eyes wide the young Rastanna lord back-stepped fearfully. The Kulls holding Val and Morgin looked at the sword flaring to life, and in that moment France appeared among them and cut down the two holding Morgin, then turned on those holding Val. He bellowed, "Get to the sword, lad, or we're all meat for butchering."

Morgin focused on the sword coming alive in Tarkiss's hands, the sword that would cut them all to pieces if he couldn't get to it and control it. He twisted past France, ignored the chaos about him and lunged at Tarkiss. The young Rastanna stood transfixed by the power in his grasp, power clearly growing well beyond his control. Morgin tore the sword from his grip, wrapped his fingers about it and immediately felt its power pounding at his soul. It had caught the scent of Tarkiss's blood and like a good hound it would not falter until it had claimed his life. It pulled Morgin toward him as he fought it, and though he cared nothing for Tarkiss, if the sword tasted just one drop of blood, there would be no stopping it.

Tarkiss staggered backward as the sword pulled Morgin toward him, until he backed into the trunk of a large tree and could go no further. The sword knew its prey was at hand and it fought even more against Morgin's efforts. But in that moment Morgin, for the first time in his life, felt just an instant of control, a small fraction of a second during which the sword was his to command. The instant ended quickly, and again the sword bucked and fought his grip. But with a cunning and malign intelligence it too had been aware of that moment, and remembering that instant it retreated, then departed completely. What Morgin held in his hands was a lifeless blade of steel with the point resting just beneath Tarkiss's chin.

Chaos reigned all about them, blades clashing, people crying out, the horses whinnying. One of the donkeys brayed and began bucking and kicking.

"Call off your dogs," Morgin snarled. "Call them off or I'll drop your head at their feet."

"Brakke!" Tarkiss shouted. "Stand down. Let them go."

It took some moments for the fighting to stop, and when it did a stillness descended upon them all. One of the donkeys was down, the victim of a misplaced sword stroke. There were two Kulls down, and Val clutched his sword arm against his side.

Morgin kept his sword at Tarkiss's throat as he barked out orders. "France, get our horses and the unhurt donkey. Cort, help my uncle into his saddle. Val, scatter the rest of the animals, but save one for Lord Tarkiss here."

They moved quickly while Morgin and Tarkiss stood like statues amidst the silently unhappy Kulls. Val set a spell to frighten the Kull horses, and they scattered into the forest bucking and kicking. And when Morgin's companions were mounted he walked Tarkiss out of the camp at sword point. They bound his hands behind his back, then helped him onto the bare back of the extra horse. And with Morgin leading his horse by the reins, they traveled for about a league before Morgin called them to a halt. "This is far enough," he said. He turned to Tarkiss. "You can climb off that horse, or I'll kick you off it."

"What are you going to do with me?"

"Nothing. You can walk back to your friends and try to find your horses."

Tarkiss stared at him for a long moment, then dismounted. "You're the Elhiyne, aren't you? The renegade wizard? The one they call the ShadowLord? Aren't you?"

Morgin ignored him. "Let's get out of here," he said to his friends, and he spurred Mortiss into a fast trot.

••••

After releasing Tarkiss they redistributed the remaining donkey's provisions among them, stuffing as much as they could in their own saddlebags, discarding what they couldn't. Then they set the donkey loose and rode hard for several leagues. They needed to put some distance between them and the pursuit that would soon follow. Tulellcoe's injury bothered Morgin more than any danger from behind, for his uncle's face lost more color with each stride of his horse, and Morgin saw an ever-widening red stain growing beneath the hand he kept constantly pressed against his side. When he leaned forward slightly, a prelude to doubling over in the saddle, Morgin realized he must be in great pain.

Morgin eased Mortiss up beside Tulellcoe's horse, leaned over and took the animal's reins, pulled the two horses to a halt. Cort too had been watching Tulellcoe, didn't appear surprised by Morgin's actions, though France and Val trotted a short distance up the road before they realized what had happened and came to a stop themselves. France shouted back, "What's wrong? We don't have time to stop."

At that moment Tulellcoe's eyes rolled back into his head and he started to fall. Morgin spurred Mortiss into a side step toward Tulellcoe's horse, and on the other side of him Cort did the same, pinning Tulellcoe's animal between them. Morgin threw out an arm and caught his uncle about the shoulders. "Keep his horse calm," he snapped at Cort.

They eased Tulellcoe out of the saddle, laid him down in some soft grass beside the road. Cort produced a small dagger, cut open his blouse near the wound, examined it carefully, shook her head and declared, "It's deep."

Tulellcoe opened his eyes, grimaced, forced words out between clenched teeth, "I know. A thrust, not a cut, though I think my ribs deflected it some."

"What can you do?" Morgin asked Cort.

Cort shook her head, looked about desperately. "With the proper spells I can do quite a bit. But my healing kit was on that injured donkey we left behind, and I also need time and that's just what we don't have."

"No we don't," France said. "Those Kulls will have a dozen horses rounded up within an hour, and they'll be hot on our trail."

Morgin pressed Cort. "You helped me once without preparation or spells, back at Gilguard's Ford."

She grimaced. "But I pay a heavy price for such wanton use of power." She looked at Tulellcoe who seemed unable to find a comfortable position. "Though I guess I have no choice. But then I'll be as much an invalid as he, though neither of us will be as bad as he is now."

Morgin demanded, "Will you both be able to ride?"

She nodded, her attention wholly on Tulellcoe. "Yes. We can ride."

Cort sat down beside Tulellcoe, took him in her arms and close her eyes. She sat that way for some time with her lips moving almost imperceptibly as she chanted spells that none of them could hear. After some minutes she opened her eyes and stood unsteadily. Her face was pale and drawn, her eyes shadowed and dark. Tulellcoe, however, was able to stand on his own, and while he did not look at all well, he looked much improved and the bleeding had stopped.

They rode without rest through the morning, and shortly after midday they left the forest behind, entering an open, grassy land of gently rolling hills. "This is Rastanna land," Val said. "Tarkiss will have no trouble getting fresh troops and mounts, so we'll have to stay well ahead of him."

"Shouldn't we turn south?" Morgin asked. "Try to make for Yestmark?"

Val scanned the horizon. "Eventually. But there's a large river between here and there that flows hard and fast coming down out of the mountains. It marks the northern border of Yestmark, and we'll find no fords or crossings until we get farther east. At least another two days of hard riding."

They continued east across a countryside dotted with small farms and hamlets, though they avoided any contact with the locals. Near midafternoon they came upon a wide valley squared off in neat little farms. They took to a small cart track that led down into it and spent the rest of the day crossing the valley floor. Near dusk, as they followed the same cart track up out of the valley, Morgin glanced back the way they'd come, and in the distance he saw Tarkiss with a dozen Kulls just entering the valley.

Cort seemed better, but Tulellcoe looked worse. The bleeding had started again so they stopped for a short rest, and again Cort applied her magic to Tulellcoe's wound. Once again, he improved while she withered.

They rode on through that night. To throw Tarkiss off their track they tried the unexpected and headed north for several leagues before again turning east. It worked, and shortly before dawn they stopped long enough to eat something and to sleep for a few hours. When they rode on the next day they were somewhat revived, though Tulellcoe still needed Cort's magic to stay in the saddle.

Through that entire day they saw no sign of Tarkiss so they slowed their pace. Tulellcoe grew steadily worse, and each time they stopped for Cort to apply her magic she withered even more, and Tulellcoe improved less.

They decided to find a place to stop and hide and rest for a day or two. They hoped to give Cort the opportunity to take proper care of Tulellcoe's wound. But without her healing kit she needed certain herbs in some quantity. "I've been keeping my eyes open as we ride, and most of them don't seem to grow wild in this countryside. We'll have to find a village large enough to have an open market. I can probably get what I need there. We can also get something to eat other than jerky and journeycake."

"I don't think you should ride into any village," Morgin told her. "Female twonames are much too uncommon. In fact, twonames in general are uncommon so Val is out of the question as well."

Morgin looked at France. "Looks like it's you and me, old friend."

Cort shook her head. "But you won't know what to look for."

"But I will," Morgin told her. "My mother taught me healing, though I certainly don't know the art as well as you, but I know the plants and herbs you'll need, and the other materials also."

"All right," Cort agreed reluctantly. She scanned the horizon. "A village the size we're looking for won't be in the middle of nowhere. It'll be where there's a fair amount of traffic. We'll have to stop cutting cross-country, and find a well-traveled road."

It didn't take them long to find a road that was more than a cart track. It forced them northeast for the rest of the day, cautiously cutting across open fields to avoid the smaller hamlets. Late in the day they found a village large enough to serve as the local market, but the day was too far gone and the market long since closed. They left the road, cut southeast across open country for a good distance, set up camp deep in one of the larger clumps of forest. That night they all got a full night's sleep, the first they'd had in several days.

29

The Swordsman Lost

AT DAWN THE next morning Morgin and France returned to the road at an easy trot. They knew they'd raise suspicion if they appeared to be in any kind of hurry, so when they were within sight of the village they reined their animals back to a walk.

From a distance the place was no more than a cluster of low-lying buildings and thatched mud-and-wattle huts sprawled on either side of the road. The morning was still and calm, with no clouds in the sky and the sun just barely above the horizon. There were columns of smoke rising from two buildings, swirling slowly up into the thin mist that hung on the morning air. As they entered the outskirts of the village Morgin heard the ring of a smith's hammer, and he sensed that the steel the smith worked was of poor quality.

The street that cut through the center of the village was deserted. In the middle of the village they paused in front of one of the few wooden buildings there, one of the two buildings producing a column of smoke. As they both dismounted France said, "This'll be the common room." He pointed at the other column of smoke rising from a building near the far end of the village. "That'll be the smith. The smith'll have more authority here, but we can get better gossip from the innkeeper."

France stepped between their two horses, looked conspiratorially up and down the street. Satisfied they weren't being observed, he lifted one of the rear hooves of his horse, and producing a small dagger he pried at the shoe for a moment, loosening it slightly. "You go in and see what you can learn from the innkeeper. I'll wander on down to the smith, get this loose shoe fixed, see if he likes to talk while he works."

Morgin stepped through the door of the inn into an empty common room that smelled of damp and mildew. There was a bar along the far wall, and a low, beamed ceiling that would have forced Morgin to crouch had he been any taller. The smells wafting from the kitchen made his stomach growl, and he thought breakfast would be a good excuse to strike up a conversation with the innkeeper.

Morgin crossed the room to the bar, rapped on it with his fist, called out, "Innkeeper. You've a hungry man out here."

The innkeeper appeared almost instantly, a short, round, little fellow, with puffy red cheeks wearing an apron that rode up high over his protruding belly, and wiping his hands in a towel. "What can I do fer ya, kind sir?"

Morgin smiled through his beard, which had grown quite scruffy. "Would the food I smell be fer yer guests, or is it private fare?"

The innkeeper looked at him carefully. "If you got the coin for it, it's yours. Fresh biscuits me wife is bakin' this instant, with butter and honey, and bacon fried up crisp and lean."

Morgin tossed a few coins on the counter. "Well I ain't a rich man, but it all smells too good fer me to pass up. And you wouldn't happen to have some hot tea to wash it all down with, would you?"

The innkeeper scooped up the coins. "We got a kettle startin' to boil this instant."

The innkeeper disappeared into the kitchen. Morgin found a table, sat down on a stool with his back to the wall where he could keep an eye on the kitchen door, the entrance to the inn, and the low stairway that led to the rooms upstairs. He didn't have long to wait; the innkeeper reappeared carrying a tray laden with food and steaming hot tea. As he transferred the contents to the table he asked, "Are you travelin' alone, sir?"

Morgin shook his head, smeared butter on one of the biscuits and thought guiltily of his friends waiting back in the small clump of forest. "No. I'm travelin' with a friend. He's down havin' the smith check a loose shoe on his horse. In fact that reminds me. He'll be here shortly, and I'm sure he'll want some of this fine food."

The innkeeper nodded. "We'll have it ready when he arrives. But there's just the two of you, eh?"

Morgin nodded. "Is that a problem?"

"Well I should warn you, sir," the innkeeper said with a serious frown on his face. "There's some Elhiyne outlaws rampagin' across the countryside. Five of them, I'm told. One of them's this ShadowLord. You know, the rogue wizard. Travelin' in small parties ain't safe, I'll wager."

Morgin frowned worriedly. "Is anyone doing anything about them?"

"Oh yes they are, sir. Why old Lord Andrew sent his own son to this very inn just last night. In fact young Lord Stetha should be down shortly. And he has a company of soldiers camped just out of town, he does. As long as you're here you should be good and safe."

Morgin tried to appear grateful, though his heart wasn't in it, and his appetite was disappearing by the second. "Well that makes me feel a lot better."

The innkeeper returned to the kitchen, and once out of sight Morgin rose to his feet, started stuffing his pockets with biscuits, crammed a handful of bacon into his mouth. But just then the door to the street slammed opened. Morgin sat down quickly, tried to look like he was enjoying a leisurely breakfast.

A young, adolescent boy stepped warily into the room. He was a large, oafish lad, and after scanning the room quickly he was unable to hide his distrust of Morgin. He sauntered past Morgin's table, stepped around behind the bar, and keeping an eye on Morgin he leaned through the kitchen door and hollered, "Malachi. Come out here. It's important."

The innkeeper appeared in the doorway instantly. He and the boy conversed in hushed tones for some seconds while frequently glancing Morgin's way. Then they appeared to come to some agreement. The boy disappeared up the stairs to the rooms above while the innkeeper remained behind the bar busying himself with some sort of work. But where he'd been friendly and open before, he was now suspicious like the boy, and he refused to meet Morgin's eyes with a direct look.

Morgin was trying to think of a way to exit discretely when again the door to the street slammed opened and France stepped into the room. He looked about for a moment as his eyes adjusted to the dark, spotted Morgin and joined him at his table. "The smith was not at all talkative, and seemed quite suspicious of me. And there were two Rastanna mounts stabled with him. Their owners are probably staying in this inn."

France reached across the table and grabbed a biscuit. "I know," Morgin said. "And I learned there's a company of Rastanna troops camped somewhere outside of town. And we're the reason they're here. Evidently Tarkiss got the word out rather quickly."

"Aye," France said. "The smith also had two apprentices when I first showed up, but he sent them on some errand. I don't like that."

Morgin looked at the innkeeper. "Was one of them a large, clumsy boy?"

France nodded. "Aye."

"Well he showed up here a few moments ago, talked to the innkeeper for some seconds, then went upstairs. I think we'd better get out of here."

France stuffed some bacon into one of his pockets and stood. Morgin stood with him, but as they turned for the door the innkeeper called out, "Don't yer friend want any breakfast?"

Morgin replied over his shoulder, "A little later perhaps."

"But it'll be cold by then."

France and Morgin reached the door, stepped out into the light of morning, but as Morgin closed the door behind him he heard the innkeeper cry out, "They're getting away!"

Up the street the smith was headed their way, carrying a large hammer like a club. But just then pounding hooves on the road broke the stillness of the quiet village. The smith stopped, turned and looked back over his shoulder. The door to the inn swung open. A young Rastanna nobleman, sword in hand, his tunic half tucked into his breeches, stood in the doorway for an instant blinded by the morning light. Morgin kicked him in the groin then spun and dove into Mortiss's saddle just as a troop of mounted Rastanna soldiers thundered into view at the northeast end of town. He and France spurred their horses into a charge away from the soldiers and out the opposite end of town. They gained a little time as the troop stopped at the inn to retrieve their master, but the Rastannas took up the chase quickly.

A short distance out of the village Morgin and France turned northwest off the road. They both knew they were on their own now, that it would do no good to lead their pursuers back to Cort, Val and Tulellcoe, so they cut across open countryside away from their companions.

For the next two days they played cat and mouse with any number of Rastanna posses, and more than once Morgin wished for his shadowmagic again. Even France expressed a desire to see a bit of it here and there. Late the second day they found another road and headed northeast on it. They traveled without rest through that night, walking their horses when the animals reached their limits. The next morning they cut off the road again, turned due east across open country, found a small forest about midday and set camp for some rest. They slept poorly through that afternoon.

After sunset they moved on, and near midnight they noticed a sharp glow on the horizon. They investigated further, and in the middle of the night, from a small nearby hill, they found themselves looking down upon Castle Rastanna. Like Elhiyne it had a good-sized village outside its gates, but here the huts and buildings of the village hugged the castle wall and spread outward from it.

Clearly, the countryside had been alerted to the presence of the outlaw wizard, for even in the middle of the night a hundred torches lit the castle while riders charged in and out of its gates. "They'll be expectin' us to go south," France whispered. "Try to make for Yestmark. So our best bet is to head north, maybe northeast."

"But that'll take us toward Durin," Morgin said.

France shrugged. "What difference does it make? You're no less of an outlaw here or there, but they won't expect you there. And we got no choice."

"Can't argue with that," Morgin said, and they headed northeast.

The next morning they ran out of trail rations, but Morgin discovered he still had the forgotten biscuits in his pockets, though they were stale and somewhat crumbled. He shared them with France.

For the next three days they rode north and east living off the land, though not living well. They snared a few hares, found an occasional bush plump with berries. Once they even came across an apple orchard and ate apples until almost sick. Finally they decided to take the chance of stopping in a village for supplies. They were now far enough north they had some hope they'd left the hunt behind.

They chose a village not much different from the one with the suspicious smith and the fat innkeeper, though this one was a little bigger and located at a crossroads. Morgin and France rode into the village just before dusk. It had more huts and buildings, and a more spacious inn. Like the other place the common room still smelled of soot and mildew, and the innkeeper was a heavyset man, though not roundly obese like the other fellow.

About a dozen patrons occupied the common room talking in low tones and sipping on some of the local ale. A wandering bard sitting in one corner strummed on a stringed instrument singing for his meal. Clearly, these people were more accustomed to strangers, for they paid no heed to Morgin and France as they sat down at an empty table. They ordered up meat, bread, cheese and ale, and ate their fill. Drowsy with fatigue and full stomachs they sat back to listen to the bard as he sang a soft love song, then followed that with a rollicking jig.

When the innkeeper brought the bard his meal he stopped playing and concentrated on eating. But someone called out, "What news have you from the south?"

The bard swallowed a large bite of cheese, washed it down with a gulp of ale. "They're searching all over the place for those Elhiyne outlaws. They haven't caught any of them though, but they've been seen a few times and chased about a bit." He tore off a mouthful of meat, chewed for a few moments and swallowed. "They think they've split up, that a few of them are headed this way, though I can't understand why Elhiynes would do that. Seems a bit crazy to me."

Someone remarked, "One of 'em's that ShadowLord, and we all know how crazy them wizards are." The speaker was answered with silence, for it could be dangerous to agree with such a remark.

Morgin and France adjourned to their room, slept well that night, arose early the next morning and bought some provisions. They stocked up on journeycake and jerky, and bought some perishables so they could do a little cooking if they found a good place for a fire. They were back on the road two hours after sunrise and riding at an easy pace.

They spent that night far enough from the road to conceal a fire, got a full night's sleep and woke up refreshed. The next morning, after a few hours of riding the road turned due east. They considered following it for a good distance then turning south and taking a circuitous route to Yestmark. But then they both heard the faint sound of a large group of men riding hard on the road behind them.

France swore. "Somebody back in that village recognized us."

At that moment the posse rounded a bend far back in the road, saw the two fugitives and pulled to a sudden halt. The leader called out to them. "Stand and identify yourselves." Several members of the posse pulled their swords.

France looked at Morgin. "I think we'd best be gettin' out of here, eh lad?"

Morgin nodded, spurred his horse into a charge with France hot on his heels. They rode hard for a league until the road turned north. There they cut off the road and continued east across open country, and every time Morgin looked back the posse had gained on them. They rode for most of the day, pacing their horses to stay just ahead of the posse. But then they topped a small rise and found themselves on the banks of a river.

The water looked cold and icy as it roared past them in a swirling froth, tumbling over rocks in places, fountaining into the air in others. "We can't cross that," France shouted above the roar. "Maybe downstream it'll be a bit calmer."

They turned north, paralleling the river, and in the distance the Rastanna posse turned north also, intending to cut them off. Morgin gave Mortiss free rein, letting her pick her own way through the brush along the riverbank. The river turned west toward the posse, and then it made an even sharper jog, forming a long spit of land bordered on three sides by a bend in the river, and too late he and France realized their mistake. The posse had closed off their only exit from the spit of land. They were trapped.

Morgin looked down at the river. The water was calmer here, smooth and glassy on the surface, with no rocks to break it up into a white-water froth, though it still flowed dangerously fast. "Well," Morgin demanded of France. "Do we fight or swim?"

France looked back at the posse. "I like me chances in the water better."

Morgin nodded, spurred Mortiss's flanks and she plunged into the icy water. She snorted, catching her breath while he gasped a few times. But then she got into the swim and started doing well. A moment later he heard France's horse plunge in behind him.

There was a certain calm on the surface of the water. The banks that rose up on either side muffled all sounds, even that of the posse after they arrived and stood on the bank cursing at their Elhiyne prey. Mortiss's exertions became a steady rhythm beneath Morgin as the opposite bank drew closer with each second.

They made nice progress, but the river carried them much too rapidly downstream, and they were only half way across when he caught the faint sound of a muffled roar. And then he rounded a bend and the river straightened out, and in the distance he saw a hump in the water where it flowed over a large boulder just beneath the surface. He spurred Mortiss and cried, "Swim, girl, swim!"

Mortiss doubled her efforts, but the river flowed too rapidly. They missed the rock itself, but the swirling, twisting water that flowed around it upended them. Morgin tumbled head over heels in a soup of white bubbles. He slammed up against something that sent a jolt of pain through his side. He tried desperately to get his head above water, managed to see daylight for an instant and catch a single breath of air, then again he plunged beneath the surface and clutched desperately for something to hold on to.

His tunic caught on a large branch and he came to a sudden stop, though he was still in the flow of the water and he tumbled around like a tether in a harsh wind. Only when his tunic finally twisted up too tightly for him to tumble more did he stabilize, but he was just beneath the surface with his lungs bursting. He struggled in the flow, managed to reach his dagger, gripped it tightly in his right hand, and used his left to guide it toward the twisted knot of tunic that held him anchored there. He sawed at the knot in the cloth.

How he managed to saw through it he could never remember, or how he managed to keep his grip on the branch, or how he managed to find the strength to pull himself out of the flow that sucked at him like the power of the *netherworld* itself. But he did manage these things, and an eternity later he crawled up on the bank of the river. He'd lost the dagger somewhere in the river.

He didn't have the strength to rise up off his hands and knees, but from that position he glanced down the bank, and a short distance away saw France's horse lying lifeless, its neck twisted at an odd angle. He saw no sign of Mortiss or France.

He heard voices, Kull voices. Instinctively he reached for his sword, but the sheath strapped to his side was empty. Like the dagger it lay somewhere at the bottom of the river, lost forever. He struggled to remain conscious, to rise up onto his feet. He managed to get one foot beneath him. But there were several pairs of Kull boots standing in front of him, and as one boot rose up off the ground and arced toward his face, he didn't have the strength to escape it.

30

Decouix Power

MORGIN REGAINED CONSCIOUSNESS sitting with his back to a tree. Two Kulls stood over him, their swords drawn. They had removed his sword sheath and discarded it, and the side of his head hurt where the Kull had kicked him. "What of my friend?" he asked the Kulls. "The swordsman?"

The Kulls stared at him and showed no inclination to answer his question. Then a familiar voice spoke, "The swordsman is dead."

Morgin turned to one side, found Tarkiss standing over him smiling happily. "He washed up on the bank of the river about a league from here. Evidently he tried to breathe water."

An emptiness formed deep within Morgin's heart and he wanted to cry, but he would not give this Rastanna the pleasure of seeing him do so.

"You're on Decouix land now," Tarkiss continued. "And there'll be no further escape."

They treated Morgin rather well after that. They gave him a horse, tied his hands to the saddle horn rather than behind his back, gave his reins to one of the Kulls. They didn't beat him, and they fed him regularly and properly.

They headed due east. Morgin lost count of the days as each morning they arose, washed up, ate, then rode on. They'd stop around noon for a short rest and a meal, then continue on until dusk, at which time they'd set camp, eat, then go to sleep. Morgin no longer cared where they took him or what they intended to do with him. Finally, they came to a wide and well-traveled road running north and south. "Where are we?" he asked.

Tarkiss grinned. "This is the God's Road."

Morgin thought carefully of what he knew of the God's Road, the main thoroughfare running from Inetka in the south, to Durin in the north. As the implication of that hit him, Tarkiss's grin broadened. "Lord Valso will reward me handsomely for delivering you in good condition."

They followed the road north through the rest of that day, camped near the road that night and rose early the following morning to continue their journey. Morgin noticed that the small farms and holdings they passed were now closer together, as were the hamlets and villages along the road. They came to a stretch of road that cut through a number of large and apparently luxurious estates, and then they entered a city of huts and low-lying buildings.

Durin had more than one market, and a lot of people busily going about their business. They paid no heed to Tarkiss and the Kulls, and as for Morgin, it would require a close examination to notice that his hands were tied to the saddle horn, that he was more than just another trail-weary soldier without sword or shield.

When Morgin first spotted the wall he thought it might be Castle Decouix itself, but it was much too long to be the outer wall of a castle. Somewhere he'd heard Durin was a walled city, but he'd never truly understood what that meant until now.

Once they passed beneath the wall the character of the city changed. The buildings behind the wall were all multistoried, and separated by narrow, cobblestoned streets. Again no one took notice of the prisoner among the Kulls.

The length of the ride from the wall to the castle impressed Morgin with the size of the city, but Decouix impressed him even more. The castle loomed above everything at the center of the city. It stood alone, with a wide parade ground separating it from any other structure and surrounding it on all sides. There were two motes, one immediately beneath the wall, and another at the outer edge of the parade ground, separating the empty stretch of land from the city proper. Decouix would be difficult to take by force.

A drawbridge had been lowered over each of the two motes, and the portcullis in the main castle gates had been raised. Tarkiss halted at the outer drawbridge, took Morgin's reins himself, then spurred his horse into a slow walk. As the hooves of Morgin's horse pounded on the planks of the first bridge, he noticed movement on the battlements above the castle gate. Looking up he saw Valso standing there, staring down at him without expression. Something hovered near Valso's head, then settled on his shoulder: the demon flying snake, Bayellgae.

The journey across the parade ground took an eternity under Valso's gaze. And just before they passed beneath the outer wall of Decouix, Tarkiss raised Morgin's reins triumphantly above his head and waved them at Valso. Valso nodded, but still he showed no expression. Then Morgin's horse stepped into the shadow beneath the wall and he could no longer see the prince of Decouix.

••••

Still, they did not treat him badly. They assigned him a suite of rooms high up in the castle, servants to cater to his needs, and several suits of fine, expensive clothing. They bathed him, threw away the tattered and grimy rags he'd been wearing, shaved off his beard and cut his hair. Standing there in one of his rooms with the servants about him, no one would guess he was anything less than a prince of the House of Elhiyne. But outside every window or door, and even on the balconies that opened off the bedroom and sitting room, there stood at least two heavily armed Kulls.

Late in his first afternoon in Decouix the servants dressed him for dinner, and with an escort of six Kulls they led him down several flights of stairs and through the corridors of Decouix. He was hopelessly lost as they halted just outside a large room with high vaulted ceilings and filled with elegantly dressed courtiers. Morgin heard them talking in low tones, carrying on a dozen conversations with an occasional laugh.

The servants indicated he should enter the room, and when he did all there looked his way, and a silence as thick as honey descended. Morgin looked back, noticed the Kulls had not followed him into the room, guessed one or two waited behind every exit.

Tarkiss stepped out of the crowd, greeted Morgin pleasantly. "Lord AethonLaw," he said. "You look much better." He held a goblet of wine in one hand, and with the other he flagged down a servant with a tray full of similar goblets. He took one and handed it to Morgin. "Drink and enjoy yourself, AethonLaw. Lord Valso is celebrating tonight."

Morgin took the goblet of wine. "What's the occasion?" he asked.

Tarkiss turned a patronizing smile on Morgin. "Need you ask?"

Morgin didn't want to talk to Tarkiss, and he felt no obligation to be more than minimally polite, so he turned away from the young Rastanna, sipped on his wine and stepped through the crowd.

The buzz of idle conversation returned, yet they were all trying to avoid staring at him. He caught the surreptitious looks and silent glances, and he knew he was a curiosity. He had no destination in mind as he walked through the crowd, so he moved slowly and let the crowd part before him.

A pretty, young girl stepped in front of him and forced him to halt. She threw her skirts out and curtsied in a very formal way. "Lord AethonLaw."

Morgin bowed. "You have the advantage of me."

She rose and stood facing him. "I am Xenya et Vodah, of the House of Vodah."

Morgin revised his opinion of her. She was young, but she was a strong and proud woman. She stood her ground before him without flinching. "What can I do for you?" he asked.

She smiled with a bit of mischief in her eyes. "I'm not sure. You're a curiosity to me."

"I do believe I'm a curiosity to everyone here."

"Well of course you are. You singlehandedly defeated an army that outnumbered you twelve to one."

Morgin shook his head. "The odds weren't that extreme. And besides, I used both hands."

She threw her head back and laughed. "And you have a sense of humor too." She looked about unhappily at the people around them. "That's a refreshing change from my kinsmen who cower under the Decouix yoke."

"Xenya!" an older woman hissed nearby, and stepped forward to grab the young woman by the arm. "Watch your tongue."

"Oh come now, mother," Xenya said. "The only reason Valso likes me about is because of my sharp tongue. In fact, I do believe . . ."

Morgin stopped paying attention, for deep within his soul he sensed something within the castle that sent a shiver up his spine and raised the hackles on the back of his neck. It drew closer with each heartbeat, something evil beyond imagining, something old beyond life itself. He sensed a chasm of power opening before him, a depth of magic so vast it threatened to overwhelm him. Thankfully, it did not sense him, not as anything more than a simple human being, not as something that could sense its true nature.

A set of large, double doors opened at one end of the room. Silence again descended upon them all as the crowd parted to reveal Valso standing in the doorway with a woman on each arm. Haleen, his mad sister, hung on his left arm almost desperately, while on his right stood an older version of Valso. Looking into the long, gracious lines of her face, Morgin understood then where the Decouix prince had gotten his beauty.

The crowd parted, forming a long aisle from Valso to Morgin. Valso and the two women walked toward him, the prince nodding politely to one side or another. When he reached Morgin the silence grew oppressive, and Morgin noted that even the brash, young Xenya had withdrawn.

"Well, Elhiyne," Valso said. His voice held no triumph, none of the bluster or bragging Morgin expected. "We've finally come to this, eh?"

"Is it final?" Morgin asked.

"Of course it is. Surely you realize I have to kill you, even if only because these people expect it of me. Though I don't have to kill you right away, do I?" He looked at the older woman on his right arm. "But I'm ignoring the amenities. May I present my mother, the Lady Merriketh esk et Decouix."

Morgin bowed politely. "I'm honored."

The woman said nothing, didn't even acknowledge him, looked through him with a stare that could have put icicles on the gates of the ninth hell.

"And of course you know my sister Haleen," Valso continued, looking at the younger woman. She in turn looked at Morgin, and her chin quivered for a moment as if she had something to say. But before she could do so Valso said, "Let us adjourn to dinner. Come, Elhiyne. You'll sit beside me tonight."

Valso and Morgin and the crowd moved to a long and narrow banquet hall containing an equally long and narrow table. Valso sat at its head, with Morgin on his left, Ladies Merriketh and Haleen on his right, and Tarkiss immediately beneath them in the order of seating, a place of honor for the young Rastanna.

Valso treated Morgin like an honored guest. There were no confrontations, no threats, no further mention of his fate. Young Xenya wisely kept her mouth shut while Tarkiss told of the hunt, chase, and finally Morgin's capture, though Tarkiss told it as an interesting story, with little bravado and no innuendo.

Morgin noticed a hint of tension between the Lady Merriketh and her son, almost as if she too feared Valso. He also noted a certain bitterness in her, a marked lack of joy. But throughout the evening his thoughts kept returning to that vast chasm of power hidden within Valso's soul.

Morgin gave up trying to understand these things. Given time, understanding would come, if he lived long enough.

••••

Surrounded by an escort of six Kulls, Morgin wondered at their destination as they led him deep into the bowels of Decouix. They'd come for him in late afternoon, and told him only, "You are to come with us."

Deeper and deeper into Decouix they led him, and he thought it possible Valso would now have him thrown into a dungeon. But the halls down which they led him had not the dank and musty smell of a dungeon, were in fact quite clean and well kept. Then he felt the pull of power at the edge of his senses, and he understood they were approaching something quite unique.

At the end of a long hall the Kulls halted before an open portal. They parted, stood to either side and waited silently for him to pass between them. He hesitated, for he sensed an enormous amount of power beyond the portal, so like, but at the same time unlike, that in the sanctum at Elhiyne.

"Come, Elhiyne," Valso called from beyond the portal. "You have nothing to fear from Decouix power, at least as long as I choose that you need not fear it. Come forth, now, or I'll have you dragged in here."

Morgin stepped forward. The power within pulled at him, and like the power at Elhiyne it demanded he take it up, allow it to enter his soul. As he stepped through the portal his stomach knotted up and he staggered under the onslaught.

"Yes, Elhiyne, the Decouix power is a fearful thing, is it not?"

Morgin pressed his back to the wall inside the sanctum, struggled to breathe, took in deep gulping breaths. Valso laughed; the prince thought him cowed by the Decouix power, assaulted by it, fearful of it, when in fact it wanted him to wield it just as the

Elhiyne power had. He didn't understand why the Decouix power, accumulated in this room for centuries, called to him like a servant to its master. He dared not trust anything about it.

Valso gripped him by his arm and led him out through the portal as one might lead a child, and once in the hall beyond, the oppressive, stifling nature of the power waned. Morgin leaned against a wall and fought to control his breathing.

"Yes, Elhiyne, I knew you would find Decouix power a frightening thing. No doubt, even terrifying to one such as you."

Morgin dare not tell him he wanted to take up that power as much as it longed for him to do so.

31

Death Ritual

THE NEXT MORNING the servants woke Morgin early, bathed and dressed him for breakfast, which, like dinner, was a moderately formal affair in the sophisticated atmosphere of House Decouix. Then Valso, accompanied by Bayellgae and an entourage of about twenty, and escorted by two twelves of Kulls, took Morgin on a tour of the city of Durin.

Durin was by far the largest city he had ever seen, making Anistigh seem like a small, backwater place. They saw so much in so little time Morgin's memories of Durin were a blur of sights and sounds. And then there was Valso, suave, sophisticated, handsome, concealing the malicious and hateful side of his nature. For some reason he allowed Morgin to see an extended glimpse of a charming and entertaining man. It put Morgin on edge, wondering when the true Valso would emerge, for there was no doubt he would show himself, and probably to Morgin's detriment.

The next morning the servants again woke Morgin early and bathed and dressed him for breakfast. Valso held court, and Morgin watched him arbitrate disputes among his vassals. Valso's style was to impose his own will on each situation, often without listening to anyone. He ordered two deaths that morning, not for criminal acts, but for some arbitrary and unclear reasons of his own.

That afternoon they strolled about the edge of a large practice yard inside the castle walls. Groups of soldiers and Kulls filled the yard, often in pairs practicing their sword skills. Occasionally Valso would stop to observe two contestants for a short time, frequently interrupting to comment and offer instruction.

"Tell me, Elhiyne," Valso said, after they'd finished observing two Kulls cutting away at one another in a rather brutal and rough form of practice. "What did you think of my court this morning?"

Tarkiss, walking beside Valso, looked at Morgin, and Morgin wondered of this was a trick question of some sort. He glanced down at the young Vodah woman Xenya, but her face showed no hint of how he should answer. He tried to play it safe. "It was efficient."

"Yes," Valso said proudly. "It was."

Morgin had to ask one question. "However, I don't understand why you ordered the deaths of those two men."

"Oh that," Valso said. He looked up in the air and cried, "Snake."

Bayellgae alighted on his shoulder, its head weaving from side to side. "Massster. How may I ssserve?"

"The Elhiyne wants to know about the deaths I ordered today."

The little demon turned its eyes on Morgin. "Death isss alwaysss a lesssson, Lord Mortal."

"Right you are, snake," Valso said, looking fondly upon the little monster.

Valso turned to Morgin. "I always order a few deaths. And if there's nothing that comes before me to warrant a death, then I find something. It keeps them guessing, and it reminds them I rule at my pleasure."

Valso had spoken in such an offhand manner, Morgin wondered if he was being humorous in some sophisticated way. But when Morgin glanced at Xenya and saw her eyes flash fearfully, he knew the truth of Valso's words.

Valso stopped and turned to face Morgin squarely. "Tell me something else, Elhiyne. You are my guest here. Is there anything you lack?"

Morgin shrugged. "The obvious: my freedom."

"Why you have freedom of a sort. Certainly more freedom than any peasant."

Morgin shook his head. "A peasant doesn't have Kulls at every turn in his path to stop him."

Valso frowned. "But you're mistaken. My halfmen won't hinder you. You have the freedom of the castle, to go where you will, to open any door not barred, and my half-men have orders to allow you to pass if that is the case. Is there anything else you lack, within reason, of course?"

"Of course," Morgin said bitterly. He looked out over the practice yard at the soldiers sweating in the sun, at the few noblemen among them exercising their sword arms. "Exercise," he said as the thought came to him. "I would enjoy the chance to swing a sword, to practice, to sweat a little in the sun. Surely, one lone Elhiyne with a sword would stand little chance of escaping in broad daylight with so many guards about."

Valso glanced at him suspiciously, but, standing next to him, Tarkiss said, "Perhaps Lord AethonLaw would like to give us a demonstration of his legendary swordsmanship. I'm told you are quite the duelist."

Morgin shook his head. "All I want is to stretch my muscles a bit. I'm no duelist. In fact I'm quite poor at it."

"Come now," Tarkiss said, and the forced politeness of the past days gave way to mockery. "I'm told you've killed many of our Kulls."

Morgin sensed a trap of some kind, and he wanted to avoid it at almost any cost. "Just a few, and that was in combat. No rules. Not even the kind you live by in practice; just survival, each man fighting for his life. It's not the kind of thing one can demonstrate."

Valso looked at Morgin and nodded thoughtfully, then seemed to come to a decision. "I see no reason why you can't, as you say, stretch your muscles a bit." He looked out across the practice yard and called loudly, "Salya."

A Kull lieutenant turned away from his charges and casually crossed the distance to the prince. "Your Highness."

"Lord AethonLaw needs some exercise. Choose one of your men—a good fighter, but not the best, and about the same size as AethonLaw. And get Lord AethonLaw a sword."

Surprised, Morgin said, "But it's not necessary this instant."

Valso looked at him. "Oh, but it is. You desire it, you shall have it." He looked back at the Kull. "Do it. Now!"

The Kull barked out orders, sent one of his halfmen running across the yard to a rack of old arms. The halfman scooped up a dozen blades, ran back across the yard and dumped them at Morgin's feet with a loud clatter. By that time Salya had chosen Morgin's opponent: an average looking Kull, meaning he looked mean, angry and hateful. He was stripped to the waist, with a sheen of sweat already covering his skin, and a cascade of straight, shoulder length hair. He looked bored by the prospect of exercising with Morgin.

Valso looked at the Kull, then at Morgin. "I do so want to see you at your best."

He turned to Bayellgae. "What do you think, snake. Can we arrange to see real combat demonstrated here?"

Morgin shook his head and frowned. "That's not possible."

Valso's lips curled upward into a mocking smile, and like Tarkiss, the pretense of civility vanished. "Oh I think it is, Elhiyne. You see, I'm giving this Kull permission to kill you as soon as you've chosen a blade. No rules, just survival, each man fighting for his life, fighting to the death. Isn't that how you described it?"

Xenya gasped, put a hand to her mouth. The Kull chuckled with a low growl. Valso called out, "Stand back. All of you." He swept his arms out, indicating everyone should give Morgin and the Kull room. There were quite a number of men and halfman in the yard, but only a few paying close attention to the events taking shape, and those few stepped away cautiously to form a ragged ring around the two contestants.

Morgin stood over the pile of old swords dumped at his feet. Valso called out to him, "Choose a sword, Elhiyne, and fight for your life. Or I'll give the Kull permission to cut you down where you stand. It's kill or be killed."

Morgin looked at the few spectators standing about, and saw no sympathy there. He shook himself, and careful not to turn his back on the Kull he unlaced the finely tailored jacket Valso had provided him. He shrugged out of it and tossed it aside.

Still watching the Kull he squatted down over the pile of derelict blades, started reaching for one to test its weight, but at the last instant a spasm in his arm deflected his hand to the hilt of another blade. And as his hand settled about the grip he experienced a single moment of surprise. But it ended almost as soon as it came, and he recognized his own sword, the old Benesh'ere blade he'd grown so used to.

How it had been retrieved from the bottom of that river he could not guess. There was no rust on it, though it had never shined. It looked even older, as if the few days it had been gone from his side had been centuries to the life of the steel. And the hilt had been rewrapped, though not recently, for the wrapping was old with time and use. That would indicate the sword had been gone from his side for a long time, perhaps years. He looked again at the steel, touched it lightly, sensed the voices within it, and any doubt he had disappeared.

The Kull's boots pounding on the hard packed dirt of the yard were his only warning that the contest had begun. He dove to one side as the halfman's sword hissed past his throat, turned his dive into a shoulder roll and sprang to his feet. The Kull was on top of him in an instant with a two-handed overhead stroke meant to split him down the middle. He didn't meet it, but remembering France's tutelage he deflected it only the amount needed, kicked the Kull in the ribs as the halfman's blade slammed into the dirt, turned the momentum of his kick into a spin and brought his sword about in a flat arc.

The Kull barely managed to duck beneath it, and even though he came up in an awkward position he did throw his own sword up and parried it strongly. Their swords rang together once and they disengaged.

Morgin bent into a crouch, and he and the Kull circled slowly. Then, as if by mutual consent, they both swung their swords up, and for a few quick strokes they traded blows back and forth. Again, they disengaged and circled slowly.

Morgin thought the Kull had a tendency to over commit his strokes, and he wondered what the Kull thought of him. Again they traded blows, their swords ringing together in a slow, grinding cadence. Morgin watched for the moment when the Kull might over commit himself again, but the Kull changed tactics and lunged at Morgin with a point thrust aimed at his heart. Morgin committed to the thrust, parried it heavily, and realized too late he'd exposed his ribs.

The Kull's boot caught him just under the armpit with a solid thud. He grunted, tried to ignore the pain, spun into a kick of his own that caught the Kull in the solar plexus. They both stumbled away from one another and fell to the ground.

Morgin scrambled to his feet with less speed than he would have liked. But the Kull moved no faster as he struggled off his knees clutching his abdomen and sucking for air. They dove at each other again, traded more blows and kicks. Morgin caught the Kull squarely in the jaw with the hilt of his sword, and was amazed that an instant later the halfman managed to dodge a flat slice meant to take off his head. Then the Kull cut him badly across the hip with a glancing thrust that just barely missed gutting him. Morgin spun inside the Kull's guard and they locked hand to hand, the Kull's free hand clutching the wrist of Morgin's sword arm, Morgin's free hand clutching the wrist of the Kull's sword arm, chest-to-chest, face-to-face.

The Kull jerked his head back, butted Morgin in the nose with his forehead. The pain brought tears to Morgin's eyes and he felt a hot stream of blood flood his lips and chin. The Kull head-butted him in the cheek just under his right eye, then the halfman's teeth flashed, going for Morgin's throat. Morgin ducked his head, drove upward and caught the halfman under the chin, driving his head back and over balancing him. The Kull tumbled backward; Morgin tumbled with him, tried to keep his head beneath the Kull's chin as he landed on top of him. They hit the ground with their sword arms still immobilized in each other's grip, Morgin's nose and cheek pressed against the exposed skin of the Kull's throat so the Kull couldn't get his teeth on Morgin's throat. Without thought he opened his mouth, and like a wild animal at the kill he buried his teeth in the halfman's throat, felt the Kull's larynx crushed in his jaws.

The Kull struggled frantically, and with a desperate effort broke his sword hand free. Morgin bit down on the halfman's throat even harder, felt his teeth sinking in as he shifted his weight to immobilize the upper half of the Kull's wildly swinging sword arm. The Kull's sword bit into Morgin's back, but chest-to-chest, and for the most part pinned to the ground, the halfman could put no strength behind it. And then inevitably, second by second by second, with Morgin's teeth buried in the Kull's throat the halfman's struggles slowed, his partially immobilized sword arm began striking down with only a halfhearted effort, and he relaxed his grip on Morgin's sword arm.

Morgin waited until the Kull grew still, then he opened his mouth and rolled off the halfman, careful to roll onto the Kull's sword arm in case there was a last breath of life in him. He lay on his back for a moment catching his breath, conscious of each of his injuries though not of how serious they might be, listening to the silence of the castle yard about him and the thunder of his own heartbeat. And in that silence he heard a gurgling rasp of breath coming from the Kull. Morgin looked at the man, at the throat half torn away. The Kull was still alive, drowning slowly in his own blood. Morgin vomited up his breakfast.

Only a few minutes earlier Morgin would never have believed he could feel pity for a Kull. But now with a great deal of effort he struggled to his feet, stood over the slowly dying halfman, reversed the hilt of his sword so he held it in both hands point down, then buried it in the halfman's chest. The Kull flinched once, and then his struggles ceased and he lay still.

Morgin looked up and found a sea of silent faces surrounding him. Everyone who had been in the castle yard had gathered to watch the spectacle, and now they all stood in a circle about him mutely staring at him. They were mostly soldiers, many of them Kulls, a few of the Kulls nodding. They approved. The Kulls accepted him and respected him for killing with such brutal efficiency.

"Very good, Elhiyne," Valso called, stepping forward into the circle of onlookers. He began applauding loudly. "Excellent. As you said, no rules, just survival."

Morgin looked at Valso, turned and started toward him, and the look in his eyes must have said something to everyone for they all flinched and reached for their swords. Even Valso hesitated for a moment, but when Morgin left his sword still standing in the dead Kull's chest he relaxed. In that instant Morgin realized he had the greatest chance, and without thinking further he dove for the Decouix prince, wrapped his hands about his throat and crushed down with all his strength.

He dug his thumbs into Valso's larynx and felt it snap and crumble, saw the prince's eyes bulge even as he sensed that vast gulf of power rise up to protect him. But Morgin didn't care. There was no power that could frighten him now, nor pry open the white knuckled death grip squeezing the life from Valso. Morgin did not care even as that monstrous chasm of power struck at him, and he cared not even as it devoured him.

••••

Morgin awoke in his bed in his suite of rooms high in Castle Decouix. He was alone, and surprisingly enough alive, and he felt much better than he should. He tested his nose where the Kull had butted him; a little sore, but not terribly so. And the cut on his hip seemed almost healed. He wondered if the memory of crushing Valso's throat was nothing more than a hallucination.

He climbed out of bed, dressed, then decided to test Valso's claim that few doors were barred to him. He stepped out into the hallway, passed the two Kulls standing guard there, and began strolling down the hall. They fell into step behind him and followed at a discrete distance.

It appeared he'd arisen a bit earlier than the rest of the castle's inhabitants. He found the kitchen with the cook busy preparing breakfast. She told him they'd all be awake shortly, were probably already awake but were bathing and dressing and doing the things nobility did to make themselves presentable. Morgin talked her into giving him breakfast then, and with the two Kulls standing guard over him he ate in silence.

He explored some of the castle itself, wandered through the stables and the smithy, checked out the kennel, though in the back of the kennel he found a barred door through which he could not pass. But as he tested the door he sensed something beyond it that had the taste of the netherlife to it. He paused at the door and wondered at that, and heard a faint and distant sound, something like the cry of an animal, perhaps that of many animals, and it sounded something like "skree."

The dungeons were also barred to him, though that didn't surprise him. Mostly, he wanted to avoid Valso. He'd had enough of the Decouix prince, and he wanted some privacy. And oddly enough, he'd grown accustomed to the two Kulls that were his constant shadows, and their presence no longer intruded on that privacy.

Late that morning, after exploring most of the castle, he was on his way back to his suite when a nearby door opened. A servant stepped into the hallway, turned and faced back through the open door, bowed and said, "Yes, Lady Xenya." The servant closed the door and walked away.

On impulse Morgin rapped politely on the door. An old matron answered it, the kind of woman mothers preferred as chaperones for their daughters. "Yes?" the woman asked.

Morgin said, "Tell the Lady Xenya the Elhiyne would like to see her."

The old woman frowned, looked at him unhappily, then curtsied and said, "Yes, Your Lordship," and closed the door. A few moments later she returned and admitted him to a large sitting room containing Xenya seated on a long couch and a young man standing near a hearth.

"What do you want?" Xenya demanded.

Morgin shrugged. "I don't know. I guess I just wanted to talk to you. You don't seem to like Valso."

"Be that as it may," she said harshly, "I like you even less. At least he doesn't rip men's throats out with his own teeth."

"Xenya!" the young man said. "He had no choice."

The young man stepped forward and extended a hand to Morgin. "I am Alta et Vodah. Xenya's brother. And I know you to be AethonLaw et Elhiyne."

Morgin shook his head. "I'm no longer of the House of Elhiyne."

Alta shrugged. "The talisman, eh? But I'm told it's lost."

Morgin looked at the young man carefully. "I'm still an outlaw, without magic, and eventually Valso will kill me."

"I wasn't there yesterday," Alta said, "but I heard about it. And the timbre of Valso's voice is a bit different this morning."

"What do you mean?"

"Why, you almost killed him."

Morgin shook his head. "When I woke up this morning I thought it was all a hallucination."

Alta shook his head emphatically. "Oh no. It was very real. Valso's just playing his games with you. He used his own magic to heal himself, though as I say his voice has changed, and he also worked very hard to heal you. Then he gave everyone instructions that no one will speak of the matter in your presence. Be careful. He likes to play with your mind."

"Did you get what you came for?" Xenya demanded angrily. "If so, please go."

Alta threw an arm about Morgin's shoulders and escorted him to the door. "Don't pay attention to her. She has this romantic idea a fight should always be by the rules of a duel, all clean and neat, though you were a bit bloodthirsty yesterday."

Out in the hall Morgin hesitated. Alta had said he'd had no choice, but he did have a choice. He was going to die anyway, so he could have just let Valso's Kull cut him down. But he'd been too frightened to do anything but fight, and now he felt unclean.

Morgin managed to avoid Valso most of the day, but late that afternoon six Kulls came for him. They escorted him out to the practice yard. They'd already assembled the circle of onlookers, with the lone Kull standing at its center. To one side Salya and Valso stood by the pile of old, derelict blades, and a knot formed in the pit of Morgin's stomach.

"I enjoyed that contest yesterday so much," Valso announced, "I thought we might do it again."

Morgin tried to talk his way out of it, but again Valso threatened to let the Kull cut him down where he stood if he didn't fight. Again Morgin was too much of a coward to do anything but fight back, and again his sword waited for him in the pile of old blades, and again it would allow him to choose no other. He fought the Kull; they were evenly matched and the contest lasted much longer. They both sustained several minor wounds, and before it ended Morgin bled from a dozen cuts, though the Kull fared no better. That day Morgin killed the halfman with a clean thrust to the heart. And when he turned to face Valso, the prince had prudently wrapped himself in his power to prevent a repetition of the previous day's events.

The next day a slightly larger crowd had gathered for the gladiatorial contest. That day Morgin killed the Kull with a cut deep into the juncture of his neck and shoulder.

On the fourth day the crowd of onlookers had grown large and varied. And the fifth saw the yard filled to capacity, people lining the battlements, standing in balconies high above and leaning from windows, wagering on the outcome of the combat. Valso and Salya always chose a well-matched opponent for Morgin, so the contests never ended quickly. And though Morgin was always victorious, he never emerged unscathed. After he'd lost count of the contests, lost count of the days of murderous battle, standing there one day soaked in the blood of the Kull he'd just killed, he understood then that this was his death sentence. Valso had an unlimited number of Kulls, and eventually Morgin would make one fatal mistake.

32

A Dark Sacrifice

TO MORDDON, WHO stood on the balcony of AnneRhianne's boudoir high in the palace, Kathbeyanne had the air of a graveyard. The streets below were now almost completely empty, and in the distance beyond the edge of the city, lines of refugees clogged the roads.

After the massacre of the First Legion and Gilguard's last stand, Aethon's forces had suffered one defeat after another. The Goath hordes, now sensing total victory close at hand, had begun making forays deep into the kingdom of the Shahotma. The inhabitants of Kathbeyanne, realizing the city itself was their ultimate goal, were fleeing for their lives.

AnneRhianne stepped out onto the balcony. A cool breeze blew down off the plains in the west, but she chose to wear nothing more than a thin, almost transparent negligee that covered her from neck to ankles. From behind she wrapped her arms around Morddon's waist, pressed her cheek against the back of his shoulder. "Come inside, my love," she said softly. "You'll catch a chill out here."

Morddon inhaled deeply, took in the scent of her, continued to watch the lines of refugees snaking out of the city. "You know," he said. "In the future they're going to have it all wrong. They'll think we Benesh'ere deserted Aethon, and the other tribes remained faithful to him. And yet now they've all gone over to the Goath, or gone in hiding."

"We still have the angels," she said. "Eleven full legions. And we have the Thane. And perhaps WolfDane will relent and allow the Dane to aid us."

That was wishful thinking, though Morddon let it stand without comment. "The Goath are gathering a great army on the other side of the Worshipers. They're forcing our hand. We have to meet them at Sa'umbra, for we can't let an army that size cross the mountains without resistance. So tomorrow Aethon is gathering what remains of his army, to take them into what may be the last battle of this war. And tomorrow I have to go with him, and you have to stay here."

She kissed him softly on the back of his neck. "I know," she said. "Just promise me you'll come back for me."

Deep within the soul of the tall Benesh'ere warrior Morgin thought of the Isle of Simpa, and of the witch AnneRhianne waiting there for centuries, waiting for him to return. And he had returned, though he now knew something would prevent him from returning in this time and place. He nodded slowly. "I'll come back for you—someday. I swear it."

He turned about in her arms, took her in his arms and held her tightly.

"You know," she said wistfully, "I've dreamt strangely for the past months, dreamt of a young girl named Rhianne in another time."

Morgin tensed as she continued. "I haunt her soul, just a passenger, and she loves a young man and they're trying to find happiness. But then it's just a dream."

Morgin said, "For me, this is the dream."

They had only this short time left to them, this day, and the night that would follow, and Morgin knew these few precious memories would have to last them for centuries.

•••

"Come Elhiyne," Valso said. The servants had awakened Morgin early at Valso's instructions, and he'd barely had time to dress before the prince arrived. "I have to feed my pets, and I think you'll find them quite interesting."

Valso had come alone that morning, though he had his usual escort of Kulls. Morgin had come to think of them as part of the furniture. Valso took Morgin by the arm as if they were close friends, smiled pleasantly and chatted as they walked down to the castle yard. "I'm told you did some exploring the other day, that you walked through almost every open door in the castle, that you even explored Xenya's boudoir. She's an interesting young woman, isn't she?"

Morgin didn't answer, for at that moment they turned into the kennels and his ears filled with the sounds of barking and yapping dogs. Valso ignored the hounds in the pens on either side and walked directly to the barred door through which Morgin had been unable to pass. The door was open now, and as they stepped through it Morgin again heard the strange, high-pitched cry of several netherbeasts, "skree, skree, skree."

Beyond the door Morgin saw two Kulls standing at the edge of some sort of pit with a man kneeling between them. They had bound the man's hands with thick rope behind his back, and he'd been beaten cruelly, his face swollen and puffy. But as Morgin and Valso approached, the pit drew Morgin's attention, for from it the cries of "skree" arose. Within it Morgin sensed a powerful netherlife.

He slowed as they approached the edge of the pit, but Valso tugged on his arm and dragged him onward. "Come, Elhiyne. You'll want to see this." He pulled Morgin forward, and at the bottom of the pit Morgin saw a confusing mass of writhing and swaying motion, all gray and formless. Then one of the little beasts climbed up on the shoulders of one of its fellows, and jumped toward them with teeth snapping mindlessly. It came nowhere near the top of the pit, managed only to rebound off the pit wall and drop among the seething mass of the rest of its ilk.

There were hundreds of them, small, dog-like, netherbeasts, standing no taller than the top of a man's ankle. Their hindquarters were small, with most of their bulk concentrated in the muscles of the neck and shoulders. They seemed all head and mouth, their jaws filled with several rows of needle-like teeth. "They're called skree," Valso shouted above the noise of their cries. "Their teeth are razor sharp, and when they get hold of you they don't let go. I'm rather fond of them."

"But they're netherbeasts," Morgin said. "How did you get them into this life?"

"I have powers, Elhiyne, powers you can't even imagine."

Morgin looked at the Decouix prince, and within his eyes he saw that chasm of power opening before him again, and he flinched away from it. Valso threw his head back and laughed. "But come. My pets are hungry." He nodded to the two Kulls standing over the man at the far side of the pit.

"No!" he cried out. "Please, no."

Morgin tried to turn away, but two Kulls grabbed him from behind, twisted his arms behind his back and forced him to watch. One of the Kulls on the far side of the pit lifted a boot and kicked the kneeling man forward. He had one instant to realize what they'd done, and as he fell into the pit his eyes widened and he screamed.

He died slowly, not a quick death, and of course not clean. Valso laughed and giggled as the pack tore the man to pieces in hundreds of small bites. The contents of Morgin's stomach boiled forth; he vomited on his own boots and Valso found that funniest of all.

••••

The big Kull's sword sliced toward Morgin in a flat arc. Morgin ducked beneath it, but he underestimated the large halfman's agility, and as he came up a boot caught him in the ribs. He went down hard, landed on his back with a thud, dust scattering in all directions. He saw the Kull's blade arcing down toward his face, threw his sword up and managed to deflect it. But it bit deeply into the side of his shoulder and for an instant he hovered at the edge of consciousness.

The crowd roared and cheered as the Kull raised his sword for the kill. Morgin threw all his remaining strength into one last effort. He threw a hand full of dust up into the large Kull's face, rolled, kicked upward and caught the halfman in the crotch. The halfman grunted and swung out blindly as Morgin rolled to one side. Then Morgin spotted the side of an exposed knee and he kicked out at it, hit it solidly and heard the joint collapse with a snap. And as the Kull tumbled to the ground Morgin threw his sword out desperately, felt it bite into something, then he rolled away from the halfman.

Morgin staggered slowly to his feet, blood streaming freely down his arm from the deep cut in his left shoulder. He looked at the wound, saw the blood pulse with the beat of his racing heart. And at the sight of so much blood the crowd cheered.

The Kull lay on his side, his sword dropped nearby, his face buried in his hands, his ruined knee twisted at an unnatural angle. Slowly he opened his hands, and only then did Morgin see that his last blind stroke had hacked through the halfman's face, destroying both eyes and the bridge of his nose, probably even cutting into the brain, though not deeply enough to finish the man quickly. Again Morgin felt pity for a Kull.

Morgin looked again at the wound on his arm, and wondered how he'd managed to survive the last two months. Every day Valso had forced him to fight for his life, each day choosing a combatant more capable than the previous one. Morgin had remained alive only because he'd always been victorious, though several times he'd sustained serious wounds. Valso always saw to it he was treated with powerful healing spells, so Morgin was fully healed and ready for the next day's contest. Today Morgin had finally faced one of the best fighters among the Kull troops. He wondered what Valso had in mind for him next.

The large Kull had rolled onto his back, was breathing raggedly. Morgin staggered up to him, barely had the strength to raise his sword and put the halfman out of his misery. The crowd screamed and roared as Morgin dropped his sword in the dust and staggered off the field of battle.

That evening Morgin stood alone at a window in his suite of rooms looking out over the city of Durin. They'd bandaged his left arm and it hung in a sling, though the healers had done a good job and most of the pain had receded. The damn thing was beginning to itch badly and Morgin fought to overcome the urge to scratch it. It would be nicely healed by morning, and Morgin would be ready for whatever Valso planned next.

A soft knock at the door pulled Morgin's attention back to the moment. "Enter," he called out.

The door opened slowly, and whoever stood beyond in the dark hallway hesitated for a moment. Then, as if coming to a decision, a woman entered the room, though a dense veil hid her face. She looked at Morgin for a moment, then turned and closed the door behind her.

Morgin bowed cautiously, though the gesture was a bit clumsy with his arm hanging in a sling.

The woman spoke, "I watched you fight today."

Morgin had heard that voice before, though he couldn't remember when or where. "Did you enjoy the spectacle?" he asked bitterly.

"Of course not," she said, in a sharp, scolding tone. "I watched because I'm curious about you. And until now I have specifically avoided watching this display of my son's cruelty."

The reference to her "son" was the final clue Morgin needed. The Lady Merriketh stood before him, Valso's mother.

She continued. "And I watched because if I did not watch today then I would not again have the opportunity to see how you survive."

"And why is that?" Morgin asked.

She turned her head sharply toward him, and even though the veil hid her face, he sensed her eyes piercing through his soul. "Your family will be here two days hence. They will bring my husband back with them, chained in disgrace, and my son will fully consolidate his power then. So I believe you have fought your last Kull, at least in such a gladiatorial way. But you know these things."

There was something odd in the way she spoke those particular words, and Morgin decided to confront her with it. "You sound pleased your husband is in disgrace, and displeased your son will see success."

Merriketh shrugged, and let out a soft, short, bitter laugh. "There is not now any love between us, though long ago there was something."

"And why is that?"

She reached up and slowly pushed the veil back from her face. She looked at Morgin proudly and said, "I am Merriketh Alaella."

"A twoname?"

"Yes," she said angrily. "Oh I loved Illalla once, but like any twoname I could love no man enough to spend the rest of my life in one place. And he coveted the power of the Decouix throne too much to wander about with me. So he decided to have the best of both worlds. He took me to wife by force, and he locked me in this castle forty years ago and has held me as a prisoner ever since. I'm still amazed how easily I learned to hate him."

Morgin could almost feel the hate radiating from her. "Why are you telling me this?"

"I'm curious about you," she said. "You've managed to survive. You managed to survive the onslaught of my son's power when you wrapped your fingers about his throat and nearly killed him. You managed to survive it even though you have no power of your own. You managed to survive it with no more than your own will, and so I am curious about you, because Valso fears you. He's always feared you, for some reason."

"Why should Valso fear me?"

She hesitated for several heartbeats. "Because you are the most frightening thing of all. You are the unknown."

"And why do you hate your son?"

She frowned wistfully. "He's like his father in so many ways, even in that I loved my son once before I learned to hate him. A mother can't help loving her children, I learned. Haleen was the oldest—I bore her forty years ago. And then came Valso a few years later, and after him his three younger brothers. But Illalla trained Valso in his own likeness, and taught him to be cruel and ruthless. And as each of his younger brothers grew into manhood, grew to a point where he might challenge Valso for the throne someday, each died a strange and mysterious death. Valso is always thorough, especially when it comes to power."

She referred to temporal power, but Morgin purposefully misunderstood and asked, "But where did he come by such power. It's unnatural. It's wrong."

The Alaella looked at him, and she understood what he was doing. Her lips curled upward in a knowing smile. "There is an old magic, an evil magic. Its price is one's very identity, one's very soul. But the spells to gain such power had been lost in the obscurity of time. Then some years ago Illalla came across a very old manuscript—how I do not know—and he memorized the spells and incantations, then destroyed it. To wield such magic one must also be capable of housing such power, and Illalla knew he could not. He found in his son a vessel for the achievement of the power he coveted.

"Finally, as part of the incantation, they had to sacrifice the life of a true innocent." She looked at Morgin and asked him pointedly. "If you assume we are all born pure of heart, and from that moment forward we begin losing our innocence by degrees, where do you find a true innocent?"

"A new-born child, straight from the womb. But where did they find such a child?"

Merriketh walked over to the window and looked out at the city. "Our two families are so tightly coupled by fate. As a young man my husband raped your grandmother's sister Hellis, and she bore your uncle Tulellcoe. And as a young man your uncle Tulellcoe and my daughter Haleen fell in love. But neither clan would condone such a union, and so Olivia and Illalla took steps to insure they would not meet again. But unbeknown to us all they had lain together and conceived a child, though even to this day I doubt your uncle knows the child existed. But when born, Valso took it from Haleen and sacrificed it to the Dark God. And now that spell is coming to fruition."

"And what will that be?"

"I know not," she said, then sighed wearily and turned toward the door. She hesitated there but did not look back as she spoke. "I have tried to love my son, but I can love him no more than he loves me, and I can hate him no less."

••••

Sa'umbra the dream: two vast armies facing one another, Aethon arrayed in his finery. Morgin had dreamt it so many times he knew every detail with intimate familiarity.

Though always before he'd dreamt it from within Aethon's soul, the great Shahotma, and then it had possessed the sense of a dream, the ethereal character of unreality. But now he dreamed it from behind the eyes of Morddon, a lowly Benesh'ere mercenary, and the dream was all too real.

Morddon looked out over the field of death, at the bodies strewn haphazardly across the Gap. A strange calm had descended, quiet and still. For the past three days the two armies had fought sorties; small and large skirmishes, like two combatants testing each other's reflexes, seeking a weakness or blind spot. But now they sought the end, the finish, and as dawn broke slowly behind the forces of the Shahotma, a new tension filled the air.

"Master."

Morddon turned to face the voice, found a young Benesh'ere warrior standing respectfully behind him with considerable awe upon his face. The young warrior bowed deeply and dropped to one knee, as they'd all taken to doing now that they thought he was the last of the SteelMasters. Morddon had tried to tell them he was no SteelMaster, that he was not righting any wrongs, but his pleas always fell on deaf ears.

"Master, the Shahotma requests your presence."

Morddon nodded. "Lead on."

He followed the young warrior to Aethon's tent, expecting to find another council of war, but instead he found the Shahotma waiting alone. Morddon dropped to one knee. "Your Majesty."

Aethon shook his head and impatiently said, "Arise, Morddon. Please don't stand on formality now. I feel too alone."

Morddon understood what the young king meant. He'd felt the same isolation all his life, especially now that he'd been elevated to the exalted status of SteelMaster.

"I'm frightened, Morddon."

Morddon looked into Aethon's eyes, saw a frightened boy hiding behind the demeanor of a young man, a young king. "There's nothing wrong with being frightened. We're all frightened. In fact a certain amount of fear is healthy before a battle."

"But we've lost so many battles lately, and there's little hope we can win this one."

Morddon shook his head. "But this battle between two armies counts for naught in the scheme of things. The only battle that counts will be that between you and Beayaegoath, and the swords you carry."

Aethon shuddered, closed his eyes. "That's what I'm frightened of."

Again Morddon shook his head. "But don't you see. On that battlefield the slate is clean. Your army is outnumbered six to one, but you and the Dark One are evenly matched. They can slaughter all of the rest of us, but if you defeat Him then we are all victorious."

Aethon frowned and had difficulty choosing his words. "There is within me . . . There is within me another soul that haunts my soul. He's been with me for some time now, though not until recently did I realize his identity." Aethon smiled, as if remembering a pleasant thought. "I met him first in my dreams. I called him Lord Mortal. He is a handsome young wizard from a time I do not know, and he was searching for the Unnamed King so he could find his own name. But now he's just frightened. He doesn't understand what he's doing in my soul, and I don't know what to tell him."

Morddon chose not to speak of the fact that Lord Mortal now haunted his soul, for then he would have to admit he already knew the outcome of the battle to come.

A guard entered the tent. "Your Majesty, Lord TarnThane sends his regards. Dawn is upon us, and the hordes are gathering for battle."

Aethon straightened and stood erect, and the image of the frightened young boy disappeared, replaced by that of a proud and mighty king. "Tell Lord TarnThane I'll be out shortly."

Morddon helped Aethon put on his armor. They worked in silence, both of them trapped in their own thoughts.

••••

The morning began with a series of skirmishes as each side struggled for position. The lay of the pass had not changed from Morgin's time, or rather, it would not change by Morgin's time. Both roads, from the east and from the west, opened out on opposite sides of Csairne Glen, the Glen clear and carpeted with grass. The center of the Glen was slightly lower than either end, both sides sloping gently down toward the middle, as if to pull the two armies together for the bloodletting. By midday both armies had drawn up at either end of the Glen, and in anticipation of the final battle all of the small skirmishes came to an end.

While Aethon's generals positioned the various units of his army, Aethon nudged his horse forward a few dozen paces and stopped to survey the landscape before him. Behind him, and a bit to one side, Morddon watched him closely, knowing what would come.

Aethon sat upright in his saddle, his head snapped toward the middle of the Glen and his attention seemed riveted there. Morddon looked that way, and though he saw nothing he knew Aethon looked upon the apparition of his own death slowly limping toward him. Morddon followed the progress of the apparition by the tilt of Aethon's head as he watched it approach, then stop just out of reach. Then slowly, Aethon drew his sword and raised it to point at the apparition, though to Morddon's eyes he pointed at an empty patch of ground. And as Morgin had said in his own past, though in Morddon's future, Aethon demanded, "Name yourself, demon."

The apparition was not meant for Morddon's eyes, and its answer was not meant for his ears, but nevertheless he knew the words it spoke. "I am AethonDeath, my lord, and I have come for you."

Morgin had panicked at the sight of MorginDeath, had said, "Be gone. Leave me. You cannot have me." But Aethon, with the bearing of a true king, merely nodded for a moment, then shrugged and said, "So be it."

Guessing that the apparition had now departed, Morddon nudged Mortiss forward. Aethon turned to look at him, his face as white as the specter that had stood before him moments earlier. But as the color returned to his face, he said, "I've seen my own death, Morddon."

Morddon nodded. "I know."

"You know so much, my Benesh'ere friend. Do you know the outcome of this battle?"

Morddon stared out over the battlefield and refused to answer the question.

"I thought as much," Aethon said.

One of the generals rode up behind them. "We're ready, sire."

Aethon looked out across the Glen. "And it looks like our friends across the way are ready also. Stay close to me, Morddon. Stay close to me."

"I will, my king."

For that day's slaughter Morddon had chosen a good-sized broadsword, and as the two armies charged at each other and met with a roar, he laid death about him with an efficiency born of years of practice. The battle raged on through that afternoon without letup and Morddon did stay close to Aethon. But near dusk the vagaries of battle separated them, and later Morddon understood fate had intervened, for as darkness enveloped them it brought with it the Dark God, and all ran screaming before the might of evil that came upon the land.

33

The Darkness Descends

MORGIN SQUATTED DOWN on his heals over the pile of derelict blades, and as always his hand could choose only the one blade that seemed to be his destiny. He stood up, didn't bother to test the weight or balance of the steel, looked at the crowd gathered about him. Like him they wondered who Valso would find to fight him now that he had defeated one of the best among the Kulls.

As always, Morgin sensed Valso shortly before he arrived. He sensed him by the vast chasm of power that opened before him whenever the Decouix prince came near. But this day the sense of that power struck him like a sword, for it had the same taste as the power that had come to Csairne Glen to devour the army of the Shahotma that day long ago, and he wondered at that.

Morgin stood alone in the middle of a large cleared space where none of the on-lookers dared venture, and as Valso joined him the crowd murmured. Valso looked at Morgin carefully, then at the crowd, and when he raised his hands they cheered riotous-ly. He kept his hands raised through the cheers, until slowly the noise died and a hushed stillness settled over them all.

When all was quiet Valso spoke, "I have no doubt you're all wondering who will fight the Elhiyne this day. He has defeated the best among my Kulls, and so I must look beyond the ranks of the halfmen. So where do I look, and who will I find?"

He turned slowly as he spoke, addressing the entire crowd and drawing their atten-tion with practiced ease. "Should I look to the ranks of my noblemen?"

"Yes," the crowd screamed, desiring a true contest, not merely an exhibition of butchery.

"No," he told them, shaking his head. "My noblemen cannot fight without using their power, and for this poor Elhiyne, who is bereft of his power, that would be an unfair contest."

The crowd murmured its agreement, for none of them wanted to see an easy victo-ry.

"Well then, where should I look?"

The crowd grumbled in confusion and disappointment, until Valso threw his hands up again and signaled for silence. "I know where to look," he said. "I know the best swordsman in Durin, a man who can fight this Elhiyne without the use of power and still stand victorious. I know where to look, because I know to look to myself." Valso finished by drawing his own sword and waving it above his head, and the crowd roared its approval.

A knot formed in Morgin's stomach. Valso was the better swordsman, and they both knew it.

Valso threw off his coat, turned to face Morgin and crouched, ready to fight him. The crowd became still.

"You know I'm no duelist," Morgin said.

"And this is no duel," Valso said. "This is a fight—no rules, just survival—to the death."

Morgin had no choice so he nodded and extended his sword. They circled for a moment, then Valso sprang forward with a flurry of blows, forcing Morgin to back step desperately. But then he saw an opening: exposed ribs waiting for a well-placed boot, so Morgin kicked out, but Valso was no longer there, and fire danced up Morgin's leg as Valso nicked him with his sword. They disengaged and began circling again.

"Good try, Elhiyne," Valso said. "But you'll have to do better than that."

Valso was playing with him. The Decouix prince could have taken off his leg at the knee, but that would have ended the match too quickly. In desperation Morgin decided to go on the offensive. He attacked Valso with a flurry of cuts, but the Decouix deflected them easily, turning one of Morgin's strokes and cutting him on the cheek. Again they disengaged.

They circled for a moment, then Valso spun in and struck down with his sword. Morgin deflected it, struck back, dodged a thrust and elbowed Valso in the solar plexus. The Decouix grunted, and as he staggered away Morgin pressed his advantage, bringing his sword around in a flat arc. But Valso regained his composure, stepped away from it easily, struck back with a combination of strokes, slipped beneath Morgin's guard and nicked him in the ribs, though as they disengaged Morgin cut Valso on the shoulder.

Valso was a born swordsman, whether dueling or just fighting for his life, though oddly Morgin and he seemed almost evenly matched in this kind of combat. But Morgin knew Valso was using a small hint of that vast power at his command, just enough to make the difference, though not enough to be detected by the crowd. And as the match progressed he made a fool of Morgin, cutting him time and again, dropping him in the dirt, kicking or punching him. Occasionally Morgin got in a blow, or a cut, but only because Valso didn't want his use of power to be obvious. Clearly, he wanted to give the crowd a good, long show, slowly wearing Morgin down. And while at first they had appeared evenly matched, it slowly became obvious Valso was in control, for Morgin had gone down into the dirt six times to Valso's one, and he was cut in a dozen places where Valso had been touched by Morgin's sword only twice.

Morgin could barely lift his sword, but he would not give up. If Valso was going to kill him, then he was determined to die fighting. He attacked the Decouix, cut down then across, down then across, kicked out at an exposed knee. But Valso sidestepped the blow, kicked Morgin in the ribs, then caught him in the back of the head with the hilt of his sword and Morgin went down.

He almost lost consciousness, lying face down in the dirt, and he did lose his sword. But as he groped for it he felt cold steel touching the back of his neck and he froze. Valso stood over him with the tip of his sword resting on Morgin's spine.

The crowd went wild screaming for his blood, but Valso raised his free hand and silenced them. "You want the Elhiyne's life?" he asked them.

The mob screamed its reply. "Yes. Kill him."

Valso shook his head. "But I want it too. We all know who is the better swordsman, and I have uses for him alive."

Valso stepped back a few paces and sheathed his sword. Bayellgae streaked across the yard and settled on his shoulder. "Massster. I am pleasssed you were victoriousss."

Valso looked at the little demon snake curled on his shoulder and stroked the top of its head with a finger. "Perhaps I'll give him to you, for who can survive your venom?"

"Only you, massster. Only you, and of courssse . . ." The snake turned its head and looked at Morgin. "And of courssse Lord Mortal there."

Valso started and his eyes snapped toward Morgin. He looked back at the snake, then back at Morgin, then screamed, "Nooooo."

He rushed up to Morgin and started kicking him, screaming and cursing as he rained vicious blows on him. Morgin wasn't sure if he should take some satisfaction in Bayellgae's revelation, though he resolved to remember the look on Valso's face as he lost consciousness.

••••

Morddon moved silently from one shadow to the next, paused to listen carefully to the sounds about him. Dawn had come almost reluctantly, as if the land wished to keep the devastation of the battlefield hidden in the shadows of the night. The still air was filled with the cries of those who were unfortunate enough to die slowly of their wounds.

He thought he knew where Aethon had gone down, but the landscape looked different littered by so many corpses. Nevertheless he searched, and he continued to search without rest, for somehow he knew Aethon still lived, and he didn't care enough to wonder how he knew.

He found him just as the sun rose fully above the mountain peaks. The young king lay unconscious, his tunic soaked with blood, so Morddon picked him up like a child, and with the help of Morgin's shadows carried him off the Glen to where Mortiss hid in a small clump of forest. The two of them were not an excessive burden for the horse.

Morddon rode with Aethon seated in front of him, his arms gripping Mortiss's reins around the unconscious king to support him. But near mid-morning Aethon cried out and regained consciousness. Morddon cupped a hand over his mouth and whispered in his ear, "Be silent, my king."

"Morddon?" Aethon pleaded. "Is that you?"

"Aye," Morddon answered.

"Ah, my white faced friend. The sword . . . my sword, it was not flawed. It didn't fail, and yet, here I am, defeated."

"I think your victory must wait for another age, my king."

Aethon drifted off into an uneasy sleep, his breathing ragged and shallow. When he again awoke he pleaded, "Can we stop and rest? It hurts so terribly."

Morddon stopped near a small stream, gently put Aethon down in the shade of a tall elm tree. Aethon burned with fever, so Morddon soaked his blouse in the cold stream and swabbed the young king's forehead. He was much too ill to travel further so Morddon let him rest, and through that day he drifted in and out of consciousness while Morddon sat next to him and tried to calm him. But late that afternoon Aethon awoke and grasped Morddon's arm. "It wasn't me he sought," he said, struggling to get the words out. "Never me."

"Don't speak," Morddon told him. "Try to rest."

"I was nothing to the Dark God. He swept me aside like a feather in a strong wind, and he coveted only Lord Mortal. Always Lord Mortal."

Aethon shuddered and gasped. "I pity poor Lord Mortal, for Beayaegoath ripped him from my soul, and even now torments him beyond life itself. I wonder if he ever found the Unnamed King . . . ever found his name."

Aethon calmed, and the shaking stopped, and slowly his body relaxed and his eyes glazed over with death. And there beneath the elm tree all life seemed to stand still for that instant, as if the soul of the land felt the loss of its king.

Morddon used his fingers to close the dead king's eyes, then he covered him with the blanket from his pack and bivouacked for the night. In the morning, while gathering stones for a cairn, he happened to glance up and saw a small, black speck high in the sky. He knew that shape well, so he stepped out into the open and waved his arms.

The speck circled and grew in proportion as it descended, until a few minutes later TarnThane landed nearby. "Well, SteelMaster," the griffin lord said. "We are come to this."

"He's dead," Morddon said.

The griffin nodded. "I know. We all felt his passing. We're preparing a crypt now, a place appropriate for the last of the Shahotma. Will you bring him?"

Morddon started to object, to say he must return to Kathbeyanne, but the griffin shook his head violently. "Your place is by his side, whiteface."

Morddon turned his head slowly from side to side, stretching the tension out of his neck muscles. "I guess Magwa can wait a few more days, halfbird."

Morddon wrapped Aethon's body in his own blanket, and carefully sat him on Mortiss's saddle. He then mounted behind him and wrapped his arms around him as if he were still alive and needed protecting. And it occurred to Morgin that, perhaps in death, he did need protection.

TarnThane led the way, always circling high in the distance ahead, guiding Morddon north toward Attunhigh. The path TarnThane chose kept them high in the mountains, always skirting the edge of some deep crevasse or sheer rock face. Morddon could not have found the way on his own, even with his vast knowledge of forest and mountain lore. But with the griffin overhead surveying the ground from the advantage of soaring heights, always picking just the right trail, Morddon found his way easily. He camped that night near an icy mountain stream, and the next morning they rose above the tree line to a barren landscape of rocks and lichen and small patches of snow.

On the third day of travel, as Mortiss carefully picked her way up a twisting trail of steep switchbacks, the path suddenly opened out onto a flat shelf of rock, a wide expanse where Ellowyn and the other legion commanders awaited them in a solemn, silent throng. With them stood the royalty of the House of the Thane and what remained of the Benesh'ere command. Morddon nudged Mortiss forward slowly and stopped just short of them.

He dismounted, and gently lowered Aethon out of the black mare's saddle. The dead king weighed next to nothing, as if he'd already begun turning to ash. Morddon laid Aethon down at Ellowyn's feet. He watched as the archangels stripped him and carefully washed him, then dressed him in the ceremonial armor of the Shahotma, the greatest of kings.

When Ellowyn finished she looked to Morddon. "You should take him to his final rest. He would want that." She nodded toward the mountain behind her and the granite that rose steeply from the shelf where they stood. Only then, with Morgin's ability to see through shadows, only then did Morddon see that one particular black slash of granite was actually a shadow filling the small mouth of an open cave.

Morddon picked up Aethon; he weighed more now that he'd been dressed in the heavy ceremonial armor, yet still he seemed diminished. Morddon had to duck, and shuffle sideways to fit through the low, narrow mouth of the cave. But it opened into an inner cavern dimly lit by flickering sconces, and Morgin immediately recognized the burial chamber of the Skeleton King, a room cluttered with swords and shields and armor polished to a brilliant sheen and studded with jewels. Thick and richly embroidered tapestries covered the walls, and in the center, surrounded by such unimaginable riches, sat the throne of the Shahotma King.

Morddon sat the dead king upon his throne, and arranged his arms and legs as if he were holding high court. But to Morgin's eye the scene remained incomplete. Morddon straightened, and looking at Aethon's lifeless form he said, "There's something missing."

Behind him Ellowyn said, "His sword. The AethonSword."

Morddon turned to face her, found her standing with a sheathed broadsword resting in her outstretched hands. Morgin recognized the jeweled hilt from his dreams as Morddon reached out and took the sword, then carefully pulled the blade from the sheath. It shone with the brilliance of the finest steel, the blade intricately worked with runes decorating its entire length. "The godslayer," Morddon said. "Why did Aethon not fight the Dark God with this blade? It must contain great power, and yet he left it behind."

Morddon, who was not a magician or wielder of sorcerous powers, could not sense what Morgin sensed: that the blade contained no power and was just a blade. He hid that knowledge from Morddon, the only thing he'd ever truly hidden from his Benesh'ere host.

"Why?" Morddon asked again.

He hadn't meant it as a real question, not one to be answered, but Ellowyn did so anyway. "He said the blade you forged, the flawless blade, would have more power against the Goath's evil."

Morgin shared Morddon's thoughts; had he doomed Aethon by giving him the blade he'd forged? Had they turned fate aside by not using the proper blade? But it was too late for such thoughts.

He turned back to the throne and his dead king, and arranged Aethon so he sat with one arm resting casually on an armrest, the other on the hilt of the great sword, its tip resting in the dust of the floor, its upper weight balanced by no more than the casual grip of Aethon's hand. He carefully set the scene so that every detail matched the tomb of Morgin's dreams.

He was the last to exit the tomb, and he stopped just outside the narrow entrance. The angels quickly filled it with rocks the size of a man's head, and then Morgin cast a shadow he hoped would deter any stranger who chanced this way.

Morddon climbed into Mortiss's saddle, and when he looked back one last time, Morgin had the oddest thought. *He could see through his own shadows as no other could. Anyone else standing at this spot would see nothing but rock and mountain, but Morgin would always recognize that cave mouth in an instant.*

34

Triumph Denied

THE BLACK DARKNESS, the rank smells of piss and shit, his own unwashed body, matted and clumped hair; all of these things were familiar to Morgin, and as he slowly struggled to full consciousness, the aches and pains in his mistreated body reminded him he was in the bowels of Decouix. It took great effort just to pull himself up off the stone floor into a sitting position with his back to a wall, and in the process he discovered a hundred bruises and aches. The Kulls had prepared him for the arrival of his family by beating him continuously through the night. His left hand had swollen badly, though he didn't think anything was broken there, but his ribs might be a different story. He explored his face carefully with his right hand. One eye had swollen completely shut, was unusable; and while the other was swollen badly, he guessed he could see out of it to some limited extent. Bruises and small cuts covered his face. He thought about trying to stand, decided it wasn't worth the effort, and drifted back into a restless sleep . . .

The cell door slammed open; light blinded him; rough hands lifted him off his feet, then chained him hand and foot. He thought at first they'd come for another beating, but they pulled him out of the cell and dragged him through the castle. They took him to a room high in Decouix, and as Morgin peered through the slit of his half-swollen eye, he found Valso waiting for him. "I have something I want you to see," Valso said.

He turned and stepped through tall doors onto a balcony. The Kulls dragged Morgin across the room and out onto the balcony with Valso, stood him up against the balcony rail. "Look," Valso said, and he pointed down into the city.

For the longest time Morgin saw nothing that should pique Valso's interest so, though time and again he tried to sight down the length of Valso's arm. But then he noticed a commotion in one of the main streets that led to the castle, a procession of riders, one of them carrying a red Elhiyne banner. The distance was too great to be certain but he thought the banner carrier might be DaNoel, and behind him rode several members of House Elhiyne.

"My father is among them," Valso said. "He thinks he's returning to his throne, but actually he's returning only to shame. And your family thinks they will use him to shame all of House Decouix." Valso looked Morgin up and down carefully. "But you're going to help me turn the cards on them, aren't you?"

Morgin refused to answer, so one of the Kulls kneed him in the groin. He cried out and fell to his knees. "Aren't you, Elhiyne?"

Still Morgin refused to answer, so the Kulls beat him senseless.

He awoke again in the dungeon, but it seemed he'd only been awake for moments when they came for him again. He didn't try to help them or resist them; his body hurt too much to take action one way or the other. They dragged him again through the castle corridors and finally dumped him on a cold, stone floor in a large room. He heard a large crowd gasp at the sight of him, and he forced open the one eye through which he could see, saw ranks of feet gathered along a wall several paces away. He'd been dumped in the middle of the Decouix throne room, and all those present feared the consequences of coming too close to him. It hurt too much to hold his head up and keep the eye open, so he closed it and lay his head against the stone floor.

He heard some sort of an argument going on. He tried to ignore it, but then he caught the sound of Rhianne's voice raised in anger. ". . . and you'll not stop me."

He heard the soft patter of slippered feet crossing the floor, then the rustle of petticoats nearby. He could smell her; the scent of her contrasted sharply with the smell of the dungeon that clung so heavily to him. He opened his eye, looked into her face. She'd sat down on the floor right in the middle of the throne room, and cradled his head in her lap. "My darling," she said. "What have they done to you?"

"Young Lady!" Olivia's voice had not changed in the months since he'd last heard it, would probably never change. The old woman stood over them both as Rhianne looked up at her. Morgin kept his one eye on Rhianne and ignored his grandmother. "It's not proper for you to just sit down in the middle of this hall like that."

Rhianne's eyes hardened. "I care nothing for what is proper, old woman."

Olivia said angrily, "You care nothing for—"

Something abruptly silenced the old woman, and when Morgin looked in Rhianne's eyes he saw magic flare so intense and angry it was something to match even that of the old witch. Rhianne spoke softly, but there was steel in her voice, "Go away, old woman, and leave us alone for the few moments we have."

Morgin heard Olivia hesitate, then turn slowly and walk away. Rhianne looked down at him and there were tears on her cheeks; they dripped down onto his face. He lost himself in her eyes as she bent down and kissed him gently on the cheek, then on the lips. And for that one moment he would have endured a thousand beatings.

••••

DaNoel stood just within the entrance of the great throne room of Decouix, his hand carefully holding one end of a symbolic chain, with the other end wrapped about the throat of Illalla. At the far end of the hall Valso sat on the Decouix throne on a high dais. DaNoel had expected to walk the length of the hall in triumph, Illalla following meekly behind him at the end of his chain. Olivia wanted it to be a grand display of Decouix defeat at the hands of Elhiyne. But just as DaNoel was ready to march forward, Valso had surprised them all by having a semiconscious Morgin dragged into the throne room and dumped unceremoniously in the middle of the floor, half-way between DaNoel and Valso.

DaNoel had thought he would feel great triumph to see Morgin humbled so, but this victory brought him no joy. He watched Rhianne defy Olivia, watched her shed tears that dripped onto the whoreson's battered and swollen face, and he wondered if anyone would ever love him so.

"How touching," Valso cried, standing arrogantly. "It warms my heart to see such devotion."

Looking past Morgin and Rhianne, he gestured grandly to DaNoel. "Come forth, Elhiyne. I long to see my dear father."

DaNoel marched forward slowly, carefully keeping to the script prepared by Olivia, though he was forced to turn aside and walk around Rhianne and Morgin. When he reached the base of the dais beneath the throne he stopped and merely nodded, refusing to bend the knee or bow to the Decouix prince.

Valso laughed and strode happily down the steps of the dais. He stopped in front of DaNoel and held out his hand. "Yield my father. I certainly paid enough ransom for him."

DaNoel placed the end of the chain in Valso's hand.

Illalla said, "Finally, I am home. Let's have these chains removed immediately."

Valso smiled unpleasantly and turned to a Kull captain standing nearby. The Kull stepped forward and Valso handed him the end of the chain. "Deposit my fool of a father in a cell next to that of the Elhiyne wizard. They can shout encouragement to each other."

The Kull jerked the chain hard, and as Illalla stumbled forward off balance, the Kull kicked him in the crotch. Illalla crumbled to the floor, gasping for air. The Kull waved two of his comrades forward, and they proceeded to kick and beat Illalla senseless, until he lay there groaning piteously. They picked him up by the armpits and dragged him away down the length of the hall. As they passed Morgin and Rhianne two more Kulls stepped out of the crowd and pulled Morgin out of her arms.

No, DaNoel felt no triumph in this charade; as they dragged the whoreson away he felt only pity, and regret.

••••

Morgin awoke again in the darkness of his cell, wondered for a moment if Rhianne had just been another delirious dream. But then he noticed a hint of the scent she'd worn still clung to him and he was thankful for that.

He slept for a while, awoke again and felt a little better. Hunger gnawed at him, so he managed to get up on his hands and knees and search the floor of his cell. He found a large bowl of gruel, which meant Valso didn't want him dead yet. It was tasteless, but it filled his stomach. He slept again, awoke and ate again, repeated that cycle several times. Then one time when he awoke a light pierced the darkness of his cell. Not much, just a sheet of rays escaping past the partially open cell door. He saw the silhouette of a woman leaning down over him, touching his forehead gently, as if to determine if he was real. "My child," she said.

Valso's sister Haleen stood over him. "He is cruel, my brother. It is a terrible thing for him to be so cruel. But then that is his nature, isn't it?"

Thinking only of the open cell door Morgin struggled to sit up, then to stand. "Yes," she said. "You must be strong if you hope to escape."

"Escape!"

"Yes, escape. You don't think I would leave my only child to him and his devices?"

Now it all made sense. Haleen, the Mad Whore, had deluded herself into believing Morgin was her long lost, murdered child. Morgin didn't want to take advantage of the poor woman, but he wasn't stupid enough to pass up such an opportunity.

She had cast a spell on the dungeon guards and they slept soundly standing up. So too did several sentries in carefully chosen corridors. She had to help him most of the way, but eventually she got him into a small carriage. The driver sat atop it with eyes glassed over in a trance. She had Morgin lay down on the floor of the carriage, and called up to the driver to proceed.

Morgin drifted off to sleep as the carriage wound its way through the streets of Durin, and when he awoke he smelled the fresh air of the countryside. The carriage had come to a stop and again Haleen stroked his forehead gently.

He climbed out of the carriage, felt stronger than he'd felt since being thrown into the Decouix dungeons. Haleen must have cast a spell upon him to sustain him temporarily. "Travel south," she said wistfully, "and beware of the skree."

She kissed him on the cheek, called up to the driver, and the carriage disappeared into the night.

Morgin looked about. He stood near a road in a lightly forested area, and her last words struck him like a blow to the stomach: ". . . the skree."

He headed south, his mind's eye replaying the image of the poor man torn apart by the small netherhounds. He kept to a brisk walk, constantly forcing himself to ignore the temptation to break into a blind panic and run. He probably had a few hours before Valso discovered he was missing, a few more hours before he forced the truth from

Haleen. He had a much better chance if he kept his head about him and kept to a steady pace rather than running until exhausted.

He followed a narrow cart track that ran south. By midday Haleen's spell had begun to wear off and he felt the effects of his treatment in the Decouix dungeon. As time wore on his physical state deteriorated until finally he could only manage a slow, limping shamble.

The cart track cut through a small village. He was in no state to be seen, so he cut off the track and circled the village. He spotted an old plow horse grazing at the edge of a field. It bothered his conscience to steal the animal, though he thought it ironic he had begun life as a thief in the streets of Anistigh. But he was desperate, and without something beyond his own feet to carry him, he would soon collapse.

Morgin hadn't ridden bareback in years, and doing so now reminded him of how uncomfortable it could be. Dozing in the saddle was one thing, but any attempt to sleep on the back of the shambling old mare would inevitably deposit him on his butt in the middle of the cart track.

Shortly before sunset the cart track joined up with a larger path that almost qualified as a road, though weeds growing out of the dirt meant it was little traveled. The old mare had begun to show the effects of the long ride, and he needed rest and food, so he traveled down the road until he found a small farm. He set up a makeshift camp in a small clump of woods nearby.

That night he snuck onto the farm and managed to steal a tattered old piece of canvas he could use as a blanket. He also found a bin full of cattle feed, picked through it without much care to what he ate, and took some back for the old mare.

He traveled for two days, not covering a vast distance, but making steady progress south. In the evening of the second day he felt he'd gained enough distance to warrant a full night's sleep. So he curled up in his canvas blanket and lay down near the old mare for some much needed rest.

••••

A heavy black cloud hung over Kathbeyanne as the city burned, obscuring a full moon that would have ordinarily lit the streets. The flickering, orange-yellow glow of fire filled the night, accompanied by the crackle of burning timbers. Wafts of smoke drifted down the streets like early morning fog, and the cries of the dying could be heard everywhere.

Morddon slipped from one shadow to the next. He moved carefully, for there were marauding Kulls, human Goath, and jackal warriors everywhere, intent on burning all that remained. Somewhere in the distance a wall collapsed with a loud crash.

With the help of Morgin's shadows Morddon had no difficulty making his way to the palace. An enormous bonfire burned in the middle of the parade ground outside its gates, with hundreds of Goath gathered around it. They seemed frantic to find something else to destroy, as if the city of the gods itself was not enough.

Morddon didn't cross the parade ground, but instead worked his way along the back of the barracks until he reached the palace wall. There he found innumerable shadows waiting for him. He slipped into one, gave it life, danced along the base of the wall toward the gates, which were wide open to facilitate the plunder of the grandest court in the memory of all mankind.

He had no difficulty finding AnneRhianne's quarters, though she had long since departed. He hadn't expected to find her there, but he had to make sure. She was resourceful and would manage to take care of herself.

Next he made his way to the throne room, the grandest of all halls in the grandest of all palaces. With the shadows of so many flames dancing about, and with Morgin's shadowmagic, he had no difficulty getting there undiscovered.

The ceiling-high doors to the throne room were open, with two jackal guards standing watch over them, though they leaned drowsily on their lances. Morddon heard voices in the throne room itself so he waited patiently. After a few minutes the conversation came to an end and several jackal officers emerged. The two guards snapped to rigid attention, and as the officers disappeared down the corridor they returned to their drowsy boredom. Morgin called up a simple spell, and both guards sat down on the floor and slipped into a deep sleep. Morddon, wrapped in a shadow, stepped past them into the throne room. As he'd expected, Magwa sat arrogantly on the throne, reveling in her victory.

Morddon closed his eyes, let Morgin's senses go out. He sensed no steel in the room other than his own and that Magwa carried. Very quietly he closed the doors to the room and latched them in place. He wanted Magwa alone.

Morgin dropped his shadow magic, and Morddon stepped openly into the center of the hall with almost the entire length of the room between him and the jackal queen. Magwa looked up, clearly unsurprised. "Well now," she barked. "The SteelMaster has come, as I knew he would. Is it revenge you seek?"

Morddon shrugged. "I seek your death, bitch-queen, and if that is revenge, then so-be-it."

"And how will you kill me, with my warriors to protect me?"

"Your warriors are locked beyond the walls of this room. And in any case, they would have some difficulty raising steel against me."

"And after I am dead, how will you escape?"

"After you are dead, I care not if I escape."

She nodded slowly. "You are a determined man, but you're also a fool." She turned her head, barked an order, "Now, captain!" and from behind the dais on which the throne rested, a jackal officer and a dozen jackal bowmen appeared in an instant to stand between their queen and Morddon. The bowmen were ready with arrows nocked, and they raised them now, drew the bowstrings taught.

Magwa waved a hand to indicate the bowmen. "This officer and these bowmen are carrying no steel. Their arrows are tipped by sharpened stone, and so these arrows will not obey your commands, oh last of the SteelMasters. And my master is done with you. He has given me permission to dispose of you."

Morddon understood then that he was going to die, and for an instant he searched within his soul to find some regret. But all his life he'd known his fate, and the fate of his people. There had never been any hope.

He sprang forward like a lion, drawing his sword in the same instant Morgin pulled a shadow about him. He heard the twang of a bowstring, but the shadow must have confused the bowman for the first arrow hissed past his ear harmlessly. But the second caught him high in the left shoulder, the third smashed into his hip and he stumbled momentarily, though he kept his balance and his momentum carried him on. The next arrow caught him low in the chest, to one side of his solar plexus, the next caught him in the thigh, and finally one slammed into his chest and he went down.

He managed to pull himself to his feet, but as he did so they put an arrow in his stomach, then one in his throat, and he collapsed in a heap. Lying on the floor he felt an arrow bury itself in his back, then another, and another. Suddenly he no longer had the strength to hold onto life and for the first time he felt free. But Magwa's barking laughter spoiled his new freedom, spoiled the last moments of his life.

35

The Dane King

RHIANNE AWOKE TO the sound of some strange netherbeast's cries. She threw on a robe and stepped out onto the balcony of her room, and down in the Decouix castle yard she saw Valso gathering together a group of noblemen and an escort of Kulls. Valso looked up and saw her, waved, called up happily. "Your husband has escaped, made a run for it. It's going to be good sport hunting him down."

The cry of the netherbeasts drowned out all other sound, and the pack of skree poured out of the kennel like a wave of death, held in check only by some magic of Valso's. Valso and the noblemen and Kulls mounted their horses then herded the skree out through the castle gates.

Rhianne turned back to her room, and in a mad haste she threw on some clothes and rushed down to the stables. She forced one of the stable master's apprentices to saddle a horse for her, climbed into the saddle and charged out of the castle, ignoring the challenge from the guards on the battlements above the gates. She didn't look back to see if they tried to stop her. Somehow she must help Morgin.

••••

Morgin awoke in the first moments of dawn to a strange sound far in the distance. He sat up in his canvas blanket, trying to shake the fog of dreams from his thoughts, and listened carefully. For some moments he heard only a continuous sort of braying at the limit of his hearing. But then out of that continuous background, one voice rose above the rest, and it sent a cold shiver through his heart: "... skree ... skree ..."

He jumped to his feet with his canvas blanket wrapped around him like a cloak. There was no camp to pack up, no possessions, no saddle to worry about. He climbed up on the old mare's back, dug his heels into her flanks and demanded all the speed she could give him. But she was old and tired, and she barely managed to put wind in his face with a half-hearted trot. His own condition had improved vastly; cattle feed apparently agreed with his muscles and bones, if not with his taste.

He kept to the road, pushed the old mare to her limits; by virtue of her longer legs when compared to the short, stubby pegs on which the skree ran, she outran them, and their barking and yapping dwindled into the distance. But after a short while she began struggling for air and her gait grew uneven. He was forced to let her drop back to a walk, and after only a few minutes his ears caught the sound of the pack on his trail: ". . . skree . . . skree . . . skree . . ."

He pushed the mare into a trot, and she struggled valiantly to obey, but there was just nothing left in her old bones to fight with. The sound of the skree grew louder and he could pick out individual voices in the pack now. There was no justice in making the old mare die with him, so he slid off her back, scratched her gently between the ears. "I'm sorry, old girl. I should have left you in your pasture. Perhaps some poor farmer will find you, feed you, and not work you too hard."

Morgin swatted her on the rump as hard as he could. It startled her and she trotted up the road a short distance, then slowed to a walk.

He turned around and backtracked several hundred paces. There was no question the skree would catch him, but if he diverted them off the old mare's trail far enough then she might live out her remaining years peacefully.

He turned off the road, began cutting across open fields, tried to run at a steady trot. But while he'd had a few days to recuperate from his treatment in Valso's dungeon, he learned quickly it wasn't enough as the pain from his injuries awoke, and his trot turned into a limping walk.

He didn't want to die, and especially not that way, torn apart in a hundred tiny mouths filled with razor sharp teeth as the monstrous little netherbeasts swarmed over him. He tried to force that image out of his mind, and limped on paying little heed to his direction. He concentrated on each step, and that it must be away from the cries of the pack. They were gaining on him, and he felt panic stirring within his heart.

He cut through a small woodland, then across a large open field to another woodland. But just before stepping beneath the leaves of the trees the cries of the skree took on a renewed urgency, and he stopped to look back.

He should have realized the old mare would follow him. She had no place else to go, and for the past few days it had been his hand that had fed her. In the distance, in the middle of a grassy field, she shambled toward him with a tired walk. But when she saw that he'd stopped, she stopped too and hesitated for a moment, and then the pack of skree broke from the trees on the opposite side of the field. They poured outward like a small, gray flood of water, and from that distance he could not distinguish individuals in the pack.

The old mare didn't seem to know enough to fear them. She just stood there watching Morgin as the fastest members of the pack reached her first. She cried out as they bit into her ankles, tripped her up, forced her to her knees, brought her down so that when the body of the pack reached her it swarmed over her, and she disappeared completely from sight beneath a seething mass of small gray bodies, as if a gray blanket had been placed over her body, with a lump in the middle as the only indication she was even there. As Morgin looked on the lump slowly dwindled, and then finally it flattened completely, and for a moment the pack lost some of its frenzy. When they moved on the only thing that remained of the old mare was a large red stain on the ground. They had devoured her, bones, hair and all.

The cries of the skree broke out anew as they swarmed toward Morgin.

He turned toward the trees, ran in among them, knew the skree would be upon him in seconds. He picked out an old oak tree, tossed his canvas cloak aside and began climbing. Beneath him the skree reached the base of the tree and went wild. He stopped and perched on a thick limb, looked down at the little monsters.

They swarmed over the base of the tree, barking and yapping at him. All he saw were mouths full of teeth turned up toward him and snapping uncontrollably. They had even managed to climb a short distance, but they'd reached a point where the trunk was nearly vertical and that stopped them, though one of them broke away from the rest and struggled upward by burying its tiny claws in the bark. The little thing was awkward, and clumsy, and slow, but it managed to climb the height of its own body above its fellows, and once there it stopped and dug its claws into the bark even deeper. Then one of its fellows climbed over it easily, and just as clumsily struggled beyond it until it had gained one more body length higher, and there it stopped. Another skree climbed easily over the two, while others beneath it swarmed over them and reinforced them. They were slow and clumsy, struggling up a vertical wall of bark, but once in place they locked their claws into the bark to provide a ladder up which the rest of the pack swarmed with ease.

When they got within range of the limb on which Morgin crouched, he kicked down at the next one that tried to climb above the pack. He managed to dislodge several of them that way, but then one buried its teeth in his calf and his leg lit up with a fiery burn. He screamed out, grabbed the little monster behind its ears and pulled, but nothing would dislodge it.

The pain was horrendous. Blood poured down his ankle, and below him they'd almost reached his limb. He began edging his way farther out on the limb, but he stopped when it became too thin to support him. The one skree still had its teeth buried in his calf, and he was desperate enough now to ignore the pain, so he raised his leg and slammed the little beast against the limb. It took five such kicks to crack the little beast's skull, and even then he had to forcefully pry its jaws open. But he managed it, and tossed its carcass aside just as the pack reached his limb.

He had nothing to lose now. There was another oak just near enough for a truly desperate man to delude himself into thinking he might jump across to it. So he stood up precariously on the limb, thinking even if he missed he was high enough to break his neck when he hit the ground, so at least they wouldn't devour him alive.

He squatted down and sprang up into the air, and for a moment was free almost like a bird. But then his fingers touched the limb he was reaching for and he caught hold of it, though only near its tip, and it bent down heavily like a fishing pole with a large trout on the hook. It snapped with a loud crack; he let go and grabbed at anything, bounced off a larger branch with his ribs, caught another and came to a stop hanging by his hands swinging back and forth.

He caught his breath for a moment, looked down. His feet dangled no more than head high off the ground. He could have easily dropped to the ground and walked away were it not for the swarm of skree gathered beneath him, snapping up at his ankles. They'd also begun bridging their way up the trunk of the tree he was hanging from. His ribs hurt and he didn't think he had the strength to pull himself up to start climbing again. He should have just let himself fall, should have let the fall break his neck.

Without apparent reason the skree suddenly stopped yapping, stopped completely; stopped moving, stopped barking, stopped snapping at his ankles, and an incredible stillness settled over them, as if waiting for something, listening. Morgin listened too, though the pounding of his heart filled his ears.

Far in the distance, though not a distance measured in length, but in time and worlds and life, a howl rose above the stillness, a sound like the cry of a wolf. But he heard something more in it, something not of this life. It rose high on the air, reached a magnificent crescendo, then died as slowly as it had come.

The skree broke into a frenzy of cries. A few started snapping again at Morgin's heels but most lost interest. Then the howl came again, this time closer. It tore at Morgin's soul, though it had an even greater effect on the skree. They abandoned their efforts to climb the tree, ran around wildly for a few moments, then gathered together and swarmed away as if they'd lost all interest in one poor, outlaw wizard hanging from a tree above them.

He could see nothing more of the skree, though in the distance he still heard their cries. Morgin hung from the tree, afraid to believe his eyes and ears. But then the howl came again, and he was just too tired to hold on longer, so he let go. He landed badly because of the wound in his leg and he fell to the ground.

He was sitting there like that, trying to gather the strength to stand and run, struggling to overcome sheer exhaustion, when the hellhound trotted up and towered over him. Morgin looked up at WolfDane, the hellhound king—he was easily the size of a horse. Morgin shook his head, struggled to hold onto consciousness. "You can't be here," he said. "Not in this time, this world, this life. You can't be here. This isn't a dream."

"Nothing is a dream," the hellhound growled. "And all things are dreams, fool, spawn of the Fallen One. I am here. That is all that matters. That is all that counts in the bargain I've made. Now come. We must be gone. The skree will soon realize I am alone and take up the hunt again."

Morgin struggled to his feet, could barely manage a limp. "Can't walk," he said. "You'll have to go on without me."

"But I can't, mortal. I'm stuck with you. Climb on my back. I'll carry you, if I must, to fulfill this bargain."

"What bargain?"

"Shut up and do as I say." The hellhound curled its lips back, showed Morgin its anger by flashing enormous, yellow teeth.

Morgin struggled to climb onto the hellhound's back. Once there the beast broke into a loping run that jarred Morgin's ribs painfully. He lost track of time, knew only that WolfDane carried him further south, and that they traveled without pause for two days and nights. Fatigue pulled at him, numbed him, dulled his senses.

He awoke lying on a sandy beach, with the hot sun blazing in the sky high overhead. He sat up, looked to the horizon and saw nothing but sand. He turned around, found WolfDane behind him standing on the bank of a wide, gently flowing river, his head bent to the water as he drank his fill. In the distance Morgin heard the cry of the skree.

Morgin turned about again and looked at the rolling sea of sand that stretched to the horizon. WolfDane had crossed the Ulbb and deposited him at the edge of the Great Munjarro Waste.

WolfDane's voice startled him. "Yes, mortal. The Munjarro. You're on your own now, and if you want to escape the skree then you'll taste the sands of the Munjarro."

Morgin looked at the hellhound. "But what'll stop them from following me out there?"

"Their feet are too small. They sink into the sand and flounder helplessly."

Morgin looked out again over the sand. "But how can I stay alive in that."

WolfDane shook his head. "I care not if or how you survive. My bargain is to deliver you from the skree, and you are delivered. And when next you meet the Fallen One, tell him I have done his bidding. Tell him this frees me of my debt to him, and never again will he bind me. Tell him the Dane King is finally free." And with those words WolfDane turned his back on Morgin, crossed the river and loped away.

The yowling of the skree pack was a constant din growing ever closer. Morgin knew he would need water out on the Munjarro, but he had no way of carrying any, so he lay down on the bank of the river and drank until nearly bloated. Then he stood, turned toward the sand and began walking.

••••

Rhianne traveled hard for days, eating nothing, sleeping little. She knew the way, simply followed the nether scent of the skree as if she had the nose of a hound. Eventually she came to a field where some poor animal had been devoured, and for some moments she wondered at the red stain that covered a large patch of grass. But just beyond that, in a small forest, she came across the bit of cloth.

It lay in the dirt where it had been trampled by a thousand tiny paws, and she was drawn to it by instinct, knew it had been something of Morgin. When she picked it up her fingers recoiled at the touch of it. It was moist with the drool of the small nether-hounds, and wet with blood.

She could no longer sense Morgin in her heart. With his magic so tightly compressed and wrapped about that of the blade, the thread of magic that had connected them had long since been severed. Since the battle at Csairne Glen, to have any sense of him she was wholly dependent upon her own magic and power.

She cast a spell of seeking, then opened her blouse and touched a dab of the blood to her breast just above her heart. An image of Morgin came to her. He was bloody, tattered, filthy and desperate. She heard the cries of the skree in the distance, and she tasted his fear. Her mind filled with a kaleidoscope of half formed images: Morgin cornered up a tree, the skree climbing clumsily after him, one of the little monsters with its teeth buried in his calf, his desperate leap for another branch, and his miss, and his fall, the skree everywhere. She sat down there in the dirt and sobbed openly, cried at the loss of the one man who had loved her, the man she had scorned and failed to love back until too late.

She grew numb to the core of her soul. Eventually she stood, mounted her horse, and in a daze she let it take her south until she reached the Ulbb and looked out across it to the Munjarro.

She sat on the northern bank of the Ulbb and watched the water drift past. Above her the sun burned hot and high in the sky, while across the river a sea of sand and heat stretched to the horizon. She was tired, hungry and dirty, but none of that mattered, for the loss of Morgin left her empty beyond belief. She wanted to walk out into the oven of sand and die, but that kind of ending was not for her. And there was no going back either, for she had failed. Elhiyne held nothing for her now, only the hateful old witch. Nor would she be welcome at Inetka.

She sat there for some hours watching the river, and came to the slow realization there was no place in this world for her. The one thing she could do was make sure the old witch would never find her. Young maidens were taught early-on how to conceal their magic from others with power, a sometimes necessary defensive tactic. And under the tutelage of AnnaRail and the old witch her capabilities had grown immeasurably. She smothered any outward signs of her power; though to make it last for more than a few days she'd have to prepare a rather complicated spell-casting. She'd worry about that later.

She stood, hunted down her horse, climbed up into its saddle and turned west. Perhaps she could find something at the Lake of Sorrows, for certainly the name of the place suited her. And if not there, then she'd seek elsewhere.

Epilogue:

Salula

THE DUNGEON BENEATH Decouix was, by nature, a damp, dark and dreary place. There were no windows, and the light of day never penetrated the darkness. During the quiet times the only sounds were the constant drip of water leaching out of the rock, or the occasional groan from one of the tortured souls confined therein. Every sound carried an echo.

High above a door slammed open, and light slashed into the darkness illuminating the top of a long stairway. The dungeon's jailer—a fat, middle-aged man who knew little of bathing and even less of polite manners—stepped through the open door carrying a spluttering torch. Valso and a half dozen Kulls followed him closely as he descended the stairs. At the bottom he moved quickly to light several torches set in the walls. The light revealed a large room containing many implements of torture. And set in each wall was the black mouth of a tunnel that led to a block of dungeon cells.

Valso looked about and barked at the jailer, "Clear a space in the center of the room and put a wooden chair in the middle of it."

He turned to one of the Kulls. "Go get the swordsman."

While two of the Kulls helped the jailer slide a rack to one side, the other four took a torch and disappeared down one of the dark tunnel mouths. There came the sound of a heavy latch thrown aside, an old door creaking open, then a scuffle and a single shout.

Valso walked over to the mouth of the dark tunnel and shouted down it, "Don't damage him. I have use for him, and need him healthy and whole."

A few moments later the first Kull emerged from the tunnel carrying the torch. Two more followed supporting an unconscious France between them, dragging his feet across the floor.

Valso pointed at the single chair sitting in the center of the room. "Put him there and bind him well."

The Kulls moved quickly, bound France's hands behind his back and his legs to the chair. France didn't move, sat with his head hanging limply against his chest and his eyes closed. "Wet him down," Valso said.

One of the Kulls filled a bucket from a barrel of foul smelling water then threw it in France's face. France threw his head back, spluttered and coughed and choked for several seconds.

"Well now, swordsman," Valso said pleasantly. "Have you enjoyed your stay here in Decouix?"

France shook the water out of his long, blond hair and smiled cockily. "Wonderful, Decouix. I particularly enjoyed the lice. They're a nice touch. It just wouldn't be right without them."

Valso nodded. "I like you, swordsman."

"I wish I could say the same about you, Decouix."

Valso continued to nod. "Yes. I do like you. I even sometimes like your friend, the Elhiyne. Like you, he amuses me. He thinks you're dead, you know. We told him you drowned in the river. I suppose that was a mistake. If he'd known you were alive he might have tried to rescue you when he escaped, and that would have given us another chance to capture him."

France threw his head back and laughed defiantly. "He's escaped, eh? Good for him."

"Yes," Valso said frowning. "Good for him. He escaped out onto the Munjarro, and we couldn't follow him there. He's probably dead already, but then I don't know that for sure and I need a hound to track him."

France shook his head and laughed again. "You won't catch him."

Valso considered France's comment and frowned thoughtfully. "Well now, with any ordinary hound it would be exceedingly difficult. But you see, swordsman, I have Salula."

France stopped laughing and his eyes darkened. "Salula's dead."

"Dead?" Valso asked. "Salula was never alive, so how can he be dead?"

France looked confused and Valso smiled at that. "Oh, the corporal body that was Salula's is dead. But he was only borrowing that. The body was not Salula, merely a vessel to contain him in this life, and the essence of Salula still exists. It still belongs to me, and is waiting for me to find an appropriate replacement for that body so it can again live among you mortals and hunt the Elhiyne."

France leaned forward and snarled, "You're mad."

Valso nodded his agreement. "Of course I'm mad. There's a certain madness that comes with limitless power. I've found that as I've risen above the rest of mortal mankind my understanding of the universe has grown beyond your comprehension, swordsman, and those like you. But I don't have time for this. I'm interested in seeing my dear old friend Salula again, and to do so I need a body for him, preferably that of an excellent swordsman with a strong will and a cold temper."

For the first time fear darkened France's face, and with his jaw clenched tight he spoke through his teeth. "Not me, Decouix. You need a willing partner for that, and I'll fight you to the grave."

"Good!" Valso said. "Good! Excellent! The more you're able to resist me the better for Salula, and in the end the stronger he'll be. Oh, without your consent it will be difficult, and it will take longer—in fact it might even take years—but I am a patient man, and when I am done you will be my hound, and together we will hunt the Elhiyne, and in the end it will be you who takes his life."

The Antiquities

It was in the springtime of antiquity that the gods first came unto the land, and there walked in mortal guise among the children of the Shahot, and blessed beyond imagining were the children who lived in the shadow of the divine.

It was in the summer of antiquity that the gods crowned the kings of the Shahot, and ordained the king of kings, the Shahotma. And with the guidance of the gods the kings reigned with wisdom, justice and mercy.

It was in the autumn of antiquity that the gods warred among themselves, and in the great clan wars that followed, the children of the Shahot lost four tribes, annihilated to the last man, woman and child, and never to walk the land again.

It was in the winter of antiquity that the gods left the land and, godless, the children of the Shahot despaired. They sought the gods throughout the planes of existence. But to no avail, for in their despair they failed to look in the heart of the Shahot, and they failed to look for the gods within.

• • • •

And so ends *The SteelMaster of Indwallin*, the second book of *The Gods Within*, in which Morgin has learned the lies of the past and the limits he faced there. In the third book, *The Heart of the Sands*, Morgin encounters the soul of the steel, and Rhianne must come to terms with her burgeoning power.

Dramatis Personae

The SteelMaster of Indwallin

Clan/Tribe	Color	Ward	Leader
Decouix	White	Tertius	Valso
Rastanna	Gray	Undecimus	Valso
Vodah	Blue	Duodecimus	Valso
Elhiyne	Red	Octavus	Olivia
Inetka	Yellow	Nonus	Wylow
Penda	Green	Quartus	BlakeDown
Tosk	Violet	Primus	PaulStaff
Benesh'ere	**Black**	**Septimus**	**Angerah**

The Greater Clans
- Decouix (dominant among the Greater Clans)
- Rastanna
- Vodah

The Lesser Clans
- Elhiyne (dominant among the Lesser Clans)
- Inetka (sworn to Elhiyne)
- Penda
- Tosk (sworn to Penda)

Clanless
- The Benesh'ere, the exiled tribe

Personae Decouix
- Illalla—King of the Greater Clans and head of all three

- Merriketh Alaella—wife to Illalla and mother of his children
- Valso—only living son of Illalla and Merriketh, and heir to the throne of the Greater Clans
- Haleen—only living daughter of Illalla and Merriketh, called *The Mad Whore* by some
- Thandin—an emissary to Elhiyne
- Andra—minor Decouix nobleman
- Degla—minor Decouix nobleman
- GeorgeAll—minor Decouix nobleman

Personae Rastanna
- Oubba—Commander of Tharsk, the fortress at Methula
- Carri—Oubba's wife
- Tarkiss—Oubba's son
- Andrew—an old country nobleman
- Stetha—Andrew's son

Personae Vodah
- Xenya—a young noblewoman with a rebelious attitude regarding Valso
- Alta—Xenya's brother

Personae Kullish
- Salula—Captain and commander of all Kulls
- Verk—a Kull captain, subordinate to Salula
- Mook—a simple Kullish guardsman
- Brakke—Kull officer in command of the Kullish forces at Tharsk
- Salya—a Kull lieutenant in Durin

Personae Elhiyne
- Olivia—Head of Clan Elhiyne
- Bertak—Olivia's father (deceased)
- Hillell—Olivia's mother (deceased)
- Karlane—Olivia's husband (deceased)
- Malka—Olivia's oldest son and heir to the leadership of Elhiyne (deceased)
- Marjinell—Malka's wife
- MichaelOff—oldest son of Malka and Marjinell (deceased)
- Brandon—youngest son of Malka and Marjinell
- Roland—Olivia's youngest son
- AnnaRail—Roland's wife

- DaNoel—1st child of Roland and AnnaRail
- Annaline—2nd child of Roland and AnnaRail
- JohnEngine—3rd child of Roland and AnnaRail
- NickoLot—4th child of Roland and AnnaRail
- Morgin—adopted child of Roland and AnnaRail
- Rhianne—the 4th of Edtoall and Matill's four daughters, and now Morgin's wife
- Hellis—Olivia's younger sister, took her own life in suicide (deceased)
- Tulellcoe—Hellis' only son, conceived by Illalla in an act of rape
- Alcoa—Marchlord of the western reaches that border on Penda
- Eglahan—Marchlord of Yestmark, sworn to Elhiyne
- Packwill—a scout, sworn to Eglahan of Yestmark
- Annen—bastard son of Eglahan
- Abileen—a sergeant of men
- Dannasul—a childhood friend of Morgin and JohnEngine
- Durado—an old man who maintains the waystation at Kallun's Gorge
- Samull—Durado's son
- Gorguh—Elhiyne stable master
- Erlin—Elhiyne stable boy
- Valken Surriot—a *twoname* who fought with Eglahan at the battle of Yestmark
- Cortien Balenda—a *twoname* who fought with Eglahan at the battle of Yestmark
- Hwatok Tulalane—a *twoname* advisor to Olivia (deceased)
- France—a common swordsman

Personae Aud
- Aiergain—Queen of the free port city, aka the Queen of Thieves
- Pandorin—a lieutenant in Aiergain's guard
- Sacress—Aiergain's physician
- Terrikle—a manservant provided to Morgin

Personae Penda
- BlakeDown—Head of Clan Penda
- ErrinCastle—Blakedown's oldest son and heir to the leadership of Penda
- Anja—a very young girl of minor status
- Tarare—a nobleman known to be a mouthpiece for BlakeDown

Personae Inetka
- Wylow—Head of Clan Inetka
- Carmet—Wylow's wife

- SandoFall—Wylow's oldest son and heir to the leadership of Inetka
- Edtoall—a minor Inetka lord and father of Rhianne
- Matill—Edtoall's wife and mother of Rhianne

Personae Tosk
- PaulStaff—Head of Clan Tosk

Personae Benesh'ere
- Angerah—ruler of the Black Council
- Jerst—WarMaster of the Benesh'ere tribe
- Blesset—Jerst's daughter
- Jack the Lesser—a bowman and scout

Personae Celestial
- Attun—a mythical god
- Unnamed King—knows all names but his own
- Erithnae—god-queen and consort to the Unnamed King
- Aethon—the last Shahotma King

Personae Angelicus
- Metadan—an archangel
- Ellowyn—an archangel
- Laelith—a faerie
- Cynaban—Metadan's senior lieutenant

Personae Common
- Raffin—a merchant, also known as Fatpurse
- Mathal—a fruit vendor
- Ott—a peasant
- Gulk—Ott's wife
- Ikth—Ott and Gulk's son
- Darma—captain of the *Far Wind*
- Bakart—first mate of the *Far Wind*
- Chiren Tesha—guardmaster of a merchant caravan out of Anistigh
- Katha—leader of the scouts reporting to Chiren Tesha

Personae Nether
- Beayaegoath—the Dark God and ruler of the ninth hell of the netherworld
- Bayellgae—the venomousss demon flying sssnake

- ElkenSkul—the demon *namegiver*
- Mortiss—Morgin's unusual horse, also known as the DeathWalker
- Soann'Daeth'Daeye—a shadowwraith that Morddon meets outside Kathbey-anne

Personae Ancient

- Morddon—a bitter and angry Benesh'ere warrior, and Morgin's alter ego
- AnneRhianne—a Benesh'ere princess and Rhianne's alter ego
- WindHollow—a young Benesh'ere boy and AnneRhianne's nephew
- Gilguard—warmaster of the Benesh'ere
- Sarker—a Benesh'ere scout
- Takit—a Benesh'ere scout
- Bendaw—a Benesh'ere scout
- Binth—the pipist, Morddon's father
- Eisla—the SteelMistress, last of the SteelMasters, and Morddon's mother
- Jander—a Benesh'ere warrior, one of Gilguard's senior lieutenants
- Magwa—the jackal queen
- TarnThane—the griffin lord
- SheelThane—the griffin queen
- AuelThane—a griffin warrior
- TearThane—a griffin warrior
- WolfDane—the hellhound king
- Perrik—a nobleman with a flawed blade

Acknowledgements

I'D LIKE TO thank Durelle Kurlinski for fixing all my dotted t's and crossed i's, Karen for both supporting my dream and being my most valuable critic, and Steve Himes, and the whole team at Telemachus, for getting a quality product out the door.

Books by J. L. Doty

Series: The Dreadmark Covenants
Dread Child (available 3/1/2024)
Dread Spirit (6/1/2024)
Dread Soul (9/1/2024)
Dread Lord (12/1/2024)
Series: The Treasons Cycle
Of Treasons Born
A Choice of Treasons
Stand Alone Novel
The Thirteenth Man
Series: The Gods Within
Child of the Sword
The SteelMaster of Indwallin
The Heart of the Sands
The Name of the Sword
Series: The Dead Among Us
When Dead Ain't Dead Enough
Still Not Dead Enough
Never Dead Enough
Series: The Blacksword Regiment
A Hymn for the Dying
A Dirge for the Damned
A Prayer for the Fallen
A Requiem for the Forsaken
Series: Commonwealth Re-contact Novellas
Tranquility Lost

About the Author

JIM IS A full-time SF&F writer, scientist and laser geek (Ph.D. Electrical Engineering, specialty laser physics), and former running-dog-lackey for the bourgeois capitalist establishment. He's been writing for over 30 years, with 19 published books. His first success came through self-publishing when his books went word-of-mouth viral, and sold enough that he was able to quit his day-job, start working for himself and write full time—his new boss is a real jerk. That led to contracts with traditional publishers like Open Road Media and Harper Collins, and his books are now a mix of traditional and self-published.

The four novels in his new coming-of-age epic fantasy series, *The Dreadmark Covenants*, are scheduled for release beginning in early 2024.

Jim was born in Seattle, but he's lived most of his life in California, though he did live on the east coast and in Europe for a while. He now resides in Arizona with his wife Karen and Julia, a little being who claims to be a cat. But Jim is certain she's really an extra-terrestrial alien in disguise.

Visit the author's website at https://www.jldoty.com/
Contact the author at jld@jldoty.com